By LEE PINI

Published by DREAMSPINNER PRESS
www.dreamspinnerpress.com

ACCIDENTAL BOYFRIEND ACQUISITION

LEE PINI

Published by
DREAMSPINNER PRESS

8219 Woodville Hwy #1245
Woodville, FL 32362 USA
www.dreamspinnerpress.com

Accidental Boyfriend Acquisition
© 2025 Lee Pini

Cover Art
© 2025 Reece Notley
reece@vitaenoir.com
Cover content is for illustrative purposes only and any person depicted on the cover is a model.

Trade Paperback ISBN: 9781641089050
Digital ISBN: 9781641088633
Trde Paperback published November 2025
v. 1.0

Chapter One

THE WINDSHIELD wipers can't keep up with the falling snow. They're whipping from side to side on their highest setting, but Walt still can't see shit. It's like the old hyperspace effects in *Star Wars*. His truck tunnels through streaks of white, the light from the headlights illuminating a pitiful amount of road.

White road. White shoulder. White coming at him in thick, blizzardy fury.

He should never have gotten off the freeway. Just another mistake in the clusterfuck of today.

Walt clenches his hands around the steering wheel and tries to breathe deep. Getting off the freeway *was* a good decision. He'd sat in a sea of red brake lights glowing through the murky snowfall, inching maybe a quarter of a mile in an hour, so when he got close enough to the next exit, he took it. The whole freeway could be shut down and he could've been trapped for hours until he ran out of gas. And if he ran out of gas, how would he have kept his new plant alive?

Getting off the freeway would've worked out fine, probably. Except his phone died, even though it was plugged into the charger, so he couldn't Google Maps his way home. Which was when Walt discovered his charger was shot.

So now he's lost on some highway or county road or something smaller, with no phone and a dwindling supply of gas in the tank.

He chews his lip and tastes blood where he's worried it raw already. The next sign of civilization he comes to, he's stopping. Directions—that's what he needs. To a gas station and then to a hotel. Or literally anywhere he can wait out this storm for a few hours.

Yeah. Okay. That's a plan.

The tight knot between his shoulder blades relaxes fractionally. Little shots of pain radiate up his neck and down his arms from the tension that's been locking up his muscles all afternoon, ever since Lia broke up with him.

Nope, no. Not gonna think about that. Thinking about getting dumped isn't useful when you're white-knuckling your way down what could very well be a goddamn dirt road in the middle of nowhere. People don't think of New York as having big stretches of nothing. They hear New York and they think Empire State Building. Times Square. Central Park. It's a whole huge state, and the only part anyone ever pays attention to is that one tiny corner all the way at the bottom.

Not that he's bitter about Lia breaking up with him over the fact that he doesn't want to live in the city, and she doesn't want to live anywhere else.

A hard knot of unhappiness pushes at his windpipe, but he grits his teeth and clenches his fingers tighter around the steering wheel. *Think about it later.* He can't afford the distraction right now.

Something glows ahead. Maybe? Hopefully. Walt squints, leaning forward in his seat. Are those lights? Please let it be a gas station, please let it be a gas station, please let it be a—

A dark shape darts into the road in front of him. "Shit!!" Walt yells, slamming on the brakes.

His Honda Ridgeline fishtails. Walt hauls the steering wheel into the turn like he knows how to do, *just like he knows not to slam on the brakes like that in a fucking blizzard*, but the truck is already too out of control. The tires get no traction, even with the frantic flashing of the ABS lights.

With a *whump* and a thud, the truck nosedives into the ditch. The seat belt catches hard, robbing Walt of air for several choking seconds.

Snow whirls around the truck as Walt catches his breath. The left blinker is clicking, orange light illuminating the dash in morse code flashes. He must have hit it while he was trying to correct. Overcorrect. The front grill is buried in so much snow that the headlights are lighting it up from beneath like one of those fancy ice lanterns.

Except this is a lot less whimsical and a lot more *oh shit*.

Walt turns off the engine, because there's a half-remembered warning ringing in his head about carbon monoxide backing up into the vehicle if the exhaust pipe gets buried. What the hell is he going to do now? He might be doomed, never mind the spider plant from his brother. Walt told him that anything left in his care isn't going to make it, and here comes the world to prove him right.

Somehow that seems like the worst thing to happen today. Walt and Tad have gotten as close as they were as kids over the last year. Maybe closer, because now Tad's out of the closet, and Walt feels like he knows his younger brother again.

With the car off, the lights he clocked before going in the ditch are brighter. Closer than he thought, too, because through the thick haze of snow, it looks like a house, not a gas station.

At least he hopes it's closer than he thought. If it's not, he's fucked. Mom always nags him to make sure he has extra winter clothes in the car in case this very situation arises. Then again, if he doesn't find help, he's going to be a Walt-cicle either way. His truck's going nowhere without a tow.

He looks at the passenger side footwell, where a box with a small, potted spider plant is sitting. Miraculously, the box stayed where it was, though the spider plant is tipped onto its side, black soil spilled across the cardboard from the pot. As he reaches over to pick it up, he says, "Sorry about this, Spidey. We have to find somewhere warm, though."

There's nothing in the car to protect the plant, so he does the best he can and tucks it under his shirt. The cold ceramic pot against his stomach makes him flinch and the plant's fronds, small as they are, tickle.

Outside, the snow is flying so thickly that it looks like a solid wall. Well, he played football in high school. He's used to running into solid walls. All he needs to do is make it to the source of that light.

With a fortifying breath, Walt grabs the keys out of the ignition and shoves the door open.

The wind slams into him, so cold that it takes his breath away. Snow stings his face and his leg sinks calf-deep into snow. It immediately gets in his shoes, biting cold before it goes to icy wet.

The longer he's out here, the worse it'll be. He moves, each step ten times more effort than normal as he trudges through over a foot of snow, fighting the wind the whole way. His face goes numb; his shivers get convulsive. He keeps his gaze fixed on the light, which doesn't seem to grow any closer until he's stumbling up wooden steps to a porch.

The porch defangs the wind enough for Walt to catch a breath. His lungs feel deflated, like he hasn't filled them since the moment he stepped out of the truck. Another shiver reminds him he's still outside, and it's still cold. With a few more steps, he's at the door, and he fumbles for the doorbell. He can't feel it against his fingers, only the pressure of depressing it.

An eternity goes by. What if no one's home? What if no one even lives here? No, the lights are on. Someone's here. Someone *has* to be here.

How long can baby spider plants survive blizzards?

He's about to ring the doorbell again, but a lock clicks and the door swings open. A man stands there, blinking at Walt in surprise. His short black hair is tousled, and the long column of his neck disappears into the slouchy collar of a CUNY sweatshirt. Navy blue sweatpants sit low on his hips, leaving a stripe of golden-brown skin exposed. His eyes are almond-shaped under sculpted black eyebrows.

"Hi, uh, my truck went off the road," Walt says, willing his teeth not to chatter. There's a tremor to his voice, despite his best effort. "C-could I come in and call a tow truck?"

"Yeah, oh my god, of course! God, how far did you walk?" The guy grabs Walt's snow-caked sleeve and hauls him through the door with surprising strength. Or maybe Walt's just that close to falling down.

His toes hurt in his soaked-through shoes, and when he looks over his shoulder, he can't see his car. He can't even see the end of the driveway he trudged up to get here. Was it that far? Or is the storm just that bad?

The door shuts with a clatter. Warmth envelops him. The house smells like a bakery. He never answered the guy's question, did he?

"I was only out there ten or fifteen minutes," he guesses.

"Come in, come in—wait, take your shoes off first."

"Sorry!" Walt takes half a step forward before he rocks back. His hands are still clutching the spider plant under his shirt, though, his legs are stiff from the cold, and his brain is also trying to get him to use one foot to pry his shoe off the other. He tips backward, his stomach swooping in dismay.

And the guy is there again, steadying him before he topples over. "Careful!" His eyebrows draw together in concern. "Let me help with the shoes. You don't want frostbite. Do you have a pet under your shirt?"

"Huh?" When the guy lets go of Walt to gesture where Walt's hands are stuffed at the front of his shirt, Walt says, "Oh, no. It's a plant."

Maybe that's kind of weird. Now that Walt's inside a house that smells like cake, and he isn't being pelted with snow and ice, it feels weird.

Carefully, he disentangles Spidey. The pot is warm where it was pressed against his skin. Hopefully the little guy makes it. After today's shitshow, he just wants one thing to go right. Proving he can keep a plant alive—a plant that Tad assured him is "really forgiving and great for beginners"—has apparently become that thing.

Dumb thing to fixate on when he's so bad at taking care of stuff.

Instead of taking the plant, the guy gets on his knees in front of Walt and reaches for his shoe. "Pull," he instructs.

For some reason, Walt focuses on the top of his head and his messy black hair. It looks like he just got out of bed.

Then the request penetrates, and Walt does what he's told. The shoe comes off with a wet suck. Walt puts his foot down in a puddle of icy water and flinches, but it could be worse. His sock could be dry instead of soaking wet.

The other shoe comes off and the man helps him get his socks off too. As he climbs back to his feet, the man gives him a once-over, making a face. "You're soaked. I'll be right back."

Which means Walt is now standing in a kind stranger's kitchen, barefoot and holding a plant, while water quietly drips off his clothes to the floor. He glances around. It's spacious, with cherrywood cabinets, white appliances, and an oak hardwood floor that looks like it might be original. The cabinets aren't; Walt's guessing 1990s, the last time cherry was popular.

The source of the bakery smell is a cake sitting on the round table in the center of the room. A vase of fresh flowers sits next to it. Walt's still trying to decide if they're the kind of flowers you buy for company when the house's owner reappears through the kitchen door, a stack of folded clothing in his arms.

"I hope this stuff fits. Bathroom's down the hall." The man thrusts the clothes toward Walt.

It seems like he shouldn't. His clothes are wet, big deal. He'll call the tow truck, he'll be uncomfortable for a while, and then he'll be on his way. He doesn't need to get comfortable in this nice guy's house and impose any more than he already has.

Instead, he hands off Spidey and obediently follows the directions for the bathroom, where he strips out of his sopping clothes and puts on the warm, dry ones. It's just boxers, flannel pajama bottoms, and a sweatshirt that says WINDHAM, NY. When he reemerges and finds his way back to the kitchen, holding his wet clothes gingerly, the man is waiting, bent over the table, studying the spider plant.

He straightens when he sees Walt. "I'll throw that stuff in the washing machine," he offers.

"The dryer's fine." Walt feels more normal now that he's warming up. The hardwood floor is nice on the soles of his feet. Homey and warm. People shouldn't be so afraid to use wood for their kitchen floors. "That way I can throw them back on when the tow truck gets here."

"Tow truck," the guy repeats. "Oh, you said that before. No, there's no way they can dig you out tonight."

"But—"

"Just throw the clothes down the laundry chute. That door to your left."

"I can't walk in this weather to find a hotel for the night," Walt insists, but he still does what he's told. He hears his clothes land somewhere below with a wet splat. "My phone's dead. And my plant won't survive."

The guy looks at him like he can't decide on a facial expression, until a smile twitches one side of his lips upward. "Yeah, I know. You can ride out the storm here. Didn't I say that?"

"No," Walt says, feeling vaguely affronted that he's being laughed at. And also vaguely like he might start smiling back. He can't make any other sense of the weird tug in his stomach. His savior has a smile that makes him feel like they're friends. Giving in to the urge to smile back, he adds, "But I guess maybe that's obvious now that I'm thinking about it. I'm Walt, by the way. Thanks for all this."

When he offers a hand to shake, the man takes it. His fingers are long and slender but he has a strong grip. "Skylar. And it's no problem. Even if you could get a tow tonight, I'd still tell you to crash here." Concern flashes across his face. "You're okay from going in the ditch, right?"

"Yeah, I'm okay," Walt assures him. "All the snow sucks, but at least it's a soft landing." He goes to check on the baby spider plant. It looks okay. Maybe he didn't kill it. That reminds him—he should text Tad to let him know what happened. Fishing his phone out of his borrowed pants, he asks, "Can I charge my phone? It died, and my cable's shot."

Skylar makes an apologetic face. "Sorry. I have an iPhone."

Walt groans at his Samsung. "Of course."

"I can text or call someone for you if you need me to."

"I don't know anyone's number."

With a laugh, Skylar says, "Yeah, me either. What about socials? You can log in on my phone?"

Brightening, Walt says, "That's a good idea! If I can remember my passwords to any of them…."

That gets another crooked smile from Skylar, and he touches Walt's elbow. The light touch draws more weight than it seems like it should, and Walt feels it all the way down his forearm. "C'mon into the living room. I was just watching *Gaslamp Market*—"

"The new episode?" Walt interrupts in delight.

Skylar's eyes widen "Yeah! Do you watch it?" There's an incredulous but hopeful note in his voice, like he doesn't dare believe that someone else likes the same show as him.

But hell yeah, Walt watches *Gaslamp Market*. "The new episode was pretty much the only thing I had going for me this weekend. I *love* that show. I'm not even a fantasy guy usually, but the characters are so good—"

"I know! Same!" Skylar grins. "Fantasy shows are usually so cheesy, but this one is—argh. Perfection. Willis and Samuel have *the* most amazing chemistry."

"Don't tell me if they kiss in this episode," Walt warns him.

Skylar makes a cross over his heart. "No spoilers."

For a second, Walt fingers one of Spidey's green-and-white leaves. "Okay, tell me if they finally kiss." When Skylar presses his lips together and shakes his head, Walt gives him puppy dog eyes. "Please? Pleeeease?"

"I'm saving you from yourself," Skylar says like he's trying not to laugh. Walt makes a concerted effort to make his eyes bigger and sadder. He's been told that his eyes are too blue to say no to.

"This day's been really tough," Walt says. It has, technically, he remembers.

They stare at each other for a few more seconds before Skylar throws up his hands in defeat. "You win! They were literally *right about* to kiss when you rang the doorbell. Something's probably going to interrupt them."

Walt beams. "Dude! I can't believe you paused it."

"Me either." Skylar sighs. "I need to see my Edwardian gay magicians get it on."

"Seriously," Walt agrees. God, it's amazing to talk about this show with someone else who loves it. None of his friends at home in Watertown care. Some of them would be actively hostile toward it if they knew it existed. They definitely wouldn't be eagerly waiting for a gay sex scene, and they'd make fun of Walt if they knew he was. His best friend Mario for sure would.

Even Tad and his fiancé, Lewis, tease him about how into *Gaslamp Market* he is. Not for the gay stuff, though. That would be weird, since Tad and Lewis are gay. No, they just call him a nerd, which is a pretty low blow, coming from them. They brought him to Disney pub trivia once while he was visiting, and their team got first place. Lewis knew the answer to every question. Tad spent the entire night looking at Lewis like he was a genius. Walt was just impressed one person could know so much about Disney.

And maybe he spent that night being a little sad and bitter, too, because Lia was supposed to go to trivia with them, but she said she needed a night to herself and bailed. It had been weeks since Walt had seen her in person, but okay. Sure. He wasn't going to make a big deal about it. Just like he wasn't going to let on that seeing his little brother so in love and happy was like a thumb on a bruise behind Walt's sternum.

He loved seeing Tad happy. It wasn't that. It was that Walt couldn't seem to pin down that same thing for himself. Now that Lia dumped him, it's further away than ever.

Skylar looks just as happy to have found a fellow fan. "Message whoever you need to, and then I'll start the episode over. C'mon, everything's in here…."

Walt follows Skylar through the kitchen doorway, but instead of turning down the hall where the bathroom is, they go into a cozy living room. There's a well-worn and comfortable-looking sofa in the center of the room facing a TV mounted on the wall, which is currently displaying the faces of the two male leads of *Gaslamp Market*, Willis and Samuel, leaning toward each other with parted lips and lowered eyelids.

Before Walt can look more closely, Skylar darts forward and uses a PlayStation controller to exit to the splash page for the episode. He sits on the sofa, his narrow frame sinking into the rich blue of the upholstery, and moves a laptop onto a coffee table covered in magazines, catalogues, and papers. Walt can see farm equipment and animals on some of the magazines and catalogues, and the letterhead on the papers is from a bank.

Floating shelves line the walls around the room with what Walt can only describe as an interesting assortment of... things. There's a lot of art—pencil sketches, Walt thinks? But some with bright splashes of color. Interspersed with the art are ribbons and plaques that look like the kinds of awards you get from the 4H Club at county fairs. And there are peacock feathers here and there, plus balls of fluff that are maybe supposed to be animals? There's also a miniature Pride flag in a mug that's shaped like a goat's head. Is Skylar LGBTQ+?

He sits before Skylar calls him out on the snooping. The guy's doing him several huge favors; Walt shouldn't creep on him. "I just need to send my brother a message on Insta," Walt says. "I'll let him know I'm in... uh... where am I?"

"Windham," Skylar says, throwing an arm over the back of the sofa. His smile is somehow both teasing and warm at the same time.

"Windham," Walt repeats, finding himself smiling back. That's in the Catskills, and it explains the shirt. There's for sure been a property on one of his favorite home improvement shows that was in the Catskills.

"I signed out of my account already, so"—Skylar offers Walt his phone with its healthy 62 percent battery—"it's all set for you to log in."

It takes a couple tries for Walt to remember his password for Instagram, but once he's in, he fires off a DM to Tad about what happened and where he is, and not to worry if he doesn't message back, because he had to borrow a phone to send this one. For good measure, he sends a DM to Lewis, too, because Tad's fiancé is better about checking his phone.

When he's done, he starts to hand the phone back to Skylar before he thinks of something. "Hey, what's your handle? I should follow you."

Or is that weird? Well, it's out there now. Going with his gut usually doesn't steer Walt wrong, and he's always had a good sense for people. Skylar is cool. Easily Insta follow material.

Skylar looks taken aback, but not in a way that makes Walt regret asking. "I'll put it in." He takes the phone back, types, and flashes the screen up so Walt can see. The profile pic is a closeup of a black-and-white goat, and the name across the top says Blue Skies Farm. "I just have my business account," he says apologetically. "I got sick of social media otherwise."

Gaslight Market beckons. Walt's intrigued by the business account, though. "You own a farm?"

"Yep."

"Around here?"

"Right here." Skylar gestures around the living room. "You would've seen it if not for, you know. The total whiteout conditions outside."

"That's cool." And impressive. Skylar seems pretty young—probably not older than Walt, who's thirty-three. Having your own business by that age isn't a walk in the park. "I run my own business too."

"Oh yeah?" Skylar looked interested, which people usually do. "What is it?"

Walt tries not to wince. Here's the part where people lose interest. "Residential fencing." And yeah, he doesn't want to talk about this. The cool, charming guy who owns a farm in the Catskills and saved Walt's ass doesn't want to hear about privacy fences, and Walt was kind of liking the fact that said cool, charming guy was looking at him like he's worth paying attention to.

Gesturing to the TV, he says, "Should we watch this? I don't want you to go any longer not seeing a WilSam makeout."

Skylar laughs and picks up the controller to start the episode. His smile settles Walt's urge to wince and deflect from Black River Fence Co. Getting lost and going in the ditch at Blue Skies Farm is a good end to a supremely shitty day.

Now, Willis and Samuel better kiss.

Chapter Two

WHEN WALT wakes up, it takes a good twenty seconds before last night comes back to him. Dead phone, getting lost, truck in the ditch.

He rubs a hand across his face and sits up in bed. The frame, white painted metal with chips showing the original gray steel underneath, squeaks as he moves. Not a great bed for sex, then.

He rubs his hand across his face again. Why is he thinking about sex? He's in pretty much the least sexy situation he can imagine: snowed in with another guy.

Skylar is a great guy, though. After the *Gaslamp Market* episode ended, they talked about the show for at least another hour. Okay, maybe two. They needed the first thirty minutes to complain that the near-kiss between Willis and Samuel got interrupted, and also to talk about the way Willis grabbed Samuel's tie and whispered, "We're not done here" before the two of them took off after the shadowy figure that's been trailing them all season.

The guest room Skylar put him in is simple: white walls, light blue curtains, and a full-length mirror mounted on the wall. The flannel sheets and gray comforter kept him warm enough that he slept in just his boxer briefs. There's a table next to the bed that doesn't fit the farmhouse vibes of the rest of the house. Walt's pretty sure it's from IKEA.

He stands, stretching his arms over his head to loosen the tight knots in his shoulders. His reflection makes him pause and stare critically at himself. It's winter, so he hasn't been working outside putting up fences, but even before that, he was delegating most of the work to his crew. These days, he spends most of his time in his business office out by the Thompson Park Vortex.

Not like he's going to seed. His stomach's more or less flat; his chest and shoulders look good. He scratches the reddish hair on his chest. There's a lot more of that the further he gets into his thirties. It used to only be his happy trail and a few hairs on his pecs. Now he has enough that he feels like he can call it body hair. Maybe Lia didn't like it.

He makes a face at himself and runs his fingers through his reddish-blond hair. It's been a couple days since he's shaved, and his stubble is starting to look sloppy. Or maybe he *won't* shave and he'll grow a beard. Every other time he's tried, it's come in patchy.

Sure. He'll grow a breakup beard. That'll make him a chick magnet.

With a snort at his own expense, he twitches aside the curtains to see how much snow is on the ground and if the road has been plowed.

It's still snowing.

It's still snowing *hard*. It might be snowing harder than it was last night. For a couple feet beyond the glass, he can make out individual flakes swirling. Beyond that, it's a sheet of white.

The unpleasant surprise is probably why he heads to the bathroom down the hall without throwing on some pants—which he doesn't realize until another closed door in the hall opens, revealing Skylar in a T-shirt and loungers, and with an adorable mop of bedhead.

Skylar stops dead in his doorway, but his eyes take a trip all the way down Walt's body and back up. There's a dazed expression on his face when he meets Walt's eyes, and then his cheeks turn rosy. "Morning," he says, his voice strangled.

By this point, Walt has decided that A) yeah, Skylar is probably into dudes, and B) he's making a colossal ass of himself by prancing out of his room in nothing but his boxer briefs.

With a laugh, Walt says, "Sorry man, this isn't my house, and I should put some damn clothes on."

Thankfully, Skylar laughs too, but his voice still sounds the tiniest bit tight when he replies, "Don't worry about it."

Walt moves for the bathroom, feeling a slow flush creeping up his chest and neck. Since he's mostly naked and pale as hell, there's no chance Skylar isn't going to notice. But where Skylar's eyes were glued to Walt before, now he seems to be trying to look anywhere else as he slips past to go downstairs.

Did he adjust his pants?

"I'll make breakfast!" Skylar calls up the stairs once he's out of sight.

Walt's pretty sure Skylar adjusted his pants. Like, an adjustment for boner-related reasons. Once he's in the bathroom, he eyes himself in the mirror again, considering himself armed with the new information that a gay (or bi or pan!) man finds him attractive. He gave another guy a boner.

Huh.

THE KITCHEN is deserted when Walt—fully clothed—goes downstairs. There is, however, a coffee maker gurgling on the counter, a pitcher of batter next to a waffle iron, and a couple plates on the table with cutlery laid out next to them. A note taped to a bottle of maple syrup beside the batter informs Walt that Skylar went outside to check on the animals.

A twinge of unease goes through Walt as he glances at the window. The animals would be in a barn, not outside in this. Right? But Walt can't see a barn. The snow is too thick, and the wind is blowing too hard. Skylar won't get lost out there, will he?

That's stupid. This is Skylar's farm. He's not going to get lost walking between his house and the barn. He could probably do it with his eyes closed.

Still, he can't relax, pacing around the kitchen and looking out the window every few seconds while he worries at his bottom lip with his teeth. This is way too much anxiety to make a waffle.

On the other side of the kitchen, a door opens, letting in the howling wind. A huff of cold air drifts through the kitchen as Walt turns. In an alcove he hadn't noticed last night, Skylar is stamping snow from heavy-duty boots and brushing it from a thick coat.

At least, presumably it's Skylar. He's also wearing a hat and a scarf wound around his neck and most of his face.

"Hey," Presumably Skylar says. His voice is muffled from the scarf.

"Everything okay?" Walt asks. He sounds nervous. Why the hell does he sound nervous? Well, because he *was* nervous, maybe still is, and that doesn't make sense. Jesus, he just met this guy twelve hours ago.

The scarf unwinds and the hat comes off, and yeah, of course it's Skylar under there. His cheekbones look ruddy where his skin was exposed to the wind, unprotected by hat or scarf. "Yeah, everyone's chilling. They have alfalfa so they're happy. And they got some treats."

"Good," Walt says. There's a weird buzz under his skin making him want to move closer to Skylar to make sure he's really okay. What's wrong with him? Skylar wasn't in danger. Walt's inventing a whole thing for no reason.

Or maybe the reason is because he got dumped and crashed his truck into a ditch during a blizzard, and now he's dependent on the kindness of this nice man. Yeah. That makes sense. Anyone would feel a little weird under these circumstances.

Shimmying out of the jacket, Skylar asks, "Did you find the breakfast stuff? How'd you sleep? You probably saw the weather. You're stuck here another day, it looks like. Sorry. I know you're anxious to get home."

He seems nervous this morning. It's probably because Walt didn't bother to put on clothes earlier. He wants to smack himself. "Nah, man, *I'm* sorry you have to put me up again. I'll get out of your hair the second I can, I promise."

Skylar's eyes dart up to Walt's. Whatever he sees there makes him less twitchy. That makes Walt relax. He's not a huge guy or anything, but he has some bulk, and he can see how it could be unnerving, especially being cornered in your bedroom doorway.

"You're not in my hair," Skylar says. "Though"—he reaches into the tousled mess, which is even more untidy than it was earlier, and plucks at something—"Thor and Loki were. Thanks, guys."

When he holds up a piece of straw, Walt chuckles. "Thor and Loki?"

"Goats."

"I figured. Either that or you have Chris Hemsworth and Tom Hiddleston in your barn. And then I'd have some questions."

Skylar lets out a surprised yelp of laughter. "If I had Chris Hemsworth and Tom Hiddleston in my barn, that would solve a whole bunch of my problems." His cheeks color again, right along the bones. They're already prominent and when he blushes, it accentuates them more. Better bone structure than Chris Hemsworth or Tom Hiddleston. "Anyway, breakfast. Did you eat?"

Now that Skylar's coming into the kitchen, running slender fingers through his hair, it seems extra silly that Walt was worried about him. "I was about to make myself a waffle when you came in." Fudging the truth isn't going to hurt anything. "Thanks, by the way. You didn't have to go to any trouble. I just eat a protein bar at home."

Waving away the thanks, Skylar says, "No trouble. I like cooking. Now that you're staying for another day, you can let me know if yesterday's experiment turned out."

"What kind of experimentation are we talking about? Is this why you need to keep Hemsworth and Hiddleston in your barn?"

Skylar laughs again. It's a nice laugh—deeper than you'd think it would be from looking at Skylar, with his thin frame. Wiry, that's the word for it. His laugh is low, rich, and warm. The kind of laugh that makes you feel good about drawing it out.

As he pours batter into the waffle maker, deftly flipping the pitcher upright so nothing drips onto the counter, Skylar replies, "I tried making a pound cake with goat cheese. I have… way too much goat cheese. There's only so many spreads you can eat. So, yeah, I'm experimenting with goat cheese baked goods."

"That must be what smelled so amazing when I got here last night."

Brightening, Skylar asks, "Did it? Good! I don't know if I want to do a glaze."

"I vote for trying it as is," Walt says. "That way you can decide if it needs anything else."

"Consider it done." Skylar's smile does that tipped-up-corner thing again, and Walt feels the same warmth he did last night.

Walt puts his hands on the back of one of the chairs at the table and watches Skylar at the counter. The way his wrist moves to twist the waffle maker looks more fluid than when other people do it. Apparently he's never seen anyone in real life who's naturally graceful.

Walt's not graceful, that's for sure.

Once a couple waffles are finished, Skylar plates them and deposits them at the table. "Coffee? It's not fancy."

"Please." It didn't hit Walt until this moment how starved he is for caffeine. "And I don't need anything fancy. There's nothing fancy about me."

"Salt of the earth?" Skylar pours two cups and brings them over before grabbing milk from the fridge and a little tureen of sugar.

With a snort, Walt says, "I don't know if Watertown qualifies me as 'salt of the earth.' Isn't that you?"

"Mm," Skylar replies noncommittally, pouring so much maple syrup on his waffle that Walt's teeth hurt. "I don't come by the farm life naturally."

"No?"

"No. It was…." Skylar looks like he's searching for the right way to sound like he's saying something while not saying anything at all. It's a shitty thing to be an expert in, but Walt's had a lot of practice with his brother, who used to look that way pretty much all the time. "It was an idea I had in college."

Walt cuts his waffle with the edge of his fork. "You made it successful pretty fast."

This time, when Skylar laughs, there's not as much warmth. Instead, there's a brittle edge that makes it obvious Walt stepped in something. "I think the hope was that it would be more successful by now."

"Oh." Walt wants to apologize for pushing on a bruise, but they've barely passed the twelve-hour mark of this relationship. Relationship, ha. That's too strong a word.

Shaking himself, Skylar says, "Sorry. How's breakfast?"

"Perfect," Walt says, raising his coffee cup in a toast. Maybe he's an almost-stranger who can't offer any kind of emotional support, but he'd like to do *something* to show Skylar how much he appreciates what the other man has already done for him. "Let me clean up. And you should put me to work. There must be a ton of stuff to do around here. Stalls to muck, or… something?"

Skylar smiles but shakes his head. "I already put down fresh straw today. You can come help me fill up the water trough later, if you really want to."

There's a note in his voice that says he can't imagine why Walt would want to. But Walt does, with a ferocity that startles him. It's just because Skylar's doing him such a huge favor putting him up. Of course he wants to repay that kindness.

"Put me to work," Walt says. "I can take whatever you give me."

Skylar's gaze flickers from Walt's face to his shoulders. Like before, it feels… flattering.

Huh.

Chapter Three

THE SNOW doesn't let up all day, not even a little. Skylar makes a face when he checks the forecast, so Walt figures he doesn't want to know. He'll ask later. Tonight. Because he really should stop imposing on Skylar.

It's funny, though, how Skylar seems to not find Walt an imposition. They get along well, so maybe it makes sense. When was the last time Walt clicked with another person the way he has with Skylar? The *Gaslamp Market* thing, that made it seem easy last night, but today it feels like it's more than that.

When it's obvious there's no hope of leaving today, Skylar offers the use of his phone again if Walt wants to message anyone. They've been playing a board game that Walt found in the closet of the guest room; something with trains. Skylar had looked surprised to see it but was enthusiastic when Walt asked if he wanted to play.

Walt logs into Instagram while Skylar goes downstairs to check on some laundry, and finds DMs from both Lewis and Tad. First, Tad's: *DON'T WORRY IF YOU DON'T MESSAGE BACK ARE YOU FOR FUCKING REAL WALT??? YOU WALKED UP TO A COMPLETE STRANGER'S DOOR AND I'M JUST SUPPOSED TO BE LIKE OK! SURE! THERE'S DEFINITELY NO CANNIBALS IN WINDHAM!*

Walt's mouth twitches in barely suppressed laughter before he flips over to Lewis's message. Definitely fewer caps there: *Glad you're ok and you found a place to stay! Hopefully you can get on insta again to message Tad. He's convinced you're going to be sacrificed by a satanic cult. Apparently the Catskills are overrun with satanic cults, who knew*

That makes Walt laugh straight from his belly. Meeting Lewis last year was rocky—but Walt loves him. He's perfect for Tad and is going to be an awesome brother-in-law.

Quickly, he messages Lewis back, The satanic cults love me, they'd never sacrifice me, before he returns to his conversation with Tad. You've been in the city too long, Taddy. Walking up to a stranger's door for help is a normal thing everywhere else

Apparently Tad's better about checking his notifications when he's anxious, because three dots appear. Guilt pricks at Walt. He doesn't want his little brother to worry.

Are you really ok? How bad was the accident? Tad asks.

For a second, Walt's brain gets stuck loading. Accident? Oh, right! He went off the road, that's why he's here.

> **I'm really ok. The airbag didn't even go off. Nothing hurt but my pride**
> *Good*
> *And you're also ok, like… with the breakup?*

Walt winces and almost logs out of Instagram. Maybe he shouldn't have told Tad that Lia broke up with him.

> **I'm not going to wander off into the blizzard because of a broken heart if that's what you're worried about**
> *I was not but thank you for that very gothic image*
> *Just like. You can call to talk, if you want*
> *If the cannibal doesn't mind you using his phone*
> **His name is Skylar and he's not a cannibal**
> *Can you be 100% sure of that tho*
> **He hasn't tried to eat me at all**
> **So, pretty sure**

He flicks up his eyes to glance at Skylar, who just came back into the room with a basket of laundry. Walt's clothes are on top, his flannel shirt looking huge. Skylar pauses and props the basket against his hip, fingers curling around the edge to hold it in place. "Did your brother get your message?"

The feeling of his brain not loading the information he needs takes over again. Walt can't stop looking at the way Skylar's hips are cocked; the curl of his fingers around the edge of the basket.

A thread comes loose in his mind that Walt doesn't want to pull, except he can't *not* pull it, because this is how it goes. This is how it's been, every time this has happened, that he finds himself liking a man's smile in this weird, fixated way, and noticing his fingers and the way he moves his hips.

The thread waves temptingly. Tauntingly, more like. Walt's done a really, really good job of not thinking about this for a long time. Years! Definitely since college. Okay, there was that one time at that rest stop, when that guy looked at him, but that wasn't—Walt stopped before he fell back into old habits that he'd outgrown.

The phone buzzes in Walt's hand, but he barely registers Tad's request for more information, because he's too busy looking at Skylar's slender hips and the strong, graceful line of his shoulders swooping down to his ass. He's pulling the thread, unraveling the certainty that he's over this.

No, Skylar hasn't tried to eat him. But maybe Walt wouldn't mind if he did. Maybe Walt wants a taste of *him*.

His mouth goes dry, and his throat feels tight and sticky. His heart lurches.

"Walt?" Skylar asks uncertainly, which is terrifying, because that means Walt's way more transparent than is good for him. "Everything okay?"

"Yeah!" His voice sounds too bright and hearty. Very *I'm saying everything's okay in a way that couldn't make it more obvious that everything definitely isn't okay!* He pushes away thoughts of Skylar's fingers and shoulders and the lean strength in his legs. "Can I give my brother your address so he doesn't worry so much?"

Once Skylar rattles off the address and Walt provides it to Tad, he types out a quick goodbye and puts the phone on the sofa. He'd give it back to Skylar, but he's worried about what will happen if he goes too close. These kinds of feelings were supposed to stop.

"Can I fold those clothes for you?" Walt asks, hoping activity will calm the jittery feeling in his rib cage. Though folding clothes might not be the best activity. His palms are sweaty. Getting sweat stains from his wet hands on Skylar's clothes wouldn't be good.

"Nah, it's fine. Is it weird that I like folding clothes? It's oddly restful."

The more Walt thinks about not thinking about it, the more he notices about Skylar. Like the bob of his throat every time he swallows, or the sharp cut of his jaw. The knobby bones at his wrist and the way blue-green veins snake over them. The shadowy divot where his collarbones come together.

"Maybe I can do farm chores then?" Walt asks, hearing—and flinching at—the note of desperation in his voice. He's acting weird, he knows it, and the worst part is, this weirdness is probably preferable to the other thing.

Skylar does have that Pride flag, though, an incredibly unhelpful part of Walt's mind points out. So if Walt *did* think about the other thing. Not that he is. But if. *If.* Then Skylar might not be against it.

In a general sense. He might be against it with Walt in particular. Which would be good, because Walt told himself he was too old for this last time it happened.

He's wringing his hands together, which Skylar has definitely noticed, because his eyebrows are drawn together and he's frowning a little. "You really don't need to earn your keep," Skylar says.

"Yeah, I know. I just want to feel like I'm doing something besides sitting around."

Skylar looks out the window. Walt follows his gaze. There's nothing to see outside except white. For all Walt knows, Skylar *is* the cannibal leader of a satanic cult, and the farm is a lie. The barn hasn't been visible at any point since Walt arrived.

"You said the goats need water, right?" Walt adds.

Chewing his lip, Skylar says, "Yeah. They should still be fine for a few hours, but I guess we can go check. And we can make sure Valentino and Elton aren't harassing anyone."

Troublemaker goats? Walt would ask, except he doesn't want to distract from the task at hand, which is doing something physical and tiring himself out so he stops thinking about all this stuff.

Since Walt doesn't have any warm clothes, Skylar digs out some of his things for him to use. Right before Skylar opens the door in the mud room to head outside, he turns to Walt and says in a muffled voice, "Stay close to me and hold on to the guide rope, okay? You can't see the barn until you're right up close to it. And the path I shoveled earlier will be gone by now."

"Got it." Walt gives him a thumbs-up. His plan is already working. Bundled up, it's impossible to see the lines and angles of Skylar's body. Of course, Walt's standing pretty close to him right now, which means he's close enough to see the color of his eyes.

They're such a light brown that they almost look hazel, or like a good, peaty whiskey. Walt's heart patters unsteadily.

Skylar opens the door, and the howl of frigid wind and snow makes Walt reconsider this idea. Maybe they should go back to the living room and fold laundry.

Too late, though—Skylar steps outside, bowing his head into the wind. His first step makes him sink nearly to his waist in a drift. As he struggles through the snow, Walt realizes those are stairs. Jesus. Are they getting this kind of snow at home? Or in the city?

Before the blizzard swallows Skylar, Walt throws himself out the door, careful to shut it behind himself. The snow is heavy and hard to walk through, and for a stupid second, he panics that he won't be able to keep up with Skylar. That's ridiculous—he may have been spending more time in the office lately, but he still has the build of a former football player. He's plenty strong enough to wade through the hip-deep snow, especially with Skylar breaking through it first.

Skylar reminds him of one of those ice cutter ships, all sharp and brave and by himself in the middle of a lot of nothing.

The wind goes right through Walt's coat, and he surges forward through the snow to catch up with Skylar, who paused to wait for him. "Okay?" Skylar asks.

At least that's what Walt thinks he said. He fumbles for the ice-encrusted rope stretched beside them at shoulder height. "Yeah!"

The side of Skylar's hat and scarf that are facing the wind are fully coated in snow, and there are flakes caught in his eyelashes too. Which is exactly the kind of thing Walt's out here to *not* notice, so he makes himself look somewhere else. Over Skylar's shoulder, he thinks he might, possibly, be able to see the barn at the end of the guide rope.

A powerful wind gust slams into them, snatching away Walt's breath and sending snow against his face like tiny, icy needles. He rocks, off-balance with the snow and the too-small boots, but Skylar catches his arm in one gloved hand.

"Thanks!" Walt shouts over the wind. Snow hits the roof of his mouth.

Through the jacket, Walt's pretty sure Skylar squeezes his arm. "Just a little farther!"

If it wasn't snowing, this walk would probably take a minute. Battling through the deep snow and wind, it takes them much longer. Luckily, the door is on the leeward side, where the snow isn't so piled up.

Skylar unlatches the door and urges Walt inside. Walt stumbles, overcompensating for the push against the wind. The door bangs shut and the latch clanks, and suddenly everything is quiet.

Well, not quiet, exactly. Soft animal noises gradually penetrate past the ringing in Walt's ears. Lights flick on, but even so, it takes his eyes a moment to adjust from the encompassing white of everything outside.

Goats bleat and run to him as Skylar says cheerfully, "Hey, guys!"

Several more goats clamber off something that looks like a cross between a playground and an elaborate cat tree, with ramps and perches, and at the top, a little house. There's a goat sitting on the roof of the house and one inside. Another is standing on top of a stack of straw bales. More are scattered around the barn.

He counts fifteen. "So you have, like, a lot of goats." He faces Skylar, who's surrounded by three, all butting their heads into him. Two are larger than the others and shaggy, with horns. One is black, and the other is a caramel color. The third at Skylar's feet is much smaller and is tan with a black stripe down its spine.

"Bah!" yells a goat as it ambles up to Walt. It's also on the small side.

"Not by goatherd standards," Skylar says. He has a happy, almost goofy grin on his face, and Walt's chest squeezes. "I have sixteen."

"Sixteen?" Walt looks around again, counting again. Still only fifteen. "Where's the sixteenth?"

Casting his eyes around the barn, Skylar says, "Wanda likes to cuddle with Squirrel."

Walt's eyebrows grow up. "You keep squirrels?"

"No, no"—Skylar points at a stall Walt didn't notice—"Squirrel is my guard llama. Fun fact, though, people used to keep squirrels as pets."

For a second, Walt is incapable of speech. Skylar murmurs to the goats, the same kind of loving nonsense Tad and Lewis say to Hetty, their cat.

"Guard llama," he finally repeats, wondering if he didn't hear right. Somehow, squirrels as pets seems less weird.

"Yeah, when the goats are pastured, Squirrel keeps them safe from predators. Coyotes, mostly, but foxes too. A fox could kill a kid."

"A fox could kill a kid?!" Walt exclaims and immediately feels like an idiot. A *goat* kid. Not a human kid. He colors. "I mean… yeah, I guess. I didn't think about that."

Somehow, Skylar isn't looking at him like he's an idiot. There's pleasure on his face. "I have Nigerian dwarf goats, which are small enough that in theory a fox could kill them. Hurt them, for sure. And Wanda's a Pygmy goat."

Most of the goats are on the small side, now that Walt's looking closer. They range in color from black to brown to white, with some spotted, some splotched, and some with that black stripe down their back. "I don't really know anything about goats, I guess. I didn't realize there were different breeds."

"I didn't either before I started out." Skylar scratches the caramel goat behind the ears, and the black one shoves its nose into his side. Skylar laughs. "Okay, okay! You get scritches too. These two are Thor and Loki, by the way. And this one"—he nudges the tan one with his toe—"is Steve."

Walt's starting to notice a pattern with the names. "You have a whole goat Avengers thing going on, huh?"

"Well, I'm Team Steve, so not all of them."

Walt laughs. "That's fair."

Freeing himself from Thor's, Loki's, and Steve's attentions, Skylar shucks off his layers and hangs them on a hook by the door. Walt follows his lead, catching sight of the water trough on the other side of the barn as he pulls his snow pants off. Skylar opens the faucet and water rushes into the trough, sloshing from one end to the other in a mini tsunami. Walt watches the water move, because he didn't stop himself from looking at Skylar's hand as it gripped the faucet handle and twisted.

"What can I do?" Walt asks.

"If you want to grab another alfalfa bale, that will last them through the night."

Grateful for a distraction, Walt follows Skylar's directions to a room at the back of the barn where the bales are stacked. He hefts one, relishing the stretch and strain in his muscles, the rush of heat it takes to lift the bale to his shoulder. He returns with it and lowers it to the feeding station.

"Do you have a utility knife to cut the string with?" he asks, absently pushing his sleeves up to his elbows as he turns to Skylar, who's still near the trough.

Skylar's eyes snap up to Walt's, and his throat bobs. Walt feels heat surge through him for a completely different reason. "Utility knife," Skylar repeats like the words are foreign to him. Then: "I mean, yeah! Here, let me."

When he returns with a knife, Walt looks at the goats instead of the play of muscle and tendons under the golden skin of Skylar's forearm. His sleeves are pushed up now too, exposing tattoos.

"Anything else?" Walt asks quickly.

"Not really." Skylar looks apologetic. "You can give them treats, if you want?"

That sounds distracting *and* fun. "I don't have to do anything special, right? I'm not going to hurt them if I feed them wrong?"

The smile Skylar gives him makes Walt's stomach tighten. It's sweet and warm and makes the corners of his eyes crinkle. "No. You won't feed them wrong. Here." He goes to get a plastic pet food storage tub filled with what looks like dog kibble.

The goats obviously know what's up. They head straight for Skylar and Walt, and it's in that moment that Walt realizes goats are a little unnerving with their horizontal slit of a pupil and the unhesitating way they walk right up to you.

"Wow, they know what treats are, huh?" Walt says nervously as the goats surround them.

Skylar gives him a distressed look. "I should've warned you. They get pushy when the treats come out."

One of the little goats butts its head against Walt's shin and looks up at him plaintively. He laughs. These guys aren't anything to be nervous about. Especially when a black fluff ball clambers over the top of the stall on the other side of the barn and careens toward them with a bleat.

"That's Wanda." Skylar gives Walt a hopeful smile. "You're okay? I'll go check on Squirrel if—"

A blood-curdling wail splits the air, rising above the stamp of hooves and crunch of straw, even above the howl of the wind.

Walt jumps, losing his grip on the treat tub and flinging treats over the goats' heads in a wide arc. The goats go crazy, throwing themselves into each other and against his legs to gobble everything in sight. Skylar claps a hand over his mouth and Walt's lizard brain kicks in and yells *DANGER!*

He pulls Skylar to the ground, covering his body with his own, determined to protect him from whatever's in here.

"Ow!" Skylar yells and then makes a noise Walt can't process for several too-long seconds. He's—crying in terror?

Oh, wait. No. He's laughing. Hysterically.

Walt pushes himself off Skylar and up on an elbow only to see Skylar curl in on himself, wheezing through paroxysms of laughter. His heart is still pounding, and he can't see what made that horrible noise because they're surrounded by goats happily chowing down on spilled treats, but Skylar's amusement makes it clear that nothing scary is happening.

"What the hell was that noise?" Walt asks. The horrible sound wails through the barn again, and Walt bumps Skylar's shoulder with his fist. "Sky! What is that?"

It must be the real fear in his voice that makes Skylar stop laughing. He shoves himself up onto his knees, shoulders flexing. "Walt—sorry."

"Glad I'm so hilarious," Walt says. The sour note in his voice is… really obvious. His heart rate is coming down, but he's still flooded with adrenaline, and it wants to go somewhere, have something to focus on. Except all he can focus on is the fact that Skylar was laughing at him.

He starts to get to his feet, but fingers close around his wrist. Warm, strong fingers, and suddenly Walt's heart rate is climbing again. His pulse is beating against Skylar's grip. "I'm sorry," Skylar says seriously. His eyes, with their amber whiskey color, are wide. "Look, I—here, I'll show you."

As he climbs to his feet, he keeps his hold on Walt's wrist and tugs Walt upright. "Look." He points to a beam overhead, so Walt looks. Two bright blue peacocks are perched there watching the goats, who have finished all the spilled treats by now. Loki is nosing at the treat tub, pushing it across the floor with a plasticky clunk on each attempt to stick his nose in.

"That's Valentino and Elton. My gay peacocks." Skylar's fingers are still around Walt's wrist, but looser now. Walt knows he should want Skylar to let go, but instead he wants Skylar's hand to stay there, his fingers to press Walt's pulse point. Walt wants to stroke the soft skin on the inside of Skylar's wrist and trace the cut of muscle up his forearm.

No. He doesn't want that. He shifts away and Skylar must get the message, because he pulls his hand back.

"I didn't know peacocks made that sound," Walt says, in possibly the most impressive understatement of his entire life. Most people don't jump on top of their companion to shield them from death when they encounter a peacock.

Skylar crosses his arms over his chest and looks up at them. One of the birds cocks his head. How does Skylar tell them apart? "Trust me, the first time I heard it, I freaked out too. They sound like angry ghosts."

Despite himself, Walt snorts. "Angry ghosts. Yeah. I still looked like an idiot, though. Sorry for throwing myself at you."

The quirk at the corner of Skylar's lips is back. Wait. Shit. "It's okay. Men don't throw themselves at me very often. It was flattering."

The back of Walt's neck heats and he looks away. "So is the Pride flag in your living room for the gay peacocks? How do you know they're gay, anyway?"

What a stupid thing to say. The first thing. It doesn't stop disappointment from sloshing thickly through him, which is even more stupid. Walt isn't gay, so he shouldn't wish, on any level, for Skylar to be too. No, not—not *too*. Fuck. What's wrong with him?

Since Walt still isn't looking at Skylar, he has no idea about Skylar's expression as he replies, "The thing about them being gay is kind of a joke. Like, 'gay,' that's a human thing. But the lady I bought them from would only sell them together, because they're pair-bonded. And they adopted Wanda when I got her as a baby. They kept trying to feed her."

Finally, Walt looks back to Skylar. His adrenaline is draining away, and now he just feels tired and sad. A joke. Yeah, that makes sense. A jokey Pride flag for his gay peacocks.

Skylar's face is uncertain. That's not what Walt expected. His whiskey eyes meet Walt's and he says, "The Pride flag in my living room is because I'm gay."

"Oh," Walt says.

Wind rattles the side of the barn. There's something warm in Walt's chest.

And then one of the peacocks wails again and busts up the moment—if it was a moment at all. It shouldn't be. It probably shouldn't be. Walt should ignore the way looking at Skylar makes him feel like he's lit from within. Like he's a hiss of something ephemeral until you hold a match to him and he bursts to light.

Walt shoves his hands in his pockets, hunching his shoulders against that feeling, which is stupid and impossible.

"Oh?" Skylar repeats. He doesn't sound worried, but there's something to his tone that carries some of the same chill as the storm outside. Like—oh no, like he thinks Walt's a homophobe. Maybe that's not so crazy—his own brother thought he was too.

That's not a misconception Walt wants anyone to have about him ever again. "I didn't want to make any assumptions." Thor the goat bumps his hand and Walt pets him. "Since, you know. Assuming makes an ass of you and me."

Warmth returns to Skylar's face like the sun coming out from behind a cloud, and he laughs. "That should be a queer covenant. Thou shalt not assume, lest thou make an ass of thyself."

"There's probably a joke in there somewhere, right?" Walt asks, which he regrets until Skylar laughs again. Making Skylar laugh feels way too good to stop.

Walt's starting to wonder what the problem is with that.

Chapter Four

SINCE SKYLAR likes to cook, Walt's happy to offer his chopping services. "Which isn't innuendo," he adds.

Skylar freezes midreach, his arm stretched over his head to snag a mixing bowl from a cupboard. "Oh no, is there a new sex thing I don't know about? I'm pretty disconnected from the scene."

There's a tilt to the corner of his mouth, sly and amused, so Walt plays along. "Yeah, definitely. You can't go to a gay bar without people chopping all over the place."

There's a slice of skin showing above the waistband of Skylar's joggers, the sharp ledge of a hip, a hint of the slope from his back to his ass.

"I wonder what chopping would be," Skylar muses. "I want him to chop me in half?"

"Wait, like with his *dick?*"

Skylar looks down at the area in question, then back to Walt, one perfect eyebrow arched. "Walt, are you telling me you've never gotten chopped by a guy?"

"Only if he's cut," Walt says primly, then grins when Skylar cracks up. "I guess maybe I'd be cut, if he was chopping me?"

Which is definitely, for sure a hugely inappropriate thing to say. But the look Skylar shoots him isn't entirely appropriate, either. There's a sudden, sparking heat to his gaze, which Walt weakly reminds himself to ignore.

It's kind of hard to take himself seriously, though, when he's talking about his cock. It's also hard to take himself seriously when he's a little hard.

Skylar finally gets the mixing bowl, along with all the other dishes and utensils he needs. "So that's my problem," Walt says wryly. "You're supposed to get everything out before you start instead of digging through drawers while a pot's boiling over?"

"Depends how much you love the smell of scorched whatever's-boiling-over." He sets aside the ingredients for dumplings—they're making stew—and unwraps a piece of beef.

"Nice meat," Walt says. He knows exactly what he's doing. And simultaneously, he has no fucking idea what he's doing! But it gets the reaction he wants from Skylar, which is eyes snapping wide and mouth parting in surprise.

"Thanks," Skylar says. His eyes drift down Walt's body. Walt tries and mostly fails not to stare at his mouth.

By the time the stew is simmering on the stove, Walt is grateful for the loose lounge pants he borrowed from Skylar. He's a lot more than a little hard and already trying to justify why it's not going to be weird to rub one out in bed tonight.

This is because of the breakup with Lia, obviously. He has a lot of excess feelings that need to go somewhere. And rebound sex fixes those kinds of feelings. Like, not permanently. Obviously. But getting laid would be good for his post-breakup mood.

Er, jacking off to the idea of getting laid. Not getting laid for real. He doesn't have sex with men. He's straight.

Obviously.

Dinner is sinfully good. Walt moans when he puts the first bite of dumpling in his mouth. It's everything a dumpling should be, both fluffy and dense, a vehicle for the flavor of the stew but also floury and delicious in its own right. Skylar's utensils twitch, and he shifts in his chair.

"Good?" he asks.

"You fucking know it is," Walt groans.

Skylar gives him a grin tinged with wolfishness. "Glad to hear it."

"Man, can I pay you to cook for me? I bet this would still be amazing even if it was frozen and reheated." Walt shovels a mouthful of beef and potato into his mouth, knowing how gluttonous it looks and not caring. Skylar can *cook*.

The expression on Skylar's face dims, but he looks down at his food and Walt isn't sure what he saw, or what would cause it. "At the rate the snow's coming down, you're going to have to move in with me, and I'll be cooking for you anyway," Skylar says.

"I mean, if I moved in with you, I'd obviously cook." Walt wrinkles his nose. "You'd regret it, but I'd pull my weight."

Skylar tilts his head like he's considering saying something, but in the end, he just takes another bite of stew.

After dinner, Walt washes up. When the dishwasher is loaded and everything else is drying in the rack, he spends a few minutes with Spidey the Spider Plant, who spent the day in the kitchen window, soaking up whatever feeble light made it through the clouds and swirling snow.

"You okay, little guy?" He nudges one of the long leaves with his finger. When it springs back, he's relieved. It looks okay. Not wilting or turning brown or anything obviously bad. Maybe he'll manage to keep it alive.

Skylar amazes him. Here Walt is, worried he's going to kill a plant he's had for two days, and Skylar's out here keeping a herd of goats, a llama, and two peacocks alive. Plus himself! Walt has the keeping-himself-alive part down pretty well, but he can't fathom taking care of anyone or anything else. His friends are having kids. Even Mario, his best friend since middle school, is having a kid soon. The thought of doing it himself turns Walt's guts to water.

When he turns, Skylar is in the door, one shoulder leaning against the frame, with his arms folded over his chest. "How's the plant?" he asks, his smile canted at the same angle as his hips.

"It seems okay." Walt bops one of the leaves gently to watch it sway again.

"Can I ask what the story is with it?"

"Didn't I tell you?" When Skylar shakes his head, Walt huffs a laugh and rubs the back of his neck. The hair at his nape is getting long. "My brother gave it to me. He's really into plants. His apartment is full of them." With pride, he adds, "He's an editor at a botany journal."

Looking suitably impressed, Skylar says, "Wow. Smart brother."

"Yeah, he is." Walt looks at Spidey again, then back to Skylar. "I was in the city visiting him and his fiancé. Well, helping with wedding stuff. They're getting married in May. I was looking at all Tad's plants and he asked if I have any, which he knows I don't because I'm horrible at keeping anything alive, and then he got a pot and put some dirt in it and pulled a couple of these guys off a huge one he has. And he said 'Now you do.'"

"Are you guys close?"

"Yeah," Walt says, his smile involuntary.

"That's cool." Skylar kneads the point of his elbow. "I always wanted a sibling."

"Only child?" When Skylar nods, Walt says, "Well, it's probably one of those 'the grass is always greener' things. Your mom couldn't buy matching sailor outfits to dress you and a sibling in."

A sad shadow darkens Skylar's face, but he says, "There better be pictures."

"Of course there are pictures."

"Good, then you can show me."

The way he says it is so decisive and unquestioning, and it makes Walt's skin heat with pleasure. There's a chance he and Skylar will keep talking after this weekend? Hell yes, Walt will show him as many embarrassing childhood photos as he wants.

Jerking his chin, Skylar says, "I thought we could watch a movie. Show me one of your favorites?"

"All the movies I like are dumb." Walt follows Skylar into the living room, sinking onto the sofa next to him. Somehow, they end up closer to each other than last night, closer than Walt sits next to his buddies. Not quite close enough to feel Skylar's body heat, but close enough to imagine he can.

Skylar hands him the PlayStation controller. All the streaming service apps gleam on the screen. For a minute, Walt's paralyzed by the amount of choice. What are his favorite movies? Does he even like any? Why can he only think of that one asinine movie from the 80s where Bruce Willis plays the talking baby? Oh, there's *Die Hard*, but everyone likes *Die Hard*. Skylar isn't going to be impressed if he suggests that.

Yeah, so he's trying to impress Skylar with his movie choice. Apparently that's a thing now.

"Walt," Skylar says. Walt looks at him. "You're thinking too hard."

With a laugh that sounds more nervous than he'd like, Walt says, "Is it that obvious?" One of Skylar's eyebrows goes up.

This is silly. It's just a movie. It doesn't have to be perfect. Except it kind of does.

The perfect choice hits him. Walt toggles into a streamer and pulls up the movie's landing page, giving Skylar a querying look.

"*A Knight's Tale!*" Skylar grins. "Vintage Heath Ledger? Yes, please."

"I love this movie," Walt says, and goddamn him, he sounds *shy*. Of all things! Shy! He's not shy, never has been. But Skylar makes him want to… to… get things right. To make things perfect.

They settle in to watch. Walt's seen the movie so many times that he could probably do most of the dialogue along with the characters, which means he finds himself paying attention to….

Skylar.

Skylar, who laughs at all the right spots with that full, deep laugh of his. By the third time he does it, shivers start going up Walt's back. There's a prickle low in his stomach, too, and a thick, pulsing heat that's unmistakable. An ache behind his spine and through his hips, an insistent tug deep and low in his body.

And somehow, they're closer. Close enough that their arms brush. Their legs knock together, first their knees, then their thighs as they get closer. Walt isn't consciously doing it, and he doesn't think Skylar is either. It's like a gravity well between them.

Since Walt knows the movie like the back of his hand, he knows when it's coming to an end. William and Jocelyn will get together, and the credits will roll. A bubble of anxiety compresses his lungs. When the movie ends, they'll move. He won't feel Skylar's arm pressed against his and the heat of his body. That's… not okay. Nothing about that is okay. Not when he wants to feel more of Skylar—more of that heat, more of the press of his body. Skin, that's what Walt wants. Skin on skin, and mouths, and—

He puts his hand on Skylar's thigh.

Under his palm, the muscle of Skylar's leg tenses and relaxes, but he doesn't move away. He doesn't move at all, except to angle his head so he can see Walt's fingers spread against his pants like an exclamation point. A neon electronic billboard in the middle of nowhere on the freeway, blazing through the dark. A white flag.

It feels like minutes have gone by, an hour, maybe, because time won't settle down and keeps stretching weirdly, then snapping back like a rubber band. It can only have been a few seconds, because the movie has hardly gone on at all.

Skylar's eyes flick up and meet Walt's. They're amber in the warm pools of light cast by the lamps in the living room, fringed with thick, dark lashes. How did he not notice those eyelashes until now? Every girlfriend he's ever had has spent god knows how much money trying to look like that, and here Skylar is, looking at Walt through them as the nanoseconds slide by and Walt's heart hovers in the empty space between one beat and the other.

Gently, Skylar places his hand on top of Walt's, and time jolts back into its tracks. The movie plays on, William and Jocelyn embracing in their happily ever after, and Walt's white fingers sitting under Skylar's brown ones.

There are calluses on Skylar's palm and along his fingers. The dusky pink shells of his nails are cut short and blunt. The thumbnail is a little uneven, like maybe he picked it. Ragged cuticles, dark spots that might be old scabs.

And his hand is warm. Warm and solid heat, bleeding into Walt's bones and the tendons strung along them.

Skylar fits his fingers between Walt's and tightens his hold. Slowly, he moves Walt's hand, sliding it higher up his leg and inward to the dark, private tops of his thighs. Walt's fingertips bump over Skylar's inseam, and it doesn't seem possible for another person to give off this much heat.

Swallowing against his rising excitement, Walt works Skylar's fingers tighter between his. Skylar obliges. He also keeps moving Walt's hand, slowly like he's giving Walt the opportunity to pull away. The slow drag of Walt's palm over Skylar's pants is sexy as fuck, the fabric bunching under his hand making his skin prickle with oversensitivity even though nothing has happened. Walt hardly wants to look at his hand's destination, like it's a Christmas present he found two weeks early—but it's impossible not to. Not when Skylar's erection is tenting his pants.

"You good with this?" Skylar asks on an exhale. His voice sounds tight.

Walt realizes he's salivating. "Fuck yes," he breathes. How did he make it twenty-four hours without doing this? He wants to touch. He *needs* to touch. He needs to get his fist around Skylar's cock, and then Skylar's cock in his mouth.

A beat goes by where Walt could still pull away if he wanted to. When he doesn't—when he nudges his hand higher up Skylar's leg— Skylar follows through on the promise he's been making and slides their joined hands over his crotch and onto his dick.

The sharp little intake of breath from Skylar goes straight to Walt's cock. He's hard. Hard as a rock and throbbing. His dick is drooling inside his boxer briefs. As he wraps his hand around Skylar, his own cock twitches.

"Like that?" Walt asks, his voice husky as he slowly jacks Skylar through his clothes.

Skylar's head drops back against the sofa cushion and his hold on Walt's hand loosens. "Yeah," he sighs. "God."

It's been so long since Walt's done this and he thought it might be weird, or like he might have forgotten how to touch another man, but it's like no time has passed at all. Or like time has looped around on itself and smashed together again. Skylar's cock in Walt's hand is hot even through his clothes, and the hard length ignites a consuming desire in him.

He varies the strength of his grip, squeezing on the upstroke and loosening as he slides back down, and Skylar's hips twitch off the sofa. A noise escapes him, a mew of pleasure that makes Walt shudder. "You feel so damn good," Walt says. His voice feels like tires rumbling over gravel, a rasp of hormones and need.

Skylar opens his eyes and makes another noise, practically animal. He shoves himself off the back of the sofa and climbs into Walt's lap, straddling him, knees bracketing Walt's hips. Walt gasps at the sudden delicious pressure of Skylar's weight on him. Skylar's hips pressing into his. Skylar's hard cock pressed against his.

The buttons of both of their pants are straining. Walt twists his wrist to keep touching, but before he can get a good grip, Skylar grabs his wrists to push his arms over his head, crowding up against him. Walt's back arches and he groans, his wrists trapped over his head by Skylar's strong grip.

"How do you feel about kissing?" Skylar murmurs, his mouth ghosting along the line of Walt's jaw, all hot breath and soft lips and Walt's stubble making everything prickle with electricity.

"I love kissing." Walt turns his head to watch Skylar's face, but then Skylar's mouth is on his, and oh. His lips are even softer than Walt was expecting, plush and full, slick and hot. When he licks against the seam of Walt's mouth, Walt opens with a quiet moan and welcomes the way Skylar fucks his tongue inside.

It's the hottest kiss Walt's had in a long time. It might be the hottest kiss he's *ever* had, Skylar rocking slowly in his lap while he keeps Walt's hands over his head. The sound of their lips smacking together and their panting is ratcheting up the ache in Walt's hips. Skylar's tongue slides against his assertively, almost aggressively, and it makes Walt so hard it's almost unbearable.

With a frantic sound, Skylar releases Walt's wrists to run his hands down Walt's chest and hook his fingers into his waistband. The press of his knuckles into Walt's bare stomach electrifies the surface of his entire body. He arches and grabs Skylar's hips, holding on for dear life as they kiss urgently and rut against each other.

Walt breaks away from the kiss to bite the cord of Skylar's neck. "Can I suck you?" His chest heaves as he asks. "I want to suck you so bad."

Skylar presses the heel of his hand over his own dick, which Walt watches with downcast eyes as he kisses and licks along his neck to where his neck meets his shoulder. "Fuck," Skylar mumbles before fumbling with the drawstring of his pants.

When he scrambles off Walt's lap to sit on the sofa, he shoves his pants down his hips. Walt slides off the sofa and drops to his knees, pulling the pants to Skylar's ankles. He pushes Skylar's knees apart and leans in, breathes in, and has to drop his head to Skylar's leg to muffle his shameless moan. The way Skylar smells is like the way his cock felt in Walt's hand. It's a smell he thought he forgot because it's been so long.

Now that he's doing this again, though, it's clear he never forgot. Never stopped loving this smell—the smell of another man's musk and his pre-cum, the sweat and the smell of arousal. And Skylar smells so fucking good. Walt's drowning in it.

He kisses up Skylar's leg to the soft inside of his thigh. Sparse black hair lies scattered across his skin, and there's a mole right at the bottom hem of his boxer briefs. Walt kisses that too, right before he reaches into the fly of Skylar's boxers and pulls his cock out.

"*God*," Skylar hisses. His cock in Walt's hand feels… feels… goddamn. Fuck. It feels so good. Hot and velvet soft and hard as a rock. His slit is wet. As Walt watches, pre-cum pulses out.

That's more than Walt can handle. With a long groan, he takes all of it down to the root.

Which isn't one of his best ideas, probably. The feel of someone else's cock in his hand? It's like he did this yesterday. The smell of another man? Couldn't have told him it's been years.

Blowjobs, though. Maybe he's gotten out of practice with blowjobs.

He chokes, gags, and has to pull off and clap a hand over his mouth because, for a horrifying moment, he's afraid he's going to vomit. With a worried expression on his face, Skylar sits up. "Are you okay?"

The urge to gag recedes and Walt lowers his hand, feeling himself turn red with mortification. "Um. Yeah. I'm sorry."

Skylar combs his fingers through Walt's hair. "Don't be sorry."

He sounds so earnest—looks it, too—that Walt's shoulders relax. Holding Skylar's eyes, he dips his head and licks a teasing line over his cockhead. When Skylar sighs, Walt does it again with more pressure. Pre-cum leaks onto his tongue, slick and salty.

Skylar's fingers are still in Walt's hair, running through it gently. But Walt doesn't want gentle. Still lapping at Skylar's slit, he reaches up to tighten Skylar's grip on his hair.

"Yeah?" Skylar murmurs. He tugs and Walt takes the head of his cock in his mouth. He tugs harder and Walt's mouth goes slack as he moans around his mouthful of cock.

Every pull on his hair makes him sink further onto Skylar's dick. The sting on his scalp and the stretch of his lips, the ache of his jaw, the pressure on his knees as they dig into the floor, is bringing him closer to the edge. Throbbing heat spreads in a pool from his hips, winching his muscles tighter and hotter.

When he hollows his cheeks and sucks, tonguing the underside of Skylar's cock at the same time, Skylar makes a desperate sound. Even without his gasped warning of "I'm coming," Walt knows exactly what's about to happen. Skylar's cock is hot and heavy and hard in his mouth, and Walt takes it as deep as he can as Skylar chokes off a yell.

Hot, thick cum floods Walt's mouth, so much that he can't swallow fast enough. It leaks out, dribbling onto Skylar's boxer briefs, and Walt sits up, not wanting to make a mess on him. Some more escapes from between his lips, running down his chin.

His own hard-on is painful, but he can't stop looking at Skylar. Sprawled on the sofa, legs spread wide, cock flushed and wet and shining while his chest heaves, he's the sexiest thing Walt's ever seen.

Walt licks his lips. He tastes amazing too.

Shoving himself up with one hand, Skylar holds out the other. "Come here. Fuck, Walt, let me—come here, please."

Walt does, falling on Skylar. They're kissing frantically before they even hit the sofa, Skylar pushing his hand inside Walt's pants and underwear to grab his dick. After sucking Skylar and making him come inside his mouth, Walt's stamina is shot. He could come untouched.

Instead, he comes with Skylar jerking him in quick, hard pulls, crying out into Skylar's mouth as he fucks against his leg.

The orgasm blasts his brain apart for a few long, syrupy minutes. All he can do is keep kissing Skylar, who's gone warm and limp beneath him, one hand still in Walt's underwear while the other strokes his back.

Chapter Five

"THAT WAS nice," Skylar finally says against Walt's lips.

Walt kisses him once more, deeply. His brain is coming back online, and something is creeping at the edges of his awareness—something gross and panicky. He doesn't want to feel gross and panicky, not when he feels so warm and sated and loose. He hasn't come that hard in… a while. Not lately with Lia, that's for sure.

He doesn't want to think about his ex when he just hooked up with someone new.

Someone with a penis.

The gross, panicky feeling crawls closer.

The last time he did this, he swore it would be the last time. And he's been good. He's hardly looked at men for years. Everyone he's been attracted to has been a woman, and that's good. It's right. There's nothing wrong with being gay, obviously. Not for other people. But it's just… it's not something Walt can be. And he isn't. He's attracted to women. He just broke up with a woman.

And he just had sex with a man.

A man who he's still lying on top of. Who opened his home to Walt and seems prepared to keep doing it as long as this storm lasts. Why did Walt have to ruin it by making a pass?

Why does he fuck up everything?

Ashamed of his own weakness, he sits up. The mess in his underwear moves too, a palpable reminder of that weakness. "I should clean up," he says, because it's true, but also because it's a good excuse to get off the sofa and away from Skylar. How is Walt supposed to face him now? It's not like he's going to be able to act normal. Skylar deserves better than that, but Walt can't see any further ahead than getting behind the closed door of the bathroom.

Skylar straightens up, his eyes on Walt. His expression isn't quite readable, but Walt thinks he looks a little knowing and a little sad. Resigned. That's the word for that. He looks resigned.

That doesn't stop Walt from hurrying upstairs and shutting himself in the bathroom to shower. He'll figure out the right way to act. He'll figure out how to pretend that what just happened between them didn't happen.

THE NEXT morning, the storm has cleared. Skylar is surprised. So is Walt, but mostly he's relieved, because he's a coward. He doesn't know how to tell Skylar that last night was a huge mistake.

It seems like Walt doesn't need to say it, because Skylar is acting like he knows. There's a brittleness to him this morning. His smile doesn't reach his eyes, and he looks tired. A notch between his eyebrows deepens every time he looks at Walt.

A snowplow rumbles down the road midmorning. The cool wash of relief that goes through Walt makes him want to hide. Then again, he already wants to hide, because he knows he's being an asshole and a coward.

The shame gets worse when Skylar tells him, "A tow truck's on the way. I'll help you shovel your car out so you can get out of here faster."

Walt opens his mouth to say—some kind of protest. Except that's what he wants, to get out of here as fast as possible. He couldn't make it more obvious. That makes him despise himself more.

The only way Walt can identify his truck is by the slightly higher mound of snow in the ditch—it's that submerged. He wades through the drifts to confirm it's there. *Wading* can't be the right word. It's more like swimming. The snow is up to his ribs, almost his armpits in some spots. At one point, he puts down his foot and the ground just isn't there, and he's afraid for one horrifying second that he's going to be buried alive.

But the truck is there, and he doesn't get buried alive. More importantly, shoveling out the car is such hard work that talking is impossible. The snow is thick and compacted along the edges of the road, but once they get through that, it's powdery and easier to move.

It would be pretty if Walt wasn't so weighed down by his own stupid behavior. The sun is out and the snow is unbroken, glittering white in every direction. The trees are frosted with it, and it makes every branch glimmer against the blue sky. Walt can finally see the barn. It's a faded green.

When the tow arrives, it's with a small crew of pickups with plow blades attached to their fronts and people with shovels. This clearly isn't their first car-in-the-ditch today. Walt's surprised by how fast they dig him out and tow him back onto the road. When they ask him to leave a review, he promises he will.

One of the pickups plows out Skylar's driveway before the crew goes on their way to rescue the next snowed-in vehicle, so Walt can't offer to help with that like he meant to. On the trudge back to the house, Walt breaks the awkward silence between them. "Is there anything I can do before I head out? With the animals, or…?"

It's an idiotic question, and it's obvious Skylar thinks so. He glances at Walt with his lips pressed tight before he shakes his head. "Thanks, but no. You should head home. It'll probably be a slow drive."

"Yeah, probably." The silence goes from awkward to horrible. Walt knows he should apologize, but the thing is, he doesn't know how to make *sorry we had sex* sound nice. It's better to say nothing at all and be an asshole for that. It's easier, at least.

His time here feels like it's been longer than the reality. Walt counts it up. He's been here forty hours, maybe. The feeling that he needs to collect a bunch of stuff and pack is a hallucination, almost like déjà vu. All he needs to do is take off Skylar's snow pants and boots, and collect his keys and Spidey.

He tucks the plant against his body, draping his flannel shirt around it, before he turns around in the door. Skylar stands in the kitchen, not meeting Walt's eyes. That's Walt's fault.

"Thank you for everything," Walt says. Which sounds like it includes the orgasm, and that's not how he means it at all. Clarifying that would be weird as hell, so he keeps his mouth shut.

"Yeah," Skylar says. A sad ghost of a smile appears on his face. "Thanks for geeking out over *Gaslamp Market* with me."

"Maybe they'll finally kiss in the next episode," Walt says. Because he's an idiot.

His face gets hot, and the only consolation is that Skylar looks red too. "It'll be an interesting one," Skylar says, looking anywhere but Walt's face. "Oh, I almost forgot—" He goes to get a paper bag from the counter near the stove and thrusts it toward Walt, still not meeting his eyes.

Walt peeks inside. There's a big piece of the pound cake that was cooling on the table when Walt first knocked on the door and several plastic-wrapped logs of goat cheese. "Thanks," Walt says.

That sad smile appears again on Skylar's face. "You're doing me a favor. Way too much goat cheese in the fridge, remember?"

"Oh. Right." How is he supposed to eat any of this without choking on his own stupidity and bad decisions? "Well, um. Bye."

"Bye." Skylar is staring at a point off to the right of Walt's shoes. Nothing is going to make this less awful, so Walt does the only thing he can do, and walks out the door.

Chapter Six

THE GREAT thing about the farm is that there's always plenty to do, so if you're, say, trying to distract yourself from thinking about the guy you rescued from a blizzard and then had sex with because you're desperate for the touch of another man after your recent divorce that isn't even that recent then... er....

Right. The farm. Plenty to do. It's great, and Skylar's been throwing himself into chores and maintenance for the past week. When he's not working, he's paralyzed by mortification. How could he have lost control like that with Walt?

He attacks a rough patch with sandpaper on the new addition to the playground he's making for the goats. It's been shoved in the back of the barn since last winter, but he's made a lot of progress on it this past week. He'd like to blame the fact that he's been shut in because of the five feet of snow last weekend's storm dumped on the Catskills, but nope. It's the mortification. If he doesn't keep busy, he spends too much time wanting to dig a hole in the floor so he can die of shame in it.

"Knock knock, is Skylar Dangda hiding in here?" a voice calls from the entrance to the barn. Daylight spills across the goat playground as the door opens wider.

Skylar puts down the sandpaper. "Back here!" At his feet, Yelena Goatlova looks up at him and nickers. Not that he has a favorite goat, but if he did, she'd be his favorite. She follows him around like a dog, and even though she's never produced any milk, he'd never get rid of her.

Or god forbid, slaughter her, like Cody suggested. It wasn't the final disagreement on the way to their divorce, but...Skylar would be lying if he said it didn't play a part. The thought still makes him sick. If he's not careful about stopping the panic spiral, he starts thinking about how if his money problems cause him to lose the farm, he'll have to sell the animals, and Yelena might go to someone who decides if she can't produce milk she might as well produce a little meat, and and and—

If he doesn't think about his money problems at all, he doesn't have to think about that horrible possibility.

The goats bleat happily as Skylar's friend Jett walks through the barn. "There you are. I thought you might've been buried alive in the storm."

"First of all, I've been texting you, so you knew I was alive. Second of all, have you ever heard of the 1972 blizzard in Iran, because whole villages actually *did* get buried alive."

Jett swings their legs over a sawhorse. "I have not, but thanks for the fun, aka morbid, fact." They brush their shoulder-length hair out of their face. It's a steely, pale gray this week, a color Skylar's been given to understand is a pain in the ass to achieve. Last week it was dusty purple.

When they notice the direction of his gaze, they tug their hair into a knot on the back of their head. "The salon was closed Monday and Tuesday. I didn't have anything to do except lighten and tone my hair, and as long as I went to the trouble, I figured I should do a color that needed that amount of lightening and toning." They shrug. "I think I'm too pale to pull it off."

"I think it works," Skylar says. "You look like a winter spirit or something. Seasonally appropriate, and topical, considering the weather."

Jett makes a face, but there's a pleased look in their eyes. "How were things out here, anyway? I was worried about you riding out the storm by yourself."

"It was fine. We're all still here." Skylar turns away, because his face hides nothing, *nothing*, and he doesn't want to talk about it.

Of course, he didn't turn away fast enough. "What happened?" Jett asks.

"Nothing!" He picks up the sandpaper again, which is the biggest giveaway that he's lying, outside of his face.

"Oh my god, *stop*. You're the worst liar on the entire planet." That doesn't need a response, because it's patently obvious. Skylar *is* the worst liar on the planet. He's bad at feelings in general. Not bad at having them—he's way too good at having them—but bad at not getting them all over everyone else within a fifty-foot radius. Jett taps Skylar's arm and asks again, "What happened?"

Yelena nickers and gets to her feet, nudging her nose into Skylar's calf. With a sigh, Skylar says, "A guy showed up at my door Friday night because his car went in the ditch. I let him stay because, I mean, what else was I going to do? And then we had sex."

"What?!" Jett yelps. Startled, Yelena bleats and scampers off. "Dude, burying the lede, much?"

"It wasn't exactly my finest moment."

"I can imagine a lot of reasons a person might say that, but why don't you just tell me why *you're* saying it."

Pressing his lips together, Skylar shakes his head and stares resolutely at the goat playground. It doesn't offer an obvious escape. Well, besides climbing on top of it and seeing if he can jump from the highest platform to the barn rafters, but his vertical leap isn't that good. Next to him, Jett leans into his peripheral vision, tipping farther and farther to the side until their head is upside-down and Skylar feels compelled to look at them.

"It feels a lot like I took advantage of him." Saying it out loud makes Skylar queasy. "What if he thought he had to suck me off since I let him stay with me?"

"Okay, these are the details I wanted!" Jett looks gleeful and Skylar wants to bury his face in his hands. Since Jett will most likely only take that as encouragement, he doesn't. "Did you make the first pass?"

"I mean." Skylar can think of a bunch of times he did something that could be construed as a pass. "I don't know. I was definitely flirting with him. He seemed receptive. I thought he was into me."

"Uh, I thought you said he sucked you off. That suggests he was into you."

"I hate talking about this stuff with you." Skylar's face is hot. "He put his hand on my leg. And I should've just… not done anything. That would have been the right thing to do. Nothing. Because we"—god, he's not saying it again—"you know, and then something obviously was wrong, because he got weird. And he couldn't get out of here fast enough the next morning, and it has to be something I did, doesn't it?"

Jett is giving him a look that's half sympathy and half pity. "Let's go inside."

Shaking his head, Skylar says, "I have to finish this."

This blatant and abject dodge fails, as it should. "It's been sitting here since last August. It'll keep." Jett grasps Skylar's shoulders and steers him toward the barn door. "Let's go inside, and I'll eat some goat cheese."

"Would you, really?" Skylar asks in relief. Fuck. He's easy, isn't he? Offer to eat some of his goat cheese, and he'll do whatever you want.

Once they're inside, Skylar gets out crackers and a goat cheese log before Jett can change their mind. It's the black nightshade one, which is Skylar's personal favorite. The nightshade preserves he mixes with it gives it a gorgeous, rich violet color that almost seems a shame to eat.

Almost. Luckily, there's plenty more where this came from. Too much. He was hoping to sell a lot of it at the winter farmer's market in town, but hardly anyone bought anything. Story of his life since Cody left.

Ugh. He'd better make some tea too. It will cleanse his palette from thinking about his ex-husband.

Once two mugs of tea are steaming on the kitchen table and they're halfway to polishing off the goat cheese, Jett levels a look at Skylar. "Just because someone gets weird after you fuck doesn't mean you did anything wrong."

"I know."

"Do you?" Jett's still giving him that same look. "Because it sounds like this guy made a pass at *you*, but you're hiding in the barn making goat furniture because you think you, what, forced him?"

Skylar mashes a couple crumbles of cheese under his finger. "It's a goat playground."

"Skylar."

"I ogled him too." His face gets hot again. "Before I had any idea if he was queer, I checked him out."

"Skylaaaaar," Jett laments. "So you checked out a hot guy! Big if true! Dude, checking out hot guys is what gives life meaning. Wait, he was hot, right?"

An image of Walt pastes itself across Skylar's brain—his broad shoulders, his thick ass, his muscular thighs, his messy hair that couldn't seem to settle on a color between strawberry blond and copper, the freckles scattered across his cheekbones and the bridge of his nose, his bright blue eyes.

"Yeah," Skylar replies reluctantly. Part of him wants to keep everything about Walt to himself, but the rest of him desperately needs to talk to another person. "He was hot."

Something in his tone must finally flip Jett's Time To Be Nice switch, because they reach across the table and cover Skylar's hand with theirs. "Hey. You did a good thing. You helped someone out, and the two of you had some fun. If he made it weird, that's on him. Who knows, maybe he's not out. Or he was cheating on his partner. Or he had a sudden case of the shits."

Skylar can't help laughing at that last one. Jett can always be counted on to put things in perspective. "Maybe," he agrees.

"Are you good now? Done spiraling? I hope the BJ was good, by the way."

"I'm done spiraling and also done talking about this," Skylar says.

Jett pats his hand. "That's my farm boy." They swipe their finger across their half of the goat cheese log. "This stuff is so good. You're gonna sell it at the Valentine's Day market, right?"

Skylar shrugs. "I don't know if I'm even getting a table."

Surprise flashes across Jett's face. "But you're always there. That's always a huge day for you."

"Not last year." The words are hard to get out. He prefers to keep the memory of last year's Valentine's Day market buried deep in the cellar of his mind. The one filled with spiders and mice because he locked it and threw away the key, and he doesn't care if the metaphor is tortured.

Jett hesitates. "Last year was your first one after Cody left. You weren't in a great place."

He'd been crying in the bathroom for part of it, in point of fact. "I'm just not any good at that stuff." Skylar sighs. "I hate trying to sell things to people. It makes me feel dirty." When Jett raises their eyebrows but keeps their mouth shut, Skylar considers it a win. "Like I just see everyone in town as potential sales and not my neighbors."

Pursing their lips, Jett asks, "Do you think I feel that way?"

"That's different! People need to get their hair cut. No one needs artisanal goat cheese." Skylar spreads another dollop on a cracker. "Even if it's delicious."

Jett plants their elbows on the table. A piece of silver hair falls over one eye. "Hey, I know Cody was the salesman between the two of

you, but the farm was *your* baby. Those markets are big money for you."
Skylar makes a noise. With a concerned line between their eyebrows,
Jett adds, "They *are* still big money for you, right? I know you couldn't
do Harvest Days this year...."

If Skylar had dug that hole for himself over the Walt Incident,
he could jump inside it now to avoid talking about this. Harvest Days
always used to be Blue Skies Farm's biggest moneymaker. They'd bring
Squirrel, a few of the Nigerian dwarf goats, and Wanda, and put them in
a little pen with some straw bales for the goats to climb on. The animals
would draw crowds to their table, and no one's ever in a bad mood after
petting a llama and goats. For a dollar, people could buy some goat
treats (it was a markup), too. Then they'd buy goat cheese. A few brave
souls even bought the small supply of goat milk that he and Cody were
starting to experiment with selling.

But their marriage fell apart, and Skylar wasn't surprised when
it did. It was for the best, but afterward, his confidence was shattered.
It doesn't matter what it is—his business plan, the farm, his skills, his
hobbies, or himself, just in general. Everything he does, he does it with
the sword of Damocles hanging over his head. He keeps flinching, and
he doesn't even do things halfway out of fear of failure.

That goat cheese pound cake was the first thing he'd done in
forever that he was unreservedly proud of. And now he can't even think
of it without remembering how Walt could barely look at him after they
fucked.

"I'm okay," Skylar finally says, knowing he's been silent too long
about the question of Windham's local maker markets and how much
income they're bringing in. "I'll be okay."

"Skylar."

"I will be." The truth is that the original business plan wasn't
sustainable anyway. Just like you can only eat so much goat cheese, you
can only sell so much goat cheese. They needed to branch out, and he
and Cody fundamentally disagreed on what that should look like.

"You will be," Jett repeats, "even though you're not going to do
the Valentine's Day market."

"I just...." Skylar shakes his head, like that will rattle loose
a feasible way to keep Blue Skies Farm afloat. If he didn't own the
property outright, he already would've gone belly-up. "I feel like I can't
do it anymore. I don't know how to talk to people."

Jett looks sad. "You're so nice, though. Everyone loves you."

Which might be the problem. Everyone loves Skylar, except he hasn't loved himself for a while. "I'll think about the Valentine's Day market, okay?"

"Commit, Skylar." Jett fixes him with an intent stare. "How can I help?"

"Become the official face of Blue Skies Farm and convince people to buy my stuff?" Skylar tries.

Jett snorts. "I'd love to, except I already have two jobs, and I don't think your nonbinary twink BFF is going to move a lot of artisanal cheeses."

That makes Skylar smile. "C'mon, people love twinks."

"They could hit me up on Grindr more often, then," Jett says, their tone aggrieved, which makes Skylar laugh. Musingly, they add, "It's not a bad idea, though."

"The twink-loving masses hitting you up on Grindr?"

"I mean, *yes*, obviously, but I meant you having an influencer-y person representing the farm." They pause, looking deep in thought. "Don't know any influencers, do you?"

Making a face, Skylar replies, "You know I don't. I barely have a social media presence."

Jett claps. "There's your new project, then. Forget the goat playground. We're going to build you a brand."

Forget the goat playground? Sure. Skylar's had no trouble forgetting that since last summer. The real thing he needs to forget is Walt. Why is that so much harder?

Chapter Seven

"I UNDERSTAND it's unsightly, ma'am, but there's really nothing we can do until spring—"

"So I just have to live with a giant hole in my fence?" the woman on the phone demands.

Walt shuts his eyes and tries to ignore the headache that's been gnawing at his temples all day. "Again, I'm sorry, but as I'm sure you know, there's three feet of snow on the ground. Between that and the ground being frozen, it's just not possible to put up a fence."

"My neighbors can see into my yard! What if they fly drones through the fence to film me when I'm changing?"

He has to squeeze his eyes shut even tighter to resist the urge to dismantle this illogical, paranoid hypothetical. "I can send a crew over to put up a tarp, if you're concerned about privacy."

"That will be even more unsightly!"

By the time Walt manages to get off the phone with the client—and she is, unfortunately, now a client—he wishes he could quit working for the day. That's kind of a problem, since it's not even ten thirty in the morning. With a heavy sigh, he adds Mrs. Tomson to the booking system, aka an Excel spreadsheet.

Mrs. Tomson goes to the top, because five years of owning this business have taught him that difficult people always get what they want. He usually has to ask Google and Yelp to take down their profanity-laced bad reviews anyway, but at least he avoids having too much abuse heaped on him. For good measure, he makes the spreadsheet cell with her name magenta. That's the color his carpenter and occasional office manager, Lizzie, chose for Karens.

The pain in Walt's head spikes, and he rubs his eyes. It's been… a week. A week that's felt like a month, between the drive to get back to Watertown from Windham (eight hours instead of four), the way work's been dragging more than ever, and family drama. Coating all of that like an oil slick from a catastrophic spill is what happened with Skylar—the sex and the way Walt acted afterward.

His stomach clenches, and he forces Skylar from his mind. There are notifications from three separate text conversations on his phone's lock screen right now: the family group chat with his parents, his brother, and him, his chat with his mom, and his chat with his brother.

It's the same bullshit it's been for months now. Tad mentions something about the upcoming wedding in the GC. Mom says something that's supportive in theory, but if you know her, you can see straight through that tactic. Tad, who obviously knows their mother, accordingly sees through it. So then separately, they both text him with their grievances.

Personally, Walt's on Tad's side. It used to make him resentful that he had to be the good son, who stuck around while his little brother moved to New York City, but man. Ever since Tad came out last year, it's hard to be mad at him for fleeing.

Tad and Lewis are paying for the wedding, so they can do what they want, he texts back to Mom. To Tad, he writes, **Don't argue with her. You know you won't win**

They both text back at the exact same time and Walt turns his phone facedown on the desk, then lets his head drop next to it. His forehead thunks on the birch veneer. It's been months of this now. Tad and Lewis got engaged in June, and a big family reconciliation followed. Things were chilly between Tad and Mom after Tad came out, but they both put it aside with a wedding on the horizon. Sort of.

It seems harder to deal with this week. His mom's comments about "that lifestyle" seem sharper, like they're equipped with little barbs that hook under his skin. Which doesn't make sense. They're the same digs as always, and Walt's the same as always.

Several more texts come in and Walt straightens, grabbing his phone to put it on Do Not Disturb. There's work to do, bookkeeping and accounting and all the boring shit he learned how to do in college while he was doing the business administration degree he wasn't interested in, but which everyone told him was the smart thing to do. His mom, especially, because SUNY Potsdam is only an hour and a half away, and he was able to do part of the program at Jefferson Community College, which is right in Watertown.

The texts from his family are there on his lock screen, of course, but another notification catches Walt's eye. *@BlueSkiesFarm has posted for the first time in a while!* Instagram informs him.

His mouth goes desert dry, and swallowing suddenly seems hard. That's Skylar's account. Walt forgot he followed it.

He should unfollow. Instead, he taps into the notification, pulling up the post. It's a closeup picture of one of the goats' faces—Wanda, maybe? The really fluffy one. Her nose is in the foreground of the photo, with her big, thickly fringed eyes focused on the lens. *Who wouldn't love that face?* the caption says, followed by what has to be every goat related hashtag on the app.

Walt's thumb hovers over the screen. This is the moment to unfollow Skylar. Maybe he should even block him, not because Skylar did anything wrong, but because Walt doesn't want the temptation. The fact that he's thinking of it as temptation proves it. Every other time he's... whatever, scratched that itch, given in to the urge, he's been good for a while, and he doesn't need to think about it after it's done. All the people, guys, whatever, that he's... scratched the itch with, he's never thought about them after it was over.

But you know what? He's probably just thinking about Skylar because they got to know each other a little bit. And they got along well. There was *Gaslamp Market*, obviously, and the fact that they both loved it, but it was more than that too. Walt just... liked Skylar. He was easy to talk to.

"Ugh!" He grips the roots of his hair and pulls. The pain isn't as grounding as he was hoping.

The front door of the office opens and thunks closed, and a man says, "Yo, Walt, are you here?"

In the waiting room, Walt's best friend, Mario, is leaning against the wall by the water cooler. "Hey, man!" Walt says, a shot of happiness going through him.

"Walter, my good sir," Mario replies with a grin, grabbing Walt's hand for a handshake/high five and pulling Walt in to clap him on the back. "You wanna grab an early lunch? I just went with Ally to her OB appointment, and I have some time before I have to head back to work."

"Yeah," Walt says. Relief courses through him. Not only will this get him out of the office, but it will also keep him from thinking about Skylar.

They end up at a nearby diner, a small former cottage with white siding that overlooks a small brook and the Watertown city limits sign. On the outside, it looks like it's been added on to at least three times. Inside, it's impossible to tell which parts are newer and which are original. It smells like decades of accumulated grease and breakfast syrup. Walt inhales deeply and waves to Kim, the waitress who he's always thought secretly owns the place. He's been coming here since he was a teenager, and he can't remember a time when she wasn't working.

"So how was the city?" Mario asks as they sit down at their usual table.

"It was great to see Tad and Lewis," Walt says.

Mario chuckles. "Real diplomatic. Still not a fan, I guess?"

Walt shrugs. "If I wanted to live with eight million people breathing down my neck all the time, I'd move there."

"I don't get why people want to suffer so bad. Just to say they live in New York City?" Rolling his eyes, Mario adds, "Weird way to live."

With another shrug, Walt replies, "I guess they like it. Tad and Lewis do."

"How could anyone like it?" Mario laughs. "I never miss Philly. I guess at the time I was pissed we moved up here, but now I'm glad."

"Well, of course you're glad. If you hadn't moved here, you would've had to survive middle school without me." Walt smirks as Mario flicks a Sweet'n Low packet at him.

A server comes by to bring them menus, but both of them know the menu by heart. They order—a Reuben for Mario and pancakes with blueberry syrup for Walt, which makes Mario shake his head and comment that you can't eat breakfast foods after ten forty-five, to which Walt responds that breakfast for dinner is one of the joys of adulthood. They both get coffee, because coffee is an all-day drink, according to Mario.

Once their food arrives, Mario clears his throat. "So, um. Hey. I actually came by today because I had something I wanted to talk to you about."

There's an uncharacteristic serious note in his voice. Walt lowers his fork. "What's up, man?"

"Well, it's—" Mario seems to fumble for words, and that's uncharacteristic too. He shoves a hand through his brown hair. "Wow, I didn't think this was going to be so hard."

"Uh, do I need to be worried?" An insane thought hits the panic button in Walt's mind: that somehow, Mario knows about what happened last weekend during the storm, and he's about to confront Walt about the fact that he was *with* another guy.

He's so busy worrying that he hardly registers Mario shaking his head. "No," his friend says, "it's a good thing. I'm just nervous, which is stupid. You've been my best friend since seventh grade. I didn't even think it was possible for me to be nervous about asking you anything!" He laughs, which seems to put him more at ease. Walt is still wound tight.

"More coffee?" their server chirps, materializing at their table. Walt wonders if Mario's messing with him and the waitstaff are in on the joke.

He has to wait while Mario pushes his mug across the table for the server to refill, and then he has to shake his head no, he's good on coffee, and by the time she bustles away, Walt's half convinced again that Mario's going to stand up and j'accuse him of being gay.

Mario downs a gulp of coffee and slaps his palms down on the speckled Formica table. "I'm just gonna say it. Walt, will you be the baby's godfather?"

A beat goes by because Walt can't process the question. Baby? Godfather? What the hell is Mario talking about?

The expression on Mario's face goes from excitement to trepidation, which is when Walt's brain finally kicks into gear. "Godfather!" he exclaims, grinning wide. It's only a little bit in relief that this has nothing to do with what went down with Skylar (of course it has nothing to do with what went down with Skylar!); most of it is happiness. "Wow, Mario, I didn't expect that."

Mario reaches across the table to punch him on the shoulder. "What do you mean, you didn't expect it? Of course Ally and me want you to be the godfather! Like I'd ask anyone else? Say yes, man."

"Yeah, I'll do it. Obviously." It's sinking in now, and Walt feels the tightness of emotion in his chest—the kind of strong emotion that he's always struggled to deal with, because he's never understood the right way to show it. The moment feels like it calls for him to say more, though, so he says again, "Wow."

"Man, it was killing me keeping that from you. There's not a single thing we don't know about each other after all these years, but I had to keep that secret."

Right, yeah. Not a single thing they don't know about each other.

The stuff he occasionally does with guys has never felt like a secret Walt was keeping. Okay, if he thinks about it, yeah, maybe it was. But he's never thought about it. He doesn't understand why Skylar's different, why he can't get Skylar out of his head.

Mario's talking again, so Walt focuses. "Ally's asking one of her sorority sisters to be the godmother. It's okay that it's not Lia, right? It's just that neither of us really know her, so we thought it was kind of weird to ask her to be godmother."

"Oh," Walt says, belatedly realizing he hasn't even mentioned the breakup to Mario. "Yeah, no, that's fine. That's good, actually, because we're not seeing each other anymore."

Silence falls at their table. The clinking of cutlery on plates and the murmur of other conversations in the diner seem suddenly loud. Mario looks stymied. "Sorry, dude. Are you okay?"

It's kind of troubling how okay Walt is. He's so okay that he wonders if he was ever that invested in Lia and the relationship to begin with. Clearly, she was right to dump his ass, because aside from the shock of it happening and the immediate comedown from that, she's hardly crossed his mind all week. "Yeah, I'm fine. It was friendly. We just want different things."

He always thought when people said stuff like that, they were bullshitting. Turns out, it's a real thing that can happen.

"Cool." Mario looks relieved and changes the subject, launching into a story about one of his frustrating coworkers.

And it's fine, because really, truly, Walt's okay about Lia breaking up with him, and there's nothing he needs to talk about. But maybe it would have been nice if Mario could have stayed on him for like, more than a sentence.

When Mario goes back to work, Walt heads back to his own office. It feels even more like drudgery than usual, and it's felt like a slog for a while. This company was never his dream, but… you have to make a living. And what else is he going to do? There aren't a ton of options in Watertown. It's not the city, where you can reinvent yourself and do whatever you want.

Walt lets out a snort of laughter as he unlocks the door to the office and lets himself back in. If he keeps thinking like that, he might start to see why Tad loves it so much.

Skylar's farm seemed like it was his dream, and that's not in the city. The Catskills are beautiful and—

And there he goes, thinking about Skylar again.

The way he acted comes back to him, too, settling like sludge in his gut. It's a bad feeling, and it makes his headache return. How long is he going to feel like this? Someone's going to notice, like his family, and they might badger him into talking, and that would be….

Walt doesn't even want to think about that. Obviously he *is* straight, and there's nothing to tell, but it might not sound that way to, say, his mom.

So he needs to figure out a way to stop feeling sick over what happened, and he needs it to happen as quickly as possible. Idly, he unlocks his phone. Instagram is still open, and there's Skylar's post again. Walt's stomach does a funny lurch that must be guilt.

It hits him. Surely the best way to get over feeling bad about the way you treated someone is to apologize to them? A face-to-face apology, because that's always more meaningful than a call, let alone a text.

Yeah. This feels good. This feels *right*. For the first time since Saturday night, Walt's churning stomach settles. This will fix his guilt, which means no one else will notice him acting weird, which means no one else will ask him why he's acting weird, and he won't have to lie or try to explain.

He exhales, already feeling lighter, and starts looking up hotels in Windham.

Chapter Eight

SKYLAR'S IN the barn mucking out Squirrel's stall when he hears the rumble of an engine and a door shutting. Putting a hand to the base of his spine, he straightens up and pauses his work. He wasn't expecting anyone, and even though Jett likes to drop by unannounced, they're at work in the salon today.

Next to him, Squirrel flicks his ears and stares in the direction of the driveway. Skylar pats his shoulder. Should he go see who it is? There was a time when someone showing up might be a business opportunity—the owner of a local store wanting to check out the farm before carrying their products, or an event organizer wanting to hire them to bring their animals—and Skylar would have gone to check.

Since Skylar's dropped the ball on the business so far that the ball is halfway to the center of the Earth, he goes back to mucking. Granted, there's a recent example of a hot, queer man knocking on his door out of nowhere, but Skylar's not lucky enough to have that happen twice. Anyway, he's not sure he'd want it to happen again, considering the way it turned out last time.

The snow may have mostly melted over the past two weeks, but there's still a storm—oh god, this is so cheesy!—in Skylar's heart. It's just, that time with Walt, from the moment he showed up shivering at the door with a plant under his shirt, to the hazy, blissed-out moments after they had sex, were some kind of magic.

Skylar *misses* Walt, and he doesn't know how that's possible when they don't even know each other. Sometimes he's afraid he made the whole thing up, except Walt still follows him on Instagram.

Yes, he checked. Yes, he felt pathetic about it. No, he didn't block Walt.

The goats' hooves clatter as they clamber up the playground, including the addition that Skylar finally finished. Someone appreciates the labor that came out of his heartbreak, at least. Jett's taken to calling it his Sad Crafting.

The car door opens and shuts again. An empty little pang drops from Skylar's chest to his stomach, even though he already knew it was just someone canvassing for votes, or someone looking for a lost pet, or someone selling something. It obviously wasn't a hot, queer man. And it definitely wasn't Walt returning because he felt the same connection Skylar did, and he feels bad about how things went down after he… er… went down.

Squirrel's ears prick forward. The llama shuffles and hums. It doesn't concern Skylar, because Squirrel will Let Him Know if he senses danger. A llama's alarm call is unmistakable and un-ignorable.

There's a knock on the barn door and a voice asks hesitantly from the other side, "Skylar? Are you in here?"

Skylar starts violently, drops his rake, and steps on the tines like he's in a *Three Stooges* bit. The rake handle doesn't swing up to smack him in the face, but it does manage to get air underneath it to swing around and smack the side of Squirrel's stall.

That llama alarm call? The unmistakable and un-ignorable one? Yeah, Squirrel lets loose with that. It's like someone blaring a broken bugle right in your ear, a high-pitched WEEEEEHHHH followed by a rhythmic bleat. Skylar grabs for the rake handle so he can get the thing out of the way and soothe Squirrel. The goats scramble toward Squirrel like they've been trained to do when the llama alarms. As long as Valentino doesn't start screaming—

The peacock, who's perching in one of the windows, lets out a wail. That makes Squirrel bray again, despite Skylar's "Shh, it's okay! Shh, don't worry, baby, there's nothing bad, just me being clumsy—"

"Everything okay in here?"

And okay, so, Skylar wasn't hallucinating the voice. Walt's standing in front of him.

The clamor of the animals fades to auditory black and white as Skylar stares. Walt. In the barn. Jeans and a puffer vest over a burnt orange sweatshirt which clashes horribly with his hair, that coppery, strawberry red-blond that Skylar can't pin down in his memory. It still won't allow itself to be pinned down in person.

"Oh my god," Skylar says.

Because he's an idiot! *Oh my god,* the sad, gay divorcé said to the hot dude who gave him the most incredible head of his life and then disappeared! Oh my god to *that.*

"I mean," Skylar says. "Fuck."

Nope, not that either. He puts a hand to his forehead, forgetting despite his surroundings that he's been digging literal shit out of a barn stall, and it's all over him. At least it is now, because while he hadn't gotten it on his face until this point, he just managed to smear filth across his forehead.

Walt looks like he's trying not to smile. There's a loose piece of hair falling over his freckly forehead, more scruff than he had two weeks ago, and his face is red. Probably not as red as Skylar's, but it's nice to know he's not the only one who's mortified right now.

The goats are settling down now that Squirrel has stopped alarming. Wanda is shivering between the llama's front legs, so Squirrel lowers his muzzle and snuffles at her. "Sorry I scared the animals," Walt says. "Did Squirrel make that noise? I was ready to go into macho protector mode again, except I remembered that last time I was only protecting you from a peacock."

He snaps his mouth shut and his face gets redder. Skylar still doesn't know what to say, only that he doesn't want to say any of it in his stall-mucking clothes. "You should come in the house," he manages.

"Oh, I don't want to put you to a bunch of trouble…." Walt trails off when Skylar looks at him. "Yeah, okay."

Skylar was almost done with the mucking, anyway. "I just have to finish up in here." And take a shower, but one thing at a time. "You can go inside the house and wait, if you want. You know your way around."

Did that sound innuendo-y? Oh god, it sounded innuendo-y.

"What else do you need to do out here? I'll help." Walt's face is earnest. He's close enough that Skylar can see the brightness of his blue eyes.

Swallowing everything else he wants to say—and doesn't want to say, but probably will anyway, at some point—Skylar points to the large metal bins where he keeps the goat feed. "You can fill the goats' feeding stations."

The feeding stations are small troughs mounted around the goats' main hangout area in the barn. Even though there's plenty of space for each one of them to eat at the same time, they'll still crowd around two or three of them. They have their favorite spots, and there's probably a good reason for it in goat logic.

Walt nods and does exactly what Skylar asked. The goats seem confused at this change in human-feeding-them, but they still scamper after Walt to the feeding stations. For a minute, Skylar forgets that he's supposed to be mucking out Squirrel's stall, and he stands there holding the rake and watching Walt. His easy smile, the way the corners of his eyes crinkle, the slight crookedness of his teeth that Skylar only gets flashes of—

Determinedly, he turns around to finish cleaning Squirrel's stall. If he's noticing that Walt's teeth are crooked, he's paying too close attention. From the look Squirrel's giving him, the llama agrees. Llamas, Skylar has learned over the course of his four years of running Blue Skies Farm, have a well-honed ability to look at you like you're the idiot, and you should know it.

Walt finishes feeding the goats before Skylar finishes mucking, so Skylar has him put out some feed for the peacocks, too. Skylar takes care of Squirrel's feed himself. Squirrel continues to give him a knowing look as he lowers his head to chow down.

With no way to put it off any longer, Skylar invites Walt to follow him across the yard and into the house. "Give me a couple minutes to shower," Skylar says once they're in the mud room. Even though he's pretty much inured to the scent of barn, he can smell himself. Presumably Walt can smell him even more. It's a miracle he isn't covering his nose.

"Oh! Yeah, definitely. Cool. I mean, you do whatever you need to do." Now that they're in the house, Walt looks nervous. That doesn't make Skylar feel any better about whatever this is.

Upstairs, Skylar strips off his dirty clothes and tosses them down the laundry chute before taking the world's fastest shower. In the past two weeks, he's indulged himself a few times with a long shower and the memory of Walt sucking him off, which isn't helpful now. Because now he's thinking of Walt sucking him, and also about jerking off in the shower, and it's making things perk up.

Fuck! He's turned his shower into a Pavlovian trigger!

He turns off the hot water entirely so he's doused with cold. That gives him regrets, too, but at least it takes care of the semi. Under no circumstances can he go downstairs and face Walt with the slightest hint of a boner.

When he gets downstairs again, less than ten minutes after he left, Walt's sitting at the kitchen table, scrolling on his phone. Skylar clears his throat and Walt's head snaps up. He smiles, then frowns, then stands, phone still in his hand, before he looks at it like he's never seen it before and puts it on the table.

The phone was obviously giving him something to fidget with, because now that he's not holding it, he starts wringing his hands. "I shouldn't have just showed up, should I have? I was just really afraid I'd chicken out if I didn't drive down here."

"Chickened out of what?" Skylar asks. He hasn't moved from the doorway. Now that they're in the house, the memory of the way he felt with Walt is sickening in its intensity. Until things got weird, Skylar felt more like *himself* than he has in a long, long time.

Walt takes a deep breath and stills his fidgeting hands. "Of apologizing. I have to. Apologize, I mean." He pauses, maybe realizing he didn't actually apologize, and adds, "I'm sorry. I'm… man, I'm so sorry. I shouldn't have acted like that."

Does he mean the sex or the weirdness after? Does Skylar even want to know? Will he be able to keep jerking off to the memory if he knows Walt regrets it so much that he had to drive three and a half hours to tell him?

"After everything you did to help me, and then I turned around and did that." Walt looks tortured. Skylar still can't parse which part he's sorry for.

Skylar shifts his weight and leans a shoulder and hip against the door frame. It feels wrong, like his body is contorted into an unnatural rictus. It feels, actually, like he has no idea how to stand naturally at all and probably hasn't managed it once in his entire life. What's he supposed to do with his arms?

Pockets. He'll put his hands in his pockets. The look Walt's giving him is full of trepidation and what looks like fading hope, so Skylar fumbles for something to say. "I'm… sorry if I, er… exacerbated things?"

Walt looks confused. "No, you just… I mean, maybe you did, a little, but I get it. We did"—he does something with his hand that's half gesture between them and half a distinct jerking motion—"um, what we did, and then I…."

"Was weird," Skylar supplies. "Was it something I did?"

"No!" Walt's voice is so loud that it reverberates in the space. Flinching, he repeats, "No. No, you were—no. It was me. I just… I shouldn't have done it. I messed up."

A possibility that hasn't entered Skylar's mind until now rears its head, and he can't believe he hasn't thought of it. "Oh no. You're seeing someone, aren't you? And you cheated on them… *with me.*" He presses the heel of his hand to his forehead and turns away. "God, you weren't messaging your brother at all, were you? It was your boyfriend!" He's party to adultery! It's the scummiest feeling imaginable, and it makes him want to shower again.

"No!" Walt yells again, looking horrified. "No, no no no, I'm not seeing anyone. I *was.* I had a girlfriend, but I don't now. I didn't when we—when I met you. And I was talking to my brother."

He looks so distressed that Skylar can't do anything but believe him. The tidbit about the girlfriend is interesting. So Walt is bi or pan, and honestly that should have occurred to Skylar already. Just because he's gay doesn't mean every guy who likes guys is.

"Okay," Skylar says. He desperately wants to ask why Walt shouldn't have hooked up with him. How was that messing up? It's intrusive, though, so he bites his tongue before the words make it out of his mouth. Whatever Walt's reasons, they're none of Skylar's business.

His heart falls, though, because—and this is very stupid, and he *knows* that—because the moment he heard Walt's voice through the barn door, hope bobbed up from below the surface of Skylar's two weeks of boggy wallowing. That hope pops like a cheap balloon at a county fair getting snagged on a branch on its way to soaring free into the wide blue sky.

"Okay," he says again. What else *can* he say?

"I felt really bad," Walt adds. There's no question that Skylar's disappointment is showing on his face, no matter how much he wishes he could hide it. If Walt's not into him, making sad faces isn't going to change that. Walt drops his eyes to the floor. "I still feel really bad. I guess the apology doesn't make up for it. It's not like it changes the fact that I did it."

"It helps." Skylar takes a step into the kitchen, then inhales deeply through his nose and goes the rest of the way to the table, pulls out a chair to sit—not across from Walt, but next to him, with only the corner between them. "I was afraid I did something to make you freak out," he admits. "Like maybe you thought you owed me for letting you stay here."

Walt looks horrified. Why did Skylar say that?

"I didn't think that." Walt puts his hand on the table and slides it toward Skylar like he wants to hold Skylar's hand. But Skylar's hands are in his lap, and anyway Walt glances at his hand like it has a mind of its own and withdraws it. "I mean, I for sure owed you. I still owe you. But I wouldn't…. What we did, that's not the way I would pay you back."

"So you wanted to." It's vitally important, for some reason, for Skylar to know this. There's a little voice in the back of his head that won't leave him alone, insisting he misread Walt's hand on his leg that night.

Walt looks somehow stymied and terrified at the same time, and Skylar's heart sinks as nausea wells through his stomach and into his throat. That probably shows on his face too. No, it definitely shows on his face, because Skylar's never hidden an emotion in his entire life.

"I wanted to," Walt replies. The words sound like they're being wrenched from somewhere deep within him.

Walt might have a lot of shit going on in his head that Skylar can't even guess at what it is. Which, you know, duh. Isn't there a word for that? Probably in German. Or French. The French always have a word for everything.

Silence falls between them. That's what Skylar wanted to know, right? If Walt thinks he shouldn't have done it, but he wanted to do it, then Skylar can't ask for any more.

Even if he wants to.

"Okay," Skylar says, for the third fucking time. Apparently he's not capable of anything else. Or just letting the silence fill the air between them. And maybe that's the best, most appropriate thing to do. They're two people who wouldn't have met, except a set of choices brought them into contact, instead of leaving them ships passing in the night like they should have been. Maybe they filled the space between them with everything there was to put in that space.

Walt looks at his lap and rubs his hand over the back of his neck. "I should let you get back to your weekend."

"No weekends on a farm," Skylar says without thinking. "I mean, yeah. I'm sure you want to get home to Watertown."

With a surprised look, Walt asks, "You remember that I live in Watertown?"

Skylar's pretty sure he remembers every detail Walt shared about his life. He's like a dragon with the saddest hoard ever. "Yeah."

Walt nods and stands, though there's a hitch to his movements, like he's reluctant. "I got a hotel room in town, actually. I'm staying a couple nights." He looks at the table and traces the wood grain with the tip of his finger. "Maybe you could give me some recommendations on things to see around here."

Is there a question there, hidden in Walt's downcast eyes and the way the sentence doesn't quite lift at the end, but hints at it?

"Sure, it depends on what you're into." Skylar stands too, because his eyes and mouth are much too level with Walt's hips, and Walt's jeans are clinging in a distracting way. He's not proud of the next words that come out of his mouth, but he can't be expected to make good choices in these circumstances. "If you want to stay a little longer, I can figure out some stuff for you to do…."

"Yes," Walt says, so fast that Skylar's brain stutters. Walt *did* say that hooking up was something he shouldn't have done, right? But there's a flare in his eyes that finds an answer deep in Skylar's body.

There's a word for this too, but Skylar knows this one: mixed signals. Okay, that's two words. The point is, Walt said the sex was a mistake, but he's standing here in Skylar's kitchen looking at Skylar like he's starving. He came all the way down here, drove three and a half hours, to apologize in person when an Insta DM would have worked just as well. Better, even. Why apologize in person to someone you regret hooking up with?

"Yes, okay, things to do," Skylar says, his eyes roaming the kitchen so he doesn't focus on the way Walt's are devouring him. Jett's entreaties for him to table at the Valentine's Day Makers Market come back to him. Despite Skylar's meager social media following, Jett's convinced that photos of the market, specifically photos of Skylar at the market, will help him get started on *building his brand*.

Sidebar: Skylar has a bit of PTSD about that phrase after attending a seminar on using social media to drive business. That's the closest he's ever been to a panic attack. Why can't he just rely on a quality product?

"There's a market thing tomorrow," Skylar says. "The Windham Valentine's Day Maker's Market. Craftspeople and artisans from all over participate."

"So, candles, jewelry, and soap?" Walt asks. One of his eyebrows arches. They're more coppery than his hair.

Folding his arms over his chest, Skylar says, "Sure. But there's food too. All kinds of small batch, local stuff. Honey, preserves, cocktail syrups, cheese—"

"Cheese?" Walt interrupts. "Are you going to be there?"

Skylar's face heats. Which is stupid, because he was completely solid in his decision not to participate. Waste of his time, waste of the fee. "I, um, no," he stammers.

"Oh." Walt looks disappointed. "Well, yeah, that sounds cool anyway. Thanks."

"Don't mention it."

"You could come with me."

The invitation is delivered so quietly and quickly that Skylar's not sure he heard right. Blinking, he repeats, "Come with you? To the market?"

Walt's face is bright red. With his freckles, his cheeks look like apples you pick from the tree yourself. "I don't know why I said that."

Skylar remembers how good things were between them until sex made them weird. Maybe they can be friends? Sure, the way Walt's looking at him makes it obvious he's attracted to Skylar, and Skylar has made Walt a permanent fixture of his spank bank, but... friends? It would be nice to have someone to geek out over *Gaslamp Market* with. Skylar felt vaguely queasy trying to watch the two latest episodes.

"I'll go," Skylar says. He can't tamp down on his smile, but he effectively shushes the voice howling that he's totally full of it about being friends with Walt. He can take some pictures and post them on the farm's social media. So it will also be a professional outing, which makes the idea unimpeachable. Jett will be proud of him. "It'll be fun."

"Yeah?" A smile spreads across Walt's face too. "Cool."

It *is* cool. It's cool and not dangerous and Skylar definitely isn't going to indulge his attraction to Walt or develop feelings beyond the friendly ones he already has.

Chapter Nine

WALT OPENS the door to his hotel room and fumbles on the wall for a light switch. When his fingers land on it, he comes the rest of the way inside, tosses his duffel bag on the floor, and locks the door behind himself.

Why didn't he tell Skylar that he's straight? Instead, he's going to a quaint, cozy, romantic country market. A Valentine's Fucking Day market. There were two things he came down here to make clear to Skylar. One is that he, Walt, was an asshole. The other is that he's one hundred percent straight, so what they did was something they shouldn't have done, and Walt's not interested in a repeat.

The problem was, Skylar had his sleeves rolled up when he was cleaning out Squirrel's stall, and he has tattoos. Complicated patterns in bold colors swirl up his arms, and every time the muscles in his forearms flexed, the tattoos just accentuated it.

Also, Walt couldn't stop staring at his shoulders? Skylar is a slender guy, but his shoulders are… built. Strong. You could grab them and hold on for dear life.

Every inch of his body gets hot in embarrassment for thinking this stuff, and also… not embarrassment. Scrubbing a hand over his face, he stomps to the bathroom, to splash cold water on his face.

Water drips off his chin and runs down his neck to the collar of his shirt, and he catches a glimpse of himself in the mirror as he reaches for a towel. He's blushing, his pupils are wide and dark, and there's a look on his face that's not just giving away his lust—it's broadcasting it on all channels. People three counties over probably know Skylar has him so turned-on that he was ready to make an exception to his one-hundred-percent-straight rule three minutes after seeing the guy again.

Well, another exception.

He groans and splashes his face again. Maybe he should take a cold shower.

The room is nice. Hell, it should be for what he's paying, but there wasn't a ton of availability. Still, Walt doesn't mind choosing an expensive historic hotel. The room is cozy, with a king bed taking up most of the space. The wood headboard complements the accent wall behind it, done up in a botanical wallpaper with shades of muted green. The other walls are sage green with half shiplap walls stained warm, dark brown. It matches the color of the wood dresser. The floors are hardwood, oak probably, from the bits Walt can see peeking out from underneath the thick rugs that cover them.

There was a flyer for the Windham Valentine's Day Makers Market in the lobby, which Walt tried not to look too closely at. It had a pink-and-red heart border.

He unpacks his weekend's worth of belongings and puts his duffel bag inside the wardrobe before taking a shower. The toiletries are all a fancy brand he's never heard of, but they smell sexy. The thought makes his skin prickle pleasantly until he remembers the person he's going to smell sexy for is Skylar, who Walt isn't supposed to want.

That time during the storm, that was just blowing off steam. A rebound.

Once he's out of the shower, a desperate urge to call his brother seizes him. If there's anyone he can talk to about this, it's Tad. Except there's nothing to talk about, because *Walt is straight*. If he calls Tad and—honestly, he doesn't even know what he wants to *say*. How did you know you were gay? But Walt knows he's not gay, because he really is attracted to women; he's only ever dated women.

If he starts asking Tad questions, Tad's going to think Walt's gay. The thought of how supportive Tad would be makes Walt queasy, because he doesn't deserve it. Tad would be wonderful, and Walt would have to say, no, you don't understand, I just had sex with this guy and can't stop thinking he's attractive and I don't know what to *do*.

It sounds gay in Walt's head. How the fuck is he supposed to convince his gay brother that it's not as gay as it sounds?

Calling Tad is out. Horrible idea. Even though Walt remembers how he felt when he found out last year that Tad was afraid to come out to him, and he doesn't want Tad to feel that way. Except that was totally different, because Walt isn't gay! He's straight.

Instead, he sprawls on the bed, pulls up the browser on his phone, and looks up the market. The website says over a hundred and fifty vendors are going to be there. There are a lot of local farms on the vendor list, which makes Walt wonder again why Skylar isn't one of them. When he asked Skylar earlier, it was mostly reflex. Local markets and small farms go together like cookies and milk.

Now it seems even stranger. Walt frowns at his phone. There's another farm on the list that sounds like they sell goat-milk-based products, at least if their name, We're The G.O.A.T! Farm is an indication of their primary livestock. Why isn't Skylar there selling goat cheese and baked goods? Why is We're the G.O.A.T.! Farm horning in on his share of the market? Especially with that stupid name.

They're probably hipsters with neck beards and scraggly man buns. Walt hates them a little bit already. He resolves not to buy anything from them.

Seriously, though, why isn't Skylar participating in this? When Walt was at his house during the storm, Skylar made a fleeting mention of having problems. Are the problems financial?

The idea bugs him—Skylar having money problems. Or any problems, really. A hard, swollen feeling in his chest makes it difficult to swallow, and it takes him a second longer to identify it as a desire to do something. To help. But it's not like he can ask. They're not even friends, really. Are they? No. Not yet? Can you be friends with someone you keep thinking about seeing naked?

God. He has to stop. He's not going to see Skylar naked, and he doesn't want to. At least, at some point he's not going to want to, even if it's not tonight.

Shit. Now he's thinking about Skylar naked. Worse, he's thinking about getting naked *with* Skylar.

And now his dick is getting in on it. Goddammit. The sexy body wash in the shower (and the matching body lotion, which obviously he used, because even if he's straight, he knows the value of moisturizing) really isn't helping.

With a groan, he gets to his feet. He'll go out and get something to eat and what he *won't* do is sit here stewing about how he can help Skylar with his unknown problems. It already sounds like the beginning of a porno, like, "It seems like you have a problem in your jeans that you need me to help with."

Or maybe Walt's projecting, because he does have a problem in his jeans, and if he stays in this plush hotel room, he's going to take care of it with his right hand. It's been exactly two weeks since he got off, because he's been afraid if he jerked off, he'd think about Skylar.

An image flashes through Walt's mind of Skylar's shoulders working under his shirt and the sinewy strength of his tattooed forearms, and he scrubs both hands over his face. It doesn't matter what he does, he just has to get out of this room.

The hotel is in a converted historic home on the east end of town. Route 23 runs straight through Windham, and traffic is puttering along significantly slower than the thirty-five-mile-an-hour speed limit in the fading afternoon light. The ski resorts in the area are probably doing a good business with all the snow from two weeks ago, even if a lot of it has melted elsewhere. And Windham is a pretty charming town, that's undeniable. It has that upstate New York, Washington Irving, quaint Catskills historic town vibe down pat.

Walt strolls down the sidewalk, hands shoved into his pockets as he dodges couples. There are *so many* couples. Valentine's Day must be a draw. Now that he thinks about it, there was a big banner on his hotel's website about a Valentine's Day dinner on Saturday and a Sunday brunch.

To the south, he catches glimpses through the buildings of the gentle rolling of the Catskills. There are still patches of white catching the sun and making the snow visible at a distance. He ducks into a diner in a building with a false front for what turns out to be a pretty decent chicken sandwich, then wanders the town. Darkness fell while he was eating, and there are fewer people out now. A cocktail bar that he passed on his way down the street the first time is doing a good business, the dull roar of conversation spilling out of the doors as someone comes out to vape.

His phone vibrates in his pocket and he fishes it out. Seeing Mario's name on the screen, he answers with, "Hey, man."

"Walt! It's Friday, buddy!" Mario yells, clearly driving. Granted, Mario only calls when he's driving, so Walt's used to how he sounds over his car's Bluetooth. Plus, he never turns his music down enough. "Ally's doing baby stuff with her mom and sister, so they turned me loose for the night. Meet me at the Paddock? I could use a G and T or five."

"Can't, sorry." Walt pauses to look into the window of a brightly painted shop. It's a little café. On their counter, they have baskets, currently empty, and mini chalkboards with names on them that sound like local bakeries.

"What do you mean, you can't? Sitting on your sofa watching Netflix doesn't count as plans."

Gaslamp Market releases new episodes at the ass crack of dawn on Fridays, so for the past month, Walt's Friday night plans *have* revolved around sitting on his sofa and watching it. Mario isn't into stuff like that, though. "I'm out of town. You'll have to get wasted on gin without me. Call a rideshare to get home, though, will you?"

"Out of town where?" Mario asks. "Weren't you just visiting Tad and the future sister-in-law? Or wait, is Tad the girl?"

Walt's stomach clenches. "Don't say that."

"I'm kidding." The music seems to get louder, like Mario turned it up. "Seriously, though, how much do you have to visit them?"

"I'm not visiting Tad and Lewis. I'm in the Catskills for the weekend." If he doesn't explain quickly, Mario will get bored with the conversation, so he adds, "It's a long story, but I went off the road during that storm a couple weeks ago, and I ended up spending a couple nights with this guy—"

"You got in a car accident?" Mario demands, which is good, because Walt only caught that he said *I spent a couple nights with this guy* once the words were out of his mouth. "Did you tell me that?"

"No." Usually Mario's attention span for the day-to-day happenings of Walt's life is only long enough for the high-level overview. If it didn't occur to him to ask about driving back during the storm, Walt feels like he's harping on his problems bringing it up himself. "Anyway, I just came back down here to, uh"—he grasps for an innocuous lie—"return something I borrowed from him."

"Cool," Mario says, in that way he does when he's ready to talk about something else. "Hey, I'm sitting in the parking lot at the Paddock, I better go. My bar nights are at a premium. I gotta get them in before the baby comes."

"Okay, see you, man."

"I'll have a drink for you!" With that, Mario disconnects, and Walt's left with a vague sense of dissatisfaction, like gray clouds piling up at the horizon on an otherwise nice day. He can't possibly confess to Mario to why he's in Windham this weekend.

Which doesn't matter, because once this weekend is over, Walt will be cured of wanting a repeat of the snowstorm blow job with Skylar. He has to be.

Chapter Ten

SKYLAR GETS up extra early on Saturday to make sure he has enough time for chores, showering, and making himself presentable. Making Himself Presentable is by far the most intimidating part of that lineup. When was the last time he had to try? The Holiday Maker's Market? He definitely didn't use aftershave or cologne for that.

He probably shouldn't have used aftershave or cologne today, either, but that bridge has been crossed. Unless he takes another shower, but then he'd have to do his hair all over again. Yeah, he did his hair too; he Facetimed Jett for help, and Jett said they'll drop by the Maker's Market so they can meet the infamous snowstorm guy.

And, okay. Confession time: Skylar's Good Sense And No Hormones Brain knows that aftershave, cologne, spending twenty minutes on his hair, and dressing like he's going on a Saturday daytime date are all bad ideas. But Skylar's Get Laid By Hot Man Caveperson Brain is telling him he looks and smells fantastic, and no way is he changing a thing.

The doorbell rings at ten on the dot, and a buzz goes through Skylar. He reminds himself that even though he's dressed for it, this *isn't* a Saturday daytime date.

Shoving down the low-grade fizzing in his stomach, Skylar opens the front door to find Walt standing there looking just as Saturday daytime date as Skylar, but like, the straight guy version of it. Which is confusing, but probably a good sign? Or a bad sign, depending on if he's listening to the Caveperson or the Good Sense part of his brain.

"You look nice," Skylar says ill-advisedly. Caveperson brain won out, apparently. But it's also true—Walt's wearing a slate blue button-up with dark brown chinos. That scruff Skylar noted on his face yesterday is still there. Maybe Walt's trying to grow a beard. A hot pulse of desire blooms in his gut. *Down, boy*.

Red creeps up Walt's neck, under the scruff to his cheeks. "Thanks," he says gruffly. "So do you."

Skylar touches his hair self-consciously and fiddles with the collar of his button-up. It's forest green with an all-over print of tiny pink flowers, and he hasn't worn it in forever. There hasn't been a reason to. His skinny camel-colored cords have similarly been languishing in a seldom opened drawer. And he got out his nice boots instead of wearing his farm boots. Manure caked deep in the tread may be the reality of his life, but he was willing to take the chance that he still cleaned up nice.

"Well," Walt says at the same moment Skylar says, "So."

They look at each other. Walt snorts and Skylar cracks a smile. "Want to take my truck?" Walt asks.

"We could take mine, but I have to admit, I'm pretty curious to ride in the car that spent that storm getting buried at the bottom of a ditch."

With a laugh, Walt replies, "Man, if that's what passes for excitement around here, we have some work to do."

"Oh yeah?" Skylar locks the door behind him as he steps outside. It's a mild day for mid-February, bright sun that promises spring and warm enough to not need a jacket. "That's you offering, right?"

"Sure." Walt offers him an easy grin as they get in his truck, a silver Honda Ridgeline. Judging by the lack of screen on the dashboard, it's on the older side. That fits, somehow. He seems like the kind of guy who wouldn't spend money on a new car with all the bells and whistles when an older model drives just fine. "But I gotta confess, I might not be the best person to spice up your life. My ideal Friday night is having a beer at home by myself and watching a good show."

"That sounds great, actually. Shockingly, running a farm by yourself doesn't leave a lot of energy for going out." As Walt does a three-point turn in the driveway, Valentino watches them from the top rung of the paddock fence, bright blue feathers glistening in the sun and his tail hanging behind him. It's almost grown back from his late summer molt. There's something knowing in the peacock's gaze, like he recognizes someone else fanning his fancy feathers when he sees it.

"It must be an insane amount of work." Walt hesitates. "You really run it by yourself?"

"Yeah." Skylar drums his fingers on the armrest and makes a concerted effort to unclench his abs. Why did he bring up running the farm when he feels like he's staving off a panic attack every time he does? Something about Walt puts him at ease, though. It feels like they've been friends for years. "I didn't used to. It used to be me and my ex-husband. We started it together."

"Oh—ex-husband. Sorry to hear that."

Talking about Cody and the divorce is so much less stressful than talking about running the farm. "I know it's cliché, but it was for the best. We met in college and he was…." *Definitely not ready to get married* is how Skylar would end that sentence, but he's getting over it, and part of that is not re-litigating why it was such a shitshow to every sympathetic audience. "We got married too young," he says instead. "I had this dream to start a farm. He handled the business stuff."

Walt makes a noise but doesn't comment. It's not obvious that the business side of the farm—aka, making a living—is tanking, but someday soon, it's going to be. With the way he's dipping into his savings, they, and the farm, aren't going to last much longer.

His dad would say *I told you so*.

"You went to school at CUNY, right?" Walt asks.

Skylar blinks. "I—yeah, I did, but did I mention that?"

"Oh, er." Sounding embarrassed, Walt says, "You had on a CUNY sweatshirt the night we met."

The fact that Walt remembers what he was wearing the night they met makes the Caveman brain very happy. With this much encouragement, it's going to expect Skylar to get laid. "Only for a couple years. I dropped out."

Up in Windham, telling people that doesn't get much of a reaction. For a lot of people here, college isn't part of the life plan. People in the city act(ed) like he just got diagnosed with a terminal disease. His peers at Hunter College in Manhattan kept hugging him, asking if he lost his scholarship, or if his financial aid wasn't coming through.

"You weren't feeling it, or…?" Walt asks. "Sorry, that's none of my business."

"No, it's not anything dramatic. I'm not traumatized by dropping out. I'm glad I did."

With another glance across the car, Walt says, "I wish I had." They arrive at a stop sign and have to wait for a bunch of cars to pass. Walt makes a face. "I've never told anyone that."

Skylar makes what is surely a bungled and sacrilegious sign of the Christian cross. "I absolve you of the sin of not loving college, my son."

One of Walt's eyebrows goes up. "Was that like, an old Wii Tennis move?"

Skylar laughs. "No, that's more like—" Screwing up his face in concentration, he slo-mo mimes diving to make a save and keep a ball from going out of bounds.

"The crowd goes wild!" Walt booms. A horn blares behind them. "Oh! Shit—sorry, bro!" He waves to the irate driver behind them and guns it across the intersection. Skylar cackles.

The market is held at a local brewery with a huge warehouse space. Despite the cavernous size of the warehouse, it's jammed full of vendors. Pun not intended, though several of the vendors are sure to be selling jam. The market started at nine, and an hour and change after opening, it's already crowded. Skylar knows from previous experience that lunchtime will draw even more people.

"Wow, this is a big deal," Walt comments as they walk through the doors. There are glittery red, pink, and white construction paper hearts taped all along the doorframe. Last year, Skylar thought the Valentine's Day decorations were tacky overkill. This year, they make him smile.

"Yeah, it's a whole thing. And the brewery sells a lot of beer, so they love it."

Walt sticks his hands in his pockets and steps aside as a determined-looking woman marches in like she's on a mission. "Plus drunk people buy more stuff."

"People who have been *loosened up* by a delicious and locally crafted adult beverage don't let their inhibitions get in the way of buying that special treasure they walked past earlier," Skylar corrects. Hopefully Walt will read the cant of his smile and the glimmer in his eyes the way they're meant to be read.

Gratifyingly, Walt grins. "I should try that at my business. Let's talk residential fencing over a glass of wine. Or beer. I guess I'd need to read the room."

"And get a liquor license," Skylar points out.

"Shh." Walt holds a finger to his lips, which is, oh no. It's distracting, because Walt's finger is touching his lips, and Skylar suddenly wants very badly for it to be *his* finger touching Walt's lips. That's so much horny for not even ten thirty in the morning and no alcohol.

They amble up the first aisle of the market. The first stall is clothes—jeans where the denim on the bottom half of the legs has been replaced by another boldly patterned fabric, jackets with the same concept applied to the sleeves. It's clever but would take a certain kind of person to pull it off, and Skylar isn't that person.

Walt stops and fingers the collar of a quilted jacket with sleeves made of a Van Gogh's Starry Night-esque patterned fabric. "My mom would love this." He checks the price and winces. "Maybe I'll come back after a beer."

The mention of Walt's mother is a reminder that Skylar hardly knows anything about this man. Whether they remain friends or… no, they have to remain friends, because Walt made it pretty clear that's all that's on the table. Even if he does look at Skylar like a starving man. "Do you live near your parents?"

"Yup." Something crosses Walt's face, and as someone who has a strained relationship with his father, Skylar recognizes it. "Born and raised in Watertown, and they're still there. I live about fifteen minutes away from them."

"And you just have the one brother? He's in the city, right?"

"Right," Walt sighs.

Skylar stops at one of the many booths selling candles and sniffs one. It's called Sexy Lumberjack and Skylar is kind of mad that he loves it and would be attracted to any man that smelled like this. He holds it up for Walt to smell. "That was a pretty serious sigh."

Walt closes his eyes as he smells the candle. There are freckles on his eyelids. Skylar's stomach flutters. "Tad used to do two visits a year back to Watertown, and now he's down to one."

"Oh," Skylar says delicately.

"Yeah." Walt opens his eyes and takes the candle from Skylar. His fingers brush Skylar's, all warm and dry and callused, and the butterflies situation in Skylar's stomach grows significantly more fluttery. "This is nice, I should get it for—" When he sees the name, he splutters out a laugh. "Never mind."

Smirking, Skylar asks, "For your mom?"

"I was going to say my dad, because he loves anything that smells like the woods." He considers the candle. "You know what, he'd deal with the name better than my mom. He might be at a point where he'd even find it funny."

Skylar winces. "Does that mean what I think it means?"

There's a pause while Walt studies the candle way more intently than it requires. "Depends what you think it means."

"I think it means that I can't say what I think it means without being insulting to your parents."

With a huff of unamused laughter, Walt says, "My mom hasn't been great about Tad being gay. My dad tries harder."

The implications for Walt annoy Skylar. "And she's the type to think 'bi' means you'll eventually settle down with a woman?" Walt's mouth opens but no sound comes out, and Skylar's face gets warm. "Sorry. I shouldn't have said that. I don't know your mom."

"No, I think you're probably right." Walt's voice sounds a little strange, and this time, Skylar's left guessing about what it means. "She kept hinting—well, honestly more than hinting—that she thought I should propose to my girlfriend. Ex-girlfriend."

"Oof."

"I guess…." Walt hesitates. "Maybe I kind of thought I was going to do it too. Eventually."

Where's that hole in the ground Skylar wanted to dig for himself? "Oh no. I'm sorry. I—shit. So it was really serious. That sucks."

Walt sets down the candle and continues to the next booth. "Thanks, but it wasn't. I mean, it felt like it was at the time. Or, no, that's not really right, either. It felt like it *should* be, because I'm thirty-three, and everyone I know is like, having kids and has their shit together. My little brother's getting married! Well, technically he's already been married once, but it was to the same person, so I'm not sure that counts."

That's definitely a story Skylar wants to hear, but he needs to go back to everything else first, because it's…. Well, Skylar's got some experience there. "It's better not to get married to someone who isn't right instead of marrying them because you feel like it's a thing you should do."

Walt winces, and Skylar realizes his voice came out harder than he meant it to. "Kind of stepped in it, didn't I," Walt says.

"No. I mean, I just get it, that's all. But speaking from experience, you don't like each other more as time goes on." His grandparents would have laughed and told Skylar that he's being too American. That in the old days in Thailand, couples barely knew each other when they got married.

"Anyway." Walt darts a glance at Skylar. "That got heavy. What about you? Do your parents live around here?"

"My mom's dead," Skylar deadpans, because he can't *not*. Walt set him up too well for it.

Walt stops in his tracks, puts a hand over his face, and then turns and makes for a gap between booths. Skylar snorts with laughter and grabs his arm. "I'm joking. Well, no, my mom actually is dead, but you know what I mean."

"That was dark," Walt informs him, and Skylar shrugs. They continue on, arms occasionally bumping companionably. "Is this what I'm going to get from you now? Morbid jokes?"

"Only if I can take advantage of you inadvertently sticking your entire foot in your mouth," Skylar says seriously.

"Better than having my head up my ass, I guess." Walt's eyebrows draw together and he looks thoughtful, then shakes his head like he's shedding whatever he's thinking about. "I'm sorry about your mom, though, man."

There's such sincerity in Walt's voice that Skylar's surprised— and he doesn't know why he's surprised, because Walt has seemed like a kindhearted man from the beginning. That night Walt showed up at his door, clutching a plant under his shirt because he didn't want it to die in the cold; the way his eyes soften when he sees the goats and Squirrel.

"Thanks," he murmurs. Clearing his throat, he adds, "My dad lives in New Jersey. I grew up in Clifton."

"And you ended up running a farm in upstate New York." Walt gives him an interested look. "Sounds like a story."

With a crooked smile, Skylar says, "You'll have to tune in next week."

That makes Walt's eyebrows go up, and a mischievous gleam lights up his eyes. "Are you asking me out on a second date?"

Skylar's stomach does something that he's positive is unhealthy. Can stomachs turn themselves inside out? "Uh," he says.

Walt looks shocked, like his own words blindsided him. "I mean," he says. Then, "It's. Um."

"I thought," Skylar begins, groping for the rest of the sentence. Surely he thought something? At some point? But all he can think, giddily, while the butterflies swoop and dive-bomb in his stomach, is that Walt just called *this* a date. Today. Right now, the two of them at this market, this is their first date.

Red creeps up Walt's neck and face. "Foot in my mouth again," he says, sounding strangled. "Or maybe my head up my ass?"

If Walt seemed horrified, or unhappy, or like he regretted what he said, Skylar would back off. But he doesn't seem any of those things; he only seems like he didn't mean, or maybe didn't expect, to say it. Like he's groping for words himself.

Trying his absolute hardest to sound casual, Skylar replies, "If you ever feel like a second date, you know where I live."

They've finally reached the end of the first aisle. Skylar can't remember anything they looked at in the last ten minutes. He also can't remember ever taking so long to explore any of Windham's Makers Markets before, nor enjoying himself this much.

"Yeah," Walt says. "I guess I do."

Possibility thrills through Skylar's veins, because that's not *no*, and it's not *I shouldn't have done it* and it's not another stop sign that says Just Friends on it. It's… it's…. Skylar doesn't know what, but it could be something, and it makes him feel light.

His phone chimes with Jett's assigned sound, which reminds him that he promised they could meet Walt. At least, Jett insisted they were going to meet Walt, and Jett has a way of making you feel like you promised something when they were the one to suggest it in the first place.

"Not to change the subject," Skylar says, because this is totally going to seem like an awkward subject change and that's the last thing he wants Walt to think, "but my friend Jett is going to stop by on their lunch break to say hi, if you don't mind."

The expression on Walt's face looks like a tug-of-war between relief and disappointment. "Yeah, no, I don't mind."

Skylar texts Jett back, and they agree to meet at one of the kombucha stands. *The good one*, Jett clarifies, *not the one that's totally just rebottling apple cider vinegar.*

While they're waiting, the kombucha people give them samples. By the time they get to strawberry basil, Walt has gone from a skeptic to a convert. He's just bought a full glass when Jett blows in, dressed in head-to-toe hair-stylist black, glittery black eyeliner with red-and-pink eyeshadow, bright pink lipstick, and their hair twisted into something that Skylar wants to call a chignon, only he thought you needed more hair for that?

Jett's eyebrows go up as they give Walt an obvious once-over. "Oh," they say, "you are *just* what Skylar's marketing team ordered."

Chapter Eleven

THE MINUTE Walt lays eyes on Jett, he knows he likes him. Or... her? They? They seems safest. Wait, no, he should ask! He shouldn't assume, he should ask.

"Oh, you are *just* what Skylar's marketing team ordered," Jett says, giving Walt what he can only call an appreciative look.

Walt holds out a hand, which Jett shakes delicately. "I'm Walt. I do residential fencing, actually, but I can give marketing a shot. Uh, is it rude to ask what pronouns you use?"

Jett lights up. "No, of course not! They/them." Turning to Skylar, Jett mouths obviously, *Keep him.*

Skylar looks both embarrassed and fond. "Jett, don't."

"Why? He's perfect. Brawny, handsome in that boy-next-door kind of way, and sexy. But like, attainably." Jett puts their hands on their hips and looks between Walt and Skylar. "You've been taking pictures together for Insta, right?"

Who is *this person*, Walt wonders as Skylar says, "No! We're just here for fun."

Before Skylar even gets the entire sentence out, Jett is holding their phone up. "Stand close just like that."

Their camera makes a shutter sound and Walt realizes they just took a picture. He's still stuck back on Jett calling him *sexy, but attainably*. "I feel like I walked into a bit," Walt says.

"It would take too long to explain," Skylar says. His phone pings and he reaches for it.

"I just sent you the picture," Jett informs Skylar. "Post it and caption it, umm, hm, is it too wintry to make puns about things growing and springing up?"

"Stop talking!" Skylar orders them, looking horrified but also laughing.

Jett takes another picture and sticks their phone in their back pocket. "Fine. I'll workshop it. And it won't take long to explain, Walt. Skylar isn't making any money, and he keeps not doing anything to change that. Blue Skies Farm desperately needs a branding overhaul. I'm helping."

By this time, Skylar's face is buried in his hands. The kombucha people seem like they're trying to eavesdrop, and Walt moves until he's between them and Skylar so they can't stare at him anymore.

"I think you might be hindering," Skylar says, his voice muffled.

"How many more followers do you have since I started telling you what to post?"

Skylar's hands are still over his face. "Ten, but one posts 'great content' on every picture, and another said she was very lonely and could I please come see her now."

"Eight out of ten new followers being real people is a good start," Walt says bracingly.

It's an almost physical struggle to say that instead of asking how bad Skylar's financial trouble is. But it couldn't be clearer that Skylar doesn't want to talk about it.

"It's not," Skylar says. He drops his hands from his face. "I'm bad at it, Jett. I have money. I'll figure something out. I'll be okay."

Jett's lips thin. "Guess who brought goats and is selling treats for people to feed them?"

Eyes widening, Skylar says, "They *didn't*. We're the G.O.A.T.?"

"Yep." Jett pops the P.

"Those *fuckers*," Skylar mutters through clenched teeth. Walt hasn't heard him swear in anger before. But if anyone deserves it, it's We're the G.O.A.T. Farm.

"You have to stop the bleed now," Jett insists. "It's not going to get better unless you do something."

"I'll help you," Walt says more loudly than he means to.

Skylar looks at him, eyebrows shooting up. "What? No, Walt, you don't—Jett's just being their typical overenthusiastic self. I'll figure it out."

That's the second time Skylar's said that. The first offer had no thought behind it besides not wanting to see Skylar distressed. But when Walt repeats, "I want to help," it has an additional fifteen seconds of certainty that Walt *really doesn't want* to see Skylar distressed. "What do you need me to do?"

For a second, Skylar's mouth opens and closes soundlessly. It's hard to tell if he's overcome with gratitude or wondering how to tell Walt to fuck off. Maybe Jett will have something helpful to add.

"I have to get back to work," Jett says. "Nice meeting you, Walt. Skylar, post the picture!"

They hurry away, leaving Walt and Skylar standing there in silence. Skylar's gaze flicks to Walt's. "You better post the picture," Walt says in what he means to be a teasing tone.

Skylar snorts but pulls out his phone. After a minute, he says, "Done."

Obviously, Walt has to look. It's a nice photo of the two of them. Skylar's laughing and Walt is grinning at him. They don't seem like a couple of people who barely know each other—they seem comfortable, like they're friends or maybe more.

"Jett knows how to take a good picture," Skylar says, sounding grudging. "They run the Instagram for the salon where they work."

"They seem like a cool—" Walt stops himself before he says guy or girl. "—Person."

With a smirk, Skylar says, "They claim 'cowpoke' is their favorite epithet."

Walt has a feeling the laugh he lets out is too loud, even for a loud, crowded market. A few people turn to look at him, but he doesn't care. Let them look. No one he knows is here; no one is going to connect him to his parents or his business.

Skylar jerks his head. "C'mon, let's go down this aisle. I think Margery's here with her quilts."

Margery's quilts turn out to be very dorky—she has *Star Wars, Star Trek,* Nintendo games, *Marvel, Pokémon*, you name it. Except *Gaslamp Market.* Walt looks, and it's not there. Not that he should expect it to be; it's not like it has a big following or anything.

"I'm so glad you came out!" Margery, an older Black woman with short gray hair, exclaims when she catches sight of Skylar. "I thought maybe you were out of town and that's why you weren't signed up to table."

Shaking his head as he stares at a quilt without seeming to see it, Skylar says, "No, I just… had other stuff going on."

Walt tries to hang back, but maybe he's being too obvious about watching Skylar, because Margery fixes him with an intrigued look.

"And who's this you brought today?" Once introductions have been made, Margery says, "This is perfect, Skylar. You can sign up for the Spring Fling Showcase after all!"

Skylar takes a deep breath, and Walt knows, he just *knows*, that Skylar's going to refuse to sign up for whatever the Spring Fling Showcase is. But Skylar needs to do stuff like that. Showcases are always a good thing for a business. "You mentioned how excited you were to sign up for that, Sky. Right?"

"I, uh…." Skylar trails off, looking at Walt searchingly. Walt gives him an encouraging nod. "Right. Spring Fling Showcase. You're doing the different animal categories again this year?"

"Of course!" Margery beams. "Oh, I'm so happy about this! I love seeing what all the couples come up with for the Spring Fling. I suppose it would make more sense to do it at Valentine's Day, but no one wants to be outside, and we'd have to cut so many of the events."

Couples?

"Yeah," Skylar says, pulling a face. "We'd probably have a blizzard if we tried to have this one outside."

Margery echoes his expression. "You were alright during the storm?"

Nodding, Skylar says, "The peacocks didn't love being cooped up, but they had to deal." He glances at Walt, hesitates another moment, and adds, "Walt was here that weekend."

"*Oh*, was he?" Margery's eyebrows waggle unmistakably. What? What's happening? Why is she acting like she knows what he and Skylar did? Christ, he didn't even think about it, but does Jett know too? Does this entire town know?

Skylar's eyes flick to Walt again. "We still have most of the market to check out. I'll email you about Spring Fling, though."

She gives him a pat on the cheek, and then Walt gets the same treatment. "Of course. You two lovebirds enjoy!"

A hand digs into the small of Walt's back and propels him away from Margery's Quilts, accompanied by Skylar saying in a low voice, "Don't say anything, don't say anything, *don't say anything*."

Never let it be said that Walt's not good at following orders. He keeps his mouth shut, even as Skylar's hand on his back becomes less jabbing and more comfortable. In fact, it's not a bad feeling at all, walking past market stalls with Skylar's hand at his waist.

They end up in the food section of the market, which is busy with noon approaching. Skylar finds a free table and gestures for Walt to sit. Walt does, but he says, "Shouldn't we get something to eat so we're not taking up a table?"

Skylar gives him a funny look before he twists at the waist to look at the food options. "What do you feel like?"

"Whatever. You choose. I'm not picky."

With one more searching look, Skylar gets up again. He returns ten minutes later with two plates of tacos and bottles of tamarind Jarritos. "Okay?" he asks.

Walt slides his phone away and digs in. "Of course. Everyone likes tacos."

"Someone out there probably doesn't like tacos."

"Sure, a serial killer. Or Elon Musk."

Skylar laughs and looks less tense. In turn, that makes Walt less tense. After taking a swig of his soda, Skylar says, "So, that thing you volunteered me for?"

"Spring Fling Showcase," Walt says, like this is a quiz. It occurs to him that he's acting stupid around Skylar. Why?

A smile breezes over Skylar's face, so that makes Walt feel less stupid. "Yeah. Spring Fling Showcase. It's like this, with the market, but there's also kind of a county fair component to it—like the different categories you can win a blue ribbon in."

"Sounds fun. I'm glad I volunteered you for it." Walt takes a big bite of taco. It's so good that he thinks he might be having a religious experience.

That one corner of Skylar's mouth is curving up. "Yeah? Well, you also volunteered yourself. The gimmick with Spring Fling is that you have to enter your categories as a couple. That's why Margery thinks we're together. Because you said I was really excited to sign up."

Walt chokes on his taco, and depending on if the afterlife is real, he might genuinely have a religious experience soon. He thumps himself on the chest several times, coughs, and asks weakly, "What?"

The tiny crook of a smile on Skylar's face turns sad, though Walt isn't sure how he knows that. The angle of his mouth doesn't change, but something happens in his eyes. "It's fine, you don't have to do it. I'll tell Margery we broke up."

"Whoa, hey, you're breaking up with me?" Walt jokes, trying to make that sad look in Skylar's eyes go away.

It works, kind of. A laugh brightens his face before he ducks his head and moves his tacos around his plate. Once they're rearranged, he starts moving them around again. "Look, it was nice of you to come all this way to apologize. And I like you. I mean, hopefully that's obvious?" His eyes dart up to glance at Walt, but before Walt can open his mouth to respond, Skylar goes on, "But Jett trying to drag you into my dumb problems, and doing Spring Fling with me, you don't have to do that."

"Sky—" Walt begins. His phone buzzes with a text.

But Skylar rushes on, "You're amazing for going along with things for this long. But c'mon, it's not like we're going to pretend to be a couple just so I can enter some contest at a market."

The text is from his mom. Absently, Walt unlocks his phone to respond so she doesn't worry. Instagram is still open, and he does a double take at the number of likes and comments on the picture of Skylar and him. "Uh, Skylar? You should look at your Insta."

Skylar furrows his brow but takes the suggestion. It's obvious when he sees what Walt is seeing, because his eyes practically pop out of his skull. "What?" he says faintly.

There are hundreds of likes on the photo, and as Walt watches, the count ticks up. There are comments rolling in, too, and not just emojis. One person commented, *Who's the hottie?* while another said, *Where do I find my own gorgeous gay farmer?*

"What… is even happening right now?" Skylar asks, staring at his phone wide-eyed.

Hundreds of likes isn't much by a big account's standards, but Walt knows from following Skylar for the past two weeks that it's more engagement than he's ever had.

"I think you gamed the algorithm just right," Walt says.

Skylar is still staring at his phone. "People are posting this to their stories." He looks up in horror, which wasn't the reaction Walt expected. "All these people think we're *together.*"

The appalled way he says it stings, which is maybe the dumbest thing out of all the dumb things Walt's thought or done or said in the past two weeks. Walt sits back in his chair and concentrates on his food, confused by how hurt he is and annoyed by both his hurt and his confusion. Nothing makes sense to him anymore.

Skylar stands. "We should go. Is it okay if we go? Sorry, I know I said I'd show you the market, but I really think—shit." He sits again and hunches. "People are pointing at us."

Walt glances at his phone again. The number of likes and comments on the post has grown exponentially over the past minute.

"Orville Peck added it to his story," Skylar says faintly.

"Wait, what? The country singer?" Walt scrolls through the growing comments section and finds that yes, Orville Peck the country singer not only apparently added the post to his story, but also left a comment.

Skylar makes a gurgling sound.

Despite his stupid hurt feelings over something that doesn't make sense to be hurt about, Walt doesn't like seeing Skylar so off-balance. "Let's go back to your place. I want to help you."

There's more that he means to add to that, clarifications about what he wants to help with and how he gets why Skylar doesn't want to seem like they're together romantically, but it all gets stuck in his throat with the way Skylar looks at him.

Heat flares in his chest and something molten slides down his spine to settle in his hips. No one has ever looked at him like that, like he's heaven-sent, or too good to be true, and like he's doing exactly the right thing without tying himself in knots from the effort of giving people what they expect from him.

He's more confused now. But it doesn't stop him from getting to his feet and waiting for Skylar to do the same.

Chapter Twelve

THE DRIVE back to Blue Skies Farm is somewhere at the intersection of unreal, awkward, and anticipatory. When they arrive, Skylar is twitchy, checking his notifications as they cross from the truck to the house, until he turns his phone off entirely and puts it facedown on the kitchen table.

Walt toes off his shoes and resists the urgent need to fold Skylar into his arms. It seems like the best way to approach the events of the past hour is the same way he'd approach a complicated job at work: methodically. Like a residential lot with janky property lines, this situation is going to require more than just slapping up some posts. Or something. The metaphor is getting away from him. Simile? Whatever.

Walt puts a hand on Skylar's shoulder and turns him toward the living room. It doesn't alleviate his desire to put his arms around Skylar and pull Skylar's body flush with his; in fact, it only makes that desire more pressing. Walt ignores it, gently steering Skylar into the living room.

"So people are assuming we're together from that picture you posted," Walt says, once they're both seated on the sofa.

Skylar laughs. There's a tinge of hysteria to it. "Twelve thousand and counting. I'm so sorry."

"That's okay. Most of them probably aren't here, right? And they're going to forget instantly, anyway. Nothing lasts on social media."

"I'm getting new followers," Skylar says. "People are following the farm because of this picture."

Walt kicks his foot. "That's good. That's exactly what you want. People following the farm!"

"But they're only following because they think we're a hot gay couple that runs it together!" Skylar pushes both hands into his hair. "Walt, I am *so* sorry. Do you want me to take it down? I'll take it down. And I'll make a statement or something. And I obviously won't tag you or anything, but I'll just say—"

"You're not doing any of that," Walt interrupts. Certainty settles in his chest. "I said I want to help you, and I was already going to pose as your boyfriend for the Spring Fling Showcase. So I'll just pretend to be your boyfriend for social media too. What's the harm?"

Even as he says it, an extensive list of the possible harm presents itself in his mind. At the top is Walter Pierce Isn't Gay, and… pretty much everything else is a subsection of that.

That's an easy thing to neutralize, though. If any of his family or friends happens to see this (he doesn't think they will; the internet is a big place), he'll just tell them the truth: he's doing a favor for a friend. Why should it be a big deal to pretend to be another guy's boyfriend? No one he knows would blink if he was doing it for a woman friend.

Skylar's eyes are wide. They're an amazing color. If he saw them on anyone else, Walt would think they were contacts, but nothing about Skylar suggests he'd bother with that. "You'd pretend to date me just to help me? Not just help me, but help me with a situation that's my own doing?"

"Running a business is hard."

A half smile quirks one corner of Skylar's mouth. "Does your business plan for your fence company involve a lot of fake dating?"

Walt runs a thumb along a worn spot in his chinos. He scraped them on a rough spot once on a job, which wasn't a place he should have been wearing one of his few decent pairs of pants. There was some reason for it that made sense at the time, but now he can't remember what it was.

Words pour out of Walt's mouth before he thinks about what he's admitting. "My business plan for my fence company involves a lot of me doing the same thing every day for the rest of my life because it's safe and sensible, and that's what everyone expects from me."

He snaps his jaw shut so hard his teeth click together. Of all the things he didn't need to add to this clusterfuck, the stifling of his own ambition is a good contender for the top spot.

Weirdly, though, some of the tension goes out of Skylar's body. The tight lines around his pretty, golden eyes ease. "So not fake dating as much as fake enthusiasm."

Walt considers his average work day. "I'm not sure I'm faking much enthusiasm."

Skylar leans back into the sofa. "So I love my business, but can't run it worth a damn, and you hate your business, but you run it well. Together we'd make one good business owner."

"I think that's what I've been saying," Walt points out.

Rubbing a hand over his face, Skylar says, "But when we hooked up, you—"

"Yeah, I know," Walt cuts him off. He knows how he acted. He knows why he acted that way. What he doesn't know is why he hasn't explained it to Skylar. Why hasn't he told Skylar that he's not gay, he's not bi, he's not pan. He's not under the big, colorful LGBTQ+ umbrella because he can't be, because that's not who he's allowed to be. He's just straight man Walt.

Skylar bites his lip. "I don't get why you're okay with faking a relationship on social media, but you weren't okay with hooking up."

Which is fucking merciless. Walt wishes he had an answer. Because yeah, this doesn't make any sense, and Skylar doesn't even know the half of it. This is the dumbest idea Walt's ever had, but he feels like a dog with a bone. Letting it go isn't happening.

"I like you," Walt says. "I want to help."

For a long moment, Skylar studies him. When a smile finally cracks his face, he says, "I bet you offer to drive people to the airport and always help your friends move."

"I have a truck, why wouldn't I help my friends move?"

There's a silence before Skylar snorts with laughter. Walt does too, because Skylar's laugh is infectious, even though he's pretty sure that's not something a straight guy thinks about his buddy.

Skylar nudges Walt's foot with his toe. "What do you want to do if it's not residential fencing?"

Walt's heart stutters. He's never ever told anyone about his secret dream. It's not a safe choice. It's the kind of thing you might end up blowing all your savings on before you give up, while everyone who was waiting for you to fail snickers behind your back. Or maybe not behind your back, depending on which circles you travel in. Watertown's not that small, but it's also not that big, and there are people who like to watch others fail because they feel like failures themselves.

Despite all that, despite this being one of his most closely held secrets, it's easy to tell Skylar. "I want to do home remodeling."

Saying it is easier than easy. It's like... like showering after a long, sweaty day working outside, or like lying down in your own bed after you've been away from home.

A relief. That's what it is. A relief.

Skylar looks intrigued. "Like flipping houses?"

Shaking his head, Walt replies, "No, I want to remodel homes for people who already live there. I just...." His face heats. Great, now he's going to get bashful about it? "I like those HGTV shows where one person does a home remodel for a family, and another person finds them a house they could buy, and at the end they have to either stay in their remodeled house or move to the new one. I always root for them to stay in their current house."

"You want to make people happy."

Walt shakes his head. "I'm not any good at that. I like to make stuff, though. Working with my hands, that's the part of putting up fences that I like. But who looks at a fence and thinks about how great it is? Fences are for keeping your dog in your yard or keeping your neighbors out. Or making sure you can't see your neighbors so you can pretend they aren't there."

Skylar's giving him a look that he can't parse. There's a little bit of expectations defied in his gaze, and people don't look at Walt like he's defying their expectations. He's expectations personified.

"You like to make people happy," Skylar repeats. There's something else in his eyes: a flicker of want, and it's everything Walt can do not to reach for it, reach for *Skylar*. It makes Walt feel like a fraud. He is, in fact, a full-blown fraud. A straight guy who lost control of his feelings and desires and hasn't had the guts to admit it. Now he's going to fake a relationship just to drive the point home.

"Have you done a lot of remodels?" Skylar asks.

"Oh, um. Well." His face heats, like he's a thirteen-year-old talking to his crush at his first school dance. "I helped my parents do their basement. That was my first project. My buddy and his wife are having their first baby, so I did their nursery. And I've done my whole house, pretty much. Not all at once, but you know. A room at a time."

Skylar's jaw drops. "Your whole house? Do you have pictures?"

Walt does. He has an entire album on his phone to show before and after shots of every one of his projects. Mario's wife, Ally, once showed interest in all the pictures. At least, she did a good job faking interest. Mario wandered off long before Walt flipped through all of them. Walt's parents made it halfway through before saying they've seen it in person.

Against his better judgment, Walt opens the album and hands his phone to Skylar. "The kitchen is the newest work," he says, trying to tell from Skylar's facial expression if he thinks Walt better not give up residential fencing. "The detail on the cabinet doors was kind of intimidating. And I mean, I painted them so you can't see the spots where I didn't get it exactly right, which is kind of a cop-out. I originally wanted to do this really pretty golden teak stain, but I messed up on one bevel. I couldn't get it to look right, but the paint hides it better than stain would."

He's babbling. "The paint color is called citrine, but I lightened it up some so the space didn't feel too heavy. Oh, and I know accent walls are kind of out, but I saw a picture of this wallpaper in this old book about Victorian and Edwardian houses, and I kind of got obsessed with it and thought it would look really cool in a kitchen. It's William Morris, I don't know if…. No, anyway, I finished right before Thanksgiving, and then I did the nursery for Mario and Ally's baby as kind of a Christmas present, I guess."

He has to stop talking. Skylar is looking between the phone and Walt. "How did you get Victorian wallpaper?" he asks.

"Oh, well, it's not technically exactly the one from the book, but there's a company in England that still has all the original design blocks, so I was able to find one that's really close. Otherwise I probably could have had it printed on demand, but I don't know if there are wallpaper copyright laws or anything."

Somehow he's *still talking*. More amazingly, Skylar's listening. Not fake listening, either, but watching Walt intently as he word-vomits about one-hundred-and-forty-year-old wallpaper.

"So, um, yeah. That's my hobby." Walt rubs a hand in his hair and wonders if he should apologize for going on about it.

"This isn't a hobby, this is a dream. Walt, this is amazing. You're really, really talented." Skylar flips back to the previous picture, then forward again, presumably comparing the before and after. "This doesn't even look like the same room. Are you sure you didn't use magic?"

The praise doesn't process. His parents were nice about the work but not effusive. They never are about anything. Mario said he didn't like the wallpaper and that it reminded him of an old lady's house. After the muted reactions of the other important people in his life, he didn't even mention to Tad that he was done with the project.

But Skylar's lips are parted as he looks at the photos, and he keeps zooming in to look at details. Walt feels, very very stupidly, like he might cry.

When Walt doesn't say anything, Skylar looks at him. His lips part further like he's about to say something. His fingers curl around the phone, and he scoots closer on the sofa until their hips touch, a flare of body heat that makes Walt's heart beat faster.

"You know what the wallpaper reminds me of?" Skylar asks. *"Gaslamp Market."*

Walt laughs, taken off guard, even though he shouldn't be. If anyone was going to make that observation, it would be Skylar. "Yeah… confession. That was why I was looking at the book about old wallpaper in the first place, because the set design in the show is so cool."

"Really?" Skylar looks delighted, and when he laughs, Walt knows he's not being laughed at, but that he's part of Skylar's joy. "That's so cool. All of this is so cool. I'd pay you to remodel my house in a heartbeat."

"No way, your house is great," Walt says emphatically. "I love these old farmhouses, and they're disappearing because no one wants to keep up with their maintenance. Plus they're not trendy, and it's hard to remodel them to make them trendy. But it's really sad, because they're gorgeous, and the craftsmanship is miles above what gets built now."

There's a smile on Skylar's face. If Walt didn't know better, he'd call it affectionate. "Then I'll never change a thing," he says. "Fun fact, the Dutch colonial style was developed in Bergen County in New Jersey."

For some reason, Walt fixates on Skylar's lips as he says it. The way his front teeth indent his bottom lip on the F sound of *fun* and *fact*, the way the corner turns up in pleasure.

"I didn't know that." The heat where their hips touch is distracting. Skylar is distracting. His mouth, his lopsided smile, the hypnotic color of his eyes and the way his dark lashes frame them. Worse, better, is the way he's interested in Walt. The way he cares about Walt's hobby— Walt's *dream*. Skylar called it a dream, and that's what it is, and the fact that Skylar sees that and said it when no one else ever has, it's….

Distracting. Too distracting for words, more than Walt knows how to deal with.

Skylar's gaze is hooked on Walt's, but he breaks the eye contact and takes a breath that looks steadying. "I guess if we're going to pretend to date, we should come up with a plan."

"Yeah," Walt agrees.

And leans forward to kiss Skylar.

Chapter Thirteen

SURPRISE KEEPS Skylar rigid for a second, but his body takes over. All he's been thinking about for weeks is kissing Walt again, and it's gotten so much worse since Walt showed up at his door yesterday.

So he kisses back, his mouth opening to Walt's, his breath hitching as Walt's tongue slides against his. When Walt lets out a quiet noise, halfway between a sigh and a moan, Skylar's done for. Walt tastes like cilantro and chiles and tamarind Jarritos, sweet with something husky behind it, and his lips are soft and demanding at the same time.

It's a kiss that Skylar would have expected to be urgent and hard. It starts out that way—urgent, a desperate press of mouths and tongues and teeth—but it mellows and gentles to a languid exploration, like they have all the time in the world, like there are so many more kisses waiting after this one, like this is comfortable. Like it's home.

When they separate, the sound of slick lips parting goes straight to Skylar's dick. One of Walt's hands brushes over Skylar's chest, then traces his collarbone to his shoulder. "Shit," Walt breathes, but he makes no move to stop touching.

It has to be said. "Was that a fake kiss for our fake relationship?"

Maybe it didn't need to be said, especially not by Skylar. "I shouldn't have done that," Walt says tiredly. More than tired. It's weary, like Walt's been battling something, and he's almost ready to give up.

"That's what you said before." If Skylar touches Walt, will he bolt like he did last time? Walt still has his hand on Skylar's shoulder, his thumb rubbing along the top of Skylar's collarbone, dipping into the hollow between bone and muscle. Heat radiates from that point of contact, and all of Skylar is vibrating with the need to add another.

A weary huff of laughter floats across Skylar's face. "It was true."

As long as Walt's still touching him, Skylar can play this right. Never mind that he hasn't played anything right in at least two years. "You can tell me why. You know that, right? Whatever's making you say you shouldn't have… maybe it's not as bad as you think. Maybe you're being too hard on yourself."

Walt sighs and pulls away. His hand drops to his lap, leaving Skylar's shoulder aching with the loss of contact.

"I'm straight," Walt says.

Skylar waits for the punchline, but Walt's lips stay pressed in a thin line. Which means that… *is* the punchline?

Either that, or Walt's mocking him. It's not funny, not even remotely. Skylar feels his face shutter, all the little muscles locking down. "You can just say I'm not relationship material. Or that I'm too much of a mess, or whatever it is. Just tell me you're not looking for anything serious."

"You *are* relationship material, though." Walt has the audacity to look wounded. "I wanted to be in a fake relationship with you!" When Skylar gives him an incredulous look, Walt groans and says loudly and crisply, "*Fuck.* I knew this would… fuck, fuck, *fuck.* I'm not making some weird excuse, Sky. I'm really straight. For real. I wouldn't make something up when I like you so much."

What is even happening right now? Straight? He's *serious*? This man that was just licking Skylar's tonsils is really sitting here saying he's a heterosexual with a straight face?

"My penis was in your mouth two weeks ago" is what Skylar decides to say, because the tonsil thing seems indecent. In hindsight, substituting *penis* for *dick* in the sentence he chose to articulate doesn't really class it up.

Especially because Walt looks stricken. "It's a habit I thought I broke a long time ago. But I slipped up with you."

"You slipped up," Skylar repeats. "With me."

"Because I liked you. Like you."

Walt both looks and sounds tormented, which makes Skylar feel bad about what he's about to say, but not bad enough to not say it. "You should go."

Blinking in incomprehension, Walt asks, "Go?"

Skylar stands, his spine hard and straight. "To your hotel. Back to Watertown. Wherever. You shouldn't be here. I'm not a toy for straight boys to mess around with whenever they get homosexual urges that they pass off as a *bad habit*."

Being closeted is one thing, but this is a level of repression that Skylar can't deal with. A bad habit is having a cigarette when you drink or eating an entire half gallon of ice cream when you have a bad day.

It's not a whole-ass sexual orientation, and it's especially not the people you hook up with.

He expects Walt to argue, but Walt doesn't. As he gets to his feet, all he does is stare at the floor. Sadness and resignation wash over his face. "I can still help you," he says to his shoes. "With the whole fake relationship thing, I mean, if it'll give your business a boost—"

"Please just leave," Skylar interrupts, because he's afraid if he lets Walt finish that sentence, he'll give in. He doesn't want to be a straight guy's dirty little secret, his bad habit, but he can also still taste Walt and feel the ghost of his thumb rubbing across his collarbone.

It's some kind of fucked-up when a straight guy is okay with pretending to be in a fake queer relationship to help prop up your failing business, but won't interrogate his own sexuality to open himself to the possibility of *actually* dating you. Maybe it's time to think about therapy. This needs an advanced degree to unpack.

There's an unbearable silence before Walt speaks. "Okay. Thanks for hanging out with me today. And, um. For all the nice things you said about my remodeling stuff."

Skylar can't look at him. If he looks, he'll cave. He can't be a repressed man's experimentation. His level of self-respect is rock bottom, but he has just enough to not fall into that trap.

Footsteps creak across the floor, out of the living room and into the kitchen until the door opens. Walt's voice floats through the house. "Say hi to the goats for me. And Squirrel, Valentino, and Elton."

Skylar's icy resolve quivers, and cracks spider through it. Walt remembers the peacocks' names. That's not fair. It's playing dirty. It's too much of a suggestion that Walt listens and cares and *fuck.*

With a hard whoosh of air, Skylar turns to follow Walt to the kitchen, to stop him before he walks out the door. There's not a single thought in his head beyond *stop*, but his heart is suddenly climbing into his throat and thrumming urgently, and here he goes again making snap decisions before he's thought anything through. *I should drop out of college to start a farm! I should get married at twenty-two! I should sink every bit of the money my family set aside for me into a business I don't know how to run!*

But by the time Skylar gets to the kitchen, the door has closed and Walt's halfway to his truck, his shoulders hunched and his head bowed.

That's… yeah, that's fine. It's for the best. He doesn't know what he would have said, anyway.

Walt drives away, his Ridgeline bumping over the gravel driveway. Skylar watches the plume of dust left by his tires for a long time.

Chapter Fourteen

ON THE drive back to his hotel, Walt sinks deep enough into self-pity to have the thought, *How could he get so upset at me for being* straight? *It's not fair to get mad at people for things they can't change about themselves!* which is when he pulls his wallowing up short. He can imagine the way Tad would look at him for saying that, and it's not a nice thought. He'd get that frozen expression that means he's hiding how he really feels, and then he'd remember that they're close enough now where he can really let Walt have it. Lewis would wince at Walt's douchery and let Tad rip Walt a new one.

Coming back here wasn't a mistake. Walt's glad he apologized to Skylar. It was the right thing to do. Everything else was a mistake, though. Getting in deeper with Skylar was a mistake. Spending more time together and his dumb idea to help Skylar with his business. Skylar has a whole town of people who would be willing to help him, Jett and Margery and probably a bunch of other people. He doesn't need a dumbass straight guy to pretend to be his boyfriend.

It was a stupid idea, but it still feels like a pit's been excavated in his chest every time it crosses his mind that it's not going to happen.

When he parks his truck at the hotel and gets out, he leans against it, the chill of the body seeping through his clothes and into his skin. The parking lot is fuller tonight. One of those rainbow All Are Welcome Here yard signs is prominently displayed on the hotel's front lawn. Right next to it is a sign advertising the hotel's Valentine's Day dinner, which is… oh, yeah. Tonight. No wonder there are more cars in the parking lot.

The All Are Welcome Here sign is bright against the dormant grass. It's good that it's here. It's good that people don't have to wonder if it's safe for them to have dinner with their partner, or stay in the hotel. It's good they don't have to worry about acceptance. He wishes he could live in a world where a sign like that wasn't necessary.

Tears sting his eyes and he rubs them away. Fucking embarrassing. He shouldn't be crying.

The sun is low in the sky and despite the unseasonable warmth of the day, the lengthening shadows bring a chill to the air. Except Walt can still feel the heat of Skylar's body in his fingertips where they traced his collarbone, and in his lips where they pressed against Skylar's.

It's not real, but the phantom of Skylar's smell is still in Walt's nose. He can't stop staring at the sign, thinking how he could have brought Skylar here for dinner, and had Skylar's warm, strong hand in his, and it would have been fine. He could bury his face in the crook of Skylar's neck as they put their coats on and left to go home together, he could breathe Skylar in, and it would be *fine*.

Straight people, a little voice says inside his brain, don't usually have sex with their friends of the same sex. They definitely don't pine this much to smell them.

It's possible he isn't as straight as he's been telling everyone, including himself.

First he thinks it's a good thing he's leaning against his truck for that revelation. Then he realizes he's not exactly reeling. He feels the way you do when you get home from a long road trip—like you can finally relax and give in to the exhaustion that's been battering you down. You can unclench your muscles and close your eyes. The crash isn't coming. You can rest.

It's funny to imagine how Tad would look at him if Walt said, *Guess what, I don't think I'm straight, actually!* At least, Walt laughs when he thinks about it. Maybe he's just losing it.

Maybe it would be good to talk to Tad. Maybe about this, but maybe just in general. When he tries to think of who else he can lean on, Tad is the only person who comes to mind.

Once he's inside his hotel room, he shoots Tad a text asking if he's free to talk and gets one back saying yes. A second later, a video call comes through from Tad. Walt must be giving off vibes that he's brooding even from a hundred miles away.

He sits at the edge of the bed and answers. Tad's face fills the screen. "Hey!" his brother says. "What's up? Are you okay?"

Stupid tears prickle at his eyes again. He hopes his image isn't clear enough on Tad's phone for Tad to see them. "Um, yeah, I'm fine. Or, well, I don't know, maybe?"

Tad's eyes widen in alarm. They're a mirror image of Walt's, the same bright blue, though Tad's are set in a narrower, sharper face. Tad's nose is longer and pointier than Walt's, and he's less freckly because he doesn't spend as much time in the sun. Privately, Walt's always envied the color of Tad's hair. It's auburn instead of the weird not quite red, not quite blond that Walt's is.

"What do you mean, you're maybe fine?" Tad asks. "You didn't get in another accident, did you?"

"No." Walt's tempted to add, *Unless an accident of the heart counts?* Except Accident of the Heart sounds like the lone hit of an eighties soft rock band.

Before Tad says anything else, Walt barrels on with a question he barely knew he was going to ask: "How did you know you were gay?"

"Face journey" isn't a good enough description of what Tad's expression does. It's a whole-ass odyssey. Tad's face goes to war, gets lost at sea, has some side adventures, before finally returning home grizzled and having Seen Things.

"There wasn't any one thing," Tad says.

"Okay, but like, what were some of the things that made you suspect?" Walt realizes he's making a fist around his thumb and squeezing the life out of it.

There's a pause as Tad chews his lip. From somewhere offscreen, a man's voice says exclaims, "Hey babe! Guess what! The giant air plant has a pup! Oh—sorry, you're on the phone."

"It's Walt," Tad says, looking to the side. A complicated series of micro-expressions flashes over his face—the silent communication of couples. It makes Walt's stomach hurt to see it.

A head leans into the frame. Lewis, dark-haired and looking kind of scruffy, smiles and says, "Hi, Walt."

Saved by the fiancé. Or not, since he wants—needs—to have this conversation with Tad. "Hi, Lew. What's having a pup?"

"One of our air plants," Lewis says while Tad gazes adoringly at him. Walt guesses he probably would too if his partner went from not knowing anything about plants to getting excited about a plant having a pup, whatever that means.

"Cool," Walt says dutifully. Even if he doesn't get it, he's glad they're excited.

"I'll let you guys talk," Lewis says. He drops a kiss on Tad's forehead and vanishes from the frame.

The smile on Tad's face lingers as he watches Lewis go. When he turns back, he seems less flustered by Walt's question. "How did I know I was gay? I guess never having crushes on girls was the first thing. You were always talking about like, Penelope Cruz and Angelina Jolie and how hot they were, and I never felt that way." He shrugs. "I started noticing guys, and eventually I figured out that the way you were talking about Jessica Alba, that's how I felt about Daniel Craig."

Walt chuckles. "Man, Jessica Alba, that's a name I haven't heard in forever."

With an answering laugh, Tad says, "Right?"

"I bet she's still hot," Walt says wistfully.

"Probably."

"I thought you didn't feel that way about her!"

Tad snorts. "Just because I don't get turned-on by women doesn't mean I can't identify an objectively hot one. Anyway." His smile fades and he says delicately, "Why are you wondering how I knew?"

Walt literally squirms on the edge of the bed. "Well. Okay. Um. So I guess… uh. You know how I, like. Have only ever been with women?"

"Because you're straight," Tad says, somehow conveying the exact opposite.

"Yeah." Walt's mouth gets sandpapery, and his heart pounds. If saying this to his brother, who he's almost completely sure is going to be cool and supportive, is this terrifying, how can Walt ever face telling anyone else? "Yeah, so the thing is, I… haven't. Only ever been with women, I mean."

Tad's face stays completely still. Walt's heart races faster. Then, Tad lets out a breath. "Wow. Okay. First of all, please breathe, Walt. Second, thanks for trusting me with that."

Strangled laughter bursts out of Walt, and he does what Tad says. "Breathing," he says, just in case Tad can't tell. Of course Tad would greet this news with acceptance and love. Before Walt loses his nerve, he blurts, "I met a guy."

"You met…. Like, in a romantic sense?"

Walt rubs a hand through his hair. "I thought it was just sexual."

"Gross."

"What? You have sex with Lewis!"

Looking horrified, Tad says, "Yeah, but I don't need to talk to you about it! Oh my god." He closes his eyes and breathes deeply. "No, okay, sorry. You're on a journey of self-discovery, so I'll deal. You met a guy, and you thought it was just sexual?"

Walt nods. "Yeah, so, like, all the times I've been with, um, men, it was anonymous, you know?"

Tad's eyebrows draw together. Slowly, he asks, "What about Cameron Greenberg?"

It's like a sucker punch to the solar plexus, hearing that name. Something gets stuck in his throat, preventing him from swallowing. "What about him?"

The way Tad raises his eyebrows makes it obvious he knows that Walt's bullshitting. What else is Walt supposed to do? He hasn't thought about Cam Greenberg in years, and it was on fucking purpose, because he screwed up so spectacularly. What happened with Cam was a disaster that almost ruined everything. It ruined enough.

In a gentle tone that Walt doesn't think younger brothers should get to use on older brothers, Tad says, "You two were inseparable, and then one summer he just stopped coming around. You never talked about him ever again."

Even though it was almost twenty years ago, Walt still feels sick thinking about it. The difference is that now the nausea isn't just because of what happened, but also because of the way he acted afterward.

Walt met Cam in kindergarten, and they were best friends for years. Inseparable, like Tad said. When high school started, Cam's parents sent him to the Catholic high school in town (Cam used to say he was the only Jewish kid there, but that it would've been the same if he'd been at Watertown High School with Walt). They still hung out all the time, though there was friction between Cam and Mario, who moved to Watertown during seventh grade.

Everything was great. Then came the August day in the summer between tenth and eleventh grade. They'd been in Walt's room, the house empty except for Tad, playing Zelda in his bedroom. The music was audible through their shared wall because he always had it turned up too loud.

In his head, Walt always blamed Cam. Cam was the one, after all, who brought it up, steering their stupid conversation about which girls from middle school had turned hot in high school to something else entirely. "Ever watched gay porn?" Cam had asked, such a shit-eating grin on his face that Walt had assumed—told himself he was assuming—that Cam was implying he wasn't acting straight enough.

"*You* watch gay porn, dude," Walt had neither confirmed nor denied.

Cam had gotten weirdly quiet, before he shrugged and said, "Yeah, sometimes."

In fact, Walt hadn't, though he'd thought about it. "Gross," he said. Then, "What's it like?"

Instead of telling him, Cam grabbed Walt's laptop and typed in a URL. The video game music from next door was so loud that it covered the moans and sounds of skin slapping on skin from Walt's computer. Walt popped a boner immediately, and, face burning, he stared fixedly at the scene playing out on the screen. When it was over, he made some stupid comment, like, "I wonder if it feels different with a guy than with a girl," which he'd tell himself wasn't an invitation, even though he always knew it was.

Walt had been staring at Cam's mouth for years, wondering how it would feel to kiss him. That afternoon, Cam read him right and did what Walt had never been brave enough to do himself. He shuffled closer and kissed Walt, and it felt good and right and like a piece that had been missing finally slotted into place.

They were sixteen and horny, and Walt ended up underneath Cam, jeans kicked off, Walt's shirt rucked up to his armpits and Cam's flung off, grinding against each other and exchanging sloppy hand jobs.

After they came, they fell asleep like that, Cam on top of Walt, Walt's arms wrapped around Cam's back.

Which was how Walt's father found them when he knocked and opened the door. Walt and Cam scrambled apart, but anyone could see what they'd been doing. Cam left. All Walt's dad said was, "For fuck's sake, Walter. Your brother was in the next room."

That was all he needed to say. The look on his face was such concentrated disgust and disappointment that it cut Walt down, carved something essential out of him that he'd just found.

When Cam called, Walt pretended that afternoon never happened. When Cam eventually confronted him and demanded to talk about it, Walt pretended he didn't know what Cam was talking about.

So Cam stopped calling. Walt hasn't seen him since that summer.

Remembering makes Walt's voice rough when he answers Tad's question. "Cameron was the reason all the other guys were just anonymous sex. I didn't... I *couldn't*...."

Except now he isn't sure what he didn't or couldn't. He's attracted to men. He's always been attracted to men. He's attracted to women too. It's not hard or complicated, but here he is, thirty-three years old, gasping like a hooked fish at the revelation.

Tad looks sadder than Walt expected him to, and he scrubs a hand over his face like he knows, or suspects, what happened with Cam. "You like women too, though, right?"

"Yeah," Walt says. He's not sure if that makes him bi or pan or what. He's not that solid on the difference. Maybe he'll see which flag he likes better before he decides what to call himself.

"And," Tad says hesitantly, "how are you feeling about... everything? Realizing, and coming out...?"

A couple days ago, Walt would have thought too hard about it. Hell, a few hours ago he might have thought too hard about it. Now he says the first thing that he feels, which is, "Good. I feel good. I feel... holy shit." He laughs and flops back on the bed. "Holy *shit*, Tad. I don't have to"—he gestures vaguely at himself, even though Tad can't see his hand—"pretend. To anyone. Including myself. Jesus, I've been pretending to myself for so long."

A huge grin splits Tad's face. "Yeah. It's a pretty good feeling. I'd give you a hug if I was there, and I'd probably be super awkward about it, but I'd do it anyway."

"Awkward hug IOU accepted." Walt laughs at Tad's expression. "Seriously, though, thanks for listening."

"That's my job. I'm your brother." Tad pauses. "Now please tell me about this guy you met. I'm *dying*."

A huge portion of Walt's good feelings flee at the thought of how he fucked up with Skylar. Again. A little glow remains from coming out, though. Maybe it always will.

With a sigh, he says, "He's the guy whose house I stayed at during the blizzard. Skylar."

"The goat farmer slash cannibal?" Tad gasps.

"How did you know he was a goat farmer?"

"I looked him up on Instagram, obviously. What else was I supposed to do when I couldn't make sure he wasn't going to kill you?"

Oh no. Instagram. "You didn't happen to see anything on there today, did you?" Walt asks nervously. Maybe he was too flippant about the idea of someone at home seeing the photo of Skylar and him.

"On Skylar the Goat Farmer Slash Cannibal's account? No, I didn't follow him." Tad's brow furrows. "Why?"

"No reason." Relief floods Walt. He doesn't care if Tad sees and makes assumptions. Well, they aren't assumptions at this point. But what if his parents see it? Or Mario, or Ally, or any of their friend group? "And he's not a cannibal."

"That you know of," Tad points out. "He just likes you."

Walt groans. "He *did* like me. Pretty sure he doesn't anymore." And thinking stuff like *What if Mario sees the picture?* is exactly the reason Skylar doesn't like him anymore. A symptom of it, at least. Walt's not ready to tell anyone except Tad about this part of him, but he'll tell them eventually. He has to, because he won't treat anyone like they're a dirty secret.

He did that to Cam, and he lost his best friend. Maybe he lost more than that. He'll never know.

Tad tilts his head. "What did you do? Wait, do I want to know? Is it really stupid? Is it dumber than something I would do?"

After considering for a second, Walt says, "It's probably dumber. You got outed to me at a wedding, so I think you get a pass for the traumatic experience."

"I don't know. I tried to break up with Lewis when he told me he loved me."

"I kissed Skylar and then I told him kissing guys was a habit I need to break, since I'm straight."

Tad looks appalled. "Oh, okay, no, you win. That's insanely stupid."

"*Wow*, thanks!" Walt says indignantly. When Tad shrugs, Walt sighs and rubs his hair again. "Yeah, I know. It was bad. I really fucked up. And I really like him. I really, really like him."

Something harder and sharper than sadness crawls up his throat on razor claws. The hot swell of tears presses against the backs of his eyes, but he's not sure he knows how to cry about this. He's lived so long with the idea that he was doing something shameful.

"If I'd known you could be this dumb about your love life, I don't think I would've let you help me win Lewis back."

"Again, wow." To be honest, though, Walt deserves that.

Thankfully, the appalled expression on Tad's face melts away to something more thoughtful. "Is there any chance you could just tell him why you acted the way you did? Would he understand? You should be with someone who's able to understand what it's like to be...."

When he just gestures wordlessly, Walt fills in, "Repressed?"

A twitch of a bitter smile ghosts across Tad's face. "Yeah."

Walt lays a hand on his stomach and thinks of the way Skylar pushed his fingers into his hair when they kissed. "You really think I should try again with him? What if I'm not telling you everything and I was a huge asshole? What if he's dodging a bullet with a dumbass who not only couldn't figure out that kissing dudes and loving it makes him not straight, but was really rude on top of it?"

"Because you're my brother," Tad says. "You're a good person. You'd never try to be a jerk on purpose. When you make mistakes, you own them. You try to be better next time. Anyone would be lucky to be with you."

The tears pressing at the back of his eyeballs find their way to freedom and leak from the corners of his eyes. Shit. He rubs the heel of his hand over them, but that only smears them over a wider swathe of skin. "Thanks, Taddy."

Tad smiles but doesn't say anything more. Neither does Walt. The two of them stay on the chat, the silence its own kind of conversation. Damn, Walt doesn't know what he'd do without his brother.

Eventually, Walt says, "I'm down here until Monday. I'll let you know how everything turns out. Oh! And hey, happy Valentine's Day. Hopefully you guys are doing something fun."

That same adoring smile that Tad had for Lewis earlier reappears. "Lew says all I have to do is trust him. You know him, he's my hopeless romantic. This is pretty much his most holy day."

Walt chuckles. His future brother-in-law is a fairy tale romance believer, a romcom lover, and a dyed-in-the-wool romantic, and it's obvious that he's crazy in love with Tad, who deserves to be showered in love and affection.

They talk for another minute or two before saying their goodbyes and disconnecting. Walt stares at the ceiling, his thoughts swirling. At their center, like the eye of a hurricane, is Skylar. Even if he rejects Walt, he's given something to Walt that's eluded him his entire life. Because of Skylar, Walt had the courage to stop lying to himself and pretending this part of him could be sectioned off and locked away. It was Skylar's draw and the possibility of what they could have been that allowed Walt to acknowledge and accept that if he found something amazing with a person, their gender or sex wouldn't matter.

Maybe that's enough. Maybe he can move on and get over Skylar. Maybe he can walk away and not regret for the rest of his life that he didn't try again for that amazing thing between them that he could sort of, just a little bit, see the shape of.

He sits up. No way. Maybe Skylar doesn't want to give them a chance, but Walt has to put all his cards on the table. He has to try one more time.

Chapter Fifteen

SKYLAR BAKES away his feelings, which is how he ends up with four dozen cinnamon swirl cookies cooling on racks scattered around the kitchen by that evening. He was too heavy-handed with the cinnamon.

The fact that they're nearly on par with Atomic Fireballs doesn't stop him from eating most of the first dozen to come out of the oven. He chases them with a few chunks of ginger to settle his stomach. And then he wonders if you could do something with ginger, cinnamon, and goat cheese, and oh god, he's spiraling again, isn't he?

Since the photo with Walt from the market is still doing numbers on Instagram, Skylar decides he should try posting something else. Content, content, content, right? He has to keep producing to keep people interested. This is how people drum up business, right? If it makes him money, then he doesn't have to worry about losing the farm and selling the animals.

His eyes drift to the cookies. That could work, right? People love baked goods! He just needs to arrange them artfully, which he's not bad at. Too bad he doesn't have some Atomic Fireballs to include in the picture.

He's in the middle of whipping up a glaze, because after his first attempt at constructing an Insta-worthy plate of cookies, it felt lacking, and a cinnamon glaze with some edible glitter in it to add a little sparkle feels like it will do the trick, when the doorbell rings. The glaze isn't quite done, but he removes the saucepan from the burner and goes to answer the door.

It's Walt.

Skylar braces the heel of his hand against the doorframe as his knees threaten to judder out from underneath him. He was prepared to never see Walt again and not at all prepared to see him so soon after kicking him out. "One of these days I'm going to stop answering the door," Skylar says.

Walt grimaces. "I deserve that."

"Yeah," Skylar agrees.

"Can I come in?"

"Why the hell would I let you back in?" Skylar pushes his hand against the doorframe until it hurts, because his instinct is to step aside and allow Walt through the door. Why do they have to get along so perfectly? Why does Walt have to be exactly the kind of repressed, closeted guy that Skylar knows not to get involved with? Why can't Skylar stop the spark of happiness that ignited behind his sternum when it was Walt standing outside his front door?

With another grimace, Walt says, "I deserve that too."

Neither of them moves. The light from the kitchen behind Skylar bathes Walt in warm honey, picking out copper highlights in his hair and eyebrows and scruff, and gemstone flecks in his eyes. Set against the darkness beyond the front porch, it makes him look like a god. Like Apollo stopping by for a chat.

Walt shifts on his feet and his eyes dart over Skylar's face, from his hair (a mess), to his eyes (red-rimmed from a crying session that went on for an embarrassingly long time), to his mouth (sticky from sampling the glaze). Clearing his throat, Walt gestures and says, "You have, uh, something there." When Skylar flings up a hand to his face, rubbing at a random spot, Walt shakes his head and taps the corner of his own lips. Skylar mirrors him, wiping the same spot, but that's still not right, apparently, because Walt reaches out to rub away the cinnamon glaze himself.

His hand freezes inches from Skylar's face. Skylar freezes too, realizing only after the feeling evaporates that his heart was picking up in anticipation of having Walt touch him.

Brusquely, Skylar wipes his entire mouth with the back of his hand and mutters, "Thanks." Then, because it's stupid to drag out the farce of him not letting Walt through the door, he steps aside and motions Walt in.

Walt carefully shuts the door behind him. "I'm sorry," he says.

"You said that before." Skylar tries to keep his voice steady, but the hurt and disappointment wants to well up again. "It didn't stop you from telling me I was a bad habit."

"No, I—I didn't mean *you*, I meant…." Walt lets out a frustrated sigh. "I'm sorry I said that. I shouldn't have. It was shitty. And unfair. I know you don't have any reason to listen to a word I say, but could I maybe try to explain?"

Like Skylar's going to say no. He decides to say nothing, just jerks his head and lets Walt follow him to the living room.

"It smells good in here," Walt says.

"You're here to explain, so explain," Skylar says flatly, folding his arms protectively over his chest. He's not going to let Walt distract him with all his interest and enthusiasm in what Skylar does. If Skylar told him what he was doing before Walt rang the doorbell, he knows Walt would volunteer to help. And he'd be excited about it.

Walt rubs his hands on his thighs. That's distracting, because it makes his chinos pull against his muscles. They're not gym muscles; they're the muscles of a guy who uses his body for work.

"I'm not straight," Walt finally says. There's a hoarse grate to his voice, like maybe he was crying earlier too. "I mean, I guess that's obvious. I've been telling myself I am for a long time, even though... even though I always knew I wasn't."

Skylar uncrosses his arms. "I'm not mad at you for saying you're straight." Even if he is, a little. "You called me a *bad habit*, Walt."

Torment wavers over Walt's face. "This isn't an excuse, because I shouldn't have said that. But when I was kid... I mean, god, I know so many people have it so much worse, but being attracted to guys wasn't something I thought I was allowed to do. I thought... I thought it was this shameful thing. So every time I had sex with a man, that's how I viewed it. Like I was doing something dirty."

Skylar takes a deep, steadying breath. "A lot of queer people feel that way, you know. And a pretty significant percentage of them don't decide to insist they're straight. Especially when they're in the middle of doing something super gay."

Walt stands very still, clenching and unclenching his fists. "I'm sorry. This was stupid. I shouldn't have bothered you again."

Skylar stomach clenches. "No—don't go." He lets out a hard blast of air. One of his hands is outstretched, which he doesn't remember doing. Dropping it back to his side, he adds, "I don't know what you've been through. Anyway, it's not the Trauma Olympics."

In front of him, Walt's frozen, looking like he's still teetering on the precipice of walking away. Walking out of Skylar's life, forever this time. Skylar's stomach clenches tighter at the thought, the certainty of it. If Walt leaves now, Skylar will never hear from him again.

"Don't go," he repeats. "That's not what I want."

"What *do* you want?" Walt asks softly. "I keep coming here and pissing you off."

I want you is exactly what Skylar shouldn't say, even though it's battering against the back of his teeth. "I want to start over." He sticks out his hand. "Hi, I'm Skylar Dangda."

With a wry smile, Walt shakes his hand. His palm is damp with nervous sweat, which is sort of gross but also sort of endearing. "Walt Pierce. Do you come here often, Skylar?"

"To my living room? Only like twenty times a day. What about you?"

"Yeah, this isn't my first time here, but it feels different this time."

Their hands are still clasped together. This handshake isn't even pretending to be a handshake anymore, and as Walt's thumb grazes across Skylar's knuckles, butterflies whirl inside his rib cage. "I want to know so much about you," Skylar admits. "I haven't stopped thinking about you since you left after the storm. I didn't even know your last name."

"I know. Me too." Walt catches his eyes. "Cards on the table. I'm bi, probably? I haven't really figured out the label part yet. I came out today to my brother. And myself, kind of. I never admitted it before."

Skylar squeezes his hand. "Congratulations." The smile that blooms over Walt's face goes a long way toward erasing his bitterness at the way Walt jerked him around. It's hard. Being queer is still hard, even if things are so much better now. Skylar knows perfectly well how terrifying it is to come out and not know how the people that are important to you are going to react.

"I, um." Walt clears his throat. "I should also mention that I just got out of a relationship with a woman. She dumped me the day I met you."

All Skylar can do is laugh helplessly. "Of course you did." If he's just a rebound….

But Walt raises Skylar's hand to his mouth and brushes his lips across the back of it. Skylar's stomach catapults into low Earth orbit. "You're not a rebound," Walt says, his breath warm against Skylar's knuckles.

"You don't get points for guessing I was thinking that," Skylar says, stomach still swooping.

"C'mon. I need the points. I'm really in the hole."

Skylar opens his mouth to make a remark about not throwing talk about holes around so freely, but then he catches the sparkle in Walt's eyes, like he knows exactly what he's doing.

Deep breath. If they're starting over, then Skylar isn't going to jump right into sex. That means they should stop touching, because Skylar's willpower isn't going to last forever if he keeps feeling Walt's warm skin against his.

Regretfully, he disentangles their hands. "Maybe a few points. I could just reset you to zero. We're starting over, after all."

Walt groans playfully, which makes Skylar smile and wish they were still holding hands. He wishes a lot of things related to those hands, which are strong and big and haven't been used to much potential on Skylar's body.

"Cards on the table for me too." Skylar has nothing but cards to lay on the table, really. He's barely told Walt anything about himself. "This farm's never been profitable. I got the money to buy it from my grandparents. They set aside a huge college fund for me, and the deal was that I could use it for that or cash out. So I dropped out, took the money, and bought this place."

"With your ex," Walt says carefully. It's almost a question, but not quite.

"He wasn't on the deed. We weren't married yet when I bought it, and I just never got around to it." Which they'd fought about. At the end, when Cody had no problem laying out Skylar's faults (to be fair, the reverse was also true), he'd snapped that Skylar couldn't even do something simple like get his name on the deed, and that if Cody ever left, the whole business would collapse.

"He didn't think I could run the farm on my own," Skylar goes on. His high-flying stomach is heading in the opposite direction now, sinking into the bedrock. "I mean, I'm sure he still thinks that. I'm sure he'd tell me if I didn't have him blocked everywhere."

"Really?"

"You don't block exes?"

"Well, yeah, but I meant, he'd really say that?" Walt frowns. "He sounds like a sack of shit. No offense."

Skylar laughs. "Yeah, none taken. And I don't know, he probably wouldn't say it. But he'd think it. The whole thing wasn't exactly amicable. Oh, and my relationship with my dad isn't great, just in case the divorce and the failing business wasn't enough."

"I think you have at least a flush in relationship baggage," Walt says seriously.

Skylar opens his mouth to respond, but Walt's stomach fills the space instead, growling loudly. When Skylar bites back a grin, Walt winces. "Sorry. I didn't eat dinner. The hotel restaurant was booked."

"Oh, they have the Valentine's Day dinner," Skylar says, remembering.

"Yeah, there was that too. I really didn't want to have a fancy Valentine's Day meal by myself."

Motioning as he heads for the kitchen, Skylar says, "I have three dozen cinnamon swirl cookies that aren't eating themselves."

Walt lets out a groan that's easy to imagine being produced in other circumstances. It makes Skylar's toes curl. "Man, I'm so glad you offered. Your house smells like a bakery. Are you selling your baked stuff?"

Skylar offers an entire cooling rack instead of answering that question, which is obviously no. Walt must know that.

Apparently Walt's willpower can withstand a full rack of cookies, because he keeps looking at Skylar, waiting for an answer.

"No," Skylar says. "I can't sell random food that I made in my home kitchen."

"Why not?" Walt asks. "You sell your own cheese, right?"

"Well, yeah, but that's different. I have a license from the state to do that. Fun fact, the dairy industry is the biggest segment of New York's agricultural industry."

"Huh, really?" Walt takes that in. "How much of it is goats?"

Skylar takes psychic damage from that question, to which he *doesn't know the answer*. "I can't believe I've never looked that up."

It's tempting to remedy that right now, except Walt finally takes a cookie. He bites into it and lets out another moan. Skylar's cock twitches. Also his ego swells, because, well, hot man enjoying his cookies. Wait, that sounds a lot less innocent than it is.

Walt closes his eyes and eats the rest of the cookie slowly. "Sky, you have to sell these. They're the shit. That goat cheese cake you made too. Hey, have you ever tried making goat cheese cookies?"

Skylar laughs, because didn't he think the exact same thing? "You don't think that would be weird?"

"It's worth a shot, isn't it?" Walt eats another cookie, his eyes fluttering shut. Gold eyelashes filigree his skin, and Skylar drinks in the sight. "There has to be a way for people to sell food they make at home. Otherwise there'd be raids on farmers' markets, right? You can't tell me all those people are getting licensed by the state. And you know what? If you *do* need a license, we'll get you one. These are amazing. Jesus H. Christ, I could eat all of them."

We'll get you one. There's that giddiness again.

"Oh!" Walt exclaims, putting down the cookie he's about to eat. "Instagram! You should post these."

"I don't...," Skylar begins, but Walt has already whirred into action.

Within a few minutes, Walt assembles a cookie photoshoot, with several cookies on a plate sprinkled with cinnamon and sugar from a ramekin that he places next to them. When he has them positioned the way he wants, he puts his hands on his hips and says, "It needs a glass of milk." His face lights up as he glances as Skylar. "It should be some of the milk from your goats! Then we can put a plug in the post for that too."

"I don't think a lot of people drink goat milk. Not in this country, at least," Skylar says doubtfully.

Walt bends over the table, reaching out to adjust the position of the spice jars in the background, and his shirt rides up to expose a freckly swath of lower back. The band of his underwear is visible above the waist of his chinos, above that, two dimples that Skylar wants to put his thumbs in. Walt's ass is gorgeous clothed—muscular and round, the perfect bubble butt, and Skylar feels faint at the image that invades his brain of himself walking up behind Walt, grabbing him by the hips, and pulling that perfect ass against him so he could rub himself off on it.

His eyes might roll back into his head, because when Walt straightens and looks at Skylar, a notch appears between his eyebrows. "Everything okay?"

"Yep!" Skylar sneaks a casual peek at the bulge situation and hopes Walt won't notice that the front of his pants are fuller than they were a few minutes ago.

Walt is, in fact, now thumbing at his phone, the notch in his forehead deepened in concentration. "Did you know that goat milk makes up two percent of the world's milk supply? I've never had it. Do you have any?"

"Walt, I have more goat milk than I know what to do with." Skylar laughs. "If you really think it's a good idea to put it in the picture...."

"I do," Walt says firmly.

"You should try some." Skylar goes to open the refrigerator and pulls out a bottle. "I can take your picture while you have your first taste, and we can post that too. I," he corrects himself. "I can post it."

Of course, he second guesses himself instantly, because he's horrible at social media. But Walt agrees, and that makes Skylar feel stupid with gratitude.

They take photos of the cookies first, then Walt eating the cookies. Last, Walt picks up the glass of milk and takes a hearty swig. Skylar loves him for that. Most people, raised on cow's milk and only cow's milk, sniff first before sipping gingerly. Skylar manages to get a picture of the moment Walt realizes he likes it. Or possibly the moment he realizes he has to pretend to like it for this photo to work.

"It's good," Walt says, like he expected it to not be. "It tastes like goat cheese, only in milk form."

"It's kind of better for you than cow's milk too," Skylar says, trying to sound casual, like yeah, this isn't a sales pitch or anything. It's not, but he knows it's going to sound like it no matter what, and he always sounds like an idiot when he's giving a sales pitch.

But Walt, as usual, looks interested. "Really?"

"Yeah!" Whoa, he needs to dial it back. "It might be more digestible than cow's milk."

Walt leans against the table, hand flat on its surface while the muscles and tendons in his arm tauten. "So I should make my post-workout protein shakes with goat's milk, you're saying?"

Oh no. Now Skylar's thinking about Walt working out. Sweaty and grunting, muscles straining. Hair stuck to his forehead. Stripping out of damp clothes in the locker room and showering.

The idea of the locker room is really getting him going. Shit, does he have a thing for locker room sex? Here he is, approaching thirty, and he's just learning this about himself. But damn, yeah, he wouldn't mind pushing Walt against a locker room shower and running his hands over all those slick muscles—

Walt clears his throat and Skylar startles out of the sex fantasy. Er. Daydream. Because he's not having a sex fantasy while Walt's standing in front of him, ha ha, nope! Especially not while Walt has a milk mustache clinging to his actual mustachey scruff, which is both adorable and somehow very sexy.

"Um, protein shake. Yes." Skylar tries to remember how to string words together when all he can think about is water sluicing down Walt's naked body.

Nice. Super smooth.

Walt smirks. "You were totally just imagining me working out, weren't you?"

"I was thinking about the science around when to have your protein shake to maximize gains," Skylar replies, so obviously full of it that Walt lets out a loud guffaw. Though, in fairness, his thoughts had mostly turned away from the workout to the post-workout shower, so it's not a complete lie.

Moving closer, Walt says, "I'm pretty boring at the gym, actually. I just go on the exercise bike."

"Oh" is all Skylar can manage, because Walt's taken another step closer, and now Skylar can smell him, amber and leather and a hint of woodsmoke. It's intoxicating, and Skylar's ability to resist Walt is nearly nonexistent, even though he knows he should try, if only because today has been a lot for both of them. Wasn't he extolling the health benefits of goat's milk? Shouldn't he get back to that? Something something may reduce cholesterol?

"Sky," Walt says, and Skylar realizes how much he likes it when Walt calls him that. His voice holds a note of uncertainty, and the same thing is reflected in the Delft blue of his eyes. "Do you… that is…." He takes a deep breath. "Do you, you know. Want me?"

"Do I want you," Skylar repeats like he didn't understand the question. He's not sure he does, entirely. In what way could he have possibly given Walt the impression that he doesn't want him? He's been checking him out since practically the moment they met.

Walt's face falls. "Oh."

Fucking *oh*, is he kidding? Skylar takes one step forward to close the distance between them, fists his hands in Walt's button-up, pulls him close, and kisses him.

Walt lets out a mewl of need, maybe a little relief, and puts his big hands on Skylar's back. His fingers dig in, cupping the crest of Skylar's shoulder blade on one side and the bottom of his rib cage with the other. Skylar presses closer, winding an arm around Walt's neck, licking at the seam of his lips until Walt opens on a gasp that cascades to a moan, kissing him with the desperate want that's been driving him insane for the last two weeks.

Skylar doesn't even realize he's backing Walt across the kitchen and against the wall until something crashes to the ground at their feet. They break apart with an obscenely wet sound and both look down. "Shit, sorry," Walt says breathlessly, reaching for the facedown frame they knocked off the wall.

He flips it over to look at it, which is good. Skylar knows this shouldn't go further than kissing, not today. Maybe not ever, depending on… god, who knows. He'll probably think of something later, but right now his lips feel sensitive and swollen, and the heat from Walt's body is a gravity well.

"Is this your grandparents?" Walt asks, finally raising his eyes to meet Skylar's. It's heady, seeing how his pupils are blown wide and black, knowing that he caused that. Not to mention the hard-on that's currently poking Skylar in the hip. He's trying not to rub his own against Walt's.

To that end, he tilts his hips back and takes the photo. "Yeah. That's their restaurant behind them. They taught me how to bake, actually. When I was a kid, I used to help in the kitchen, especially on weekends. By the time I was thirteen, I was doing most of the baking. It was a Thai restaurant, but Yaa—my grandma—had a bunch of American desserts on the menu. So people would order lava cake after their gaeng pa. But I make a mean khao thoum too." An only slightly bitter smile twists over his face. "My dad didn't want me working there."

Something about the way Walt meets his eyes makes him think Walt's very familiar with the weight of familial expectations too.

Walt's shoulders drop back to brace against the wall as his hands settle on Skylar's hips. The weight of them there feels comfortable and right, like something he's been missing, or that was lost but is where it's supposed to be now. "I want to ask why," Walt says. "But I also want to keep making out."

Skylar lets the picture hang against his side as he slides a hand behind Walt's neck. "How long are you in town?"

"I'm checking out of the hotel tomorrow."

Soft hair at the nape of Walt's neck tickles Skylar's palm. In the warm kitchen light, the thick scatter of freckles across Walt's face reminds Skylar of a cinnamon dusting. "Come back tomorrow and I'll tell you all about my daddy issues."

This close, it's easy to see how Walt's chest hitches with the catch of his breath, the sharp bob of his throat. Dark gold stubble trails down the underside of his chin. "What are we going to do now?" he asks, the blue of his irises almost eclipsed by hungry black pupil.

Tugging Walt's face closer so he can brush their lips together, Skylar says, "I thought you said you wanted to keep making out?"

Walt groans helplessly and dips his head the last half an inch to close the distance between them.

Chapter Sixteen

WHEN WALT arrives at Skylar's house the next morning, Skylar's on the phone. He shoots Walt an apologetic look as he opens the door, saying into the phone, "I still have your address, so it's not a problem to get there. It might take me some time to get the ladies in the trailer, and then driving over there…. Let's call it two hours? If that's okay?"

When he hangs up, he looks at Walt. "So, probably not what you were planning on doing today, but want to come along on a trip to get some goats pregnant?"

Which is how Walt finds himself sitting in Skylar's truck, watching the Catskills stream past the window and a trailer in the side mirror. It's another sunny day, but much colder than yesterday. The bare branches against the blue of the sky make it seem even colder, even though that doesn't make any sense. "Do goats always have to take a road trip to get some action?" Walt asks.

Skylar laughs. "Some don't. There are probably some lucky people who are surrounded by prime studs."

Is that a joke? Walt glances at Skylar, whose eyes remain steadily on the road. There's a pull to one side of his mouth, so that's a yes. Walt stretches his arms behind his head and pushes his chest out, watching for Skylar's reaction. "I guess it's farther from Watertown to Windham than it is from Windham to… where are we going?"

"Andes," Skylar replies. "Fun fact, not named after the Andes mountains."

"I was going to say, that's overstating how impressive the Catskills are."

They cross a small river with ice clinging to both banks, but an open channel in the middle. The trailer they're towing rattles at the change in road surface from the bridge back to regular pavement. "You're a really good sport to come with me for this," Skylar says. "Going on a trip to hopefully get some goats pregnant would be a hard pass for most guys."

"What's more romantic than the miracle of conception?" Walt deadpans. When Skylar snorts with undignified laughter, Walt adds, "Is it weird if I say I'm kind of interested in all this farm stuff?"

"Do you really think I, a literal farmer, would think it's weird to be interested?" Shooting Walt a pleased look, Skylar adds, "If anything, I feel like I'm…."

When he trails off, Walt prompts, "You're what?"

Skylar shrugs. "Using you, I guess. Like I'm all, *look at us, doing farm stuff!* Hashtag miracle of conception, hashtag goatstagram."

"Is goatstagram really a common hashtag?" Walt looks for himself on Instagram and immediately gets sucked into scrolling through a grid of adorable goats. "Oh my god. Sky! There are pictures of people doing goat yoga. Do you offer goat yoga?"

"Three times a week, with a special vernal equinox session," Skylar says. "No! Of course I don't offer goat yoga. Do you think that should be a thing I do? Goat yoga?"

Walt puts a hand on Skylar's shoulder and rubs encouragingly. "We'll figure it out. It costs money to start new things. We'll concentrate on the stuff you're already set up for." He thinks for a second. "If you're comfortable with it, I could take a look at your books."

"Er." Skylar flushes. "I'm, uh. Pretty bad at keeping track of all that stuff. Also isn't there something about not mixing business and pleasure? Or romance and finance?"

Yeah, that was overstepping. Walt winces. "Forget it. It was a dumb idea."

They drive in silence for a mile or so before Skylar says, "It wasn't dumb. And I guess we're already mixing business and pleasure, since we're putting our relationship on social media."

"Our relationship?" Walt repeats, his heart crowding out his lungs so suddenly that he can't get a breath. There's a stupid, irrepressible smile on his face too. He can feel it, and no amount of trying to bite it back will make a difference.

Skylar's face flushes further. "Technically we have a relationship. That's like, the most basic label to apply to people who are interacting."

"But it's a pleasurable relationship." The grin is going nowhere. "That's what you said—we're mixing business and pleasure. No take backs, Sky. This relationship gives you pleasure."

Skylar cuts a look to Walt's side of the car. "Well, I'm not going to deny that you do pretty wonderful things with your mouth."

Now *Walt's* flushing. If everything hadn't happened the way it did between them, Walt would be tempted to say, *How about I do something wonderful with my mouth right now*, and go down on him right here on Route... whatever they're driving on.

But things still feel up in the air. They didn't go any further last night than heavy making out. It was all over-the-clothes and above the waist, and though Walt wants more, he keeps feeling a hum of possibility every time he and Skylar are together. Like maybe this could be something, if only Walt doesn't screw it up.

The sly, canted smile that Walt loves so much slips from Skylar's face, and Walt knows he was quiet for too long, overthinking what should have been an easy, flirty line. He's always tried to avoid situations that lead to overthinking. Things shouldn't be that complicated. If you have to think too hard about something, it's probably not worth thinking about in the first place.

Yeah right. That's how he ended up not understanding he's bisexual until the age of thirty-three. What else is he putting off understanding because he doesn't want to think too hard?

"Sorry," Skylar says, staring fixedly out the windshield. "Bad joke."

"No, I—" Walt fumbles for an explanation and remembers his conversation with Tad, how telling Skylar the truth about his own confusion is the best way forward. "I just get in my head. I don't know how to flirt with guys. And I thought maybe what I was going to say was skeezy or something."

"Okay, now you *have* to tell me," Skylar says, bouncing right back to his good mood.

Heat creeps up Walt's neck again. He just managed to stop blushing! "I was going to offer to give you car head."

Skylar makes a strangled sound and shifts in his seat. His voice comes out tighter than usual as he says, "Let's table that for now."

Dark heat floods Walt's body and his dick wakes up. "So I could have said that? Good to know."

"As long as your follow-through is good, yeah. You can say stuff like that whenever you want." Skylar's tone is edged with hunger, but then he groans. "Dammit, now I'm thinking about sex!"

Walt frowns. "I thought that was good."

"Not when we're bringing goats to get bred! That's weird. Oh my god, me talking about this is weird. What if Tom can tell I'm thinking about sex? What if he thinks I'm into watching goats have sex? Walt!"

Walt's laughing, which he'd feel bad about if Skylar wasn't laughing too. Even though he doesn't say it, laughing with Skylar is just as sexy as talking about sucking him off. Has he ever felt that with anyone else he's been with? Because it feels like this is something very specific to Skylar. It's that hum again, pointing him toward a conclusion he doesn't know how to arrive at: Skylar's special. This is special.

They eventually arrive at their destination, a farm that's obviously a bigger operation than Blue Skies Farm. The barn is bigger, and there are tanks and lines and equipment that Walt doesn't know the names of populating the property. Chickens strut around inside a large wire enclosure attached to another barn building. A fenced paddock holds several horses, one of whom saunters over to check out what's going on as Walt and Skylar get out of the pickup.

At the sound of the doors slamming shut, a tall, rangy white man emerges from the barn and waves to them. "Skylar! Good to see you, kid!"

"Hey, Tom." Skylar holds out a hand and gets a hearty handshake in return. "Thanks for giving me a call. I couldn't decide if I wanted to breed the girls with a stud service this year, but if this is Triton's final hurrah, that's an easy decision."

With a loud laugh, Tom says, "The big guy's earned his retirement. I wanted to see if you were interested in breeding any more of your does before I put him out to pasture, though. You're my favorite farm to work with." As Skylar blushes, Tom turns to Walt and adds, "This guy has the best herd in central New York. Great stock, super healthy, and they get the best care I've ever seen. Plus he gets an incredible amount of milk out of them. Even the breeds that aren't big milk producers! I don't know how you do it, Skylar." He offers Walt a hand and adds, "I'm Tom, by the way. Tom Leonard."

"Walt Pierce." He moves forward to shake Tom's hand, and when he returns to Skylar's side, he lets their arms bump. Tom's gaze catalogues the closeness, but he doesn't comment on it. "I bet Skylar has the best herd in the entire state."

"Stop," Skylar groans. "I run a tiny farm that no one's ever heard of."

Tom laughs again, another loud laugh straight from his belly. "I don't know about that. Looks like plenty of people have heard of you on Instagram."

"Of course you saw that," Skylar says, sounding resigned. Walt elbows him, and Skylar elbows him back, shooting him a flicker of a smile. It lodges like an arrow between Walt's ribs.

With a shit-eating grin, Tom says, "Sure did." He claps Skylar on the shoulder. "I'm going to head on in and finish getting things set up. Bring the girls in when you're ready."

He heads back into the barn and Skylar offers Walt a sheepish smile. "Guess I should've known he'd have seen Instagram. I know we didn't actually come out and say we're dating on there, but he probably assumed just like everyone else."

"Don't worry about it," Walt assures him. "How do we do this goat breeding thing?"

"Let's get them out of the trailer, first." Skylar unlocks the back door and swings it open. The two goats inside bleat greetings at him and clamber to their feet. As he climbs into the trailer, he says over his shoulder, "Cool thing about goats—you can induce out-of-season breeding."

Walt comes closer. "I guess I didn't even think of that. If they get pregnant now, they won't have babies in the spring, right? How long are goats pregnant?"

"A hundred and fifty days." Skylar slips harnesses over the goats' heads. "So they'll kid in mid-July if they get pregnant."

Giving one of the goats, a black one, a scritch behind her ear, Walt asks, "And what's the big deal about this Triton guy?"

With a crooked smile, Skylar says, "I feel like that's my line. Triton might not be good enough for my girls."

"Well, is he?" Walt rubs the goat's nose as she butts it into his palm. "You can't just let any dude get them in a family way, right?" When Skylar laughs, he adds, "Is this how it usually works? You bring your goats somewhere to get them pregnant?"

Skylar hands Walt one of the halters, which he holds tightly, surprised Skylar's trusting him to hang on to one of the goats. Not that the black goat seems likely to bolt. She's nosing at his elbow, whuffling in the denim of his jacket. Skylar makes a clicking noise, starting toward the barn, and then says in a singsong voice, "C'mon, babies! This way, Peggy! Natasha, no eating clothes!"

The affectionate look on Skylar's face makes Walt melt and want to do something he can't put words to, but which would almost certainly be stupid. He tugs the black goat's halter to follow Skylar, and she comes willingly.

"I like to do things this way," Skylar answers. "Pen breeding, it's called. You put the ram in a pen with the does and they do their thing. I like Triton for a lot of reasons—the kids from him always do well, which is the most important thing. But they also have a lot of the traits you look for in the breed."

"These are Nigerian dwarf goats, right?"

Skylar's stride stutters as he shoots Walt a surprised look. Is it that shocking he'd remember? "Right," Skylar says. "Nigerian dwarf goats."

"You told me the weekend we met," Walt reminds him. Skylar looks more surprised. Maybe it's not that that Walt remembers—maybe Skylar's surprised that Walt paid that much attention to the things he said.

The barn is large and airy and warm enough that Walt sheds his jacket once they get inside. It smells like goat—the sweetness of hay and the earthiness of growing things. Peggy and Natasha seemed interested but unfazed in their new surroundings. Maybe they've been here before. Do goats remember stuff like that? Hell, Walt doesn't even know if dogs remember stuff like that. They never had pets growing up. Tad begged for a cat, but their parents always said no. That's probably how Tad ended up loving plants so much—he was allowed to have those. It's nice that Tad ended up being good at taking care of things. Walt was the son who was taught that nurturing wasn't for men.

Feeling silly, Walt asks, "Hey, Sky? Do goats have good memories?"

As usual, Skylar seems happy to share his knowledge. "Yeah! They're super smart, actually. There's been new research in the last decade or so about their intelligence."

Listening to Skylar talk about his animals—watching him light up with passion—feels special, suddenly. Walt already knew Skylar was special, but it just… hits him hard at that moment. Skylar's ex-husband is an idiot for walking away from this.

They head all the way to the other end of the barn, where Tom is leaning against the metal railing of a pen. A single goat is standing inside, placidly eating hay. His nostrils flare as Natasha and Peggy approach and he comes over to the railing, rearing up to put his front hooves on one of the rungs. Natasha and Peggy seem more restless too, shuffling and tugging at their halters.

Tom points toward the wall and the ceiling. "Cameras so I know how many times he breeds them." Walt resists the urge to make a smartass comment. "Where do you figure they are in their cycle?"

Stroking Peggy's nose, Skylar replies, "It I timed it right, they should come into estrus tomorrow or the day after."

With a laugh, Tom says, "Good thing I gave you a call, I guess." He opens the pen as Skylar removes the halters from Peggy and Natasha and ushers them inside. The gate isn't even closed before Triton trots over to check them out.

"We'll let them get reacquainted," Tom says. "C'mon inside for the housekeeping stuff."

The house is yet another beautiful Dutch colonial on the outside. Inside is a tragedy. Walt pauses on the threshold to the kitchen, where Tom and Skylar go without reaction. Somebody in the nineties got their hands on this kitchen, ripped the history and soul right out, and replaced it with charmless McMansion fixtures.

It takes him a second to come back to himself. That cabinet color is shockingly ugly and was only in style briefly when Walt was a toddler. The counter is granite, probably, and it's a sort of reddish brown, which isn't a terrible color on its own, necessarily. It's really, really not working with the cabinet stain, though. It puts Walt uncomfortably in mind of livestock excrement.

There's a stone alcove for the stove that doesn't match anything, and the stone is ugly, anyway. And for some reason, the interior of the alcove isn't even stone, it's tile. There's a too-big chandelier above the island, where Tom and Skylar are looking at an iPad.

Before Walt can make himself move, Tom looks up at him and takes in the subject of his staring. "Like the castle hearth?" he asks, gesturing at the stove alcove.

Oh no. Walt knows he's not the most self-aware guy out there, but there's no way the expression on his face could possibly be played off as "like."

Tom chuckles. "Relax. I know it's bad. My wife and I put all our money and energy into the farm after we bought this place. No time to do anything in here."

Walt hesitates. "It's a little dated."

This time, Tom outright laughs. "You're not gonna hurt my feelings. It's ugly as hell. Whoever designed it has no taste. Makes me look like I have no taste, too, but we don't do a lot of entertaining."

Skylar signs the iPad with a finger and passes it to Tom. "Not in here, at least. All your entertaining goes on in the barn."

"Yeah, that's why we put all the money into making it nice!" Tom locks the iPad. "We've been talking about maybe doing something about the kitchen. It's just finding the time to sit down and research designers, you know?"

God, Walt would love to get his hands on this kitchen. He'd rip out everything and bring it back to its architectural roots, but he'd make sure it still looked modern. Modern and timeless. It's one of those phrases that everyone says, but Walt can see it so clearly in this kitchen, like it has its own Ghost of Kitchen Future overlaid on top of it.

"Walt does remodels," Skylar says.

Walt's mouth drops open. Before he can clarify that he really doesn't, Tom looks at him with interest. "Oh yeah?"

"Yeah! He redid his whole house. You should show him your pictures!" Skylar sounds excited and... proud? "And he just finished a nursery for his friend's new baby."

"That's the only time I've ever done something for anyone besides myself or my family," Walt says quickly. Presenting himself as anything besides a hobbyist feels like lying or trying to take advantage.

Tom looks at him like he's taking stock. "Are you any good?"

"Um," Walt says, feeling the back of his neck get hot.

"*Yes*," Skylar says emphatically, giving Walt a look that dares him to contradict. Walt does not, though he feels like he should. "He's incredible. His house is really interesting. It's classy and unique. Not just following trends."

Does Skylar really think that about Walt's remodel? He's not just saying that to get Walt some business? That's nice enough on its own; Walt would never expect Skylar to talk up his home design abilities.

But Skylar thought Walt's designs were good just on their own, didn't he? Something huge and light behind his sternum makes it hard to breathe for a second. A good hard-to-breathe. The kind that you get when someone important does something special for you.

"Let's take a look," Tom says, so Walt pulls up the photo album of his projects and hands his phone over. Tom takes his time looking at each photo, along with the befores and afters. Eventually, he hands the phone back, his face assessing. "My wife Molly's visiting her brother in Savannah this week, but I want her to meet you. I like what I'm seeing here."

"You do?" There's something else he should say, Walt's sure of that. "I mean, you do! Okay, yeah, I'd love to meet her. Meet with both of you, I mean."

"She'll be back on Friday. What does your schedule look like?" Tom asks.

Considering he's already bailing on the office at least one day this week, he probably should show up the rest of the time, even if it's only to take appointments for consultations in the spring. "How about next weekend? I can drive down." Which means he can see Skylar again. "I'll check with the hotel I'm at in Windham to see if they have a room next weekend."

"You're not from around here?" Tom asks at the same moment Skylar splutters, "You will *not*!"

"I'm from Watertown," Walt answers first, before he turns to Skylar. "I can't keep expecting you to put me up."

Tom coughs and puts a hand over his mouth, obviously hiding a grin. "Is that what they're calling it these days?"

"Rude," Skylar says, and Walt's not sure if he's talking to him, Tom, or both of them. There's a smile on his face, though, so he can't be too offended.

They settle on a time for Walt to swing by the following weekend, and then Skylar and Tom get everything settled with the goats. Tom walks them back outside to the truck, and Skylar closes and locks the trailer before they leave, waving at Tom out the windows.

"You're staying with me," Skylar says with finality before they even make it out of Tom's driveway.

Walt grins and leans back against the seat. "I am, huh?"

Skylar glances at him. "Unless there's a really good reason for you not to."

There was a moment in high school when Walt realized that his feelings for his best friend went so much further than friendship. It was a leap over a cliff, a terrifying drop into the complete unknown. But it was exhilarating at the same time. Maybe there were sharp rocks waiting at the bottom of the fall, but maybe he'd learn how to fly.

That's how Walt feels right now, only it seems a lot more like he might learn how to fly this time. Is there a good reason for him to stay at a hotel next weekend? Is there any reason at all?

Walt's pulse speeds up and he can't stop the smile that's blooming on his face. "I can't think of one."

Chapter Seventeen

TIME HAS never passed this slowly in the history of time. That's Walt's opinion by Wednesday, and he's not taking questions, thanks. It's Wednesday and it feels like it's been eighty-four years since he saw Skylar on Sunday night.

They'd stood in the kitchen door kissing for a long time, longer than Walt's ever stood around kissing anyone goodbye. Every time he took a breath and convinced himself he was going to walk out the door for real, he'd twist his fingers in Skylar's hair and lean in for another kiss.

Sure, he didn't get home until after midnight, but it was with Skylar's taste in his mouth and the feel of Skylar's body still tingling across his skin. What's exhaustion in the face of that?

Tonight he's having dinner with his parents at a pub downtown, and he's definitely *not* planning on telling them about being bi. That's going to take planning. When he tells them about Skylar, he wants it to be something more special than a pub that thinks it's fancier than it is.

He runs a comb through his hair before he heads out, because Mom gives him a hard time if he looks "unkempt." He doesn't bother reminding her anymore that he has a physical job. Also that the neat, slicked comb-over isn't exactly the hot look she thinks it is.

After the comb makes him look like a sixth-grader getting his portrait done at church, he musses his hair with his hand. Better. Mom won't think so. But he looks more like himself.

He considers his reflection in the bathroom mirror. His stubble has grown out enough that it can almost be called a beard. At least, you can tell he's trying to grow one. He runs a hand over it, unused to the softness of a beard instead of stubble. Does Skylar like beards?

Mom is for sure going to give him a hard time about the sort-of beard. The almost-beard. He sighs and reaches for his electric razor, pausing before he touches it to his jaw. The beard looks good on him. The important thing is that he thinks so, right? Not what his mother might think. Is he a thirty-three-year-old man or not?

When he arrives at the restaurant, his parents are waiting outside. His mom hugs him. "Oh, you could have shaved, we wouldn't mind waiting!"

"I'll remember that for next time."

Mom sighs. "I know the scruffy look is in, but I think a clean-shaven man is so much more appealing. A lot of women feel that way."

"Yeah, I know." Walt smiles, because what else is he going to do? This is his mom. She's always been this way; she's not changing anytime soon. "Just trying something new. Maybe it's not working."

"It looks fine," Dad says. "C'mon, I'm hungry. Let's go in."

Walt opens the door for them. They're seated promptly in an oversized leather booth with an electric tea light flickering in a hurricane lamp in the center of the table. Their waitress takes their drink orders (a glass of Riesling for Mom, beers for Dad and Walt) and they all busy themselves with the dinner menus. It's nothing exciting, just the same pub food fancied up with coulis and aioli. And there are brussels sprouts, of course, because every single pub that thinks too highly of itself has brussels sprouts now.

They do sound good, though. Dammit, he's going to order the fucking brussels sprouts with their balsamic glaze, isn't he?

"I talked to your brother today," Mom says once the waitress returns with their drinks and takes their orders (and yeah, Walt got the sprouts). "He wants us to visit him in the city."

"Him and Lewis," Walt says.

"Yes," she says, the vaguest note of exasperation in her voice.

"Are you going to go?"

Mom looks at Dad, who looks back at her. "Your father thinks we should," she says.

"We haven't met Lewis's parents," Dad says. Walt gets the feeling it's not the first time he's said it. "They're going to be family."

"Oh." Mom waves her hand. "People don't know their children-in-laws' parents."

Dad takes a drink of his beer and wipes the foam from his upper lip. "Our parents went on vacations together, Kathleen. They did that Danube River cruise."

The fact that a hint of pink rises to Mom's cheeks is the only surprising thing about this exchange. "Things were different in those days."

Neither Walt nor Dad asks how things were different. It's not worth it. Walt's spent his entire life with that message firmly internalized. "You should go," Walt offers. "Lewis's parents are nice. His sister's cool too. Has Tad told you she's having a baby in June?" His mom loves babies, so that feels like a winner of a conversation topic.

"Isn't she Lewis's maid-of-honor?" Mom asks, sounding horrified. "She'll be so big in the pictures!"

The thing is, Walt's pretty sure she wouldn't say that if Tad were marrying a woman. Jesus, at least he hopes not. Being scandalized by a pregnant woman in a wedding party seems pretty 1950s, even for her. It's just that she's determined to nitpick and find problems with every single aspect of Tad's wedding.

"One of his maids-of-honor," Walt says instead of addressing the other thing. "His friend Stacy is the other one." Actually, Stacy has been calling herself Lewis's best man, since Lewis was the maid-of-honor for her wedding, but that joke would be lost on his mom.

Mom sighs. "Well, if we have time, we'll go. It's just such a long drive."

"We're going the last weekend in March," Dad says.

That's the weekend of the Spring Fling Showcase in Windham. "Nice," Walt says. "Maybe the weather will be good."

Dad makes a face. Walt sympathizes. The weather is never good in New York City. It's either cold and damp, or it's hot and humid. There's no in-between, as far as Walt can tell, and the hordes of people all living on top of each other don't help with the heat. It doesn't help with the cold, either, but the crowds seem less stifling when it's cold. Probably because there aren't as many tourists.

"How's work?" Dad asks. "Got many jobs lined up?"

Walt shrugs. "Yeah. We're scheduling out through July." He hesitates, weighing whether he should bring this up, whether his parents will even care. "I'm maybe getting a job outside work, though. Something I can do while it's still cold."

Raising his eyebrows, Dad asks, "Work not keeping you busy enough?"

Yes. No. That has nothing to do with it. "It's our slow season." Walt rubs a thumb on his glass, clearing a window of condensation so he can watch bubbles stream to the surface of the beer. "It's just something different to do."

Dad grunts. Mom shoots him a look. "That sounds nice. What is it?"

"A kitchen remodel. Maybe. It's not a sure thing yet. I'm meeting with him and his wife on Friday. Maybe nothing will come of it." Walt clears a wider space in the condensation on his glass. Does he believe that? Tom Leonard seemed legitimately interested.

And Skylar is excited for him getting the job like it's already a done deal. In his words, "Tom doesn't dick people around. He wouldn't want to meet with you if he wasn't serious."

"Are they paying you?" Dad asks.

The excitement and pride drain from Walt like a slow leak. "If he hires me. Yeah, of course."

"Kitchen remodel. That's a lot less straightforward than fences." Dad drinks more beer, and Walt resists the urge to do the same. He'd like this one glass to last through dinner. "Always over budget too. Then people want you to work for less than you're worth."

As far as Walt knows, his father has never done any kind of major home improvement project, let alone a remodel, double let alone (if that's even a thing) a remodel for someone else where money changed hands. The man spent forty years working for Jefferson County, sitting at a desk day in and day out. This isn't something Walt's proud of, but to this day he's not sure what Dad actually *did* at work. His office always seemed kind of *Parks and Recreation*-esque, only less funny and more boring.

"Yeah, we'll see," he says. On HGTV, the budget is usually a plot point. That's probably true in real life too. It's not like Walt doesn't have experience with this stuff, though. Fencing jobs can go over budget. When that happens, Walt talks to the client and figures something out. It's not hard. Or, it sometimes *is* hard, but Walt's good at it.

"What part of town does this person live in?" Mom asks.

"It's out of town, actually." Walt does drink some beer for this part. Mom hates it when her children do long drives on the freeway. "Do you know where Windham is?"

Both his parents shake their heads, and Dad asks, "Is that near Albany?"

"Not really." Is it? He'd have to check. It's closer to Albany than it is to, like, Buffalo. "It's in the Catskills."

He can see the dilemma on their faces. The Catskills aren't *the city*, and in theory there are good salt-of-the-earth people there. But there are also rich outsiders, people who came from the city. Some city. *Any* city. A city bigger than Watertown, that is, because Watertown doesn't count as a city in the same way. They haven't lost sight of their values here, or something.

Walt likes living here, but man. There's some stuff he'd change if he could.

Mom leans forward. "Where did you meet someone who lives in…."

"Windham," Walt supplies. He never told them about getting stranded by the blizzard, because he knows better than to freak his mom out about driving unless he has to. She already wants both Tad and him doing forty in the right lane; telling her he got in an accident—kind of— is going to turn her into a mess anytime she knows he's driving more than ten miles.

Trying not to sigh, he tells the whole story—the traffic on the freeway, getting lost with his dead phone, the snowy ditch and the house he approached with the helpful stranger.

Well. Okay. He doesn't tell them the *whole* story.

As expected, Mom's horrified. Dad chides him for not having a paper map in the car. It's not a bad point, but it's still kind of annoying. This is his parents, though, showing they love him by telling him how he could have done better. They mean well. They always have. Walt's always understood that, whereas Tad never did.

Or maybe Tad understood perfectly well and just wasn't as willing to forgive it the way Walt is.

"So yeah, the meeting with the potential client is on Friday," Walt eventually says, after they've both run out of steam. "I'm going to spend the weekend down there."

"You can't be making that horrible drive all the time," Mom frets.

"Yeah, no, I won't. I'll stay for weekends. Or whatever. It depends how they want me to work and how fast they need it done. I can have Lizzie watch the office if I'm down there full-time until the remodel's done. I don't really need to be around during the winter. All the important stuff is online, anyway."

Which is also one of Dad's favorite subjects to harp on. Mom still looks concerned. "Won't that get expensive, staying in a hotel for so long? Don't those places charge a small fortune with all the skiers?"

"I'd be staying with Skylar. The guy who helped me during the storm." Why does he feel the need to clarify who Skylar is? He literally just told them the whole story. Seventy-five percent of the story. "He runs his whole farm by himself, so I can pay him back by helping out. It's kind of fun, anyway. He has all these goats and they're really funny. And a guard llama. I didn't even know llamas guarded herds until I met him! Fun fact, right?"

"It sounds interesting," Mom says. Walt's not sure he believes her.

"He has peacocks too," Walt says. Nothing about his parents' reactions suggests they'll care, but the words come out of his mouth anyway. This is what he does. What he's always done. He tells his parents what's going on in his life, which is usually not much. His parents tell him what's going on in their lives, which is also usually not much. Something in that dynamic feels broken lately, though. Maybe it's the wedding.

He tries to remember if it was like this before Skylar and has a feeling it wasn't. Which means maybe what broke things was Walt coming to terms with who he is. That's not a great feeling.

"Sounds like a hobby farm," Dad says.

"It's not," Walt says, defensive without meaning to be. Both of his parents look surprised. "He makes a living, I mean. It's not a hobby, it's his livelihood."

"I'll go on his website," Mom says in a bright voice. Walt tries not to flinch.

Their food arrives, so they can concentrate on eating instead of talking, thank Christ. Everything feels off tonight, like he just got to the corner in his cabinet installation and the angles don't match up right.

It must be him, right? Nothing about his parents has changed.

When they're all slowing down, their waitress swoops in with an offer of to-go boxes. While she disappears to get them, Mom chews her lip, eyeing Walt like she wants to ask something, but knows he isn't going to like it. "What's up?" he asks.

"Oh," she says, then starts to speak before abruptly cutting herself off. That's how Walt knows he's really not going to like whatever it is. He also knows she'll say it anyway if he gives it another second. "I was just wondering if you've thought about who you're going to bring to the wedding?"

Who he's bringing to the wedding? They already decided this months ag—oh. Right, he and Lia broke up, so obviously they're not going together. "I haven't really thought about it." Except now he *is* thinking about it, and all he can see is Skylar next to him.

"Charlotte Stevens's daughter moved back recently," Mom says, her pulse on the movement of every one of his former high school peers like usual. "Emma. She got divorced a year ago."

"Thanks, but I don't need you to set me up, Mom."

She opens her mouth before apparently deciding not to say whatever she was going to. Instead, she finishes her wine. "I guess I don't have a very good track record with setting my children up. Considering I tried to set Tad up with a woman, maybe I should butt out."

There's a spark of rueful amusement on her face, so Walt fosters that. "Yeah," he says, trying to hit the perfect balance between gentle and final. "I'm not Casanova or anything, but I do okay."

"I hope you don't do *too* okay," Mom says.

Dad lets out a cough into hand that sounds suspiciously like a laugh. "I remember you having plenty of boyfriends in college, Kath."

When Mom flushes and waves a dismissive hand, Walt laughs, then makes a face. "Okay, but I don't want to hear about that."

They pack their food into the to-go boxes. Dad insists on paying, even though Walt argues. It's a familiar routine, including the part where Dad tells Walt he can get the next one at the Ritz. Obviously Watertown has never seen a Ritz-Carlton and never will, but it's a well-worn joke.

In the parking lot, Walt hugs his mom but not his dad. That, too, is well-worn; the acceptable bounds of masculine affection in their family so deeply ground into the Pierce sensibility that breaking them would be like jumping deep tire grooves.

Once he's in his car, he waves to his parents as they drive away. He closes his eyes and lets his head thump back against the headrest, a long exhale carrying away even more tension than he realized he was holding on to.

His breath is clouded and sparkling when he opens his eyes and turns the ignition. One more day to go, and then he can see Skylar again.

WALT WALKS into the meeting with Tom Leonard and his wife, Melanie, jittery and convinced this is, at best, an acquaintance of Skylar's being nice, and at worst, a joke that's going to end with Walt getting laughed out of Andes, New York.

It's neither. It's actually… good. On the drive back to Windham, Walt almost calls Skylar at least five times, unable to contain his excitement. Except he thinks about the way Skylar's going to look at him when Walt tells him the news, and he wants to see that. Tom and Melanie are going to pay him—they're going to pay him really, really fucking well—but the amount they agreed to is nothing compared to the way Skylar looks at him when he says Walt's amazing.

By the time he makes the turn into the gravel driveway of Blue Skies Farm, it's dark. The Catskills are lightly dusted with snow, and the gentle mountains and rolling pastures are luminous under a bright crescent moon. The barn sits solid and black to one side, the house in jeweled counterpoint, with each window a warm, bright square of lamplight.

Walt gets out of the car and stands in the still, cold night, letting his excitement settle to something calmer and deeper. His breath glitters as he exhales, shot through with moonlight.

Movement across the pasture catches his eye. Three deer are threading their way, single file, from the stand of woods on the far side of the field, across the open space. When they get closer, their ears swivel toward him. They stop, one after another, and stay so still that they could be lawn ornaments. The only thing that gives them away is the vapor of their breath clouding at their noses.

The one in the lead—the biggest one; she might be the mother of the other two—snorts, the sound carrying over the thin layer of snow crusting the ground. Another fog of glittering breath puffs around either side of her face. Walt doesn't move. The seconds slide by, nothing to measure them except the snick of cold branches against each other and the imperceptible movement of the moon in front of the fathomless ocean of stars.

The deer continue their silent passage, silvery pale in the moonlight. They disappear behind the barn and Walt waits for them to reappear as they cross the road. They stay in single file, the smaller two following the larger one, until they slip into the woods again.

Walt shivers and grabs his duffel bag from the car, then heads for the house. The door opens barely two seconds after he rings the bell, which suggests that Skylar was waiting there. It's a little thing, but Walt's chest glows with it.

"Did they hire you?" Skylar asks before Walt can say anything. "You just texted you were on your way. Rude, FYI, I had to sit here for a whole hour in suspense!"

"Are you in suspense?" Walt asks.

"Yes! Obviously," Skylar replies. "I mean, I know they hired you. They had to've hired you. It would be really, really stupid if they didn't hire you. They hired you, right?"

With a grin that turns to an irrepressible laugh, Walt steps through the door. With his duffel bag still hanging off his shoulder, he puts a hand to Skylar's jaw and leans in for a fierce kiss. Hands grip his biceps and Skylar tugs him closer, kissing back just as hard. The cold at Walt's back feels like nothing compared to the blaze of heat between them.

Fuck, he missed Skylar.

"I got the job," Walt says when they break apart for a breath.

Skylar whoops. "I knew it! Your work is amazing. They *had* to hire you. It would be embarrassing for them if they didn't. Walt! This is the best news. Oh my god, come in! Sorry, you're about to become a famous home remodeler and I'm making you stand in the cold!"

Laughing, Walt comes in, moving aside so Skylar can swing the door shut behind him. "I'm not going to be famous. I don't think people who remodel houses really get famous unless they get a TV show. And I don't want a TV show."

"Frank Lloyd Wright was famous."

Being compared to Frank Lloyd Wright would definitely be on Walt's list of Things He Won't Ever Hear if he kept a list like that. All he can do is smile so wide it hurts and laugh again. "Frank Lloyd Wright was a genius. I'm just a guy."

"Frank Lloyd Wright was just a guy at first too," Skylar says, like this is a serious comparison. Like Walt's more than a dude who remodeled his home in his spare time and did a good enough job that someone else wants to hire him to do their kitchen.

It's obviously ridiculous to use Walt Pierce and freaking Frank Lloyd Wright in the same sentence—or even the same conversation, to be honest, but the fact that Skylar did makes Walt feel so... full. Like all the empty spaces inside him that he's been carrying around for years just opened up to let in bright, golden light.

Not because Walt thinks he's ever going to be on the level of one of the most storied and influential architects of the twentieth century (he won't be; it's okay), but because Skylar believes in him.

"Thank you," Walt says, his throat suddenly tight, even though it doesn't make sense to respond to what Skylar said that way. It makes even less sense to cry right now.

Skylar looks like he maybe gets it, or at least part of it. He cups Walt's face, his hand warm and rough with calluses. They rasp over Walt's beard as he turns his head to kiss Skylar's palm.

His skin smells good. Warm and dry, with the sharp green scent of herbs. Walt covers Skylar's hand with his own to keep it in place so he can kiss the center of Skylar's palm again, then the pad under his thumb, then the soft skin at his wrist, where his veins stand out against his golden skin and the swirling ink of his tattoos begins. Walt leaves his lips pressed there, feeling the steady beat of Skylar's heart.

The kitchen smells good too. "Did you make dinner?" Walt asks, threading his fingers through Skylar's so their hands remain together, still against Walt's beard.

"What else were we going to eat?" Skylar's pupils are wider than they were a minute ago. Walt wonders what he'd find if he slid his other hand down Skylar's stomach to the front of his jeans.

Walt raises his eyebrows suggestively and Skylar's smile cants to one side. "I'll bring my duffel up to the guest room," Walt says. "You can figure out what else we could eat in the meantime."

"Can you think of a really good reason for me to sleep in my room and you to sleep in the guest room?" Skylar asks, his voice dropping at least a whole octave to a pitch that turns the bottom of Walt's spine to electric shivers.

It's the kind of voice that makes Walt want to do things he never has, not with a man at least. Things like taking his time, like amping up the burn of arousal and the hot tension between them.

He turns his head back into Skylar's hand and traces the opposite path he followed before—the inside of the wrist, thumb pad, center of the palm. But he keeps going, brushing his lips along the length of Skylar's first two fingers until he gets to the tips, and once he gets there, he lets just the blunt head of Skylar's index finger slip between his lips.

Skylar lets out a sound that makes Walt's cock jump. He sucks Skylar's finger and swirls his tongue over it. Skylar traces another finger over Walt's bottom lip and Walt takes that one in his mouth too. If points were being awarded for subtlety, Walt would be in the negative.

"Dinner," Skylar says, his voice hazy and his pupils blown out completely. It sounds like some earlier version of him programmed the reminder, but this current version of Skylar doesn't care.

Walt sucks Skylar's fingers deeper before drawing off. "Can dinner wait?" He puts a hand on Skylar's hip and takes a chance, sliding it around to his firm ass. "Because I really want to fuck."

It's the first time in his life he's said those words out loud to a man. All his previous same-sex encounters were arranged with meaningful looks and touches. Saying the words is amazing.

More amazing is Skylar's reaction. He digs the fingers of his free hand into the waistband of Walt's jeans and yanks their hips together so Walt can feel his hard-on, before he crushes his mouth to Walt's.

Walt lets out a sound that's half surprise, half groan of desire, and drops his duffel bag to the floor behind him. Skylar makes a noise too, a growl deep in his chest, before he pulls back. His face is flushed. Walt's feels hot too. "Yeah," Skylar says. "Dinner can wait."

Chapter Eighteen

SKYLAR STANDS up to his libido long enough to turn off the oven and yank out the roast chicken. It's hard to do even that much, because Walt's behind him the entire time, running his hands over Skylar's stomach and chest. The roasting pan clatters on the stovetop as Skylar drops it and turns in the same motion, pushing Walt against a cabinet so he can feel that hard, strong body against his.

You wouldn't know Walt's new to this by the way he kisses, tongue fucking into Skylar's mouth, teeth nipping at Skylar's lips. Skylar catches his wrists and pins them over Walt's head, and they kiss messily. It's wet and hot and sloppy and Skylar wasn't expecting this right now, but he isn't complaining.

He releases Walt's wrists so he can fist the hem of his shirt instead and yank it over Walt's head. Walt's arms and head get tangled, and he laughs breathlessly. When he emerges from the shirt, his sandy red hair is tousled and his eyes are bright. They hold Skylar captivated for a second before his own gaze drifts down.

Damn. Skylar's mouth goes dry. He forgot what an amazing body Walt has—all those muscles covered in a healthy layer of bulk. It's not a gym body, it's real. No six-pack abs, just obvious healthy strength. Freckles cascade over his pale skin, peeking through the mat of red-gold hair covering his chest.

A flush spreads from Walt's chest up his neck to his face. "Is it okay?" he asks, awfully shy considering he just told Skylar he wants to fuck.

"Your body?" Skylar clarifies. "Are you asking me if your body is okay?"

"Yes?" Walt rubs a hand across his hairy stomach and up to his pecs. "Is this the kind of thing gay guys like?"

"Oh. My. God." Skylar gives Walt a push toward the door. "We're going upstairs, and I'm going to take the rest of your clothes off, and you're going to see exactly how much I like 'this kind of thing.'"

The look Walt gives him could melt steel, it's so scorching.

It's a miracle they get up the stairs without tripping. Skylar leads Walt by his loosened belt into his bedroom and they fall, kissing, to the bed. Walt's big hands grab Skylar's ass and squeeze. Skylar pants. Then Walt smacks one ass check, and that makes Skylar groan long and low.

There was this idea in Skylar's head that when they had sex again, when Walt wasn't ashamed that he wanted this and Skylar could let himself want without feeling guilty, it would be slow and tender. Skylar would take his time with Walt and show him how it was when you didn't have to rush—when it wasn't a hurried encounter in a bathroom but instead a thorough fucking in a bed. When you could let yourself go because you were with someone who you trusted to have you.

The strength of Skylar's yearning to be the someone who holds Walt steady through everything surprises him.

He can't think about it now. He also can't think about the slow and tender lovemaking he'd fantasized about, because he needs to feel Walt's body against his right this second. Walt seems to feel the same, because he's frantically getting Skylar's jeans open to shove them off.

"Shirt," Skylar gasps as he goes for Walt's jeans. Luckily Walt understands the fractured command, because he works Skylar's shirt over his head. It's more work than it should be, since Skylar doesn't want to stop sliding Walt's pants down his legs.

They roll on the bed. Skylar ends up on top, hands braced on Walt's biceps, hips pushing into Walt's. More importantly, their cocks are pressed against each other's.

Neither of them moves for a breathless moment. Walt's eyes are wide, pupils blown out. He's flushed red from the roots of his hair all the way down to his stomach and his shoulders are heaving. And Skylar just… he wants Walt so much, but he has to remember that Walt's never done this with a guy.

Walt reaches up to put his fingers on the knob of Skylar's wrist bone, following the curves and swirls of Skylar's Kranok tattoos up his arm. When he gets to the inside of Skylar's elbow, he rubs light circles into the sensitive skin there. The hairs on Skylar's arm stand on end as he shivers. A pleased smile pulls at the corners of Walt's lips, but he keeps his eyes on the path his fingers are tracing, up along the swell of Skylar's bicep to the arc of his shoulder, where the tattoo sleeve ends in tendrils and filaments.

As his touch slides along Skylar's collarbone, Skylar fights not to close his eyes in pleasure. They're hardly even doing anything, but he can't stop himself from shuddering, especially not when Walt traces the cords of his neck, along his jaw, and into his hair. "You're so beautiful," Walt says wonderingly, like he doesn't know how he got here.

Skylar smiles down at him. "You're not so bad yourself."

The smile Walt gives him is blinding. Skylar's chest hurts.

Slowly, Walt lifts his hands over his head and lays them on the bed. The position pulls his pecs taut, and Skylar wants to run his tongue along the furrow it creates from chest to shoulder. The hair in his armpits is the same curly red-gold as the hair on his chest and stomach, and the same as the thick line of hair disappearing under the waistband of his boxer briefs.

"You're *really* not so bad yourself," Skylar breathes, drinking in the sight of him.

Walt swallows and Skylar follows the movement of his throat, the sharp jag of his Adam's apple making his cock throb. "You should do something about it, probably," Walt says, his voice hoarse.

Yeah. Yeah, he probably should. Skylar rolls his hips once, and the pressure and tiny amount of friction feels so, so good. Better for Walt, maybe, because he groans as his eyelids flutter shut. Skylar does it again, looking for the same reaction, and then again. Walt meets him this time, his hips thrusting up, and if it felt good before, it feels amazing now.

Walt's arms are still over his head and Skylar can't resist the temptation of that any longer. He covers Walt's body with his, using one hand to pin Walt's wrists to the mattress, while he finally lets the other wander.

And oh god, Walt's body feels as good as it looks. Hard and soft in exactly the right places, strong muscles under the skin, hair Skylar can sink his fingers into. He kisses Walt hard, touching everything he's been fantasizing about for weeks.

Walt wraps one leg around the backs of Skylar's thighs and rocks against him. The friction is overwhelming; the rubbing of their dicks against each other makes his mouth drop open in a low moan, even with two layers of fabric between them.

"Wanna feel you," Walt pants, lust turning his voice to gravel. "I wanna—fuck, Sky, I wanna be naked with you so fucking bad, so—"

He cuts himself off with a gasping, openmouthed kiss that's mostly tongue, arching against Skylar. Who is he to deny a hot man what he wants?

The bad thing is that he has to unpeel himself from Walt to get his boxer briefs off; the good thing is that Walt gives him a look that almost makes him blow his load right there, then snaps the waistband of his own underwear. Skylar takes a hint and strips them off.

They catch on Walt's cock, which, if Skylar's being totally honest, he did on purpose, because he wants to see it bounce on Walt's stomach.

It does, and it's just as good as Skylar thought it was going to be, hitting with a thick, fleshy sound. Pre-cum dribbles into the hair on Walt's stomach.

If Skylar's brain was in charge, he'd freeze with the options open to him right now. But his brain isn't in charge. It's one hundred percent his dick, which just wants Walt touching it. He crawls over Walt and Walt wraps his strong arms around his back, pulling him down.

There's no technique anymore. There's just hunger and the need to touch as much of each other as possible. Walt's hands are all over him, running up and down his back, grabbing his ass and squeezing, slapping, stroking. His fingers trace along Skylar's crack, shying away from any serious contact, and Skylar's too out of his mind with need to encourage more exploration. Their hips thrust into each other's, cocks rubbing and slipping together. Sweat and pre-cum slicks them up enough for this, no lube needed.

Skylar grabs Walt's hair and tilts his head back so he can kiss the expanse of freckly, hairy jaw and neck, so he can run his tongue along the cords of his throat and bite the spot where neck meets shoulder.

"Yeah," Walt whispers. "Yeah, goddamn, Sky. Fuck, aw fuck, fuck me...."

Skylar gasps and reaches between them with his other hand, getting it around both their cocks. It's not a perfect grip, because Walt's cock is thick, just like the rest of him. Definitely the kind of cock you look at and think, *hell yeah, it'd be some work to take that*, while you salivate about getting the opportunity.

Next time. Next time. Because he's close, and he can tell Walt is too from the way he's all hard and tensed under Skylar.

"Gonna come," Walt groans, his hips pistoning into Skylar's while he fucks Skylar's fist.

"Me too," Skylar manages. It's barreling toward him, but he wants to hold out to see Walt go first. He clenches every muscle in his body to hold back. Just until then. Just until Walt comes.

"Come on me," Walt says.

Which blows Skylar's plan to hell, because *come on me* are magic words, and the spell they cast is Giant Orgasm. He sails over the edge, flinging himself into free fall as his vision telescopes and release explodes through his body.

He keeps working their cocks as he shudders through his orgasm, his hand now slick and wet with his own cum. It's smearing as Walt writhes and thrusts beneath him, and Walt's breathing is all harsh and panting and sexy and—

"Fuck yes—!" Walt grabs Skylar's entire face in his hand and crushes their mouths together, his tongue thick hot muscle in Skylar's mouth, his breath Skylar's breath. He moans long and loud into the kiss, shuddering and rutting into Skylar's fist. Pulse after pulse of cum pours over Skylar's hand and cock.

With one more moan, Walt goes limp under Skylar, the hand on Skylar's face drifting down to his shoulder. He cups it gently as their kiss gentles, as the teeth and tongues give way to lips brushing softly.

When they finally stop kissing, they just lie together, lungs and hearts settling back to normal. They're going to be stuck together when they move, but Skylar can't remember the last time he felt this relaxed and this good. He could lie here forever, cocooned in the afterglow with Walt.

But the more gluey their mingled cum gets, the worse it's going to be, particularly for Walt. Of the two of them, he has a lot more hair to get ripped out.

Skylar pushes himself up on his hands and looks at Walt. The flush is fading from his skin, but his hair is damp with sweat. It turns the color closer to auburn and brings out curls that aren't normally there. They frame his face in surprising ringlets. Skylar wants to twist them around his finger and keep them like a lock of hair in a locket.

He wants to keep Walt, and that's crazy, isn't it?

Walt's eyes are hazy, like the sky in high summer. Blue gauzed with heat haze. "Wow," he says softly. All Skylar can do is laugh happily, which is its own kind of release.

The haze in Walt's eyes coalesces to something more solid. He stretches underneath Skylar, extending one arm over his head but leaving the other slung heavily across Skylar's back. If Skylar hadn't just had one of the most intense orgasms of his entire life, his dick would probably be perking up at the feeling of Walt's muscles moving against him.

Walt puts his hands on Skylar's ass, cupping both cheeks. It's another thing his dick wants to perk up at. "Gonna think about how it felt for you to shoot all over my chest next time I get myself off," Walt says huskily.

Again. The dick. It's helplessly limp, no matter how much Skylar wishes it would wake up. "I'm going to think about you *saying* that next time I get myself off," Skylar says. "Jesus Christ on a cracker. For some reason I thought you'd be shy."

With a wicked grin, Walt rolls them over so he's on top. There's an audible sucking sound as their bodies unstick from each other, and Walt winces. Sure enough, a few ruddy curls remain in the sweat-and-cum mess on Skylar's stomach. The momentary pain vanishes from Walt's face, though, the grin returning as he says, "You thought I was going to be some blushing virgin?"

"I mean, no." Not exactly.

"Because I sucked your dick in the first twenty-four hours of our…." He thinks. "Acquaintance."

"Our acquaintance," Skylar repeats, smiling and linking his hands behind Walt's neck so he can steal another kiss. Is it really stealing a kiss when Walt comes so willingly, though? "Fair, though."

"There's like a whole genre of man-on-man dirty talk I've never gotten to whip out," Walt goes on.

"Ooh, let's hear more about whipping it out."

Walt laughs loudly and buries his face in the crook of Skylar's neck. Skylar can feel the shape of his mouth curved into a smile. "I guess we should get cleaned up and eat dinner. It smells amazing. Did I already say that? I can't believe you made dinner for me."

Skylar almost deflects the praise with *it's not a big deal*. The habit is ingrained after so many years of his dad complaining that by cooking he was inviting white people to see him as even more of an Asian stereotype. *I'm cooking dinner for us, Dad, not riding an elephant down Route 46. It's not a big deal.*

"I like cooking for the people I care about," he says instead. And god, he cares about Walt more than he should. Definitely more than what's safe. It's too easy to imagine cooking dinner every night for the two of them.

The feelings are a hazard. It's too soon to feel this much. Skylar needs to deal with his failing business and probably some lingering baggage from his divorce. He needs to manage his social media and the unexpected viral fame that's been blowing up his phone since last Saturday. A week ago they were negotiating a fake relationship, now Skylar's fantasizing about a weekly meal schedule.

"I'm people you care about?" Walt asks tentatively, and there's something so achingly vulnerable in this big, masculine guy wanting to make sure that Skylar can barely hold in the tenderness flooding his rib cage.

"Yeah." Skylar reaches up and twines one of Walt's sweat-damp curls around his finger. "Yeah, Walt. You're people I care about."

Walt smiles and kisses Skylar softly.

Skylar ignores the orange signs and flashing caution lights.

Chapter Nineteen

BETWEEN WORKING on the Leonards' kitchen, documenting his and Skylar's relationship for Instagram, and preparing for the Spring Fling Showcase, it's easier for Walt to stay in Windham. In theory, Walt's staying in the guest room. In practice, he's been waking up to Skylar's soft black hair spread across a flannel pillowcase and his smile.

It's a good opportunity for the social media offensive. The picture Skylar posts of the two of them sharing a pillow, dual bedhead illuminated by a sunbeam, becomes his most-liked post faster than any of the prior photos.

The first weekend of March is going to be the first test of Operation: Make Blue Skies Farm An Instagram Star, because there's another makers' market in town. They've been hyping the event on Skylar's Instagram, with Windham's social media accounts getting in on the fun too. Skylar's growing confidence with managing it makes Walt proud. Lately, he jumps on opportunities for pictures of the two of them before Walt does. It's a huge difference from the guy who made pained faces at the idea of maintaining an active online presence and had followers that were mostly bots.

Farm chores aren't conducive to lazy mornings in bed, and market days mean an even earlier start. Walt's a morning person, but he still has to stifle a yawn as he slides another cooler full of perishables into the bed of Skylar's truck. "There's so much cheese," he can't help observing.

"Told you," Skylar says. When Walt grabs a crate, this one full of jars of nightshade preserves, Skylar's eyes follow him hungrily. Walt puts some muscle into it to make the show worth it. "You think goats don't produce that much milk until you have to figure out what to do with it." He worries his lip with his teeth. "I really hope we can clear out all this old stuff. Jane and Darcy are kidding soon, which means more milk."

"We're going to move the hell out of this old stock," Walt says confidently.

"We," Skylar repeats, smiling. "Yeah. Thanks for getting up for this today."

Walt shrugs and heads back to the porch for the last few crates, Skylar accompanying him. "That's what a good boyfriend should do, right?"

It's still scary saying the B word to each other. At least it is for Walt. It's always these kinds of oblique references. On Instagram it's easy; in real life, Walt wonders if that's really what they are to each other, or if they're tricking themselves.

Hefting a crate full of goat cheese pound cakes and tubs of goat cheese frosting, Skylar says, "I think shoveling llama manure and crating goat cheese is probably going beyond the boyfriend call of duty."

"Not sure I agree," Walt says.

Skylar opens his mouth, but nothing comes out. He closes it and one corner quirks up in that half smile that makes Walt's heart hiccup.

After making sure everything is secure in the truck bed, Skylar closes the tailgate and the truck topper. They both make one last trip to the barn to make sure the animals are good for the day. Most of the snow is gone so they have access to a paddock now, under Squirrel's supervision. Elton and Valentino are the only ones using it, sitting on the top rail of the fence preening each other's feathers.

The drive to town is relaxed, though Walt realizes he's starving when they're halfway there. Maybe he should have had some goat cheese pound cake before they left. Or one of the tubs of goat cheese frosting. That stuff is delicious. Skylar's sitting on a gold mine. Once people taste it, he's not going to be able to keep any in stock.

At the market building, the only activity is other vendors unloading. Walt unbuckles his seat belt, but before he can open the door, Skylar leans across the center console and kisses him.

Walt sinks into it. They wake up together every morning, but he'll never get used to this, and he doesn't want to. Kissing Skylar makes him feel settled. Quiet. Like there's all this static in his brain, but when Skylar's lips are on his, it fades to nothing.

"I'm really glad you're here," Skylar says, his lips still brushing Walt's. "I just—yeah. You should know that."

Walt breathes in the scent of him—the sweetness of hay and straw, the earthiness of being around animals, the strong, sugary coffee he chugged before they went outside this morning. "I like being here," he replies, inadequately. He's not sure what the better response is, but that doesn't capture how he feels.

Skylar leans his forehead against Walt's and lets out a slow breath. "Do you really think people who see our Instagram posts are going to come to this?"

"Yeah," Walt says. "And they're going to post pictures and tell their friends about your food, and even more people will come to Spring Fling. And we're going to get Blue Skies Farm making money."

"But if people don't come today…."

"If people don't come today, they'll come to Spring Fling."

Skylar straightens and lets out another big breath. "You're so confident."

"Well, I know how good the product is." Walt reaches for Skylar's hand and interlaces their fingers. "Also, keep in mind I run a residential fencing business that I don't even like, and I'm successful at it. So think about how good I could be at running a business I love."

Skylar's eyebrows shoot up. "You love Blue Skies Farm?"

Something jams itself in Walt's throat. "Yeah," he says. "I love Blue Skies Farm."

Blue Skies Farm isn't a metaphor. Walt's not speaking in code. He doesn't really mean *Skylar* when he says *Blue Skies Farm*, because that would be nuts.

Inside, they find Skylar's table before unloading everything from the truck and bringing it in. There's a Blue Skies Farm banner for the front of the table, which Walt hangs as Skylar unpacks. Over the past few weeks, they've sketched out a plan for the table's display. Walt pointed out that there should be an aesthetic to the Blue Skies Farm booth, and when Skylar said helplessly, "Isn't it just… farm?" Walt took the wheel.

He is *not* doing farmhouse chic. As a decor choice, it's fine. Overdone and close to played out, if you ask him, but if someone wanted him to do a kitchen install in that style, he'd smile and do it. But this is Windham in the heart of the Catskills, and Walt wants Blue Skies Farm to stand out in a sea of farmhouse chic.

When he suggested they take inspiration from *Gaslamp Market* and do a whimsical Edwardian vibe, Skylar's eyes lit up and he exclaimed, "Yes! That's perfect! Maybe we could incorporate peacocks somehow? Because it's pretty whimsical that I have a pair of gay peacocks."

Walt hadn't been able to contain his enthusiasm as his brain started whirring through ideas. "We could use a lot of jewel tones but focus in on blue, like peacock blue. And feathers, obviously. Oh, you know what would be really cool? If we could find an Edwardian wallpaper design that fits with the theme...."

It all came together really nice, and as they set up the baked goods, Walt can't help admiring how the table stands out. They found some bric-a-brac to fill out the table, the coolest things being a pair of Edwardian vases patterned with blue flowers. A bouquet of peacock feathers fills one, while the other holds a handful of thin dowels with cotton balls glued on the end to look like fluffy clouds. Against the backdrop of a blue Victorian-esque wallpaper (it turns out it's a lot easier to find fake Victorian wallpaper patterns to print than Edwardian ones), they're totally nailing the vibe of whimsical, interesting farm booth that everyone is definitely going to hit up.

They have a small refrigerator on one corner of the table, filled with a selection of Blue Skies Farm's signature goat cheese roundels (the rest is in several coolers, out of sight under the table and behind a tablecloth). Reverently, Skylar places a plastic goat figurine on top.

"What's that?" Walt can tell it's important. The way Skylar waited until the end to put it out, like it's a special ritual, was obvious enough even for Walt to pick up on.

Skylar flushes. "Oh. It's... a thing. That I always do. A tradition, I guess."

Walt waits, but Skylar doesn't elaborate. So he doesn't push, even though he wants to know. The figurine doesn't look like anything special—just a plastic toy, the kind of thing you'd get at a zoo gift shop. The paint is worn off it in a few places, like it's been played with a lot.

Taking a few steps back to survey the table, Skylar breaks into a bright grin. "Man, before, I just put everything out on the table and arranged it nicely. But this looks artistic." He turns his smile on Walt, and even though it's still technically winter, it's like spring leafs out into summer under the warmth of Skylar's gaze. "You're so good at making things look nice. No, more than nice. *Inviting*. You know how to make something look like a place people would want to be. Like your house, and the remodel you're doing for Tom."

Now Walt's face is hot. "I like doing it." He clears his throat and gestures. "We should get some pictures. Instagram needs to be fed."

Skylar snaps some photos, taking pictures of the same things over and over until he gets the ones that are the most Instagrammable. Then he spends a few minutes putting the post together, probably editing it into a reel. While he works on that, Walt putters around the table, fiddling with things to make them look perfect, checking the tablet and payment app that Skylar uses, and chatting briefly with the vendor next to them, a Black woman with tied-back locs who's selling jewelry.

"Done!" Skylar announces. "Sorry! Someday I'm going to get way faster at that. At least I know what I'm doing now."

Walt gives him a quick kiss on the cheek, and Skylar turns his head to turn it into a kiss on the mouth. Even though this is a family friendly event, Walt can't resist slipping in a little tongue, which earns him a tiny whimper from Skylar.

They separate just as the first market-goers stroll down the aisle, looking at the items on offer. Skylar darts behind the table, standing behind the refrigerator and watching an approaching middle-aged couple. There's a young family behind them: a mother and father and three kids under the age of five. They have their hands full and it's barely nine in the morning, all three kids pulling on their parents' arms and the parents hanging on to their hands for dear life.

"Morning!" Walt calls to them. "Do you guys want a sample of cake?"

"Cake!" the oldest child hollers, yanking her mom toward the Blue Skies Farm table.

Walt grabs the cake they set aside for samples. It's presented beautifully on a Victorian glass cake plate—Skylar frosted it with goat cream cheese frosting last night and decorated it with dried flower petals and edible gold foil. It's highly Instagrammable.

"It's so pretty!" the middle kid says. He's wearing unicorn barrettes in his pale blond hair and a rainbow tutu. Wait, maybe they're not a "he." Walt should ask for pronouns. Except is it weird to ask a little kid their pronouns? Should Walt ask the parents?

"It is, right?" Walt says. Pointing proudly over at Skylar, he adds, "My boyfriend baked it *and* decorated it."

The father looks impressed. "Wow. It looks like something from a fancy bakery."

"Maybe it's too pretty to eat," the mom tries, but the kids set her straight. She seems happy to lose the argument, accepting a plated sample just as eagerly as the rest of her family.

When they're done, they buy a cake and a tub of frosting, Walt upsells them on some goat cheese too. Once they walk away, Walt turns around to give Skylar a high five. "First sale!"

Skylar doesn't let go of Walt's hand, instead pulling it to his mouth and swiftly kissing Walt's knuckles. "You're a miracle worker."

Shaking his head, Walt replies, "I just tempt people with sweets. That's my secret."

"I could have a hundred of the most beautiful cakes sitting on this table, and it would take me half an hour to sell anything." Skylar kisses Walt's knuckles again. "You make people want to talk to you. It's not even anything you do, it's just you being you. People are drawn to you."

"I don't know about that." Walt ducks his head as his face heats.

Luckily, he doesn't have to think of a way to deflect the praise, because the crowd is growing. Between people drawn in by the sight of the cake and those whose eyes are caught by the table's display, they find themselves dealing with a steady flow of customers.

The first person to recognize them from social media shows up an hour into the market. A young woman approaches the table, towing a man behind her who Walt assumes is her boyfriend. She locks eyes with Walt and lights up. "Oh my god, can I hug you?"

Without waiting for a response, she throws her arms around Walt, squeezing tighter than he would if he was hugging a stranger. Awkwardly, he pats her upper back.

"You too!" the woman announces when she lets go of Walt, reaching across the table to wrap her arms around Skylar. Her boyfriend rolls his eyes. She lets go of Skylar. "You guys are *so* cute. I had to come down here to see you!"

"Where are you from?" Walt asks, trying to turn the charm back on, no matter how weirded out he is by the unsolicited hug.

"Albany!" She beams at her boyfriend. "We're having a country day date."

"Cool date, meeting a couple gay guys," the boyfriend mutters in a tone clearly meant to carry.

She ignores him. "I *love* your Insta. You're super inspiring, and your story is the best thing ever!" She puts a hand over her heart. "You're incredibly brave living your truth in a place like this."

Walt looks at Skylar, at a loss. Skylar's eyes are wide and the expression in them turns beseeching as he meets Walt's gaze. "Um, thanks," Walt says. That seems like the easiest thing to say. It's not confirming or denying. "Do you want to try a sample of anything?"

"Oh, I'm sure it's all amazing!" She picks up one of everything and presents it to Skylar, who totals it up before she pays with her phone. "Hashtag gay farm life!" she says, flashing them a peace sign as she leaves.

They don't have time to talk about it, because from that moment on, they're swamped with business. They sell out of cakes and frosting by noon, nightshade preserves by mid-afternoon, and there's a point when Walt thinks they might actually run out of goat cheese.

In the end, they don't, because there is *so much cheese*. But they make a serious dent in it, thanks to the number of people who seem to have turned out just to visit the Blue Skies Farm table. The majority of them buy several items, but the draw, time and again when Walt talks to them, is Skylar and Walt themselves.

Even though it was Walt's idea in the first place, he can't believe it worked this well. Jett stops by on their break and comments on the crowd around the table, leaving with a jar of nightshade preserves that they insist on paying for, even though Skylar tries to give it to them for free.

By the time the market winds down at the end of the afternoon, Walt's voice is hoarse from nonstop talking. His feet hurt and his stomach aches after forgetting to grab lunch. And his eyes feel strained from looking at camera flashes all day, because so many people wanted pictures of them. Skylar looks exhausted and shellshocked, and he's absently rubbing his cheeks. Now that Walt sees him doing it, his own cheeks hurt too from all the forced smiles for the cameras.

Still. "What did I tell you?" Walt asks, the smugness in his tone undercut by how raspy his voice comes out.

With an incredulous laugh, Skylar says, "I can't believe all those people were that excited to see us. God, I hope they like the cheese."

"If they don't, that's a them problem. You should win awards for that stuff."

Skylar grins. "First Spring Fling, then the world?"

"We could stop at some county and state fairs first," Walt muses. He keeps saying *we*, doesn't he? But Skylar doesn't correct him, and the idea fills Walt with energy and excitement for the future. The last few weeks have proved that they work as a *we*, haven't they?

"Fun fact," Skylar says, "the New York State Fair is the oldest one in the country."

"Seriously? That's cool."

"Yeah!" Even if Skylar's fun facts weren't genuinely fascinating, Walt would be just as enthusiastic about hearing more, because he loves how Skylar lights up when he shows interest. "The first one was in 1841 in Syracuse, but it traveled around the state after that."

The only time Walt ever went to the state fair was when he was in ninth grade. Mario's family invited him to go along with them. "It's in Syracuse now, isn't it?"

Skylar nods. "It moved there permanently in… I can't remember. The late nineteenth century sometime."

A gross feeling accompanies the memory of going with Mario's family. When Mario invited Walt, Walt assumed Cam would be invited too, but Cam wasn't in the Suburban when Walt got picked up that morning. Walt asked if they were picking him up next, even though that didn't make any sense, because they'd need to backtrack. Mario's dad chuckled and said this was a guys' trip, no fairies allowed.

For years, he's told himself he was just a kid, and it's okay he didn't say anything. It doesn't matter; he knew it was wrong at the time, and some part of him has felt sick over it since.

Walt shakes himself, sending the remorse back to where it lives permanently in the back of his mind. "We should go someday."

We and *someday* are rays of light. Walt's relationships usually don't last long enough for somedays to come true, but it feels possible now. Especially with the way Skylar enthusiastically agrees.

Hardly any guests are coming by anymore, so they dismantle the table. The empty crates and coolers are a testament to how incredible their sales were today. Even in Walt's wildest dreams, he didn't think they'd do this well.

As Skylar consolidates the remaining products into one cooler, he says, "I should probably feel worse about the fact that some of those people were totally like… fetishizing us."

Walt blinks at him. "What's that?"

Waving a hand, Skylar says, "You know." But Walt doesn't, so he just shakes his head, and Skylar makes a face. "It's like, reducing us to our queerness, which then they see as for them. Like we're not real people or something."

"Oh." Well, now that it's been explained, it does sound kind of gross. Walt didn't realize that was a thing, but he probably should have. People always find a way to make others less human. "But we're kind of encouraging it, aren't we?"

Skylar sighs. "Yeah. I *should* be mad, but we made a lot of money today. I might have to compromise my principles a little."

Walt smiles and wraps up the glassware before stowing it in a box. On his way to get the glass cake plate, he bumps Skylar's shoulder with his own. "You're not compromising your principles. You're just bending them." Taking money from people who see them as, what, dolls to play with? That hardly seems like compromising principles at all. Not compared to what Walt's done.

Stewing over the past and getting stuck in things he can't change hasn't ever done him much good. His high school transgressions are too far in the rearview mirror to do anything about. This thing with Skylar, though, this is something good that he wants to do right.

While they're carrying everything to the car, Walt comes to a decision. If they're going to be a real thing, a real, serious, long-term thing, he can't keep Skylar in a bubble. The bubble is nice, but where can they go together while they're in it?

The truck tailgate slams shut, and Skylar brushes off his hands on his jeans. Walt lets himself get distracted by the glimpse of lean wrists and tattoos as Skylar's sleeves ride up. "Hey, Sky? What would you think about meeting some of my friends?"

Skylar's eyebrows rise, but he smiles. "Really? In Watertown? But you're not out, are you? Oh." His smile dims. "Not as your boyfriend. Right. Probably not even as your fake boyfriend. Just as a friend."

"No," Walt says firmly. "As my boyfriend. My real boyfriend. We were only fake boyfriends for twelve hours anyway, that would be stupid."

The blue-sky summer brightness returns to Skylar's smile. "Fake dating for the farm was your idea. Now it's stupid?"

"It would be stupid of me to say you're my fake boyfriend!" Walt laughs. "For a lot of reasons. But seriously, Sky. I want people to know what you really mean to me."

"What I mean to you?" Skylar repeats, his voice softer.

Walt's mouth goes dry. He's talking without thinking. Does he even know what Skylar means to him?

"I want you to meet my brother," Walt says. "And his fiancé, and my buddy Mario. Would that be cool? It can be low key. We can go bowling or something." Bowling. Walt hasn't been bowling since middle school birthday parties.

Somehow, though, Skylar's smile is even brighter. "Yeah. I want to meet them. When?"

"Next weekend?" It might take some wheedling to get everyone in the same place, but Walt doesn't mind. Because he *does* know what Skylar means to him, even if he's not ready to say it.

Skylar nods, a big grin on his face. Then, he opens the camera on his phone and holds it out. "We should post to Insta to mark the occasion."

Walt laughs and pushes his face into the side of Skylar's, giving his ear a gentle nip as he breathes in Skylar's scent.

The post has ten thousand likes by the time they get back to Blue Skies Farm.

Chapter Twenty

"ARE YOU nervous?" Skylar asks as Walt makes the left turn into Seaway Lanes. The parking lot is surprisingly full, but then again, it's Saturday night, and maybe bowling is still a cool thing to do in Watertown. It's kind of nice to see the old place still doing a good business.

Also, concentrating on how full the parking lot is distracts Walt from how nervous he is. "Is it obvious?" Walt asks. Now that they're in the floodlit parking lot, probably. His heart is pounding, and it must be visible somewhere on his body.

"Not until the last few minutes," Skylar says. Walt thinks that's generous. He's been a wreck since they got off Route 12, all along Huntington Street, with the iced-over Black River glinting in the streetlights off to their side. "Should I be nervous?"

"No," Walt says with more confidence than he feels. If this is the worst idea he's ever had and everything goes to shit, he's sure he can settle Skylar with Tad and Lewis while he goes and hashes stuff out with Mario.

Walt's normal nervous about introducing Skylar to Tad and Lewis; the standard nerves anyone gets when they're introducing their significant other to their family. There's an extra layer of anxiety since for the first time in his life, Walt's introducing a boyfriend, not a girlfriend, to people—but then again, he's hardly introduced any of the women he's dated to his family.

Mario's a different story. Walt doesn't know what to expect. He's hoping for the best. Mario's his best friend. They've been best friends for twenty years. Even if Mario isn't the most PC about LGBTQ stuff, their friendship should override anything bad he might say or feel.

Whatever else happens, Walt has faith that their friendship will get them through it. Their friendship is one of the most enduring things in his life, right after his family.

He pulls into a parking space and shuts off the car. Its creaks seem loud in the silence after hours of road noise. "Ready?" Walt asks. His hands are still gripping the steering wheel, and he lets go. It takes more effort than it should.

"Are *you*?" Skylar asks. So he noticed Walt's death grip. He unclips his seat belt and leans across the center console, slipping his hands inside Walt's puffer vest and pressing them against his ribs. "This will be good. It's going to be a good night."

"Yeah?" Walt huffs out a breath of laughter. "I mean, yeah. Yeah, you're right. I'm excited." When Skylar's mouth twitches, he adds, "Really. Just. Okay, yeah. It's a little nerve-wracking."

Without warning, Skylar's hands dip under the hem of Walt's shirt and dig into his sides. His hands aren't *cold* cold, but they sure as hell aren't warm, either, and Walt yelps, hitting a note he's pretty sure he hasn't heard out of his own throat since sixth grade. "No!" he yells, batting ineffectually at Skylar, who commits an even worse betrayal than cold hands and starts tickling.

Skylar cackles, pushing his body into Walt's, so the harder Walt struggles, the more he ends up pinned against his door, Skylar holding him there, their bodies locked together. Even though Skylar's lean, not an extra ounce of fat on him, he's heavy, and his weight presses down on Walt intoxicatingly.

Maybe Walt isn't struggling that hard. Or maybe—this is probably the more accurate way to put it—he's struggling in a way that's designed to look like struggling but is really about rubbing bodies together. There's some good body-on-body rubbing going on, even through their winter clothes. Walt's cock is filling.

"It's going to be a good night, baby," Skylar says again, stroking his fingers down Walt's bare sides.

Walt blinks at him. "You've never called me that."

Skylar's eyes go wide and he winces. "Sorry."

"No, no, don't say sorry." God, Skylar has pretty eyes. Even in the harsh light from the parking lot floodlights, they're the color of amber. Something about the quality of the light makes the contrast between the shadows and illuminated parts of his faces more intense, so his eyelashes look even longer than they normally do, and the sweep of his eyes is more dramatic.

Skylar makes a lip-zipping motion. "I won't say it aga—"

"I like it," Walt interrupts. He does. It makes something hot and needy throb inside him. Separate from his dick, though, that too. It's a turn-on when men call him baby, which he learned about himself once when he sucked off a trucker in a truck stop shower.

"Yeah?" Skylar gives him that sunny smile that turns Walt's insides into some kind of sweeping vista. "Then I'll keep saying it." He leans forward and kisses Walt's neck slowly as Walt tips his head back to give him better access. "I love that you want me to meet Tad, Lewis, and Mario. I think it's really brave, baby." When Walt makes a helpless little noise, Skylar drops another slow kiss, this one closer to his Adam's apple. "And sexy."

Walt groans and wraps his arms around Skylar's back as Skylar kisses him on the mouth and works a hand between them to cup Walt's cock, which is half hard. Maybe more like three-quarters hard. "Sky," he mumbles.

Giving Walt a squeeze, Skylar says, "Later." Even though Walt's eyes are closed, he knows Skylar has that hot, lopsided smile on his face. Skylar plants another quick kiss on Walt's lips and returns to his side of the car. And yeah, there's the smile. Walt wants to trace it with a finger but manages not to.

Once both their bodies settle down, they head inside. Walt scans the parking lot but doesn't see Mario's car; Tad and Lewis don't have one, so the Kia sedan with California plates might be their rental.

Walt pulls open the door and is hit with Megan Thee Stallion blasting on speakers that can't handle the bass, fuzzing out so audibly that even Walt, not exactly a music guy, winces. The bowling lanes are dark, lit only with black lights and whirling light thrown by disco balls.

It smells like musty carpet, floor wax, grease, and long-stale cigarette smoke, and between the smell and the thud of bowling balls hitting the floor, then the crack of pins flying, that door might as well have been a portal to 2002. The speakers probably were just as bad then, too, but Walt didn't notice.

"Walt!" At a table near the shoe rental, Tad waves and stands up, nudging Lewis, whose back is to the door.

As Walt makes his way over to his brother, his heart pounds all over again, though he also can't stop himself from grinning. It makes him wonder if this is what it's like to have a manic episode. Luckily, he doesn't have long to dwell on it, because a few strides get him to the table, where he and Tad hug. Tad's definitely holding on tighter than he usually does.

Tad steps back, a happy smile on his face and his curly auburn hair falling across his forehead. "I'm so ready for Rock After Dark. Honestly if it wasn't for the music, I'd think we were in a time warp."

Walt laughs. "I was thinking the same thing! This place hasn't changed."

Lewis joins Tad, and Walt gets a hug from his future brother-in-law too. Then, gulp, it's time for introductions. It takes a couple coughs to clear his throat enough to make his voice work, but Walt puts a hand to the small of Skylar's back and says, "Um, so, yeah. This is Skylar. Sky, this is my brother Tad"—Tad waves—"and his fiancé Lewis."

Both Lewis and Tad try to shake Skylar's hand at the same time, so they just end up smacking their hands together and laughing before Lewis withdraws his hand to put it around Tad's waist, squeezing him close. The easy affection between them, and the fact that they're in Watertown and Tad isn't worried about anyone seeing that affection—makes Walt's chest feel tight with both happiness for them and the sharp desire to have the same thing himself.

"It's so amazing to meet you," Tad's saying as he shakes Skylar's hand enthusiastically. "Are you in the market for embarrassing stories about Walt? Because I've been compiling a list on my phone since last weekend."

"Asshole," Walt says without rancor, giving his brother's shoulder a light punch.

"Payback," Tad retorts, though his face gets bright red. "Sorry, Skylar. I think I psyched myself up too much to meet a new person."

Skylar gives him a warm smile. "You're good. I'm for sure the most awkward person here, so don't worry."

That just makes Tad turn even brighter red. "Oh god no. My awkwardness knows no bounds. Boundless awkwardness. I can't believe I just admitted to having a list of embarrassing Walt stories. Lew, make me stop talking."

As Lewis takes his turn shaking Skylar's hand, he says, "There's really a list, and he dug pretty deep into the childhood humiliation. Walt, who's Mrs. Mortinson? That's all the list says."

Walt's head snaps around so he can glare at Tad. "You wouldn't."

"I would," Tad says.

Skylar laughs and leans into Walt's side. Then the knife comes out. "I love embarrassing childhood stories."

"Betrayed," Walt says aggrievedly.

Patting Walt's shoulder, Lewis says, "It's okay. You're about to see me bowl, so I'll be the most embarrassing thing here tonight."

"I think they do bumpers in the gutters here," Walt says.

"Not during Rock After Dark." Lewis sighs and adds sadly, "I already checked."

Tad motions at the shoe rental desk. "Should we get our lane?"

Walt glances over his shoulder at the door. "We should probably wait for Mario."

A flicker goes over Tad's face. It's gone too fast for Walt to read, but he doesn't need to, because he already knows Tad isn't Mario's biggest fan. The dislike isn't totally unwarranted. Mario hasn't exactly tried to be friends with Tad, and when they were all in Las Vegas a little over a year ago, Mario said some downright shitty things. At the time, Walt mostly let it slide, which he's not proud of.

It's a testament to the newfound strength of his and Tad's relationship that Tad was willing to drive all the way up here, even though he knew he was going to have to see Mario.

"Didn't we have to do this in Watertown because Mario didn't want to drive anywhere else?" Tad asks, an acid bite to his tone that usually comes out when anything Watertown-related is the subject of conversation.

"Yeah, let me text him." Tempting as it is to make excuses for Mario, Walt bites his tongue. Tad has a point. He and Lewis came from Manhattan, a five-hour drive, and Walt and Skylar came from Windham, which is closer, but still hours. Mario lives fifteen minutes away, and he's ten minutes late.

He texts Mario, **Yo where you at**, not expecting a response. It's mostly an optics text so Tad knows Walt has his back.

They stand there chatting for a few minutes, just small talk about their respective drives, the last time they all went bowling, and in Skylar's and Lewis's cases, where they grew up. Walt totally forgot that Lewis is also from Jersey, and it turns out Clifton, Skylar's hometown, and Weehawken, where Lewis grew up, aren't that far apart. They quickly determine that Skylar's grandparents' restaurant was Lewis's family's favorite Thai restaurant. "Totally worth the drive," Lewis assures Walt and Tad.

"Maybe we crossed paths," Skylar muses. "I helped out in the kitchen a lot."

"Maybe!" Lewis looks charmed by the idea, which is classic Lewis. He loves fate and meant-to-be, and he'd love the possibility that he encountered his fiancé's brother's future boyfriend years before Walt and Skylar would meet.

Lewis has just asked Skylar how long he's been running Blue Skies Farm (after Tad's initial embarrassing-Walt-story-driven talkativeness, he's receded into his usual shyness and is letting Lewis do most of the talking), when Mario finally arrives.

Tad hunches his shoulders and sets his mouth in a thin line, looking away as Mario joins them. "I feel like I haven't seen you for months, man!" Mario says to Walt. They do a bro hug, and Walt quickly introduces everyone. He can't help analyzing Mario's expression as he shakes Lewis's hand and gives Tad an awkward high five/handshake thing. Is that a tiny smirk on Mario's face? Or is Walt just worried and imagining things?

"Should we bowl?" Walt asks, now that they're all here. They buy unlimited games, get bowling shoes, and head down to their lane. A teenage waitress comes by to check if they want anything to eat or drink, and they get pizza and a couple pitchers of beer.

Walt makes sure he and Skylar have a minute alone as they go to choose bowling balls. As Walt reaches for a swirly purple one labeled with a 16, he says in a low voice, "I have to tell Mario I'm bi before I tell him we're together."

The holes on the sixteen-pound ball are too small for his fingers. Or maybe his fingers are too fat. He crouches to put the ball back on the bottom rack, and as he does, Skylar's fingertips brush the back of his hand.

"I get it," Skylar says, his smile so understanding that Walt wants to wrap an arm around his legs and press his face into Skylar's body. That would put his face right in Skylar's crotch, which Walt would like, but probably isn't great for a public place. Though if he did that, it would take some of the pressure off the "Hey Mario, can I talk to you for a second?" conversation, since it would be obvious that Walt's now the kind of guy who puts his face in other guys' crotches.

"I won't post anything on Instagram until you tell him," Skylar adds. "Not that he'd see it anyway. If he ever saw any of my posts, he'd know about us already."

"You're going to post on the farm Instagram tonight?" Walt asks, weirdly blindsided.

"Well, yeah." A line appears between Skylar's eyebrows. "We lost a bunch of followers this week, and I think it's because I didn't post enough of us. I have to keep the content going, right?"

"Right," Walt says. He doesn't know why the idea of Skylar posting pictures of tonight is getting to him. This is exactly the kind of thing Walt told him to post.

Skylar picks up a glittery turquoise ball, testing his range of motion with it. His bicep flexes and the muscles in his forearm tauten, the stark ink and clean lines of his tattoos accentuating every dip between muscle, tendon, and bone, and highlighting how strong Skylar is. His shoulder blades knife under his T-shirt, and the curve of his shoulder bunches and extends.

And Walt's mouth is literally watering. He drops his eyes to Skylar's hands on the ball, his hand cupping the swell of it, his fingers sliding into the holes and fitting snugly; the curve of his thumb—

A hot throb in Walt's gut and balls clues him in that far from making his drooling situation go away, he's exacerbating it.

Plus, now he can't stop thinking about Skylar's fingers in holes. They haven't crossed the butt barrier, but now, *now* of all times, as they're about to bowl with Walt's brother, future brother-in-law, and best friend, he realizes how much he's gunning for butt stuff. Skylar's fingers look good jammed in the bowling ball's holes. They'd look good in Walt's ass too.

His cock would look even better stuffed in there.

Walt's face burns. Jesus Christ. He hasn't even had any beer. Bowling balls shouldn't be making him horny.

Skylar curls his arm around the ball and looks at Walt expectantly. Why? Is Walt supposed to be doing something? Oh! Bowling ball. Right. He needs to pick one out. He fumbles for one, red and magenta swirls to Skylar's glittery turquoise, and decides it's good enough. It's not like he's going for the win here. Mostly what he's going to be doing is ogling his boyfriend.

It's clearly obvious to his boyfriend, because one of Skylar's eyebrows creeps up, and his crooked, sexy little smile appears, a hint of wickedness to it. "I'm not sure about this ball," Skylar says, holding it straight out in front of him, which does all kinds of interesting things to his arms. Raising it over his head, he continues, "I better make sure I can handle it. It's important to me to handle big, heavy balls the right way."

His shirt is riding up, exposing his toned stomach and the sparse line of hair trailing from his belly button and under the waistband of his jeans. "No complaints about your ball handling from me," Walt says, his voice too strangled to be cool.

Skylar grins, and the strobe of the black lights make his teeth look purple. It's not sexy, but it makes Walt's stomach twist with happiness anyway. Because he's here. He's with Skylar; he introduced Skylar to Tad and Lewis, and it went well. Granted, introducing his boyfriend to his gay brother and his brother's gay fiancé is a gimme, but Walt knows to take the wins when they present themselves.

"You two are taking forever! Just grab some balls, man."

Mario's voice startles Walt out of the private bubble he and Skylar have spun around themselves. Mario slaps Walt on the back and belatedly laughs at his own words. "I should've saved that for your brother and the missus."

Skylar's eyebrows shoot up. Walt's heart falls. "Mario," he says warningly.

"I'm joking! Jesus, if you can't joke about gay dudes grabbing balls, what's the point?" A sour expression crosses Mario's face, and he grabs a ball from the rack. "That's heterophobia. C'mon, I'm ready to whoop your ass."

Walt wants to say something or try to make a joke out of Mario's heterophobia comment, because Walt's positive that's not a thing. It sounds like straight pride. But Mario's obviously annoyed that Walt called him out on what he said about Tad and Lewis, and he doesn't want to get into it with Mario tonight, not when tonight's supposed to be about coming out to the people he's closest to. So all he says is, "You're on."

As they return to their lane, Skylar says in a voice just loud enough for Walt, but not Mario, to hear, "And here we see the fight for dominance in males of the species...."

Showing affection toward Skylar is a risk—not only is Mario *right there*, but there's a non-zero chance that someone here will recognize Walt, even through the strobe lights and disco balls. When Walt looks at him, though, there's such a bright, mischievous smile on his face that Walt can't help himself from leaning over and kissing him quickly.

Mario turns around. Luckily, Walt's leaning back from Skylar, so Mario doesn't see the kiss. At least, Walt hopes Mario didn't see the kiss.

For a second, he thinks he's wrong, as Mario's eyes dart between the two of them. He doesn't say anything, though.

Walt takes a deep breath. That's a sign that he needs to stop stalling and tell his best friend what's up. They'll bowl a few frames, Walt will down a beer, and they'll talk.

Chapter Twenty-One

"Ohhhhh yeah, turkey, baby!" Mario square-dances in place as an animated turkey flashes up on the TV screen overhead.

Walt boos while Lewis groans and buries his head in his hands. "We need more beer," Lewis says. "I have to drown my sorrows."

Resting a wrist delicately on Lewis's shoulder, Tad says, "We'll go bowling during the day sometime and get you gutter bumpers, sweetheart."

"Thanks," Lewis says, voice muffled by his hands. Then he raises his head. "Gutter bumpers sounds like the new drug of choice in gay bars."

Skylar cracks up and flags down their waitress. "I definitely need more beer. I used to think I wasn't a horrible bowler. Joke's on me."

Dropping into the chair next to Walt, Mario says, "Ally's dad loves bowling. Haven't I ever mentioned I go with him sometimes?"

"Oh, so you're a ringer," Walt says.

As the next pitcher of beer gets delivered, Skylar asks, "Is Ally your wife?"

"Yeah. Love of my life." Mario puts his hand over his heart and pats it. "When she's not eight months pregnant, she bowls three hundred."

"Is that good?" Lewis asks. Tad rubs his back.

Skylar swallows a mouthful of beer, and Walt tries not to stare so obviously at the movement of his throat. "How'd you meet?" Skylar asks Mario, which makes Walt love him even more. Mario's his best friend, and Skylar's trying to get to know him.

Waving a hand, Mario says, "High school. Same story as everyone else around here. She was a couple years ahead of Walt and me, though, so she didn't look twice at me in school. After I finished college, we ran into each other at Tim Horton's."

"Excellent meet-cute," Lewis says.

"What's that?" Mario asks.

The scandalized expression on Lewis's face almost makes Walt spit beer back into his glass. "That's where you have a particularly adorable first meeting with your significant other. Like, romcom level adorable."

Mario leans back in his chair and points between Lewis and Tad. "So did you guys have a meet-cute?"

"More like a meet horny," Tad mutters.

"The cutest," Lewis says.

"They rode a mechanical bull together," Walt volunteers. "I've heard it described as 'fornicating on a mechanical bull,' if I'm remembering right?"

When he looks at Tad, his brother's face is a mixture of bright red and smug. "So much for what happens in Vegas stays in Vegas," Tad mumbles.

Lewis bumps his shoulder into Tad's, and Tad leans into him. Since Skylar doesn't know the Tad-and-Lewis love story, Walt says, "We all"—his finger circle encompasses Tad and Mario—"went to Vegas about a year ago. Tad wandered off, got wasted, and married Lewis."

"Wait, where was the mechanical bull in all this?" Mario asks.

"That was before we got married." Lewis looks thoughtful. "And I guess on the way to getting wasted."

"I thought you were engaged?" Skylar asks.

"We got divorced so we can have a wedding we remember," Lewis says, like this is a totally normal trajectory for a romantic relationship. Skylar seems to accept it.

Mario shakes his head. "Wild. And Walt kind of met Lia on that trip too."

Walt takes a too-fast drink of beer that goes down hard. "Yeah, that wasn't meant to be, obviously."

"There's a chick out there for you, man." Mario grasps his shoulder and shakes it. "You'll find her."

Certainty coalesces with crystalline precision in Walt's chest. This is it. They're all having a good time; this melding of the people he loves could have been the most awkward night ever, but it's working. Walt wants to be able to share his and Skylar's meet-cute. More importantly, he wants to be able to grab Skylar's hand and say he's pretty sure he found his person.

He stands. "Mario, wanna come with me to the bar to order some more food?"

Mario points across the bowling alley. "We can just get our waitress—"

"No, let's go order at the bar." He catches Skylar's eye and Skylar smiles encouragingly. It must be obvious what he's thinking.

By the time Walt and Mario get to the bar, Walt's heart is hammering harder than it ever does while he's building fences or tearing out cabinets. It's tempting to chicken out. It would damn sure be easier. But then he'd have to go back to everyone else and shake his head, and they'd all have to keep pretending Walt and Skylar are just buddies.

As Mario orders the pizza, Walt tries to breathe deeply to bring his pounding heart back into a non-cardiac episode range. Lia tried to get him to do yoga, and for the first time, he regrets not taking her up on the invitation. There's probably some deep breathing he could do right now to calm down or center himself or whatever.

"Okay, let's get back to me embarrassing the rest of you," Mario says, slapping the bar and starting back toward their lane.

Something makes Walt's body move; he's pretty sure it's not him. His arm feels like it's on strings as he raises it and puts a hand on Mario's shoulder. Once it's there, though, the words are too. "Can I talk to you before we go back?"

Mario's forehead crinkles. "Uh, okay. You're not gonna tell me you have three days to live, are you? You have to be my kid's godfather, man. We'll beat this thing together."

"I'm bi," Walt says.

Shaking his head, Mario says, "Nah, I'll get the tab. You all drove up here."

There's a silence so empty that the ambient noise of the bowling alley rushes in to fill it like the ocean flooding a sea cave. The crack of balls hitting pins, the squeak of shoes, the clink of glasses, the hum of conversation and occasional cheers, all of it is suddenly so loud that Walt feels like he needs to physically push it away.

"Did you hear me?" Walt finally asks.

"Yeah, you said you're buying." Mario looks both amused and exasperated. "Is that what you wanted to talk to me about that? Pretty sure we could have done it in front of those guys."

Oh Jesus fuck. Walt came out to his best friend, and now he has to come out to his best friend *again*?

"No, I said"—deep maybe-yoga breath—"I'm bi. Like bisexual. Like, I'm into guys too."

This time, it's clear Mario heard him. His face is frozen in a half smile, caught between Walt's ridiculousness in making their bar tab into a whole thing and the reality of what Walt was trying to tell him.

"Are you serious?" Mario asks after the silence goes on for at least three hours.

Okay, not the worst response. Not the best, either. "Yeah." Walt wipes his palms on his thighs. "I wouldn't joke about that."

"Didn't seem like you would. Since Tad's, you know. All fairy princess."

"Don't," Walt says, something jagged spiking up his throat.

Mario raises his hands before rubbing them over his face. "Fuck, man. You're—other guys, really? I mean, Tad and Lewis, I can see it. But you're not...."

"What?" Walt forces his voice to stop shaking.

Shrugging awkwardly, Mario says, "Feminine."

If Walt had learned how to do yoga breathing, maybe he'd be able to get a full breath now. "Just because a guy likes other men doesn't mean he's feminine."

"No, I know." Mario rubs his hands over his face again. "I know. Fuck. Sorry. I just don't know what to say. I never thought... I never would've *guessed*. Not you. Not in a million years. So is this, like, something you've been keeping on the DL forever?"

Now it's Walt's turn to shrug awkwardly. He shoves his hands into his pockets so Mario doesn't see how bad they're shaking. He hates confrontations with his friends, especially Mario. "I guess."

"So why are you telling me now?" Realization strikes Mario's face like lightning. "Skylar. He's not just your buddy, is he?"

"No." Walt glances toward their bowling lane, but between the darkness and the strobe lights, it's impossible to tell if Skylar's looking this way. "We're, uh, together, I guess."

Why is he waffling? They *are* together. There's no *he guesses* about it. The expression in Mario's eyes just makes it hard to hold the line of his principles. Or the simple truth.

Even though he'd like to say he looked Mario in the eyes and was brave about coming out, Walt decides he'd rather say what he needs to than be courageous about it. He looks toward their bowling lane again, and this time, he's sure he sees Skylar turned toward him, watching.

"Skylar's my boyfriend," Walt says, both trying and not trying to see Mario's reaction in his peripheral vision. "I'm serious about him."

Mario doesn't say anything for what feels like forever. Walt's hands in his pockets are clammy with sweat. It's disgusting. If they go back to bowling after this, he's going to be lucky if the ball doesn't slip out of his hands and fall on his toes.

"If you're with someone who makes you happy, that's what's important," Mario says. Walt snaps his head around and Mario gives him a wan smile. "Nothing else really matters, right? I guess people can think shitty stuff, but screw other people."

"Yeah," Walt says. His voice breaks and he clears his throat a couple times, like that's the problem instead of the fact that his emotions are hanging on to the outside of a jet by their fingernails. Weird metaphor, but his head is in a weird place right now. "You're cool with it? Me? And him?"

"It's not like you'd stop being into dudes if I wasn't cool with it, right?"

"Right," Walt says. Muscles he didn't even know he had unlock in his shoulders with relief.

Mario drums his fingers on the bar, glances at Walt, then looks away again. "You're not into me, though, are you?"

"What?" Walt laughs. "No." Gross, but Walt doesn't say that out loud. Mario's friendship is incredibly important to him, but the idea of desiring him carnally is ridiculous.

"Damn, you could have thought about it for a second." Mario's indignation rings false, though Walt can't put his finger on why. There's just something hollow beneath it, like he knows it's a joke he should make, but his heart isn't in it.

"Sorry," Walt says, laughing. It comes out with the same hollowness.

Or maybe it doesn't, because it seems to put Mario more at ease. "So," he says, "when you played football in high school, did you... you know?"

For a split second, Walt thinks Mario's asking if he fantasized about locker room group sex with the entire football team. Before he opens his mouth to answer—because yeah, he did, and he's still kind of ashamed and turned-on by it—it occurs to him to stop and clarify what *you know* is. "Did I what?"

Rolling his eyes, Mario says, "Sneak a peek, man. Were you checking other dudes out in the showers?"

Walt kind of wishes the question had been about his teenage spank bank. Checking his teammates out in the shower, though, that makes a sting rise to the surface of Walt's skin in a different way. It's too reminiscent of all the freaking out over trans people in bathrooms, like if you fit somewhere in the LGBTQ+ spectrum you're totally sex-crazed, unable to find sex in a normal way, and also probably a predator.

The truth, which Walt feels jammed at the base of his throat, is that he was too terrified of someone seeing him looking too long to look at anyone at all. Walt had a reputation for being really into the game, because he'd get to the locker room early and stay late to avoid changing with everyone else as much as he could. There are probably locker rooms in the world where guys can freely check each other out, but Watertown High School wasn't one of them.

The fact that Mario would say something like that bugs him so much that an objection almost breaks through the logjam of unsaid things blocking up his throat, but it's not worth it. Mario will brush him off. Maybe more, considering the way he reacted to Walt's lack of amusement at the ball-grabbing joke.

He can see the moment Mario goes from maybe joking to disgusted, which Walt can't help being afraid is what he's felt this whole time. It's Walt's fault, though, because he took too long to answer. Mario says, "Fuck, you did. That's nasty."

"I didn't," Walt says quickly. "Sorry, I was just…. High school was kind of weird for me. I was just thinking."

Mario opens his mouth, then closes it again. He drums his fingers on the bar again before shrugging. "I mean, I don't know. I guess everyone probably looked once in a while. I never saw you checking anyone out when we changed for gym. Not like Cameron Greenberg."

Walt's stomach clenches unpleasantly at Cam's name. "What do you mean?"

"Don't you remember how gay he was? He totally perved on everyone."

"I don't…," Walt begins, with no clear idea of how he's going to object. He just knows he should, because he's pretty sure Cam didn't.

And because he was horrible to Cam all those years ago, and he wants to have the guts now to take a tiny bit of weight off his side of the karmic scale. That's stupid, obviously. Cam doesn't care what Walt does or doesn't say right now. Walt threw away their friendship and the seed of everything else that had been growing between them.

The bartender delivers their pizza and Mario grabs it, turns, and walks back to their lane without waiting for Walt to answer.

Walt stands there for another few seconds, something sad rushing through his veins. Maybe this is what anxiety feels like—an indistinct feeling that something's wrong, but you can't pinpoint what and it's only going to get worse. By all accounts, that didn't go badly with Mario. He said some of the right things, and the rest of it… well, Walt will give him the benefit of the doubt. Their friendship deserves that.

He follows Mario back to their lane, where Skylar, Tad, and Lewis are laughing about something. Tad seems more comfortable and talkative. As Mario puts the pizza on the table, he asks, "What's so funny?"

Walt slides onto the booth on one side of the table, where Skylar's sitting. He puts a hand on Skylar's leg and squeezes, but then—fuck it. Deliberately, he moves his arm to rest loosely around Skylar's shoulders instead. The smile Skylar turns on him makes it worth it.

There's no reaction at all from Mario, so that's probably good. Skylar's smile goes from bright to a little evil. "I was telling them about the fake dating plan."

"It was a good plan!" Walt's chest warms when Skylar laughs and leans into him.

Lewis takes a piece of pizza. "I think it's fair to say that none of us would have expected you to live out so many romance tropes in such a short amount of time."

"I'm not living out romance tropes," Walt says, but he's grinning. He's sitting here in a Watertown bowling alley after successfully coming out to his best friend, and now he has his arm around his boyfriend. How can he do anything except grin?

"I tried to tell them it wasn't like that at all," Skylar says.

Shaking his head, Tad says, "No, Lew is right. Seriously!" Ticking them off on his finger, Tad goes on, "You had a meet-cute. You got snowed in. And then you faked a relationship!"

"Barely," Walt says.

Mario keeps looking at Walt. Actually, it's Walt's arm around Skylar that Mario keeps looking at, then away from quickly, like he's afraid he's going to get eye damage if he looks too long. "They know?" Mario asks, jutting his chin toward Tad and Lewis.

"Yeah. They're the only people I've told besides you," Walt says. Giddy relief spreads through him like helium. It was just on a time delay; that's why it didn't hit when he came out to Mario. He's been carrying the secret so long that his body couldn't let go of it.

"Cool." Mario looks up at their scoreboard. "Should we keep playing?"

"Sure, I'm ready to keep making the rest of you look good," Lewis says cheerfully.

Tad wrinkles his nose as he studies their scores. "I think the only person you're making look good is Skylar."

That's embarrassingly true. Tad, Lewis, and Walt are all within ten points of each other, and none of them have broken fifty points.

"I'll take it," Skylar says with a laugh. Before he gets up, he kisses Walt chastely but lingeringly. For the rest of his life, Walt will associate the taste of beer and pepperoni with doing something that he's been scared of forever. His whole life, or close enough. He cups Skylar's jaw in his hand, warm skin and the prickle of stubble.

The crack of pins intrudes on their tiny, shimmering space. Walt draws back and looks down the lane. Mario just got another strike, and the sweep bar at the end of the lane clears the fallen pins from the deck. "Nice," Walt says, rising to his feet and lifting a hand to high-five Mario.

For a second, Walt thinks Mario's going to ignore him—but he accepts Walt's high five with the same force as always. Maybe Walt imagined that split second of hesitation.

Chapter Twenty-Two

IT'S AFTER midnight when Walt rolls into his garage and turns off the truck. Skylar's that weird cocktail of wired and exhausted, and his eyes keep wanting to close even though his body isn't tired at all.

Before he gets out of the car, Walt takes Skylar's hand. "Thanks for being cool with Tad and Lewis crashing here. I know it's not really, uh… you know."

"Conducive to me sucking your brains out through your dick?" Skylar asks. He's going for sultry, but then he yawns, which ruins it.

Walt chuckles. "Yeah. That." He shifts in the seat and adjusts his jeans—the pants-pluck that says more than a thousand words. "Uh, is it too late to send them to a hotel?"

"Yes," Skylar laughs. He pops his door open. "C'mon, I want to see your house in person."

He swings his legs out as the headlights of Tad's and Lewis's rental car bathe the garage in white light. On the drive up from Windham, Walt talked more about his relationship with Tad than he has the entire time Skylar's known him—about how they were practically estranged for years, only seeing each other on holidays.

"We pretty much spent a decade talking past each other" is how Walt sums it up, and it makes Skylar a painful mix of happy and sad. Being an only child has meant spending his entire life wondering, and frequently wishing that he had a sibling. Listening to Walt talk about how he and Tad contributed in equal parts to the fucking up of their relationship puts the hard parts of having a sibling in stark relief, but there's also something gleaming in the way they repaired it.

They wait for Tad and Lewis to troop into the garage. Tad yawns and rubs his eyes, which makes Lewis murmur something to him. Tad smiles sleepily in response. Walt flips on lights inside, takes coats and hangs them up, and then insists on taking the single roller bag that Tad and Lewis brought, as well as his own duffel and Skylar's backpack. Skylar takes the opportunity to appreciate the ripple of muscles under Walt's shirt.

"Hey, Skylar." Tad sounds shy again, like their relationship reset during the drive. "In case I didn't say, it was really good to meet you. I, um—sorry, this sounds really corny, but Walt seems happy. Like, really happy. So, yeah. I'm glad you two are together."

More warmth spreads through Skylar. "That means a lot. Thanks. I'm pretty sure if you'd hated me, that might've been it for us."

Tad snorts. "No way. He doesn't put that much stock in what I think."

"He definitely does." Skylar looks to Lewis for backup, because Lewis has to see it too.

Lewis nods. "Yeah, babe. Your opinion matters a lot to your brother."

"Not as much as Mario's," Tad says stubbornly.

Walt comes back at that moment. "What about Mario?"

Before anyone can answer—because Skylar doesn't trust himself to answer, and he doesn't want to put Tad or Lewis in the position of having to answer—he says, "Can I have the tour?"

"Yeah!" Walt says brightly. "You guys can come too, if you're not too tired…."

"Yeah, obviously!" Tad says, though his enthusiasm is undercut with another huge yawn. "I want to see the remodel."

It's a good save. You couldn't pay Skylar to say anything, but he got a weird vibe from Mario tonight. Nothing creepy or anything, just… something not exactly right. Something that felt a lot like resentment looking for an outlet. But he seemed to be saying the right things after Walt talked to him, and Walt's happy with the way it went. If Walt's happy, that's all that matters.

Except Skylar's hackles are still up, because he kept expecting the strange vibe to spill into outright hostility, and Skylar won't let anyone hurt Walt, even if they *are* his best friend.

Seeing Walt's house in person sweeps Mario right out of Skylar's mind. The pictures don't do it justice. The house itself is a two-bedroom bungalow with a full bathroom upstairs and a tiny powder room downstairs, but from the moment they walk in, it's obvious Walt's made it his own. The galley kitchen is small but doesn't feel tight, with light-colored cabinets and a big window. The bathrooms have all new fixtures with clean, unassuming lines. The tile in the large-enough-to-fit-two-people shower is pretty—shimmering greens and blues in a botanical pattern—and when Skylar says so, Walt flushes with happiness and says he designed the pattern and did all the tiling. Like it's nothing. Like that's just a thing you do—throw on a YouTube video and become a master tiler.

The smaller bedroom is bright and straddling the line between clean and ornate, with white chair rail, sky blue walls, and a dark blue border with a Greco-Roman-looking geometric design in gold. The queen bed is neatly made, covered with a duvet in the same dark blue as the border and edged with a similar design, like they were meant to go together.

Walt's room is the stunner, though. The Victorian wallpaper is lush and detailed, the rich spectrum of greens and sumptuous pattern drawing you in like there's an entrance to a secret garden hidden in all the foliage. The king mattress is set in a sturdy, dark frame with floral accents on the posts and the center of the headboard.

Skylar normally isn't a person who thinks of furnishings as masculine or feminine, but this room feels like a space that uses a lot of elements that are traditionally "feminine," while clearly being a man's bedroom. It all looks immaculate. Maybe Skylar should hire Walt to redo his house too.

They all gush over the house, especially the master bedroom. Tad's especially delighted by the plant on the dresser, positioned to get as much light as possible through the window. It's the same plant Walt was protecting under his clothes the night of the blizzard, Skylar realizes, but it's grown since then.

For a second, he feels like he's dissociating, or maybe seeing everything in double, past and present overlaid like ghosts on top of each other. Like echoes of different universes, where Walt never showed up at Skylar's door clutching that plant. It would have been so easy for them not to meet, but here they are, standing together in Walt's bedroom.

He wants to snap a picture for Instagram—his followers should know how talented Walt is, in addition to being hot.

Within a few minutes, Tad and Lewis retire to the second bedroom. Taking turns in the bathroom reminds Skylar of being a kid and sharing the single full bathroom in their house with his parents. Stuff like that usually just depresses him, but this time, it's bittersweet.

"My mom would've really liked you," he says once the two of them are behind the closed door of Walt's bedroom. Those fancy old-fashioned Edison lightbulbs give the room a golden, relaxing glow. It feels luxurious, and it feels private, and it feels like this, right here, Walt pulling his shirt over his head so the light caresses the planes of his muscular shoulders and chest, so it glimmers off his chest hair and his short beard, is something Skylar wants to keep for a long time.

He might want to keep it forever.

Walt gives him a soft look that makes Skylar's insides turn to warm honey. "I wish I could've met her."

Skylar pulls off his shirt too, then steps out of his pants, folds them up, and sets them on the dresser next to the plant. "Me too. And my grandparents. They'd probably already have convinced you to shut down your fence business to concentrate on remodeling houses instead."

When Walt's eyebrows draw together, Skylar wonders if he went too far. His grandparents *would* have tried to convince Walt to ditch the business he doesn't like for the one he loves, and if that happens to also be what Skylar thinks, well, he always was on the same wavelength as his grandparents.

They'd have gotten Walt, too, but they wouldn't understand why he keeps doing something that doesn't make him happy, especially when there's no one depending on him. They'd ask, *Didn't your parents work hard so you could do what makes you happy?* That was always the American dream to them, being able to do what you loved, instead of what you had to do to make money. It's why they put all that money aside for Skylar, so he could pursue his dreams instead of feeling cornered into doing something because of necessity.

"Fences aren't very exciting," Walt says. He chews on his lip. "Do you think I should sell the company?"

"I don't have any thoughts about it," Skylar lies. He definitely has thoughts, but now doesn't seem like the time. He throws back the duvet on the bed and looks at Walt meaningfully. Walt grins and takes the hint, sliding under the midnight blue sheets with a slither of skin against what Skylar's sure is a high thread count. Eagerly, Skylar follows him, sinking into the soft mattress and pillows. It's like floating on a cloud. "I need one of these," he says dreamily.

The mattress dips as Walt shifts. "Yeah, your mattress isn't the best. Good company in it, though."

Skylar opens his eyes to see Walt on his side with his head propped on a hand. His eyes are a darker blue than usual in the dim light—closer to the velvety midnight of the sheets than his usual sky blue. Skylar rolls onto his side, too, so now they're facing each other, a space between them that's waiting to be spanned by an arm. A crazy thought pops into Skylar's head—that he could ask Walt to move this bed to Blue Skies Farm. He could ask Walt to move himself to Blue Skies Farm— permanently.

That's crazy, of course, so he doesn't. Instead, he reaches across the space to put a hand on the broad curve of Walt's shoulder, then traces a finger down to the crease of his armpit. Hair peeks out, dark gold in the shadow of Walt's pit. "Too bad we're not here alone," he says, dropping his voice to a fuck-me growl.

A shiver chases over Walt's skin. "Yeah."

Skylar strokes his thumb over Walt's chest where it curves into his pit, tangling it in that little peek of hair. "Watching you bowl made me hard." Thank god for the dark and the strobe lights; he's pretty sure no one noticed.

Walt lets out a tiny groan and slides his calf between Skylar's legs. "We really shouldn't. Tad and Lewis are right on the other side of this wall."

"Mm hm." As Skylar drags a finger from Walt's pit to his nipple, Walt's skin pebbles. His nipple hardens as Skylar draws slow circles around it, blushing dark rose to go with the red flush spreading across Walt's chest. "How thick are the walls?"

"Not thick." Walt puts a hand on Skylar's wrist but doesn't put much effort into removing his hand. Skylar pinches his nipple and Walt's eyes flutter shut as he lets out a gust of air. "Fuck, Sky…."

With a grin, Skylar puts his fingers in his mouth to slick them up, then plays with Walt's nipple again, tugging and rolling it, pinching then stroking to soothe it when Walt gasps. Closing the distance between them, Skylar puts his mouth close to Walt's ear and murmurs, "We can do whatever we want if you don't make any noise."

Walt puts one of his big hands around the back of Skylar's head, fingers sinking into Skylar's hair and massaging his scalp, and Skylar shifts closer until they're chest to chest and hip to hip. The hard ridge of Walt's erection through his boxer briefs presses against Skylar's groin; he wiggles so it's pressed against his own hard dick, which is straining against his briefs. "Sky," he says again, and Skylar feels like he's being offered a prayer. Maybe a benediction.

Skylar tongues Walt's earlobe, behind his jaw, the bristle of hair under it, and Walt wraps his other arm around Skylar's back as he rocks his hips. At the press and friction between their cocks, he lets out a low grunt, and that—Well, even if Skylar was inclined to stop doing what he's doing, which he wasn't, that noise flicks his libido into overdrive.

"Can you be quiet for me, baby?" Skylar's voice feels like it's coming straight from his balls.

"Yeah," Walt breathes, pushing his hand inside Skylar's underwear. His hot palm grabs Skylar's ass, squeezing and kneading, as he tilts Skylar's head to bring their mouths together.

It's ridiculously hot how Walt comes apart for Skylar—this big, brawny man is Skylar's to do what he wants with. Making Walt stay quiet? Feeling how he stifles his moans, the thrum in his throat and jaw as he suppresses them down to sub-vocal levels, is even hotter.

He works his hand between them, rubbing Walt's coarse chest hair, tweaking his nipples, and loving each shudder and choked-back sound he draws out. His hips ache, though, and his cock is throbbing and stupid hard, so he moves lower, pushing his briefs down so he can take his dick out.

He gives it a couple pulls and almost breaks his no noise rule. Being pressed up against Walt like this, sweat starting to slick their skin and the close air smelling like pre-cum, is the kind of situation that's hard to stay quiet in. Especially with the way Walt's touching him, thick, blunt fingers stroking over his crack, exploring a little deeper with each pass.

If Walt fingers Skylar, there's no way he's staying quiet. Just the thought of those fingers stretching him makes him whimper softly. He'll never be able to look Walt's brother in the eye again, probably, which wouldn't be ideal.

He lets go of his cock and gets his hand on Walt's, taking him out through the fly on his boxer briefs. It's hot and steel-hard in his palm. So damn sexy. Skylar swipes his thumb over the head and it comes away slick with pre-cum, which he paints down Walt's length before going back for more, massaging into Walt's slit as Walt writhes.

Fuck, Walt's leaking so much. Skylar presses the heads of their cocks together. They slide against each other, both drooling. Skylar bites Walt's lip and tugs to stop himself from groaning from the sheer fucking filth of coating both of them in their mingled pre-cum. There's so much, Skylar bets he could jack them without any other lube.

But Skylar's not going to complain about wetter sex, so he lets go of them long enough to spit in his hand. When he closes it around both of their cocks again and strokes, it makes a thick, wet, squelching sound. "Fuuuuuck," Walt moans, his entire body tightening.

"Are you gonna come for me?" Skylar asks, pressing his nose into the side of Walt's face and kissing, kind of. It's more like his lips and his tongue on Walt's skin, the tang of sweat in his mouth as Walt fucks up into Skylar's hand and against his cock.

"Fuck yes." Walt's voice cracks.

Skylar pumps them faster. "Are you gonna come all over your briefs? Gonna make a mess of yourself?"

"Oh—*fuck* yeah, fuck yeah—" Walt throws his hand back and grabs the back of Skylar's neck, hips thrusting wildly as his cock pulses in Skylar's hand.

The hot splatter of thick, sticky cum across Skylar's hand and stomach, over his aching, throbbing cock, sends him over the edge too, and he's kissing Walt without even realizing he moved. It's not enough; it's not *close* enough; he wants to devour Walt. To be inside him, so this blazing supernova of sensation can be shared between the two of them. It's so much that it needs two bodies.

Their kissing slows and Skylar's blood cools. Walt's fingers stroke through Skylar's hair. Everything is warm and soft and perfect, and when their lips drift apart, Skylar mumbles, "Best end to a good day."

Every day with Walt is good, but today was even better because Walt brought him to his hometown. Walt wanted Skylar to meet Tad and Lewis, and it feels like Walt's inviting Skylar into his family. And Mario—Walt came out to Mario so he could introduce Skylar to him honestly. No pretense.

It was brave. It was romantic, too, because Walt sort of came out for Skylar, but also because Walt embracing his whole self makes him even more gorgeous.

He snuggles close to Walt and thinks, *I love you.*

Something keeps the words behind his teeth. Exhaustion, energy he can't muster to open his mouth and make the words come out. A dim sense that it's too early to be in love with Walt, but that last one doesn't seem so important anymore.

The admission floats on the tip of his tongue, though. "Walt," he says, his voice thick with sleep and sexual satiety.

Walt grunts and wraps his arms tight around Skylar, and Skylar breathes him in. He'll tell Walt in a second.

Chapter Twenty-Three

AN INCESSANT itching on his stomach drags Skylar awake, and once he's conscious, the light beyond his eyelids won't let him drift off again. He scratches his stomach and dried cum flakes under his fingernails. On the way back down, the back of his hand grazes warm, naked skin, so he turns onto his side and opens his eyes.

Walt is sitting up in bed next to him, phone in his hand, smiling down at Skylar so affectionately that Skylar wishes he could curl up in it. "Morning," Walt says.

"How long have you been awake?" Skylar asks, his voice hoarse with sleep.

"Not that long." Walt rubs his foot along Skylar's calf. "I never get to watch you sleep. You get up so early usually." He pauses. "That sounded really serial killer-y. I didn't mean it in a serial killer-y way."

Skylar laughs and wiggles closer, pressing his face into Walt's side. He smells like warmth and sex and Walt. "Maybe just in a stalker-y way?"

"Maybe. But just a mild stalker. Not a really creepy stalker." There's a clunk as Walt puts his phone down on the bedside table, before he slides under the sheets again to take Skylar in his arms. "Thank you for yesterday," he says and kisses Skylar slow and deep.

The kissing makes Skylar's morning wood more urgent, and when he reaches for Walt's cock, he finds it hard and ready. They jack each other lazily as they kiss, and Skylar's orgasm rolls through him like a breaker on a reef, frothy and slow.

They shower separately, which is disappointing, but Skylar guesses they have to leave something for later. The shower at home is an old clawfoot tub that two six-foot men won't fit in together, especially not when one of them is as bulky as Walt.

When they go downstairs, Skylar raids the refrigerator and cupboards to find ingredients to make breakfast. There are eggs that aren't past their expiration date, an open package of bacon, and half a carton of milk that still smells okay. With the dry ingredients he finds in the cupboards, he whips up pancakes and uses the rest of the eggs and milk to make scrambled eggs.

Tad and Lewis wander into the kitchen just as the first batch of pancakes come out of the pan. The bacon's in the microwave because Walt only has one frying pan, and that goes against everything Skylar stands for, but he's already scrambling eggs in a wok he dug out from the very back of the pots and pans cabinet, so he's being flexible.

"Can I ask a dumb question, Skylar?" Tad says once they're all squeezed around the table in the dining room and everyone's exclaimed over how fluffy and delicious the pancakes are, and how these are the best scrambled eggs they've ever eaten, and Skylar even managed to make microwave bacon good!

"It's probably not dumb, but sure." Skylar stuffs another wedge of pancake into his mouth, smothered in maple syrup. There was a bottle of the real stuff hiding in the back of the pantry.

Taking another piece of bacon, Tad asks, "What happens to all the farm stuff if you're not there? Does it just not get done for the morning? Is that okay?"

"He's worried about the animals," Walt supplies, shooting a teasing smile at Tad. Tad wrinkles his nose but doesn't deny it.

"Well, I don't really get to take vacations," Skylar says. He wonders if Walt realized that before now. "But going away overnight is fine. My friend Jett went over to check on the animals last night and this morning, so they have plenty of food and water."

"Jett mucks stalls?" Walt asks, shocked.

"Never let them hear you suggest that." Skylar laughs, though the answer is yes. Jett sent pictures of the animals from both their visits, so Skylar shows Tad and Lewis. Tad's enraptured and asks shyly if he can visit the baby goats once they're born, which Skylar agrees to right away, both because he likes Tad and because he wants Walt to *see* that he likes Tad.

Lewis looks adoringly at Tad and says, "We're going to end up with a baby goat in our apartment. I just have a feeling."

"Lewis, please," Tad says. "You can't keep a goat in a Manhattan apartment. We won't get one until we move out to the suburbs."

As they're cleaning up from breakfast, Walt's phone buzzes. His eyes light up when he checks it, and he types something before putting it away again.

Tad and Lewis get ready to go, and Skylar hears Walt say something about visiting their parents in a bracing tone. "You just have to let it roll off your back," Walt adds.

Tad shakes his head, hesitates, and hugs Walt. "You're the good son, not me."

Lewis, straightening up from tying his sick Pride Chucks, snorts and mutters, "Not so much anymore," with half a glance at Skylar.

And—oof. There's a lot lurking under those four words, like a shark's fin cutting the smooth ocean's surface. Though maybe that's not a good analogy, because sharks are mostly misunderstood. Sharks actually only kill five or six people a year on average. And here he is, illustrating exactly what the *Jaws* effect does!

Okay, so, what's a better analogy? Whatever, it's not important. There's clearly a whole realm of baggage around Walt's and Tad's relationship with their parents, and Skylar's going to find himself in the middle of it at some point.

At least they don't seem to be on social media. Or if they are, they don't follow Walt. They're not going to go scorched earth on the Blue Skies Farm Insta.

Once Tad and Lewis leave, Walt says, "I know we have to get back today, but how would you feel about going to a baby shower?"

Skylar blinks. "I... don't know?"

Walt laughs and rubs the back of his neck. "Yeah, maybe more information would help. Ally's having her baby shower today, and Mario was wondering if we want to come over and keep him company."

"Oh! Um." Wrong response. You can't even generously consider "oh" a response, and Walt's expression falters. "Wouldn't I be intruding? He barely knows me. And I don't know his wife at all."

Walt shakes his head. "He asked if we wanted to come over. You're not intruding."

Yeah but, Skylar wants to ask, *did he invite both of us, or did he invite you, and you're inferring that I'm welcome too?* No—Skylar shouldn't assume the worst just because he got an off vibe from Mario last night. "I should probably get a present."

"You don't have to."

"Walt, I'm not going to show up at a baby shower with no gift!" Skylar puts a hand over his heart in mock horror. "Can I do a Target gift card? Is that tacky? Wait, is there a Target around here, or is this a Walmart town?"

"Target?" Walt repeats in a confused voice. "What is this... Target... of which you speak?" When Skylar shakes his head, trying to look stern, Walt grins. "Baby, this is the county seat. We have Walmart *and* Target."

All Skylar can do is laugh, sling an arm around Walt's neck, and kiss him. "Okay, let's hit up this baby shower. After we stop at Target."

FIRST OF all, Skylar thinks gendered parties are odd. Baby showers in particular don't make sense to him. It's not like the mother is the only one having a baby. Unless that's the situation, but for all the times when it isn't. What about when it's two guys? What about people who don't fit in the gender binary? When two women have a baby together, which one gets to have the baby shower? Is it for both of them? Why is it a Woman Thing?

Second of all, somehow this baby shower manages to be more odd, because it's all women and small children, plus Mario. And now Walt and Skylar. There was this idea in Skylar's head that Mario was banished to the basement or something, but no—he's part of the shower. He has his piece of paper that's been handed around for the games they'll be playing.

Skylar wants to ask Mario why none of his friends are invited, but that seems like it's overstepping the boundaries of their almost nonexistent relationship.

Third of all, when they arrived, Mario introduced Walt as his "buddy from way back" and Skylar as Walt's "friend."

So. Yeah.

Ally is nice, though. She's very pregnant, seems overwhelmed by all the people in her house, but takes a moment between games to introduce herself to Skylar.

"You're the person who pulled Walt out of a snowbank during the blizzard, right?" she says with an amused twinkle in her brown eyes. She has to crane her neck to look up at him; she can't be more than five two.

With a friendly laugh, Skylar says, "He got himself out of the snowbank, but I helped him dig his truck out."

She glances at Walt, who's piling a plate with finger food. "It's cool you're friends now."

"Oh, well—" Skylar doesn't want to make waves, but he also doesn't want to hide who he is. But also, he doesn't know if Walt wants to come out to Ally and all these people, and it's not his place to make that decision. They should have talked about it before they came in. He wishes Walt would have brought it up, but Skylar also didn't ask. He's not used to dating someone who's not fully out, and Walt isn't used to dating a man.

Ally's looking at him, waiting for him to complete that thought. He clears his throat and says, "Yeah, it is." He looks at Walt, hoping Walt will meet his eyes and they can telepathically communicate the right play here.

"Or maybe I should say"—she does air quotes—"'friends.'"

Thank god, Walt comes over at that moment. "Hey Ally, thanks for letting us crash the party."

"I'm glad you could come! Mario's been moping about being the only guy here and having to do 'girly stuff.'" She makes a face, though clearly she's amused instead of exasperated.

"Bro code," Walt says with an admirable level of confidence for a phrase that contains the word "bro." Gesturing between Ally and Skylar, he adds, "I'm glad you guys got a chance to talk."

Ally rests a hand on her belly. "I had to talk to the person that got Walt Pierce to leave Watertown."

A flush appears on Walt's cheeks. "I haven't *left*. I'm just staying in Windham for a few weeks."

It would be super helpful if Skylar knew what Ally knows vis-à-vis Walt's closet status. Was she just guessing before? Has she suspected Walt isn't straight when apparently no one else did? Or did Mario tell her, which wouldn't be surprising, but would still be kind of shitty?

He looks at Walt, hoping he's conveying his question without looking like a boyfriend looking to his boyfriend for direction on how to act around his friends. It's possible he just looks panicked, because Walt's eyebrows draw together.

Laughing, Ally says, "I don't think you've left this town for more than a week! Suddenly you're 'staying with a friend' in the Catskills. I had to meet them."

The calculation in Walt's eyes is visible. He's embodying the confused Math Lady meme, his gaze flicking between Skylar and Ally, and once over his shoulder at the rest of the women in the room.

His arm slips around Skylar's waist, his hand coming to rest chastely on Skylar's hip. It feels like they're undressing in front of all these people. They may be strangers to Skylar, but Walt probably knows all of them.

"Not just a friend," Walt says. There's the tiniest quaver to his voice, but his hand on Skylar's hip is steady.

Ally looks thrilled. "I knew it!" she says in a voice that's quiet but triumphant. "Mario said I had pregnancy brain but I *knew* there was something going on. Especially since you broke up with Lia."

"That was unrelated." Walt's fingers dig into Skylar's hip and Skylar realizes he can't just stand here like he's a prop on the Walt Show. Despite the laidback way he's playing this off, this has to be scary for Walt. It's going to be scary every time he has to come out to the people he's known for his whole life in the town he's never left.

Until Skylar. The guy who made him finally admit he's not straight. It probably made it easier that it wasn't in Watertown. It gave him the freedom to experiment. That's not all he is, right?

That's a crawly, icky thought. And it's unfair too. Walt's come out to his best friend and his best friend's wife in the space of twelve hours. Anyone who looks over here and sees Walt's arm around Skylar is part of the tally too. Straight men don't put their arms around each other the way Walt has his arm around Skylar.

It's unfair, maybe, but now it's in Skylar's head, and—what if this is like Cody, who wanted to be married, wanted to run a farm, until he found out what being married and running a farm was actually like?

Skylar covers Walt's hand with his, partly to steady Walt and partly to ground himself. There's no evidence that Walt's thinking, or even unconsciously motivated, by those thoughts. Not once has Skylar thought Walt was like Cody. Cody was a kid who thought he was smarter and more grown-up than he was, just like Skylar. That's not Walt.

Skylar takes a breath and smiles. "He might be staying with me in Windham because of the goats. They're pretty cute."

For good measure, he squeezes Walt's hand, and it's clearly the right thing to do, because Walt gives him a small, grateful smile. "You promised baby goats. You don't think I'm going to miss that, do you?"

"What I just heard is you're offering to help when the goats kid." Skylar pokes Walt in the chest, which has the added benefit of letting him squish a finger into one of Walt's thick pecs. "No take backs."

The small smile on Walt's face broadens into a grin. "Hell no, I don't want to take it back. Can I seriously help?"

When the first kidding season rolled around for Blue Skies Farm, Skylar had to beg and plead with Cody to help him. Why would Skylar think even for a second that Walt had anything in common with his ex-husband?

"Of course," Skylar says. "I'd love you being there to help."

He's saying *I'd love that*, but it suddenly occurs to Skylar that he might as well be saying *I love you*. Because he does. Oh god, he's in love with Walt. How can he realize that he's in love with Walt two seconds after getting worried that he's just an experiment?

"Walt, you're actually glowing." Ally's voice yanks Skylar back to the real world. There's a big smile on her face as she looks between them.

"I am not." Walt blushes. "We're taking up too much of your time. You should get back to your party. Brittany's holding a bunch of pens and paper and looking over here."

"Oh, games! You guys have to play!" Before either Walt or Skylar can say anything, Mario saunters up to Ally's side, where he squeezes her butt before putting an arm around her. "C'mon, Mario. You three will play a couple of the games, right?"

Mario's eyes linger on Skylar's waist. He's looking at Walt's arm nestled there and his hand still gripped firmly on Skylar's hip. "They didn't come over to play baby shower games, Al."

"Sure we did," Walt says, bumping his shoulder against Skylar's. "If Sky's up for it."

Has Skylar told Walt how his insides melt every time Walt calls him Sky? "Yeah, I'm up for it! Sounds fun."

Once they get into the swing of the games, he has regrets. The first one's okay—they have to match the fictional mother (it's always mothers) to the fictional child. Walt's horrible at it, and Skylar's only marginally better. Game two, though, is where it gets rough. They have to bob for pacifiers. Their hands get tied behind their back as they stand in front of bowls full of pacifiers, and Skylar can't get over the fact that it looks like they're all bobbing up and down while giving head.

Game three is changing a diaper on a watermelon blindfolded, which the women with kids are good at. Everyone else sucks. There's a lot of cackling at the way Mario's diaper looks—which is indisputably bad—and jokes about men not being able to do basic childcare. Which is…. Okay, well, Skylar doesn't have kids and didn't have younger siblings or cousins, so he doesn't know how to take care of kids. But he could learn. He *will* learn, when he has kids. If he has kids. Whatever. Kids of the human variety, not goat kids, which he's very good at taking care of.

It's just, why are these women giving their husbands a pass on taking care of the children that they both produced? Why is it funny that Mario can't change a diaper blindfolded, but not funny that Ally can't (hers is worse than his, and it took her longer).

"We're bad at this," Walt observes, looking between his misshapen diaper and Skylar's. He laughs, though he doesn't sound very amused. "More proof of how terrible I am at taking care of anything."

Walt's diapered watermelon isn't the worst in the room. "Luckily, watermelons don't usually need to wear diapers. Anyway, what about your spider plant?" Skylar asks. "You saved it from freezing and you've been taking good care of it since then. It's way bigger now than it was when we met."

Walt looks at him like Skylar's speaking a different language. When Skylar waits, the expression on Walt's face transforms from resignation—good-natured resignation, but still—to realization. At least Skylar hopes it's realization, because Walt's said more than once that he doesn't know how to take care of anything, whether it's children, animals, or plants, and Skylar doesn't think that's true. Didn't Walt volunteer to help with kidding? And isn't he out in the barn doing chores every day?

"Tad says they're for beginners," Walt says, almost shyly.

"So what? You're still taking care of it."

It makes Skylar sad that Walt thinks he's not a caregiver when he so clearly has the capacity to be one. No, it doesn't make him sad. It makes him angry. It pisses him off that men are told they can't be caregivers and that women are forced into the role.

Maybe that's why it's rubbing him the wrong way how all the women at this baby shower are acting. Like it's funny instead of deeply toxic. Like it's fine for Mario to never know how to change his kid's diaper. Skylar likes Ally, and it pisses him off to think about her shouldering the bulk of the childrearing. It's not fair to a single one of them—not Ally, not Mario, and not their child, who's going to lose out on the love and nurturing of one entire parent because of stupid gender roles.

It's fucking dumb. Skylar lost out on one parent's love because his mom died. These people are just cutting it out of their kids' lives voluntarily, because it's not manly to take care of people.

No wonder Walt was afraid to be queer. Skylar and his dad don't see eye to eye about a lot of things, but his father raised him after his mom died. Skylar's a better man for seeing that a man can be the primary nurturer of his child.

Walt leans into Skylar, their shoulders pressing together with a little starburst of warmth. "Are you okay? Your blind diaper changing isn't the worst thing ever. Ally's is way worse."

Skylar wants to lean harder against Walt. He wants, fiercely, to kiss him, just for the hell of it. Just a quick kiss to reassure Walt that everything's fine, and to reassure Skylar that... what? He doesn't really know, but his emotions feel spidery, and he wants the grounding solidity of Walt's mouth against his.

He doesn't know if it's okay here, though. "Good thing most people don't put on blindfolds before they change their baby's diaper."

"That's why they had to stop using safety pins for diapers," Walt says seriously. "Sticky diaper closures were invented because people kept jabbing their babies with the safety pins when they were doing blindfolded diaper changing."

Skylar bites back a laugh—unsuccessfully—and tries to answer in as grave a tone. "When did they figure out they could just take off the blindfolds?"

"Someone was trying to invent a helmet for space travel and discovered non-blindfolded diaper changing instead."

Walt's eyes are sparkling and he's obviously trying not to smile, but he's not succeeding. There might not be anything in this world cuter than Walt's smile breaking through his attempt to cover it up. This isn't helping Skylar's desire to kiss him.

The smile breaks through and Skylar doesn't have to stop himself from kissing Walt, because Walt puts a hand on Skylar's chin to hold him in place, then leans in and kisses him. It's just a second, soft lips pressing gently against Skylar's, before he pulls away and looks at Skylar like he doesn't ever want to look anywhere else. Skylar's stomach crests the top of a rollercoaster and swoops.

A harsh scoff of displeasure fractures the moment. At the other end of the folding table where the two of them and Mario have been participating in the games, Mario is glaring.

Walt turns his gaze to Mario, a smile still on his face. It takes him a second to process the way Mario's looking at them. His smile falters, sticking but turning confused, then fades. It breaks Skylar's heart, and he *still* feels like he can't say anything, because this is Walt's town, Walt's friend. The little kids running around screaming are the children of people he went to school with. Walt has a million big and small connections here to navigate.

It's not a surprise when Walt removes his arm from Skylar's waist. Skylar wishes it was, but come on. It's way easier to slip back into the closet than it is to stand up to your best friend glaring at you.

But then Walt *does* surprise him. He puts his arm back around Skylar. "What?" Walt asks Mario.

Mario shakes his head. His jaw looks clenched hard enough to crack his teeth. "Nothing," he grits out.

Walt stares at him. Skylar can feel his breath coming faster. "Okay," Walt says eventually.

A toddler runs by laughing, naked except for a diaper on their head, followed by an older kid, also wearing a diaper on their head and holding a purse. A harried-looking woman who must be their mother rounds out the parade, chasing them with a wineglass in her hand. Skylar wonders if she forgot she was holding it. "Noah, Sophia, get back here!" she commands to absolutely no avail. "Nicole said you could *look* at her purse, Sophia, not take it!"

It brings a smile back to Walt's face, and oh no. Walt and kids. Walt would be a great dad, wouldn't he? It doesn't take any effort to imagine it. Somehow it takes less than no effort for Skylar to imagine himself there too. Walt and him and a couple kids, who they could trust Squirrel with because he's the gentlest guard llama in the world. Maybe a dog or a cat so the kids could have a pet whose only job was to be a pet.

"Jesus Christ, there are kids here," Mario says sharply. "Stop groping each other."

Walt's mouth falls open. Instinctively, Skylar pulls away. Walt's arm tightens around him, not with enough force to keep Skylar there if he really wants to move, but firmly enough to make it clear that he wants Skylar to stay. "We're not groping each other," Walt says.

There's a hint of shakiness to his voice. If Skylar can hear it, then Mario, who's known Walt for decades, can hear it too. Mario's expression hardens. "I wouldn't have invited you if I knew you were going to be all over your—whatever. You know I have a hard line against that kind of stuff in my house, especially when there are kids around. You were there when I kicked Chris out."

"Are you seriously comparing me to Chris and his random Tinder hookup that he brought over?" Walt asks. "Really?"

Glaring, Mario snaps, "Your hand is way too fucking low. It's inappropriate."

Walt's hand hasn't even gotten to first base. It's been above the waistband of Skylar's pants this entire time. Accusing Walt and Skylar of groping would take a specific type of person, and Skylar's clamped-shut lips can't quite stand up to the blaze of anger that burns through him.

"You literally touched Ally's butt!" he bursts out, because he's an idiot who's decided to make a bad situation even worse.

Until now, Mario has mostly ignored him, like he's an accessory. Like Walt's just trying him on or something, and Mario doesn't have to treat him like a full person. "What did you just say?" he asks, a dangerous glitter in his eyes. "Don't you dare mention my wife's fucking butt."

Another toddler wanders over, staring up at Mario in that unblinking, mesmerized way kids do. Skylar takes a deep breath and moves to head the kid off, maybe herd them back to the women around Ally.

Before he gets there, the kid announces, "Fucking butt!"

Skylar isn't built to hear that and not lose it—especially not when his emotions are already stretched tighter than a guitar string. He lets out a loud laugh before clapping a hand over his mouth. Too late. The kid understands that saying *fucking butt* at volume gets attention, so they say it again even louder, then once more.

They run back to their mom, chanting, "Fucking butt fucking butt fucking butt!" Skylar has tears in his eyes from trying to stifle his laughter, his hand jammed so hard against his teeth that he wouldn't blame Mario for calling him out for fisting his own mouth.

He has just enough time to catalogue the varied reactions from the women—horror from some, embarrassment from others, and laughter from a few, who are definitely the cool ones in the room. The other kids who are old enough to talk have taken up the call, spurred on by attempts to get them to stop. Then a hand closes firmly around his arm and pulls him toward the door.

"We should go," Walt says tersely, his fingers gripping tighter with each kid that joins in the chorus.

"That seems like a good idea," Skylar agrees, tears of laughter still in his eyes. He catches sight of Walt's face as they hurry out the door, though, and his amusement dies sharply and suddenly, the tightened guitar string of his emotions snapping with a discordant twang.

Chapter Twenty-Four

ON THE drive back to Windham, Skylar seems to understand how much Walt doesn't want to talk. Walt doesn't know how to process what happened with Mario. His best friend came at him for something so stupid that part of Walt wants to laugh, while the other part wants to cry. He doesn't understand. He feels like he just got roundhouse kicked in the chest and never saw who did it.

They get off I-90 at Canajoharie, which Walt loves to say when he's in a better mood. Now he just thinks about what a dump the town looks like from the interstate, and how annoying the exit is. Going this way is nice, though. The small highways are a slower drive, but a more beautiful one, too.

Something in Walt's chest eases when they cross I-88 and the land rises into the Catskills, like he's coming home. Maybe he is. He glances at Skylar, whose fingers are linked together in his lap as he watches the scenery pass. The feeling Walt gets with Skylar… that feels like home too. Skylar glances at him and smiles tentatively. "Want me to drive?"

"Nah, I got it."

Skylar nods. Another mile spins by beneath the tires. "Want to… talk about it?"

If Walt could, he'd cover his eyes with both hands and live in the warm darkness. But he's driving, so he can't. "Not really," he says, staring fixedly at the road ahead so he doesn't have to see Skylar look disappointed. He's not stonewalling or trying to be macho. He just… hurts. How do you talk about that? That's what crying's for, but he's driving, so he can't give into the urge to cry, either.

Maybe there's a little avoidance going on, after all.

"When Mario said that thing about having a hard line against that stuff in his house." Walt tightens his grip on the steering wheel and doesn't realize how hard he's clutching it until his fingers start falling asleep. "That was really shitty."

"Am I allowed to ask who Chris is?"

It takes Walt a second to rewind the conversation with Mario to remember why Chris came up. "He's an old high school friend. He cheated on his wife and dumped her for the lady he was cheating with—she was married too—and then ended up dumping her." Walt rolls his eyes. Calling Chris an old high school friend is generous. It's one of those friendships he's been holding on to more out of habit than affection. "Anyway, he brought a Tinder hookup to Mario's one night, and they had sex in the kitchen while the rest of us were watching the Bills game downstairs."

Skylar guffaws, which, fair enough; it's ridiculous. "Someone must not have been downstairs, since you know it happened."

"Yeah, Ally's nephew walked in on them. He was nine, I think." Glancing over at Skylar again, Walt adds, "Mario comparing us to that was really... really not cool. We weren't being gross. And Mario *did* touch Ally's butt right in front of us. He does that all the time."

"We weren't being gross," Skylar agrees.

"I mean, unless...." Walt feels sick, and then something hard lodges in his throat. He clears it a few times. "Unless he just thinks anyone who isn't straight is gross."

"I don't want to talk shit about your friend," Skylar says in a way that makes it very clear that he'd have plenty of shit to talk if he let himself.

That's fair too, though—both the not wanting to talk shit and the wealth of shit available to talk about. Walt doesn't want to talk shit about Mario, either. He's starting to worry that he *did* do something wrong. Like maybe he said something that Mario took the wrong way. Or like putting his arm around his boyfriend was offensive and icky.

The swirl of thoughts accompanies him all through the rest of the drive. The fear that he was wrong, that he didn't do the right thing, that something was expected of him and he failed at it, gets bigger and bigger until it's all Walt can feel or see.

When he turns into Blue Skies Farm and parks next to Skylar's truck, the giant, stormy collection of fear and gnawing anxiety and sludgy misery slaps right up against the reality of Walt's life for the past month and a half. If he failed at something, maybe it wasn't worth doing right, because he can hear Skylar breathing steadily next to him when he turns the car off, and he can smell Skylar's deodorant.

Being with Skylar isn't wrong. His pride in being with someone as wonderful as Skylar, wanting everyone to know that this amazing guy wants to be with *him*, Walt Pierce, who never had much to be proud of before—that's not wrong. Wanting Walt to hide it is wrong, though. Walt knows in his heart that if he'd been at the baby shower with Lia, Mario wouldn't have had a single problem with them showing affection.

He grabs Skylar's hand. Words crowd his mouth, drawing lines on the backs of his teeth because the gaps aren't enough for them to slip through. He can't tell Sky that he loves him right now. The words want out so badly, though.

He squeezes Skylar's hand. "I can do all the chores."

"You don't have to."

"I kind of need the distraction."

Skylar opens his mouth, but he shuts it without saying anything and nods. "I'll find something for dinner."

The goats bleat happily when Walt opens the barn. Their uncomplicated, enthusiastic greetings can't help but bring a smile to his face. They run to him, butting their heads against his legs. He doesn't have enough hands or pets to go around, but he does his best, laughing when Shuri rears onto her hind feet to shove her nose against his hand.

He checks on Jane and Darcy first, who are both heavily pregnant and expected to kid in the coming weeks. They're content, though Jane seems restless. He'll mention that to Skylar. Both goats eat pellet feed out of his hand, their soft lips and whiskers tickling his palm, so hopefully Jane's okay. He gives them head scratches before moving on to Natasha and Peggy. Neither are showing their new pregnancies yet, but he gives them some pellets too, because they deserve an extra treat for assembling more goats in their bodies.

Squirrel comes to look things over while Walt takes care of the goat chores and also supervises while he puts out feed for the peacocks. When Walt gives his fluffy neck an affectionate pat, Squirrel hums. That's one of Walt's favorite things that he's learned since meeting Skylar—llamas hum to show all kinds of emotions. Judging by Squirrel's calmness right now, this is a happy hum.

By the time Walt cleans Squirrel's stall and feeds him, the light outside has gone from bright to golden to purply twilight. He looks over the animals one more time, but they're all happily eating or bedding down for the night, so he steps out of the barn and locks up behind himself.

The sky is a work of art tonight; delicate pink clouds suspended against a violet sky and the first few stars quietly shining. Walt looks for Venus, which is one of the only stargazing lessons he remembers from camping trips with his father and Tad. It's there, a bright, steady pinprick of light above the tree line.

A shadow shutters across the lit kitchen window. Skylar is standing there, his profile picked out and sharp against the warm illumination. He looks outlined in light as he works at something—maybe cutting bread, with the way his shoulders and arms are moving.

He's changed out of what he was wearing earlier and is in a basic white tee now, tight across his biceps and showing every flex and roll of the muscles in his shoulders. A bolt of desire burns through Walt. It's followed by a painful clench in his stomach that he can't identify for a second.

Then he does. It's shame, fucking *shame*, and guilt mixed in. He was supposed to be over this, but Mario brought it all back. Don't look at a guy as an object of desire, because your best friend might disapprove. He might see you showing a tiny amount of normal physical affection and get uncomfortable.

Well, fuck that. Walt's done holding back on everything he wants because the people he wants to love him might not approve. The shame and guilt melt away. Both will probably return. He's thirty-three years old and has spent twenty years denying and making excuses for his bisexuality. A month and a half, no matter how good it is, isn't going to fix that. It's going to take time and confronting each one of his stupid, tangled knots of self-loathing.

Watching Skylar move, Walt knows which one he wants to untangle tonight.

The smell of pie crust and fresh-baked bread hits him when he steps inside, but better than that is how Skylar's face lights up. After the way Walt was in the car, the happiness on Skylar's face is already a surprise; Skylar wrapping his arms around Walt's neck is even more unexpected.

But god, Walt's grateful. He pulls Skylar close, burying his face in the side of his head. Silky hair tickles his nose and lips as he breathes, sinking into Skylar's scent. Even though he used the stuff in Walt's shower this morning, he still smells like himself.

Aaaand Walt probably smells like animals, straw, and sweat. "Sorry, I should have gone straight upstairs to shower. How long do I have before dinner's done?"

Before he can take more than a step backward, Skylar grabs his arm. "It'll be done in a couple minutes, and you don't smell. Sit down. Do you want a drink? I could use one, personally. How are the goats?"

A drink sounds so good. "Whatever you're having. And the goats are fine. Jane seems a little restless, maybe."

Skylar pauses before he gets a bottle of whiskey and a couple tumblers from the cupboard. "How restless?"

"Not much. She ate from my hand." He scratches his chest. "I guess I'll shower after dinner."

"If you insist."

Walt gives his armpit a conspicuous sniff and waves a hand in front of his face. "I smell like I've been putting up a fence all afternoon."

Skylar thunks the glasses down on the table and meets Walt's eyes. "Maybe I like when you get all sweaty and I can smell it on you."

Heat throbs in Walt's gut, sliding and spreading until his balls get heavier and his cock starts hardening. "Good to know," he says, not making any effort to keep his voice from going lower and more suggestive.

Skylar pours healthy doubles of Jack Daniels and hands one to Walt before raising his own. "Here's to getting through days like today."

"I'll drink to that," Walt replies, clinking his glass against Skylar's. Walt's more of a Jameson guy, but you can't go wrong with Jack when you just need the burn of oak and rye sliding down your throat. He swallows the whole glass in one gulp, puts it down with a heavy clunk, and rubs a hand over his face. "Did you ever have to deal with stuff like this?" he asks.

"Not like this, exactly." Skylar finishes his whiskey more slowly. When his glass is empty, he sets it next to Walt's. "I came out in high school, so it was… I don't know. Different shit, I guess. My friend group was fine. No major betrayals. I kind of fought over this one dumb boy with one of my friends, but she wasn't that serious about it."

"You never talk about friends from high school."

With a shrug, Skylar says, "None of them were close friends. I was kind of a weirdo. I mean, I dropped out of college to start a goat farm. And I was never into social media the way everyone else was." The oven timer buzzes and as Skylar pulls out dinner, he adds, "A couple of my old high school friends have DMed me on Instagram since we blew up. One's in Seattle and wants to know if I ship that far."

"That's the next thing to figure out, I guess," Walt says. Dinner is a pot pie, probably one that Skylar made ahead and froze for exactly this kind of night.

"People keep asking me if they can visit, too." Skylar puts the pot pie down on the table and laughs. "It's crazy that this all started with a picture of us that people mistook for a couples photo."

"They saw the obvious." Walt waggles his eyebrows, and when Skylar lets out another huff of laughter, Walt rubs his foot against Skylar's.

When they finish eating, Walt pushes his chair back to go upstairs and shower. Even if Sky thinks sweaty is sexy, there's… other stuff Walt needs to take care of.

Before he gets to the stairs, though, Skylar catches up to him with a hand on his shoulder and a, "Hey, Walt." When Walt turns to face him, Skylar surprises him with a kiss. "Really, if you want to talk about what happened today…."

Walt takes one of Skylar's hands and traces the complicated pattern of spirals, waves, and lotuses up the inside of his arm. "Not now. Sometime, though. Maybe." Worry flashes over Skylar's face, like he thinks he's failing Walt or something, so Walt moves his hand farther up Skylar's arm to the inside of his bicep, where he rubs slow circles. "I'm gonna take a shower, and then you should come upstairs."

There's nothing subtle about the tenor of his voice, and he sees the moment Skylar's brain and dick connect. Granted, that's not subtle either. Skylar bites his lip before licking it and giving Walt a slow up and down look.

Everything south of Walt's waist tingles, including his virgin ass. He squeezes Skylar's bicep before turning for the stairs and what he plans on being the fastest shower he's ever taken.

Chapter Twenty-Five

IT'S NOT the fastest shower he's ever taken, because he needs to make sure he's clean. And making sure he's clean... well, *down there* isn't something he's ever bothered with.

The cleaning doesn't feel great. Hopefully it will feel better when it's Skylar's finger. Finger*s*. And cock. Because fuck every single bit of internalized homophobia Walt's been dragging around behind him for decades.

When he leaves the bathroom in a cloud of steam, towel wrapped around his waist, he pads down the hall to find Skylar sprawled on their bed, scrolling on his phone. Skylar sucks in a breath and gives Walt that appreciative once-over again. "How are you so hot?" he groans, dropping his phone.

Walt takes it and puts it facedown on the bedside table before he sits on the bed. Skylar slides a hand along the top of the towel, brushing his fingers along Walt's stomach, taking a moment to linger where the hair is thickest in the middle. "Manual labor," Walt says, earning him a light smack against his hip.

He sprawls next to Skylar and slips his hands under Skylar's shirt, running them over all that soft, warm skin stretched over lean muscle. Skylar smiles and loosens the towel around Walt's waist, but not all the way. It's just enough to make Walt ache for it to be gone, so he can feel the friction of Skylar's clothes and skin instead of the towel.

The light trailing of Skylar's fingers along his body makes him chase the friction of the towel anyway. Skylar lets out a low chuckle and leans in to mouth kisses along Walt's jaw. "Love your beard," he mumbles.

"I'll keep it." He pulls Skylar's shirt off and flicks his nipples, which makes Skylar swear. Wanting more of that, Walt takes one of Skylar's nipples in his mouth, teasing and biting it to hardness before working the other one into the same state. As he licks and sucks, he unbuttons Skylar's pants and pushes them down, moaning when he grabs Skylar's cock through his boxer briefs.

He licks a fat stripe up Skylar's chest and neck, right to his mouth, and then they're kissing hard and openmouthed. The hard press of Skylar's body makes Walt arch closer, closer, but not close enough.

Skylar shoves Walt onto his back and yanks the towel open. His hand closes around Walt's dick and he strokes, the pressure and the friction driving Walt out of his mind. He lets out a loud, fractured moan and breaks their kiss, only to lose it even more when Skylar pushes his face into his armpit.

Hot breath and a hotter tongue move against the hair and skin of Walt's pit. He lifts an arm to give Skylar better access, head spinning. "Still smell you," Skylar growls. "Soap and Walt. Yum."

"Jesus fuck," Walt gasps, thrusting into Skylar's hand while he grabs at Skylar's head, his shoulders, the flexing muscles on his back. "Sky—Sky, I want you to fuck me."

Skylar's head shoots up, his chin slick with saliva and his eyes round and black. "You want me to…. Are you sure? Like, *fuck* fuck you?"

Even though his hand on Walt's cock has slowed, it hasn't stopped, and he rubs his thumb across the head, into the slit. The wet slide is so hot and so good. "Yeah, like fuck fuck me." He wraps his legs around Skylar's back and arches his hips up until Skylar's cock rubs against his balls. A little more, and it's rubbing against the crease of his ass.

With a shudder, Skylar reaches up to twist his fingers in Walt's hair. "I'll get the condoms and lube," he says, his voice rough.

The space and emptiness he leaves when he peels his body off Walt's is physically painful, like somehow that emptiness got inside Walt. Pretty soon Skylar's going to be literally inside him. Walt whimpers at the thought and gives himself a slow stroke. He's rock hard. Has he ever been this hard? Is this the hardest it's possible to get?

The lube and a box of condoms lands on the bed next to Walt right before Skylar flings himself down. "I haven't been with anyone since Cody, and we were both monogamous," Skylar says. "But I'll suit up if you want me to."

All Walt can do is shake his head, because now that the idea of barebacking is in his head, he can't accept anything else. "I don't," he says when he realizes the head shaking has gone on too long. "No condom. Please. I mean, unless you're worried about me. But I'm good. I mean, nothing funky going on with my junk."

Well, if he could go back in time and not say that last sentence, he would. By some miracle, Skylar grins before swooping down to kiss Walt, slow and sultry at first, building to heavy and gasping, their bodies moving against each other's.

"Let's get you ready, baby," Skylar finally breathes. "Goddamn, I've been fantasizing about this."

The possibility hadn't even occurred to Walt, despite his own mind vault of Skylar fantasies. Hearing Skylar say out loud that he wants this, *has* wanted it, as much as Walt, accomplishes what Walt thought was impossible and makes him harder. Which, god, if he can get harder just from that, maybe the sky's the limit. Maybe his cock will be hard enough to hammer nails.

Skylar kisses down Walt's body, licking both nipples, rubbing his face in Walt's chest and stomach hair, licking a path along the groove of his leg. His cock goes untouched.

While Skylar moves lower, Walt whines at the lack of attention being paid to his cock, lifting his hips off the bed. Firmly, Skylar pushes him back. "Down, baby. Let me take care of you."

"You're gonna kill me," Walt groans.

Warm breath puffs against his balls as Skylar laughs. "That's not until you're bouncing on my dick."

"Not helpful." Walt clenches his abs to make sure he doesn't blow his load just from listening to Skylar's dirty purr.

It's a good thing he has them clenched, because Skylar touches his tongue to Walt's hole, and Walt's entire body jerks. "Holy *fuck*," he gasps, straining toward Skylar to get more of that sensation, unfamiliar and amazing.

But Skylar moves away, swiping his tongue across Walt's asscheeks and into the crease, moving away from where Walt needs to feel him again. It's embarrassing how fast he's been reduced to a whiny wreck.

No, it's not, actually. It's not embarrassing. He feels good. *This* feels good.

The wet muscle of Skylar's tongue reaches Walt's hole again, and oh. Oh, fuck. He circles slowly, doing—doing something. Flicking, or licking, or—or oh god, that's kissing, he's definitely kissing. A man is kissing Walt's asshole and it feels incredible and he wants more; he wants everything.

"Sky," he moans.

"Getting there," Skylar says, his voice muffled. Muffled from the fact that he has his lips pressed into Walt's ass. "You taste so good. I want more. You okay with me tasting more?"

"Unnnh," Walt grunts, a guttural, animal noise that he didn't know he could make.

Hands push his thighs wider. Walt's never felt so vulnerable and exposed. That feels good too, though. Didn't Skylar say he'd take care of Walt? All Walt needs to do is lie back and take it.

Skylar tongues Walt more firmly, and the moment it slips inside Walt is like embers bursting back into flame. The noise he makes is more animal than the last one, and Skylar must rightly take it as encouragement, because his tongue slips deeper. The sensation is—wet, hot, amazing.

"More," Walt manages breathlessly.

Since Skylar's tongue is buried in Walt's ass, he doesn't respond, except to stroke his hands along the tops of Walt's legs. The sensations are starting to overwhelm Walt—fingers on his taint, a palm on the curve of his ass, a hand fisted around his cock before cupping his balls, rolling them, tugging them.

When Skylar withdraws his tongue, the emptiness from before hits harder. "Lube," Skylar says, sounding breathless himself as he sits up. It takes Walt a moment to fumble for it, and Skylar seems a little clumsy as he pops the cap and drizzles it over his fingers.

Walt's legs are still looped loosely around Skylar. He's still open and exposed. It heightens everything. His skin is buzzing. Crackling. He could conduct electricity right now. Skylar touches a slick, warm finger to Walt's hole, his eyes locked on Walt's. "If you don't like it, I'll stop," Skylar says.

"I'm gonna like it." Walt sounds drunk. Feels drunk too.

With the canted smile that made Walt fall in love with him, Skylar says, "I want you to like it, but what I want most is to make you feel good. So tell me what feels good."

"Finger fuck me already, Sky."

Skylar makes a strangled little sound and presses his finger slowly into Walt. It's a strange feeling. Pressure and tightness, but wet and hot. It's not bad. "Okay?" Skylar asks. When Walt nods, he sinks his finger in deeper. That feels stranger. There's a burn that borders on painful.

Walt breathes out and makes a conscious effort to relax. He's pretty sure he read once you should bear down, so he tries that.

It helps, brings the sensation from the edge of unpleasant back to strange again. Strange and maybe good. Skylar stays still and the burn fades. As Walt's muscles relax, the tightness does too, and he's left with the feeling of stretch and fullness. But it could be more. It seems like it would feel good if it were more.

Skylar moves his finger out and back in, a slow, steady slide. And oh, oh fuck. Yes. There's a burn again, but not in Walt's ass. His entire body feels flushed and hot. He runs his palm over his chest. His skin is slick with heat and sweat, his chest hair damp with it. He can only imagine what he looks like. Messy, wrecked, legs spread wide while a man fingers the most private part of his body.

Instead of the shame he's half-expecting to follow the image, he feels sexy. Hot. Powerful, because when he opens his eyes, Skylar is staring at him ravenously, his lips parted and his cock flushed dark.

Walt tilts his hips up. "More."

There's more lube, and then just as carefully as before, Skylar slides a second finger in. This time, Walt's ready for the sensations that skirt the boundary of too tight, too much burn, and they transform more quickly to pleasure. Because yeah, *yeah*, he likes this feeling, likes the fullness and the stretch.

Slowly, Skylar fucks him with two fingers. Walt tilts his head back and winds his own fingers in the duvet.

Then Skylar presses both fingers against a spot inside Walt that he technically knows exists, but the bolt of bone-melting pleasure that rushes through him wasn't something he knew his body was capable of feeling.

"Fuck!" he gasps, back arching and hand flying to his cock to—he doesn't know what. Pump himself to orgasm or squeeze until he's not so close to one?

"Yeah," Skylar growls. "Feels good?"

"Fuck," Walt repeats. Skylar laughs and bends over to take the tip of Walt's cock in his mouth. "Oh god. Sky. Am I ready? I'm gonna… I'm gonna die. Can you fuck me now? Please."

The squelch of more lube. More pressure, more stretch. Three fingers moving in and out, brushing his prostate, sending deep rumbles of pleasure through him. How can something that feels so similar to his dick being touched feel so different at the same time?

Having three fingers inside him only makes him want what they're building up to. He squirms, trying to move down on the bed, to make Sky fuck him harder. Maybe to somehow get himself impaled on Skylar's cock. God, yeah, he fucking wants that. Held down, legs spread, completely at Skylar's mercy. Why was he ever ashamed of this? Sex has never made him feel so complete, and they aren't even done yet.

Skylar pulls out his fingers, and it's the worst emptiness yet. Mindlessly, Walt hooks his hands behind his knees and pulls them up. The feel of his asscheeks spreading wide is beyond dirty, and it makes Walt feel like he's flying. Especially when Skylar moans and says, "You're so hot. How are you real?"

Walt bounces his legs and his ass. "If you don't put your dick in me—"

Skylar falls on him in a ferocious kiss, tongues and teeth and lips so swollen they ache, cocks grinding together and every part of Walt's body wound tight and sparking with pleasure. Everything feels good; every place their skin rubs together, every slide of their dicks against each other, the contrast of saliva and lube cooling on Walt's exposed hole.

As roughly as Skylar kissed Walt, he pulls back and squirts lube all over his cock, then Walt's ass, working it over his dick with one hand while he smears it over and into Walt with the other.

Finally, finally, he braces his shoulders against the backs of Walt's thighs and lines himself up. Right away, his dick is different than his fingers. Blunter. Broader. Softer, probably, but all Walt can feel is how big it is, and that's kind of scary but mostly it's exciting, because he just wants to take it. He *wants* it to be too much.

Skylar doesn't shove his dick in. He inches inside with slow, shallow rocks of his hips, which is maddening and sweet and also incredibly hot to watch as his abs tighten. A drop of sweat runs between Skylar's pecs and there's something incredibly dirty about thinking it's from Sky holding himself back.

As Skylar's dick enters him inch by inch, Walt tries to concentrate on the good feelings and not the bad ones, because—yeah. Skylar's cock is a lot bigger than his fingers. "Is this okay?" Skylar keeps whispering, and Walt keeps nodding, because it is. It's so good. Even the weird, kind of bad sensations keep swinging like a pendulum into good, and he already knows one of these times they'll stay there.

Skylar stops. His chest heaves, and his eyes are just black circles. Another droplet of sweat has joined the first one between his pecs. His hands are clenched around Walt's thighs, dimpling the hairy skin. "You look—god. Walt. I knew you'd look good taking my dick, but you look so much better than I imagined."

"Love that you imagined this," Walt says. His words slur. He's never felt drunk on lust and pleasure like this. "Are you—in?"

Skylar lets out a distinctly unsexy, snorty laugh, which is also simultaneously incredibly sexy, because it's Skylar, and his smile and voice and laugh is the sexiest thing Walt can imagine. "Yeah. Should I be offended you wanted more?"

"I don't want more," Walt says.

For a moment, Skylar only stares. Walt wonders if he said the wrong thing. Actually, yeah, he definitely said the wrong thing. Asking if your boyfriend has his dick all the way inside your ass is for sure the wrong thing to say when your boyfriend's dick is in your ass.

"Sorry," Walt starts, since he just ruined gay sex—or bi sex?— whatever, he definitely ruined it. He's going to do a good apology, even though he can't think because he feels—god, he feels so good, full and stretched and floating—but he's going to make it clear how sorry he is for saying the wrong thing yet again. "Sorry I ruined gay sex."

Skylar's shoulders jump and he bends forward, cupping his hands on either side of Walt's face. The angle change does incredibly interesting things to Walt's insides, so he can't process for a second that Skylar is brushing his thumbs over Walt's lips. "You could never ruin anything, Walt," he whispers. "You're definitely not ruining gay sex."

"Are you sure?" Walt whispers back.

"I could fuck you and you'll find out." Skylar closes his mouth over Walt's, swallowing his moan.

And he does. Skylar's thrusts start slow and shallow, and. Yeah. No. Walt couldn't ruin this by saying something stupid. Nothing could ruin this. This is—this is—he never imagined. Or he did, but he was wrong. Because this is beyond the wildest of Walt's imaginings.

As Walt arches and writhes, Skylar pushes himself up, his knees bracketing Walt's hips as he lifts Walt's legs to hang over his shoulders. His next thrust isn't shallow. It's long and deep, his cock sliding all the

way in until he's buried balls deep and Walt's panting, "More, Sky—
please—"

Finally, Skylar stops holding back. He grips Walt's thighs hard,
sweaty hands slipping on sweaty legs, hair stinging as it gets pulled
under Skylar's palm, and slams into Walt.

Walt lets out a howl and lets go of the last shreds of civilization.
Skylar fucks him, grunting and moaning, sweat dripping from his
hair and chest and shoulders, and Walt's just an animal made for this.
Without Walt saying anything, Skylar adjusts his angle again, and now
every thrust is hitting him in that spot, that amazing spot inside him.
Walt hears how the cadence of his moans changes, gets more guttural
and wanton.

Skylar makes a noise that might be a laugh, but he's breathing too
hard for Walt to tell for sure. There's a smile on his face, a bright, gorgeous
smile like the spring sky, so this is probably good for him too.

From somewhere deep inside his core, the swell of his orgasm
rises higher, the crest frothing as he nears its peak. It feels different than
any orgasm Walt's ever had, so much—more, and also like he doesn't
know how to get there, like he's standing at one of those cracks in the
earth where the updraft is so strong that it can hold a person up. But he
wants to fall. He wants to step off and fall, because he's pretty sure he's
going to fly.

"So close," he groans.

"Yeah? Me too." Skylar laughs breathlessly again. "Wanna see
you come—all over yourself. So hot."

He closes his hand tight around Walt's cock and pumps it hard and
yeah. That's what he needed, that's exactly what he needed, because now
the wave is rushing toward shore; the wind is receding. "Say something
dirty," Walt keens. Like Skylar's been talking like a choir boy this whole
time? But Walt likes it, likes Skylar talking like he owns Walt, like Walt
has to lie back and take it.

Skylar pumps his hand faster, rails Walt harder. "I'm gonna come
inside you, baby. Fill you up with my—"

That's the knockout punch. Every muscle in Walt's body winds
impossibly tight, and his world explodes.

Waves of wringing, gutting pleasure heave out from his center,
from some place inside him that he can't identify. The orgasm rips
through his whole body, up his chest to his neck and dropped jaw, down

his spread legs to his curled toes. He's shooting, too, ropes of hot cum splattering his stomach, his chest, his *chin* for fuck's sake. He's never come this hard in his life. He might never come this hard again, because this might kill him, and if it does, it's an okay way to go.

With a cracked yell, Skylar shoves deep inside Walt and stays there, shuddering through his own orgasm. Walt thinks he can feel it, Skylar's cock pulsing and filling him up. Maybe that's wishful thinking. Maybe it's just rumbles and aftershocks still rocking every part of Walt's body.

Skylar's muscles go soft, and he falls forward to lie on Walt. His arms tangle with Walt's legs, and they both laugh. Walt's boneless. Loose. He feels so good that he might literally be glowing. He feels like he's giving off at least enough light to read by.

Lazily, Walt reaches for Skylar's head, burying his fingers in Skylar's hair and pulling him into a slow, languid kiss. Fingers cradle Walt's jaw and Skylar sighs.

When they come up for air, Skylar settles more comfortably on top of Walt, an arm and leg splayed across Walt's body possessively. Walt strokes his fingers through Skylar's hair and finally says, "We should do that again."

Skylar laughs. "Give me a minute."

Which makes Walt laugh and wrap his arms around him. "That performance deserves more than a minute."

"Yeah? That good?"

"A-plus. Five stars. Best sex I've ever had." Whoops, that last one wasn't that funny, even if it's true.

But Skylar snuggles closer. "Me too."

The orgasm was good. Great. Incredible. Like nothing Walt's ever felt before, an all-encompassing, body-wide feeling of transcendence. The feeling curling through him now is better. He's in love. He's in love with Skylar. It's time to tell him.

He opens his mouth to say the words, but Skylar groans and sits up. "I better check on Jane and Darcy. I know they're not supposed to kid for a couple weeks, but if Jane seemed restless...."

"Okay," Walt says instead of *I love you*. It's not exactly the best time, anyway, if Skylar's worrying about the goats. "Want me to come out there with you?"

"No, I've got it." Skylar pulls on a pair of sweats with no underwear, which Walt immediately files away for future jerking off material. "I'm just being paranoid. I always get like this right before my girls kid."

Walt stretches, half to work out the pleasant ache in his muscles and half to enjoy the way Skylar stares hungrily. "I'll be here," Walt says, scratching slowly at a patch of cum drying on the underside of his pec. The naked lust in Skylar's eyes makes Walt's cock twitch.

"You better be. Keep the bed warm." Skylar considers. "Don't get dressed. I might be ready for round two when I come back."

That makes Walt's cock twitch again, and he gives it a pull just to watch Skylar's hitched breath.

"Goats," Skylar says like he's reminding himself of why he's standing up and not in bed with his hand on Walt's dick too. "Be back soon."

Walt grins and settles back on the bed as Skylar goes outside, drifting in a sated, warm haze. After a few minutes go by, the cum he shot all over himself has turned decisively uncomfortable, so he gets out of bed to clean up.

Maybe it's stupid, but as he stands in front of the bathroom mirror with a wet washcloth, he can't help studying himself for differences. Two hours ago, he wasn't a man who got fucked to within an inch of his life. Now he is.

Yeah. Probably no physical difference. Maybe there's something in his face, though. In his eyes. Something that, even if you didn't know what happened, might make you say that something good and important happened in this guy's life. Like maybe he put something aside that's been holding him back for a long time.

He finishes in the bathroom and goes back down the hall. As he's deciding whether to get under the covers or to lie on top of the duvet in a debauched sprawl, the door crashes open downstairs.

Walt jumps as footsteps pound up the stairs and down the hall, until Skylar appears in the doorway, wild-eyed. "I need my phone! I have to call the vet! Jane's in labor!"

Chapter Twenty-Six

SHIT. SHIT shit shit shit. Skylar ends the call to the vet after it goes to voicemail again. Dr. Lennox isn't answering, which means she's probably out on a call at some other farm where another animal is having an emergency.

From the kitchen table, Walt watches him pace. When Skylar stops and presses his phone to his forehead, Walt asks, "Can you help Jane give birth without your vet?"

Skylar lets his breath out slowly and deliberately. "Maybe?"

This is the part he's supposed to be good at, the actual animal part of running a farm. As a business, he may have almost run it into the ground, but he can take care of his animals. Right? So why does he sound like he has no clue?

"Yes," he says more confidently. "Yeah, I—everything's ready. I've just—" Here's the embarrassing part. "I've never done it on my own. Dr. Lennox has always been here in case something goes wrong."

"So you know exactly what to do," Walt says.

Having someone as steady and level-headed as Walt show so much faith in him makes it feel like there's more oxygen in the room. "Yeah, I do."

"I bet you know what to do if something goes wrong too?"

All the articles and books he's read flash through Skylar's mind. Words on a page aren't the same as experience, but, yes. None of his does have ever had a difficult birth, so he's never had any need for that knowledge, but it's all there.

"Okay." Skylar takes a couple gulping breaths. "Okay. Yeah. I can do this."

Walt pushes off from the table and puts his hands on Skylar's shoulders. "You left a voicemail for Dr. Lennox. When she calls back, you'll tell her what's going on, and she'll be able to come over if it'll make you feel better. So you just have to do the stuff you know how to do, and you'll have backup soon."

Skylar slips his phone in his pocket and rakes his fingers through his hair. "You don't have to help. I know you said you wanted to earlier today"—was that really only today?—"but I don't consider that a binding promise. Just so you know. If you'd rather stay inside…."

Walt shrugs on an old jean jacket. "You'll have to tell me what to do. That won't make your life harder, will it? I don't want to get in the way."

Skylar could kiss him. He does kiss him on the way to the door, hoping it conveys the depth of his gratitude, because suddenly his throat won't work.

In the barn, Jane is in the same shape she was when he left her: lying down, panting, with discharge leaking from her vulva. Her side ripples and she bleats weakly when she sees him. He kneels by her head, scratching behind her ears. "Hey, Janey. We're going to get through this." Looking at her centers him. Her eyes have that glazed look goats sometimes get when they're in labor, but she's watching him with complete trust.

"Walt, over in the corner there are a couple plastic totes with pink duct tape on the lids. Can you bring those over?" Skylar keeps petting Jane as Walt hurries to the other side of the barn. Softly, just to Jane, he says, "Can you stand up for me, sweetie? We're going to get a nice clean tarp under you."

With his urging, she heaves herself to her feet. He guides her to the stall he's been preparing for kidding. It's swept clean, and two big pails stand sentinel on either side of the open door.

Just as Skylar gets Jane to the stall, Walt returns carrying both totes. Skylar allows himself a tiny moment of appreciation for the fact that Walt isn't exerting any effort at all to carry two full plastic totes before pointing to the side of the stall. "Can you get the tarp out?"

"Your tarp, sir," Walt says once he has it.

"Thanks. Let's spread it out and get her to lie down on it."

Once that's accomplished, they let Jane get comfortable again. Since the amniotic sac hasn't appeared, Skylar takes advantage of the lull to get out the rest of his goat-labor kit. He arranges it in the order he's likely to need it, even if he hopes he doesn't need some of it. The surgical gloves and K-Y Jelly are close at hand. If something goes wrong, he wants to be able to snap those gloves on as fast as possible.

There's also scissors, dental floss, iodine, and the Disneyland ashtray he uses to hold the iodine while he dips the cut umbilical cord. The clean towels stay within easy reach too, in case Jane's too tired to clean off the kid when it's born.

Walt sits on the ground next to him, looking over the supplies. "Lube and an ashtray, huh? Should I ask what kind of operation you're running here?"

Skylar laughs, not realizing how much he needed something to release the tension. "Did you really just make a bestiality joke?"

"Did you really just laugh at my bestiality joke?" Walt shoots back. His smile shouldn't be so reassuring. No one's smile should be that reassuring, but somehow Walt's brings Skylar's heart rate down and makes him breathe easier. He's even able to shake out some of the tension in his shoulders. Maybe it works on goats too. Jane seems calmer.

Leaning over so their shoulders bump, Skylar says, "Thanks for being cool about this. Especially since we were...."

A little blaze of heat lights Walt's eyes, but it mellows to banked warmth. It's hard to be turned-on when you're sitting on the floor in a chilly barn with a laboring goat in front of you. "You don't have to thank me. This does kind of feel like a very special episode, though. Like we're facing the consequences of unprotected sex."

"Oh my god," Skylar groans, but he's laughing again.

They fall into comfortable silence, the barn rustling and creaking around them. Straw crunches as the rest of the goat herd sleeps, shifting occasionally. In the neighboring stall, Squirrel shuffles. Little pitters from the beams overhead mean mice, and Skylar thinks for the millionth time that he should get some cats. The problem is, they'd very quickly become spoiled pets instead of mousers.

If he does all the stuff Walt thinks he can do, though—farm tours, goat yoga—cats would probably be a draw.

Should he be documenting this for Instagram? He hasn't posted a single thing today, and if he's not creating content, then he's not driving engagement. The algorithm won't push his posts to the top of people's feeds, and people will forget Blue Skies Farm exists.

He's about to reach for his phone when Jane gets agitated again. The discharge leaking from her is thicker now, more like jelly than mucus. "Is that normal?" Walt asks, looking at it in concern.

Skylar nods. "It's her mucus plug. It's always come out a lot earlier with all the other does, never when the labor's this advanced. But all does are different." He chews his lip and repeats that to himself. *Just because this labor is a little different doesn't mean there's anything wrong.*

The discharge gets more yellow. If Walt is grossed out, Skylar can't blame him. Not everyone is into the Miracle of Birth pavilion at the state fair.

Jane stands and paws at the tarp. Skylar lets her do her thing. She doesn't seem distressed. Well, she seems distressed, but normal *I'm about to push the small goat I've been growing inside me through a very small tube and hole.* Kidding is stressful for everyone, but sometimes Skylar thinks he's the one that's the most stressed out of all.

"Let's fill the buckets with warm water," Skylar says. Jane's behavior is pointing to her giving birth soon, and he wants to be ready in case he needs to assist. While the water streams into the buckets at the faucet, he looks at his clothes to remind himself what he threw on before coming outside. Good—just a long-sleeved tee that he can't even remember the origin of. If it gets all bloody and afterbirth-y, no big deal.

They mix soap into the warm water and lug the buckets back to the stall. Jane makes a moaning sound and lies down again. Walt bites his lip and looks from her to Skylar. "What do we do now?"

Skylar shoves his hands in his pockets and reminds himself that he's done this before and it's all gone fine. He just can't stop his mind from worrying at one fact like it's a loose tooth—she shouldn't have gone into labor for at least another week. Darcy isn't showing any signs of going into labor. When they came into the barn and turned the lights on, she blinked sleepily at the two of them, just like the rest of the herd.

"We won't have to do much, hopefully. Animals do everything themselves, if everything goes right." *Things already aren't going right* says the least helpful part of Skylar's brain. He tries to project confidence as he adds, "Like in the wild. There's no one to help them out there."

Or like on a big ag farm, where Jane would be nothing but a commodity, her worth assessed against how much she costs, the least helpful part of Skylar's brain chimes in again. *Which is where she'll end up if you don't make enough money.* Skylar shoves the thought away.

Walt nods and thankfully doesn't point out that stuff still goes wrong for animals giving birth in the wild—it's just that having no one there to help them means the death of the baby, maybe the mother too.

That's not going to happen. Jane's going to be fine.

Her side ripples again in a wave, and she bleats plaintively. This is the hardest part about breeding the does. The kids are amazing. They're cute and lovable and if there's a person on this planet who doesn't find their antics unflaggingly delightful, Skylar doesn't want to meet them. But man, it's hard to watch his girls in distress. Even if most animals are built to give birth more easily than humans, it's obviously not fun for them.

Mucus continues to leak from her, more yellowish than white now. She starts to rock and strain to push. Skylar holds his breath and watches, hands still in his pockets. They're clenched into tight fists, so much so that when he makes a concerted effort to loosen them, his fingers hurt as blood rushes back in.

Jane tenses hard with the strain of pushing before her body abruptly goes slack. She's panting with the effort, but Skylar's heart leaps at the sight of a liquid-filled bubble appearing at her birth canal.

His shoulders loosen with relief. "That's the amniotic sac," he tells Walt. "We should see the kid's hooves pretty soon."

"There's really going to be a baby goat," Walt says, like baby goats are just as mythical as Santa Claus.

"Could be two," Skylar says.

Walt's eyes go wide and lit up. The analogy is pulling double duty, but he looks like Christmas is coming early.

They wait, Skylar's body thrumming with an anticipatory current. Not long now. Once the amniotic sac appears, the kid isn't far behind. If a doe keeps pushing and there's no kid, that's a problem. But Skylar isn't going to look for trouble. Jane's doing exactly what she's supposed to do, pushing, stopping to breathe, pushing some more.

And more.

And even more.

The minutes pass, turning to quarter of an hour, then half, then a full hour, then another. Skylar gave up standing and watching by forty-five minutes in. It's too stressful, and he knows it's not time for him to intervene. His does have taken this long to give birth before. Just because he wants it to happen faster because it would be less nerve-wracking doesn't mean there's something wrong.

He just has a bad feeling. He wishes Dr. Lennox would call back.

Like he manifested it, his phone buzzes in his pocket. Not wanting to stress Jane out more by talking loudly, he moves to the barn door, maneuvering himself so he can keep an eye on Jane but also not speak in her direction. "Thank you for calling back! Jane's in labor and I didn't expect it for another week and it would really help if you were here," he babbles before Dr. Lennox has a chance to say a word.

The connection is crackly, which isn't unusual around here. The mountains aren't that tall, but they still interfere with cell signals. Skylar begs the cell phone gods not to let this call drop. "How far into labor is she?" Dr. Lennox asks. She's a no-nonsense older lady who's been practicing large-animal veterinary medicine for much longer than Skylar's been alive, and she has the kind of presence that reassures you she's going to get the situation under control if she hasn't already done so. Skylar finds her scary but incredibly comforting.

Skylar makes a conscious effort to talk more slowly. "Her amniotic sac appeared almost two hours ago. She's still just pushing."

It's practically possible to see her nodding—her short iron-gray hair always kind of flops around in a way that seems a little too whimsical for her demeanor. "Sounds like she's doing good. You're going to do fine."

"I mean, maybe, but it'll be good to have you here just in case." The relief flooding Skylar's body is making him shaky. So much tension, and now the release, knowing he's going to have professional help.

"I'm not—be able to get—there—n time," Dr. Lennox says briskly. At least, her tone sounds brisk from what he can hear through the sudden dropped signal. "You've always done great before with your herd, though. You know what to do."

For several seconds, Skylar's brain just buffers. Finally, he says, "Sorry, the connection was breaking up. It sounded like you said you're not going to be able to get here in time?"

Ha! Ha ha. No way. That would be really bad. It would be *really really bad* if Skylar let himself believe everything was going to be okay, only to have the rug pulled out from underneath him.

"I'm way up near Dingley Dell. Got a lame cow that I need to get loaded into a trailer and down to Syracuse where she can go into surgery."

Skylar's stomach doesn't sink so much as implode. Or maybe an anvil just yanked it out of his body and off a cliff, *Looney Toons* style. Driving from Dingley Dell to Syracuse and back will take hours. "Oh," he says and waits, like she's going to pop out from behind Squirrel's stall and yell *Sike!*

"I can give you the number of a vet in Schenevus who I trust," Dr. Lennox says.

"Schenevus," Skylar repeats. He reminds himself that he has to speak more than one word at a time if he wants to have a conversation. "Um, sure. I guess." Schenevus is an hour away, but it's better than not having anyone here if he needs help.

After giving him the number of the vet in Schenevus, Dr. Lennox tells him she has to get back to the cow. The line clicks as she disconnects, but Skylar stands there holding the phone to his ear, sweat sticking the screen to his cheek, his ear aching as he jams the edge of the phone into the cartilage.

This isn't the time to fall apart, so he takes a deep breath, holds it for eight seconds, and releases it slowly before returning to Jane.

Walt gives him a hopeful look. "Is the vet coming?"

Skylar shakes his head. "We have to deliver the kid ourselves."

Chapter Twenty-Seven

THE VET isn't coming to save Skylar. This is on him.

There still aren't any hooves visible in the amniotic sac poking out of Jane. No hooves, no fuzzy little nose. She's still pushing, but nothing is happening. Her eyes are glazed, and her sides are heaving with the physical toll. So much effort and so little to show for it.

Looking from Jane to Skylar and back, Walt asks, "What do we do? Should we just keep waiting and letting her do her thing?" His voice is hesitant. "She seems really tired."

"I know." The words come out creaky. He clears his throat and tries again. "I know. She's trying, but"—oh god, he has to admit it; pretending everything is fine is going to get him a dead doe and a dead kid—"she needs help."

In the silence after those words, Jane's labored breathing seems loud. Skylar pushes the heels of his hands into his eyes and sees the neon backsides of his irises. "There's another vet but he's an hour away, and there's no guarantee he isn't out on a call. I have to assist."

And not fall apart. He has to assist and not fall apart. Where's that confidence he managed to find earlier?

"Hey." Footsteps approach and Walt's warm, strong hands settle on Skylar's arms. "Remember what happened in the season finale of *Gaslamp Market*?"

Skylar can't help the little smile that sneaks onto his face despite his low-grade panic. "The gratuitous shirtless scene?"

Rubbing Skylar's shoulders gently, Walt says, "No, the part where Samuel thinks he's not going to be able to get to Willis in time. Remember how he does it?"

It's weird to think about a TV show while he's hyping himself up to stick his arm inside a goat, but he thinks back to the episode, which they watched together a couple weeks ago. "He uses magic to get out of the basement he's locked in."

"Because?" Walt prompts.

"Because...." Skylar closes his eyes and shakes his head, smiling more now. "Because he finally believes he'll be able to do magic. There's finally an important enough reason for him to break through all the barriers he's put up for himself."

"Yes!" Walt squeezes Skylar's shoulders. "So you have to be like Samuel."

"There aren't any special effects to make up for the stuff I don't know how to do," Skylar points out, but he's already rolling up his sleeves.

"You know how to do this," Walt says with such complete, unshakable confidence that it fills the cracks of Skylar's fear. That's the part of the episode Walt left out in his pep talk. It was Willis who gave Samuel a reason to trust himself and believe that he was capable of realizing his potential—just like Walt's doing for Skylar now.

Skylar takes one more deep breath and sets his shoulders. "This is going to be messy. There's going to be blood and fluid and a bunch of gross stuff. Are you going to be okay helping me?"

Color drains from Walt's face, but he nods. "Just tell me what to do."

That will be the trick. Does Skylar know what to do well enough to tell someone how to help him?

He snaps on surgical gloves and tosses a pair to Walt, who puts them on shakily. As he squirts K-Y Jelly on his fingers, he cycles through all the different ways a birth can go wrong and what needs to be done to fix it. There are some alarming blank spots, which he pushes aside. If he can identify the problem, he'll remember how to fix it. There's not another option.

As he kneels behind Jane, he says, "Can you hold her head and keep her calm? I have to figure out where the kid is."

Wide-eyed, Walt does as he's told. He leans over Jane's head, stroking her and murmuring softly. Skylar looks at the amniotic sac, swallows hard, and inserts one finger into Jane's birth canal.

There! Oh thank fuck, he can feel hooves. The kid is in the birth canal; that's something. He identified something that's happening! It's a win, and he's going to take it.

It's hard to tell what's going on with just one finger, so he uses a second, and what he finds takes that win and squashes it. Instead of feeling a head, he feels a tail.

The kid is breaching.

Skylar's heart hammers but his brain miraculously produces the solution crisply and clearly. "The kid's turned the wrong way," Skylar says, amazed at how calm he sounds. "I have to turn it around so it comes out front first."

Walt looks up from murmuring to Jane, his eyes wide. Any second now, he's going to nope out. Who wants to see their boyfriend with his arm up a goat's vagina? Cody was disgusted by a fraction of that, and there was a legal contract keeping them together.

It doesn't matter, because Skylar needs to get this kid out of Jane.

Stroking Jane's muzzle, Walt asks, "What do you need me to do?"

The fear and uncertainty dripping through Skylar like poison suddenly doesn't have room to move, because an expanding pocket of happiness and love is crowding it out. "Keep her as calm as you can." He offers Walt a smile, knowing it can't possibly convey how much it means that Walt's here. Not only here, but helping. "You're doing amazing."

"So are you."

The happy bubble in Skylar's chest gets bigger. "When I pull the kid out, I'll have to get it breathing, and then there's a bunch of aftercare stuff to do. Can you be ready with a towel to dry the kid off?"

"Um." Somehow, *that's* the thing that makes Walt look really scared—but then Skylar remembers all the times Walt's said he can't take care of things, from kids to pets to plants. "Are you sure you want me doing that?"

With zero hesitation, Skylar says, "Yes. Are you okay with it?"

Walt's pulse visibly hammers in his throat, but he swallows with a hard jag of his Adam's apple and nods. Skylar nods back and turns his focus back to Jane.

The two fingers he has inside her are not, unfortunately, going to be sufficient for what he needs to do. "Sorry, sweetie," he murmurs as he eases the rest of his hand in. Maybe she's just exhausted, but she barely reacts. Skylar maps the kid's position by touch. It's mostly in the birth canal. That makes his job harder.

There's no time to sit here and psych himself up. The kid is in breach; the nearest vet is an hour away. He'll lose the kid and maybe Jane as well if he doesn't act.

So he gets a hand on the kid's back end and slowly, carefully, pushes it back inside Jane. He needs to get it into a position where he can turn it around so the front feet and head can come out first. He also needs to be really, really careful not to get the kid stuck worse.

The kid inches back into Jane's womb. Slow and steady. Rushing won't help, as much as Skylar wants to do this as fast as possible.

Once the kid is back in its starting position—which is rough; all that pushing for nothing!—Skylar turns it carefully. There's its ribs, shoulders, neck and head, and then yes. There are the front feet.

Also, if he's not mistaken, there's another kid. He hopes to any deity who feels like listening that the second one comes out in the right position, and that Jane has enough strength to deliver it.

"Okay, Janey, I'm going to pull now." He wraps his hand around the kid's front legs and pats Jane's flank with the other hand.

Just as steadily as he pushed the kid back in, now he pulls it out. It's paramount that the kid's head doesn't get caught stretched back, so he makes sure to maneuver it to be tucked against the front legs.

It seems to take forever. Like he'll pull and pull, and the kid will never emerge. Sweat trickles down his back between his shoulder blades, despite the chill in the barn.

The front hooves appear, followed by Skylar's hand wrapped around the legs. Now there's enough body outside Jane that Skylar can use his other hand to pull too. A nose appears, and then the rest of the kid's face, its little eyes closed.

Somewhere along the line, the amniotic sac burst, which is just fine, because it means Skylar doesn't have to do it now.

He's about to pull the kid the rest of the way out when Jane tenses and pushes, delivering the kid's back half with a whoosh of birth fluids. Skylar scoops it up, stands, and grips it firmly by its back legs before giving it a couple swings.

Whiiiiich makes Walt look at him like he's insane. "Have to clear its air passages," Skylar explains.

Walt exhales hard, like he was holding his breath. "I thought I was about to see some kind of weird Catskills sport."

"That's just with cows—no, sorry, kidding!" Birthing fluids spatter the ground around Skylar and the kid snuffles, and Skylar realizes he just made the worst pun ever. He bites back the urge to laugh hysterically and wipes the kid's nose and mouth with a paper towel just to be sure most of the fluids are clear.

He brings the kid around to Jane's face, kneeling next to her so she can smell and see it. Wait—Skylar checks—her. So Jane can smell and see her.

Jane still has that glazey look in her eyes, and at first she doesn't seem to know what to do with this tiny, wet thing that Skylar's holding up to her. "That's your baby," Walt tells her softly. "You made that."

Jane lets out a small bleat and nuzzles the kid. The kid wiggles in Skylar's arms and without being asked, Walt grabs a clean, dry towel from the tote and then spreads it on the floor near Jane—who, after a few more nuzzles, begins licking the kid.

Tension releases across Skylar's shoulders like driveway firecrackers. He lays the kid on the towel and Jane keeps cleaning her, licking her from her head all the way back to her tail.

Walt watches for a moment, then looks up to meet Skylar's eyes. Skylar can't process what he sees on Walt's face. It's too much.

"There's another kid, I'm pretty sure," he blurts out instead.

The emotion on Walt's face doesn't go anywhere. If anything, it gets… more. "What do you need me to do?"

Pushing himself to his feet, Skylar says, "Just keep an eye on Jane. I'm going to mix up some molasses water for her."

"That sounds weirdly good."

"I can mix up a cup for you too, if you want."

Shockingly, Walt demurs once Skylar brings back the bucket of molasses water. Jane's happy to drink it, though, sticking her muzzle over the rim and slurping noisily before Skylar even steadies the bucket on the floor.

"Do you mind holding the kid and drying her off some more?" Skylar asks. "I need to get her processed and help Jane if she's having trouble delivering the second one."

Even though Walt still looks worried, he does what Skylar asks. Dr. Lennox has always helped him with the kid processing in the past, but this part isn't stressful. He ties off the umbilical cord with floss and snips off the extra, then uses the Disneyland ashtray to dip the end of the cord in iodine. With that done, he prepares the antibiotic shot he'll need to give Jane and mixes some electrolytes up for her.

"Sky? I think Jane's having contractions again," Walt says, drawing Skylar straight back.

Walt's right. She is. Within a few minutes, the amniotic sac appears, but this time, the front hooves and the face of the second kid follow. Skylar's legs wobble with relief. There was no way in hell he was going to lose a goat tonight, but holy shit is he glad he doesn't have to pull another kid.

Jane delivers the second kid beautifully. As Skylar brings it to her face, he says, "You just had to be dramatic, didn't you?" No response is forthcoming from the new mother.

The second kid gets processed; Jane gets a couple shots and then water with electrolytes. While he's working, Skylar keeps sneaking glances at Walt. His legs are splayed in front of him and both kids are in his lap. He's still drying the second one while the first snuggles into his stomach, and he looks—

The riptide of feeling that hits Skylar is so intense that his legs shake. Walt doesn't look like a person who's bad at taking care of the small and weak. There's such care in his movements, such concentration and instinctive affection on his face. He looks like a person who takes care of those who need him to, whether they're a plant, a newborn goat, or a child.

When Jane delivers the placentas, Skylar catches them on a fresh tarp and puts them off to the side of the electrolyte bucket. Walt looks at him like he thinks Skylar's losing it, so Skylar says, "Fun fact, goats eat their placenta."

Walt looks at them. "I think Ally wants to eat hers after she has her baby."

"It's probably not as gruesome when people eat theirs."

They look at each other, and suddenly Skylar's laughing so hard he can't breathe. Walt quickly becomes just as hysterical and when Jane turns her head to stare at them, that sets both off again.

Soon, the kids are dry and attempting to stand on trembly legs, looking around at their new world in bewilderment. Baby goats are always cute, but there's something uniquely adorable about them right after they're born, as they work out how their limbs work and how to use them together.

Within an hour, they're both nursing while Jane licks their rear ends and baas softly at them. Skylar can't help getting teary—he always does after a successful delivery.

Skylar and Walt sit next to each other, leaning against the wall and watching mother and babies. It's peaceful and feels right. This is the way things should be. Walt should be here with him. They should do this together and have nights like this, sitting on the barn floor while their animals thrive.

"You know what I just realized?" Walt says a while later.

"Hm?" Skylar asks with a start. He wasn't falling asleep. Okay, maybe he was falling asleep a little.

"Our names start with the same letters as the characters in *Gaslamp Market*. Samuel and Willis. Skylar and Walt."

Skylar giggles. "Oh my god." The giggle turns into a laugh and he repeats, "Oh my *god*."

Then Walt's laughing too, and somehow things are even more right.

Walt interlaces his fingers with Skylar's and holds tight. "I love you," he says.

"I love you too," Skylar says back.

And, well. Things can't get more right than that.

Chapter Twenty-Eight

THE NEW kids are a big hit on Instagram. Walt suggests they have a contest to decide on their names, because people love stuff like that. There are some wild ones—the person who suggests Henry Kissinger makes Walt worry for a good ten minutes that his mom follows @BlueSkiesFarm. A lot of people want the baby goats to be named after their kids, which is a little strange. Enough of their followers have picked up on the theme of the goats' names, so what happens is Skylar picks his favorites out of that pool of suggestions. The post that officially introduces Agatha and Billy becomes the most liked one so far.

They decide the kids will be be their entry into the Spring Fling contest even though, as Skylar says, "Baby animals don't win blue ribbons." They draw crowds, though. Margery stops by one day to pick up an order of cheese and tells them to keep doing what they're doing, because the town's Facebook event has more people "interested" and "going" than the city council has ever seen.

In the weeks between the kids' births and Spring Fling, Walt helps Skylar set up a website with goat cheese order forms—one for local restaurants and shops and another for individuals. So many orders come in that it's not clear at first if Skylar will be able to keep up with the demand, not to mention the deliveries. Walt takes care of as many as he can on the way back from the Leonards' house in the afternoon. Jett's doing some too. Skylar takes care of the business ones himself. A couple restaurants in town put in decent-sized orders, and an upscale general-store-ish place wants to carry a few different flavors of cheese.

The kitchen remodel for the Leonards is going well—so well, in fact, that it hits Walt that he'll be able to finish right before Spring Fling. He's not sure what will happen then. There won't be any real reason to keep staying with Skylar. Plus, it's mid-March now. The weather's getting warmer; the ground is thawing. Warm weather means Black River Fence Co. can spin back up. His work email is picking up with requests for quotes, and some of his crew have called him to ask when he wants them to come by the office.

Walt hates the idea.

Remodeling the Leonards' kitchen has been a dream. Drawing up the plans, going over the budget, making adjustments, sourcing the materials, and of course the actual work—he's loved every second. Collaborating with people and designing a space that will make them happy is satisfying in a way putting up fences never has been.

Maybe there are people out there who are passionate about residential fencing. Walt's not one of them. He's never going to be. He never should have bought the company from the old owner; he knows that now. It seemed like a good decision at the time, but he's had nothing but slowly mounting regrets ever since. His feelings about his business are like a landfill with more and more garbage being dumped every year he sticks with it.

Why *is* he sticking with it? Because he feels like he can't leave Watertown? For years he patted himself on the back for being the good son, for staying close to his parents, for putting this weird idea of hometown loyalty above everything, especially his own happiness.

Not that he's made the decision to leave. He has a house that he's poured a bunch of money and time into remodeling, and a business he can't just walk away from. Most importantly, his parents are there. He'd include Mario in that list, except in the last few weeks, Walt's done his best to not think about Mario.

He hasn't made the decision to leave Watertown, but Walt doesn't know what other outcome is possible. He doesn't want to spend the rest of his life putting up fences to keep people's dogs in their yards or their neighbors behind a seven-foot privacy barricade. He's in love with Skylar. And Skylar's in love with him. Imagining a life here on Blue Skies Farm, the two of them and the animals and… okay yeah, he's getting way ahead of himself with this, but he can imagine a family. Kids—human ones, not goats. A dog they don't have to fence in. Maybe a cat or two.

Walt's never allowed himself to dream. Suddenly, he's filled with the possibility of all the dreams he's always locked away.

The morning of Spring Fling, Walt wakes up Skylar in his favorite way: slowly licking his dick to hardness and taking him down to the root so Skylar gets to start the day with an orgasm.

When Skylar finishes, coming down Walt's throat, he flops back on his pillow, his arm over his face. "You have a really impressive talent for deep-throating."

Skylar's musk lingers in Walt's nose. "Thanks. You have a really impressive talent for being insanely hot."

They kiss for a little bit before rolling out of bed. The sun is just starting to shine through the bare branches of the trees on the other side of the pasture when they finish loading the truck and trailer. Agatha and Billy chase each other in and out of the trailer before Walt's able to corner them and get them to stay. Jane placidly watches his struggles. She might be laughing at him.

When he slides into the truck's passenger seat, Skylar's staring at his phone with a funny look on his face. "What's up?" Walt asks.

Skylar turns the key in the ignition but doesn't put his seat belt on, his eyes still locked on his phone. "My dad texted and said he's driving up to see me at Spring Fling today."

"Is that good or bad?" Walt knows how he'd feel if his parents texted and said they'd be there today.

"I guess we'll see when he gets here." Skylar sighs, starting the truck.

It's a beautiful early spring day, warm enough for people to leave winter coats at home, but cool enough that the sun feels amazing. Perfect for the first outdoor market of the year. It's a relief to set up outside, though, and makes things easier with all the animals around for the contest.

They don't win a blue ribbon for Agatha and Billy, but they win second place. One of the judges tells them it's mostly for the cheese they entered alongside the goats. It was Walt's suggestion that they make limited edition cheeses for the kids' births, so they rebranded the nightshade one for Agatha and the strawberry one for Billy. Skylar assured Walt it was nerdy and clever.

The upside is that the nightshade cheese is becoming one of their top sellers. Walt meets an artist when he's making his rounds in the market who, when she finds out he's involved with Blue Skies Farm, gushes that she's never had anything like it and how it's her favorite cheese. He asks her if she'd be willing to draw a label for it, and she says she'll do it if they'll pay her in cheese.

When Walt returns to the Blue Skies Farm table, excited to talk to Skylar about the potential labels, there's an unfamiliar Asian man standing there with his arms folded over his chest as he talks seriously with Skylar. Well—maybe not completely unfamiliar. Walt can see Skylar in the angle of his jaw and the shape of his eyes.

Okay. This is fine. Walt can do this. He can meet Skylar's dad! He's good with people. He never has trouble with stuff like this.

Skylar catches sight of him and his eyes light up. He reaches out a hand for Walt, and Walt knows this is going to be fine.

"This is him," Skylar says, his voice brimming with so much love that Walt can't do anything but smile like an idiot.

He extends his hand to Skylar's dad and decides to just go for it, even though the man looks stern and serious and still has his arms crossed over his chest. "Hi, Mr. Dangda. I'm Walt. I'm crazy about your son."

To Walt's surprise, Skylar's dad smiles and accepts Walt's handshake. "You can call me Aroon," he says, his Jersey accent broad and unmistakable. It throws Walt. For some reason he expected Skylar's dad to sound… foreign. Shit, does that make him racist? Maybe he has some stuff to interrogate. "Good to meet you, Walt. I feel like I know you from Skylar's *Instagram posts*."

"I didn't even know you were looking at them!" Skylar says aggrievedly. "You never liked any of them!"

"I don't think you would've seen 'em if I had. You're a celebrity on there. Too big to notice one measly like from your father." Mr. Dangda—Aroon—shakes his head and gets these big, doleful eyes that Walt's seen Skylar do. Now he knows where Sky learned it.

Skylar covers his eyes with a hand for a second, then probably realizes he's chomping with gusto on the bait his dad is laying out. "I'm not a celebrity."

"You two are like the Kardashians," Aroon says. "What do they call it? Interferencers?"

This time, Skylar covers his face with both hands and mumbles something that sounds like, "This is why I don't invite you up here more."

Walt can't help laughing, which he tries to stifle for Skylar's sake. There's a line of customers forming, though, so he says, "Maybe we can grab dinner later, Mr. Dangda?"

"Aroon," he reminds Walt. "And let's do that. But while Skylar deals with his fans, I want to get to know the man he's been hiding from me."

"I haven't been hiding him from you, Dad—hi! Just the nightshade cheese for you today?" Skylar shoots his father a look that's both exasperated and affectionate, and Walt gets a weird moment of aching jealousy. If his parents showed up somewhere and met Skylar out of nowhere, it wouldn't be like this. There wouldn't be any simple acceptance of the fact that Walt's significant other is a man instead of a woman.

Despite Aroon's ribbing, he happily releases Walt to help Skylar get through the line of customers. Several of them want pictures. They're asked by almost everyone where Agatha and Billy are and if they can pet them. Walt puts on his *No we can't give you a discount on your fence because your neighbor's kid can still throw a soccer ball over it* face and tells them to check on social media for opportunities to meet the goats.

Once there's a lull in their customers, Skylar puts together an impromptu tasting board for his dad. When Aroon is complimentary about everything—downright effusive about the lavender one, even—the happiness and relief on Skylar's face makes that ache spider through Walt again. There's something about their interactions that's... what?

Healing in progress. That's what it is. You can see where all the cracks were in their relationship, and how they've accepted the things about the other that they can't change and are making an honest effort to meet each other where they are, instead of where they wish each other would be.

That's so far out of reach for Walt with his parents that he wouldn't even know where to begin. It didn't seem so terrifying and insurmountable when he thought Mario was on his side. Now that the ground under that friendship feels more like quicksand than granite, it's cast all his future comings-out in uncertainty.

"Skylar says you remodel houses?" Aroon asks as he smooths strawberry goat cheese over a cracker.

Shooting a surprised look at Skylar, Walt says, "It's more of a hobby."

"He's amazing," Skylar says proudly. "You should see some of the work he's done. It could totally be a career."

Walt nudges Skylar's foot under the table. "You have to say that."

"Why?" Skylar's crooked smile makes Walt's stomach swoop. He hopes that never stops happening.

"Because." When Skylar nudges Walt's foot in return, Walt wants to grab his hands under the table too. "People always say nice things about the person they're in l—"

Just in time, he realizes they're in front of Skylar's dad, and maybe Skylar's not the kind of guy who's cool with his significant other casually dropping the L word in front of a parent.

Skylar pops a blob of goat cheese into his mouth. "I'd say it even if I wasn't in love with you because it's true."

Aroon looks between them. "You two seem serious." There's a careful note in his voice, and Walt isn't surprised. Not when his son has already been married and divorced. Now here comes Walt, and how is a parent supposed to know whether this guy is better than the last one?

Walt reaches across the table and clasps Skylar's hand. Unfortunately he forgot that Skylar has goat cheese all over that hand, which is now squished between their fingers. Skylar grins and makes it easy for Walt to say, "Yeah, I'm pretty serious."

Aroon regards him. "You help him out with the farm?"

"Dad," Skylar sighs.

"I get up and do chores with him before I leave for the day," Walt answers steadily. "And I do whatever needs to get done when I get home."

"Well." Aroon licks cheese off his fingers. "That's the kind of thing I like hearing."

"Yes, Dad, my boyfriend does his share of the chores," Skylar says, looking vaguely amused. "It's a perfect match, obviously."

Aroon gives Skylar an extremely parental look—that expression full of pride, worry, love, and exasperation that parents seem to do better than anyone else. "I'm glad he works alongside you. I meant I like hearing you call Skylar's home your home, Walt."

Walt's not expecting that. Did he call Blue Skies Farm *home*? He did, didn't he? It's not just Blue Skies Farm—it's Skylar. *Skylar* feels like home. Sure, Windham's the kind of place Walt would like to live, but even if Skylar wanted to pull up stakes and move to Brooklyn, Walt would want to go with him.

It rocks him, knowing the most important thing that makes his home isn't a big yard, or a solidly built house from the 1950s, but Skylar.

It's a big realization for a small-town makers' market. Walt eats some more cheese to cover the fact that he has no idea what to say.

"I like hearing it too," Skylar says, gripping Walt's hand hard. Walt meets his eyes and sees nothing but fierce love. It's probably inappropriate to think this while he's in front of Skylar's dad, but Walt can't wait to get Skylar home so Sky can fuck him into their mattress.

Yeah, definitely inappropriate.

He clears his throat. "Well, it's true. I mean, yeah. It is. Home, I mean."

That hardly qualified as a complete thought, let alone a sentence. Before he can get better words out, a woman says from behind him, "Excuse me, can you recommend the best cheese for a groom's dinner?"

The voice is ingrained into the folds of Walt's brain, but he can't process the fact that he's hearing it right now. How could his mom's voice be here? That would mean his mom was here, and that's impossible.

He turns his head and faces the proof that it's completely possible for his mother to be in Windham, because she's standing right there with his father.

Chapter Twenty-Nine

HIS PARENTS. His parents are *here*. Not just in Windham, but at the Spring Fling Market. The Spring Fling Market, where Walt is currently sitting with his boyfriend and his boyfriend's father, talking about how serious this relationship is. His mom looks gleeful that she surprised him.

Walt doesn't think he's a bad person, but he can think of enough stupid shit he's said or done that makes this feel like karma.

"Mom. Dad." His voice comes out too croaky. Even if Mom wasn't super attuned to her children's emotional states, she'd be able to tell something's up. The trick is to talk too much for her to ask what it is. "What are you doing here? Why didn't you text? How did you even know I was here?"

"You told us about it! And this was our weekend to visit Tad in the city, remember?" She gives him a meaningful look, and it takes Walt a second to realize she's waiting for him to stand up and hug her. He does, feeling guilty it took him so long.

"You should've told me you were coming," he repeats. Or, wait, he didn't say that, did he? He's just thinking it on a loop. *You should have told me you were coming so I could hide the life I'm building here from you.*

Shame twists his stomach, and this is a new experience—it's not because he's ashamed of his desire for men, it's because he's ashamed that he wants to hide the best thing that's ever happened to him from his parents.

Dad clears his throat. "Are you going to introduce us to your friend?"

Did Walt imagine a tiny hesitation before Dad said *friend?* "Uh, yeah. Sorry." He looks back at Skylar and reaches for him, then stops himself and shoves his hands in his pockets. That's not better. Instead he lets them hang at his sides as Skylar gets to his feet. "Mom, Dad, this is"—*my boyfriend*—"Skylar. The guy I've been staying with. Skylar, this is my mom and dad."

This must look terrible to Aroon—*Yes sir, I'm serious about your son!* Right, so serious that his parents have never met Skylar, let alone know that he's so much more than just the guy Walt's been staying with.

Dad gives Skylar a hearty handshake and says, "Good to finally meet you, Skylar. I'm Bill, and this is Walt's mom, Kathleen."

"It's good to meet you too!" Skylar starts to offer his hand to Mom, but her posture, tight and distant, must make him think twice.

Mom smiles, but it looks off. "See, Bill? Lynn Berdeau's daughter was just confused."

Walt stares at her, forgetting about the death glare he's sure Aroon is boring into his back. What does Lynn Berdeau's daughter have to do with anything? Walt hasn't seen Nicole Berdeau in years; she was in his high school class and got into MIT, then never moved back. She's probably still in Boston, where Walt's never been.

Wait, that's not right. He *has* seen her. She was at Ally's baby shower, sitting on the other side of the room. He never had the chance to say hi. Her presence didn't click until this second; he registered her as someone he didn't know, but no, it was her. She laughed at the kids repeating *fucking butt.*

Which means she saw him put his arm around Skylar. And she told her mother, who told *his* mother, who's now standing here daring him to contradict her. Does she know he knows?

The Walt he's always been would defuse this situation, smooth it over so they're not on the brink of launching emotional nukes at each other. The Walt he is now wonders why telling his parents that he's in love with an amazing man has to be an act of war.

"What did Nicole tell her mom?" Walt asks. "She was valedictorian, so I don't think she gets confused easily."

Skylar gives him a look that Walt can't decipher, something between trepidation and surprise, and maybe a little bit of *you don't have to do this,* but Walt's pretty sure he does. He's pretty sure he can't lie about who he is to his parents for another minute, not just for Skylar's sake, but for his own.

"Well," Mom says, a splutter in her tone. "She said—it's silly. It's not worth repeating."

"No, I want to hear," Walt says.

"I shouldn't have said anything," Mom says, touching her hair. She looks at Dad, who won't meet her eyes. He meets Walt's, though, just for a second, just enough for a beat of understanding to pass between them.

Walt's insides shrivel with instinctive panic, the leftover response of a confused, embarrassed teenage boy who would have done anything not to let his father down. It took a long time to grow up and stop being that ashamed kid, but Walt's finally there.

He looks at his dad as he says, "Mom, please tell me what Lynn Berdeau said to you about me."

The silence might be the most painful of Walt's entire life. Finally, voice quavering, Mom replies, "She said that Nicole told her you brought a—a male friend to Ally's baby shower."

"A boyfriend?" Somehow, Walt's voice comes out steady, which is in complete opposition to how he feels. His heart is pounding so hard that he's amazed he can breathe without it crushing his lungs. "Nicole told her mom she saw me with a boyfriend at Ally's baby shower, right?"

"She was confused," Mom repeats.

A chair scrapes on the asphalt behind Walt, and he glances over his shoulder to see Aroon attempting to sneak away, a guilty look on his face. He coughs and mumbles something about this seeming like a family thing. At least he doesn't look like he despises Walt, but that's such a faint silver lining that it hardly matters anymore.

This isn't how Walt imagined coming out to his parents. The scene had never been fully formed in his mind, but he sort of liked the idea of doing it at his house, having them over for dinner. He would have grilled in the backyard, and they could have eaten dinner outside. Mom would've had a glass of wine; he and Dad would've had beer. Skylar wouldn't have been there, but Walt would call him the second his parents left for home.

Okay, so maybe he did have a pretty clear image of it.

He breathes deep through his nose and his heart slows. "She wasn't confused." Reaching for Skylar's hand, he holds it tight and adds, "Skylar and I are together. I'm attracted to men."

The air between all of them is so still and brittle that it feels like it could shatter. Skylar grips Walt's hand even though Walt's palm is getting steadily slicker with sweat, and Walt's chest swells with love, urgent and fierce, and he just wants his parents to *understand*.

"I know you're probably surprised," he begins.

Mom's crack of laughter is whip sharp. "Surprised!" she cries. "How could you say something like that?"

Somehow, Walt's hand gets sweatier. "Say you're surprised?"

"That you're attracted to—that you—" She shakes her head, her mouth pursed like she's eating something sour. "You like women, Walter! You've always liked women! You've had so many girlfriends. When you were little, you were always talking about all the girls you wanted to marry!"

"I was a little kid," Walt says, trying to keep his tone level. "I didn't even know what being married meant."

"You can't feel that way!" Mom says again, her voice rising higher.

"Kathy," Dad says, putting a hand on her shoulder. "Let's go somewhere quieter. Walt, we can talk about this over there—"

She shrugs out of his grip, her eyes bright with angry tears. Oh, Jesus fuck, he made his mom cry. That's every son's nightmare, right? "I don't need to go anywhere. I came here to see my son!"

"You're seeing me," Walt says, and he doesn't mean to sound like he's soothing a wild animal, but that's how his voice comes out. "Do you want to see the kids?"

Her eyes widen. "Kids?!"

Dad looks horrified, too, so Walt scrambles to clarify, "Goat kids! Not kid kids. Like children. Not children. Wow, no, we don't have kids yet."

Skylar squeezes Walt's hand, but it's hard to tell if it's a comforting squeeze or more of a please-stop-fucking-this-up squeeze. A text from his phone buzzes through the bones of Walt's wrist where it's pressed against his pocket, and it's really tempting to use it as a distraction.

"Yet!" his mom echoes, laughing in that frantic, wild way that means the conversation is so off the rails that there's no chance of recovery.

"No, I mean—we entered them." Oh god, does that sound like they're into bestiality? "In the competition! Entered them into the competition today."

Why is he even engaging with this?

"I thought you were spending so much time down here because you'd met someone!" Tears spill out of Mom's eyes and slip down her cheeks.

Walt's phone buzzes again. His hand, clutched in Skylar's, is slippery with sweat, and the last thing he wants to do is fight with his mom while she's crying, but he can't let that go. "Mom, I *did* meet someone. Please don't—just please don't."

"I thought you met a *woman*." More tears. Walt's phone keeps buzzing. They're attracting attention now, people around them pausing to see what's causing the drama. "Not a man! How could both of my sons turn out to be—"

Her voice strangles itself to nothing. Good thing, Walt thinks distantly, because she didn't say something that she couldn't take back.

"Kathy," Dad says again.

She ignores him. "Did I do something wrong? This is my fault somehow, isn't it?"

The buzzing of Walt's phone has become so insistent that he takes it out of his pocket to turn it off. When he sees the notifications on the screen, his stomach gives a nasty twist. Mario has called three times and texted several more. The last one says *Answer your phone*

Walt jams the phone back in his pocket. That's just what this situation needs—a conversation with Mario. From no contact to *answer your phone*, which obviously Walt isn't going to do while his mom's doing the whole "what did I do wrong to turn my children gay" song and dance.

No wonder it took Tad ten years of living hundreds of miles away and meeting the love of his life for him to come out to their parents.

And suddenly, Walt has had it. For his whole life, he's done everything in his power to be a good son. Mom didn't want him going away for college? He stayed nearby. Dad wanted him to get a useful degree? He majored in Business. They didn't want him to move far away like Tad did to pursue better opportunities? He put down roots in Watertown.

For every one of the thirty-three years he's been on this planet, Walt has been who his parents wanted him to be, and he feels the bands holding that mask in place snap.

"So you're saying I turned out *wrong*," Walt says loudly. "Tad too. We're wrong because we're not straight."

His voice carries. All the color drains from Mom's face as she glances around. "Let's not talk about this here."

"You wanted to talk about it here a minute ago, so let's talk about it." A hard knot of repression and expectations is unfurling into something wild in his chest—so wild that it might be hysterical, but Walt doesn't care. "What do you think you did to make your kids turn out the wrong way, Mom?"

"Walt," Dad says in the same tone he's been saying *Kathy*, like if he just says someone's name, that's the only effort he needs to put in. He's such a voice of reason that they'll see the disapproval on his face and they'll stop whatever silly, stupid thing they're doing.

"You wanna chime in, Dad?" Walt gives him a hard, blazing look. "I know *you* didn't want me turning out queer. I'd say thanks for not outing me to anyone, except I'm pretty sure you never told anyone because you were too ashamed."

Now Mom's bloodless, agape face turns to Dad. "You knew he was… homosexual?"

"We don't need to talk about family business with the whole world watching," Dad says, gruff and uncomfortable.

Pressure on Walt's hand tethers him to his surroundings again. That's Skylar, squeezing, trying to bring him back. "People are videoing," Skylar says in a tone that's obviously supposed to be bright and cheerful.

In his pocket, Walt's phone vibrates with another phone call. Fucking fine. Shit can't get worse, so sure, he'll take the fucking call from Mario.

Without a word to his parents, he lets go of Skylar's hand and heads for the edges of the market, squeezing by several people holding up their phones to capture the whole sorry scene. When he gets far enough away, he mashes his thumb on the missed call notification. The lack of physical feedback is incredibly unsatisfying. He misses corded phones and the way you could make the motions of calling someone an outlet for your feelings.

The phone rings several times before Mario answers, which just pisses Walt off more. "Hey," Mario says when the line clicks, as though he called four hundred times just to shoot the shit.

"Hi," Walt replies tightly. His battery is almost dead, so hopefully this is fast.

"Were you ignoring me or something? I sent you a bunch of texts."

Walt considers and discards *I was in the middle of something* and goes with, "It's that market I told you about." Which seems like forever ago. "Spring Fling."

"Huh?"

"Spring Fling. The thing with the contest?"

"You definitely never told me about that," Mario says with a confidence that Walt suddenly finds grating.

"Yeah, I did." A group of people walks by, talking and laughing loudly, and Walt hunches his shoulders as he turns away from them.

"You didn't. I'd remember something like that. It sounds like a middle school dance." Mario laughs, but it's not very nice.

The memory of texting Mario the information is clear as day in Walt's memory, so he says, "I have the texts. I told you. Skylar and I entered the competition together." Even as the words leave his mouth, he knows there's no point. Every time he's had one of these conversations with Mario over the years, there's no winning. If Mario doesn't remember Walt saying anything about it, then it didn't happen.

"Seriously? You have to be right so bad that you're digging through our texts?"

"No, I don't care about—I just know I told you!" And some stupid part of Walt thought that maybe Mario would care enough to make the drive down here to see what Walt's been doing for the past month and a half.

There's a loud sigh, then Mario says, "Whatever. That's not the reason I called."

It occurs to Walt that his parents can probably see him standing here, which is the last thing he wants. He heads to the vendor parking area as he asks, "Why did you call?"

"I want to talk about what happened when you were here the other week," Mario says.

The weight that's been steadily building on Walt's chest for the past fifteen minutes lessens. He hasn't come up with a way to start this conversation. It's good they're finally going to clear the air.

Leaning against Skylar's truck, Walt says, "Yeah, okay. Cool. We should talk about that." Words flip through his head, attempts to open the conversation in a way that makes it clear he's coming into this ready to apologize, and be conciliatory, and make sure everything's fine at the end and no one has any hurt feelings.

Except him, right? Because a lot of these conversations over the years have ended with Walt's feelings being hurt, and him pushing that aside as a casualty of maintaining good relationships with the people he cares about.

So even though it goes against every one of his instincts, he stays silent. Several beats go by while he grips the phone tight. Silence. Maybe a delay with the signal? Except no, because Mario makes a sound over the line and snaps, "So… you're not going to say anything."

It's almost enough to jolt Walt into an apology. But that part of him that stayed silent gets more determined, grabs him by the shoulders and shakes him and demands, *What are you getting out of this friendship?*

"You wanted to talk," Walt says. "I figured you were going to start."

"So you cut off communication with me for a month—"

"It's been two weeks, man," Walt cuts in. "You know it's been two weeks."

"Yeah, well, it feels like it's been a month!" Mario retorts. "You cut off communication with me and you're not even going to apologize for that?"

"I didn't know what to say." Walt picks over and discards words like he's picking up stones on a beach, looking for the perfect one to fling into the water. Does he want one that's going to slip smoothly into the still surface of a lake, or one that's going to make the biggest splash possible and send waves all the way to the other shore? "The whole thing really took me by surprise."

Mario makes a frustrated sound. "How do you think I felt? My best friend turns gay and doesn't tell me? That's a huge thing to drop on someone."

"I'm bi, not gay, and I didn't turn—" Walt's temples pound with anger and stress and unhappiness. "Are you mad at me because I didn't come out to you sooner?"

There's a silence and Walt knows he's right. But instead of sounding ashamed, Mario says, "You're supposed to be my best buddy. I can't believe you kept that from me."

"You're making this about you," Walt says, just to make sure he's understanding, because he doesn't want to.

Another frustrated noise. "Stop twisting my words."

"I'm not, though." Walt's heart pounds but if he's going to throw a rock, he's going to lob a huge one. "Me coming out was about me. It had nothing to do with you. My sexual orientation and when I decided to tell you? Not about you, Mario."

Mario sputters. "You know what? It's been pretty obvious lately that our friendship doesn't mean much. You've been cutting me off and this is just the latest thing."

"You were the second person I came out to! I made a special trip just to tell you!"

"Yeah, well, I didn't like the way you told me, okay?"

"*You* didn't like the way *I* came out." Walt laughs, because it sounds like a joke. It's not. He knows Mario better than anyone else in his life, and this isn't Mario's kind of joke. "I don't know how to say this any other way, but I don't care. Do you want me to apologize or something?"

"Yeah," Mario says bluntly. "I figured if you weren't going to call me and apologize, I'd call you."

Walt clenches his free hand into a fist and grinds his knuckles into his sternum, willing his heart to stay inside his ribs. "You need to apologize to me. You were a dick to Skylar and me at Ally's shower, and you're being a dick now."

Mario lets out a loud, angry laugh. "You're being a big fucking baby. I've been a damn good friend to you for a long time. I let you practice your HGTV shit in my house! And I've looked at all your stupid pictures of your projects, when you were lying to me all this time!"

Under his knuckles, Walt's heart stops. "My stupid pictures," he repeats dully. The fight roaring through him abruptly flickers out. "Sure. Yeah. Sorry I wasted your time."

"You sound like your brother with that passive aggressive shit," Mario snarls.

Walt closes his eyes. "I gotta go. I'll—" *Talk to you later*, he was going to say, but will he? Is this what it feels like when a friendship founders on rocks and sinks? "Give Ally my best," he says instead.

"If you fucking hang up on me—" Mario starts.

"Bye, Mario."

"Your boyfriend's Instagram followers wouldn't be too happy to know your relationship isn't even real!" Mario shouts.

The cold that runs down Walt's spine is worse than any of the whipping snow from the blizzard that brought Skylar and him together. "It *is* real."

"Is it?" There's smugness in Mario's tone that makes Walt want to put his fist through something. He should've hung up. He should've fucking hung up instead of giving Mario the attention he wanted. "Because Tad said you and Skylar are faking a relationship."

"That's—no. It's not fake." *Hang up!* Walt's brain screams, but his mouth keeps talking. "People assumed we were together in this one picture he posted, and it got so much attention that I suggested we pretend for Insta. But it was real within like, twenty-four hours."

"All I'm hearing is you lied to people for clout." The smugness in Mario's voice has a mean edge. "It would really suck for his little business if people found out and weren't happy about it."

That mean edge would still crumple under the weight of a really good rock. Walt's just not sure he has a good one anymore. The splash is settling back down to little ripples, and he's still stuck here feeling like he needs to apologize to minimize the damage. "Skylar doesn't have anything to do with this, so leave him alone. We're together. You don't have dirt on us."

"I guess it depends on how I feel," Mario says. "Bye."

The line goes dead. Walt leaves the phone pressed against the side of his face for a second until the helix of his ear protests. Head pounding, Walt rests his forehead against the cold glass of the truck's window. He just… needs a minute. Between his parents and the scene in there, and Mario—

A minute. That's it.

The scuff of a shoe on the asphalt makes him raise his head. In the reflection on the truck window, he sees Skylar, mouth set and thin and eyes wide.

Chapter Thirty

VIDEOS ARE already sprouting online of Walt coming out to his parents. That's why Skylar came to find him. That, and he's worried. He wanted to give Walt space. Except Skylar's not very good at giving Walt space, it turns out, especially not when he started getting tagged in people's Instagram Stories.

He doesn't expect to find Walt standing at the truck, looking like he's having an even worse time than he just did with his parents, and saying into his phone in a tight voice, "That's—no. It's not fake. People assumed we were together in this one picture he posted, and it got so much attention that I suggested we pretend for Insta, but it was real within like, twenty-four hours."

There's a pause. Walt's facing away from Skylar, but it doesn't matter that Skylar can't see his face. The tension and despair radiating along the taut cords of his neck and fanning across his shoulders are as clear as any facial expression. Why is he talking about their short-lived plan to fake date? *Who* is he talking to about it in this obviously distressed way?

In a harder voice, Walt says, "Skylar doesn't have anything to do with this, so leave him alone. We're together. You don't have dirt on us."

Something unpleasant crawls up Skylar's spine, and his stomach tightens. Whoever it is, they're threatening him. What? Who could he have pissed off enough that they're *threatening* him? And to Walt? This doesn't make any sense.

Well, Walt's parents probably hate him, but they don't need to call Walt when they're still here. Probably. If Skylar's being totally honest, he came looking for Walt partly to make sure he wasn't within a fifty-foot radius of them.

Walt drops his phone to his side and his head against the truck. When he raises it, their eyes meet in the reflection on the window.

"Shit," Walt says and turns around. "Sky—"

"Are you okay?" Skylar's moving toward him without thinking. If Walt's neck and shoulders were tight with tension, his face is worse, drawn into unhappy lines from his forehead all the way to his mouth. "Who was that? Why are they threatening us?"

Walt closes his eyes and takes a long breath. When he opens them, he asks, "Are my parents still here? No, sorry. It's not your job to keep track of them for me. Shit," he says again, more forcefully.

The light seems too cheerful and perfect for this moment. Afternoon sunshine is spangling across the mountains, just starting to gild their tops, and the sky is bright spring blue.

"Who was on the phone?" Skylar asks again.

Walt rubs a hand through his hair before letting it drop to his side. "Mario."

At this point, Skylar's pretty comfortable saying he doesn't like Mario, but the dark anger on Walt's face is a surprise.

"Mario? What is he threatening us about?"

"The fake dating thing."

How did Mario even know about that? Whatever; that's the least of Skylar's concerns. The chill that went down his spine before becomes a fist of ice in his stomach. "Why? Isn't he supposed to be your best friend?"

Walt shakes his head. It looks like disbelief, like maybe he doesn't even know he's doing it. "Yeah, I don't... I'm not sure if we're friends anymore. He's pissed about... I don't know. Me being bi? Me not telling him I'm bi?"

"You did tell him you're bi," Skylar says, trying to process the absurdity of this.

"Yeah, I guess I didn't tell him soon enough." When Skylar lets out a disbelieving laugh, Walt adds, "He's threatening to, I don't know, expose our fake dating scheme on social media. Even though we're dating for real. It's stupid."

The fist of ice in Skylar's stomach expands. These last few weeks, he hasn't worried so much about losing the farm, because it's finally making money. They're not in the black yet, but Skylar can see a light at the end of the tunnel, and it all started with that picture of Walt and him. The world loves #farmboyfriends. It would love #farmboyfriends who faked a relationship for money a lot less. "It's stupid, but if he got traction, it could create a pretty huge headache for us."

Looking unhappy, Walt says, "Mario thinks so."

"Yeah, he's right." That ice is crawling up Skylar's throat now. Losing the farm means losing the animals. Losing little Agatha and Billy, and Jane who worked so hard to bring them into the world. "Does he want something? Is he just being an asshole?"

Angry fear thrums through Skylar, and he doesn't understand how Walt looks and sounds so defeated. "I don't know what he wants." Walt shakes his head. "Or, maybe...."

"Maybe what?" Skylar asks. And okay, he's a little sharp, but Walt doesn't seem to care about this as much as he should.

Chewing his lip for a second, Walt says, "He might just want me to apologize."

"For?"

"For—I don't know!" Finally, Walt sounds frustrated. "For not making everything about him, I guess! For being bi without him knowing? Maybe for pursuing my dreams? Maybe for finally being happy when I'm pretty sure he hasn't been for a long time?"

Skylar exhales a huge breath. "You don't owe anyone an apology for any of that."

"Thank you," Walt says, relief tumbling from his mouth. Reaching for Skylar's hand, he adds, "I was trying to hang on to that fact, but I started second-guessing myself, like maybe I was rubbing his face in my happiness or something. Or like I kept everything from him because I wanted to cut him out of my life, even though I definitely never wanted to cut him out of my life, and I—dammit." He squeezes Skylar's hand. "Just, thanks."

"But... maybe you need to talk to him and tell him you're sorry," Skylar adds. When Walt looks at him, flabbergasted, Skylar feels like a jerk, but not enough to stop him from going on, "Not like, an *apology* apology. But that you're sorry for making him feel like that."

"How is that not the same as an apology?" Walt asks.

Discomfort runs a dull blade along the back of Skylar's neck, but he can't stop remembering Jane struggling to kid, and what might have happened to her at another farm where she was just another nameless animal. "You'd know you didn't do anything wrong. But, you know. Maybe just say the words to smooth things over with him."

"Why?"

How is Walt not getting this? "Because he threatened to spread the fake dating thing around specifically to hurt my business, and that's something I don't want to happen?"

Walt squeezes his hand. "People know we're together for real. And if he really wants to post that our relationship is fake, we'll just say he's lying."

"They'd just think we're lying," Skylar says, trying really, really hard to be patient. The last thing Walt needs right now is someone else making him feel like shit. But he has to get why this is bad, right?

There's not any one reason Skylar stopped using social media, but this is a big one. The proliferation of lies that fit more neatly into what people want to believe than the truth does; the differences of opinion that people wield like moral cudgels; the personal beefs that turn into harassment campaigns. Skylar hates all of it.

It wouldn't take much to change Blue Skies Farm's image. Skylar's seen it happen to his friends. He once consoled one of them through a nerve-wracking follower bleed when someone spread lies about everything from their political opinions to their sexual habits, and they eventually had to go on an anti-anxiety med because they were so afraid they'd irrevocably damaged their career prospects in the animation world. All over a disagreement about who a fictional character in a TV show should be romantically paired up with, too!

He takes a deep breath. "You can say whatever you want online, and it doesn't matter if it's true. The only thing that matters is if people believe it."

"Sky." Walt's tone is gentle, which doesn't seem fair, considering what he's been through today. It seems especially unfair when Skylar's heart is pounding. When had that started? "I'm not going to apologize when I didn't do anything wrong."

"But he's going to ruin our business." Skylar's grip on Walt's hand tightens, not because he's seeking comfort, but because of his pounding heart and the tightness in his chest.

Walt shakes his head. It's like they're caught in a reverse feedback loop—the more panicked Skylar gets, the calmer Walt becomes. "He's not going to hurt Blue Skies Farm. People can see how real our relationship is. They can come here and see for themselves if they think there's a chance we're not for real."

"Walt!" Skylar pulls his hand away. "That's not how it works! No one's going to say, 'Oh, I'm not sure if I can believe Instagram User MarioSucks, let me fact check him by taking a road trip to Windham, New York.' No one's going to do that!"

"People here will back us up."

How is Walt so *calm*? How does he not see how completely and utterly wrong he is? How can he not see the damage this will do, not just to the business, but to the animals counting on them?

"It doesn't matter, that's what I'm trying to tell you!" Skylar doesn't mean to yell, but somehow, he is. "It doesn't matter if we tell the truth, or if people who know us personally tell the truth! The only thing that matters is *who people believe*."

Walt flinches and Skylar feels like the biggest jerk on the planet. "Why are you so convinced that people are going to believe Mario? And even if they do, so what? Who cares what they believe?"

"I do!" Skylar's voice bounces off the surrounding cars. "It's my farm, it's my business, and I can't afford to lose all the customers I'm getting through social media! We have to start posting more content. Or better content. We need to post enough that even if Mario tries to out us, we drown him out."

The lesbian couple who make felt cat toys walks by on the way to their car, carrying plastic totes full of merchandise. On the other side of the park, people will be starting to pack up, which is what Skylar should be doing.

Walt shoves his hands into his pockets. "I don't want to document every single second of our relationship for social media. And I don't think that's the answer to this, anyway."

A small part of Skylar's brain tells him to take a deep breath and walk away, maybe see if anyone's selling cookies at an end-of-day discount. Instead, he says, "Faking a relationship was *your* idea in the first place. I never would have thought of using a fake boyfriend without you suggesting it. And now you're getting squeamish about putting our actual real relationship online because it doesn't matter for you, but this is my livelihood! I need that content to keep driving people to the farm's website, so—so—"

Fuck, he's totally lost the thread of this conversation, and mortifyingly, he's tearing up in his growing panic. "So I just need you to apologize to Mario, or whatever you need to do to keep him from blowing up Blue Skies Farm!" He fumbles for his phone. "And we should post a picture of us right now."

He's writing the caption and hashtags in his head already. *Great day at Spring Fling with the bf! He's the G.O.A.T.!#farmboyfriends #smalltownromance #makersmarket #shopsmall*

Before Skylar can open his camera, Walt steps away. "I don't think this is going to make a very good picture."

"Yes it is!" Skylar finally pulls up the camera app. "Anyway it doesn't matter if it's a good time for a picture or not. You have to feed the algorithm. That's how it works!"

"Sky, you're crying," Walt says.

"I'm obviously not!" He obviously is.

Taking another step back, Walt says, "I really don't want to start putting up fake content about us."

There's a clatter as something falls on Skylar's boots and bounces off the asphalt. It takes him a second to realize his hand is empty because he dropped his phone, which is now laying screen down, camera ready to take a picture of blackness. And the reason he dropped his phone is because his fists are clenched at his sides. "It was *your idea to post fake content about us*!" he yells, his voice cracking.

"Well, I was wrong, okay?" Walt looks exhausted and shattered. "It was a bad idea!"

"What else are you going to decide is a bad idea?" Skylar demands. "Coming out, since it's not all just hearts and rainbows from people on the internet?"

His brain feels like a derailing train. Every word coming out of his mouth is carnage. This was what it was like the night Cody said that they weren't working, that he wanted a divorce. It was the pity in his eyes when Skylar pulled out that Mignon McLaughlin quote that sent Skylar over the edge. "A successful marriage requires falling in love many times, always with the same person," was pretty much the most last-ditch thing he could have said to save a marriage that had been over for a while, but the pity and Cody's little head shake made Skylar lose it.

Now he's doing it to Walt, and the flood of anger and devastation and panic snaps something in him. "I have to pack up the table," he says.

Walt opens his mouth, and Skylar gets ready to rebuff his offer of help. "Okay," Walt says.

Wait. What? He's not going to offer? That's—well, that's good! That's what Skylar wanted!

There's a thick, sludgy silence between them before Walt drops his gaze and walks away. Something wild claws its way into Skylar's throat, but he turns around and marches back to the market.

Chapter Thirty-One

HIS DAD helps him pack up, insisting on carrying everything to the truck while Skylar deals with the goat kids. Agatha and Billy are cuddled together, sleeping off their big day. They're adorable, and Skylar resists, barely, the temptation to hug them close. If he hugs his goats, he'll burst into tears again, and that's not something he needs to see immortalized on the internet. It doesn't seem possible at this point that it wouldn't be.

When he doesn't have them anymore because Mario killed his business, he'll be able to watch himself sobbing and clinging to them. Great.

"Let me take you out to dinner," Dad says once they're both in the truck. Skylar shakes his head and turns the key in the ignition. The engine rumbles to life. "Skylar, we're going to dinner. Do whatever farm stuff you need to do with your cows back there, and we'll drive out to that diner on Route 87."

The laugh Skylar lets out is watery and snotty. "What diner on Route 87?"

"I don't know. We'll find one. This is greasy spoon territory."

Skylar laughs again, somehow in an even snottier way, and swipes his sleeve across his eyes. "They're goats, but okay."

Somehow, his dad hasn't asked him what's wrong or what happened. Or where Walt is, for that matter. Which is good, because Skylar doesn't know where Walt is, and every time he thinks about texting or calling him, he starts shaking too much to go through with it.

Back at Blue Skies Farm, Walt's truck is still in the driveway, which is... something. If it had been gone, Skylar wouldn't have been surprised. He was expecting it.

After he gets the kids settled in the barn and feeds the rest of the animals, he climbs back in the truck, where his dad has been waiting. "Head east on Route 23," his dad says.

Skylar put his hands on the steering wheel. "Where are we going?"

"Just trust me, kid." He leans over and brushes Skylar's hair off his forehead. "I may not know about this farm stuff, but I can find a halfway decent diner."

Even though Skylar almost bursts into tears, he also laughs, starts the truck, and heads off into the unknown.

THEY DO, in fact, end up at a diner off Route 87, with neon lights illuminating the building, vinyl booths along the walls, and thick, spiral-bound, laminated menus. It's just like all the institutions he grew up with back in his Jersey suburb.

They both get breakfast for dinner. Not that anyone has to explain why breakfast for dinner is comforting, but after Skylar's mom died, it was about the only thing his dad was able to cook.

Once they both have their plates full of pancakes and bacon, his dad asks, "Want to talk about it?"

Cutting into his pancakes with the edge of his fork, Skylar replies, "You already know it's another one of my screw-ups."

His dad slathers his pancakes with the perfect little scoop of butter before drowning them in fake maple syrup. "You don't have screw-ups." When Skylar laughs incredulously, his dad eats a too-big bite of pancake and says with his mouth full, "You don't. Geez, kid, you have your own business. And you couldn't choose an easy one to start. You had to go and buy a farm and get a bunch of animals. Did you ever even see a live animal when you were a kid?"

"We had squirrels," Skylar says. The pancakes are fluffy enough to give him a little sunburst of joy. "And come on, Dad. I'm twenty-eight and divorced. I dropped out of a great college to go live in the country and devote my entire life to a hobby farm, which you hate. You wanted me to have a nine to five and try to swing a work from home position. And I couldn't handle running the farm by myself, so you were probably right."

"No I wasn't," Dad says. Skylar gives him a surprised look, and he looks down at his plate, concentrating harder on eating pancakes than anyone really needs to. Finally, he goes on, "Don't get me wrong, my heart was in the right place. I just wanted you to have an easier life than your grandparents did. I didn't want you giving up your youth to a business that just takes and takes and uses you up by the time you hit forty."

There's an old, knowing pain in Dad's voice. Skylar hesitates before he says, "That's not how Blue Skies Farm is. I love it."

"Yeah, I know you do. I couldn't stop seeing myself in you, working at the restaurant, not having time for anything. All my white friends were going to college, figuring out who they were. You know I had to miss Nirvana at the New York Coliseum? We had a big dinner rush that night at the restaurant. I gave up my ticket so a friend of a friend could go." A little smile appears on his dad's face. "I guess it worked out in the end, though. The friend of a friend ended up being your mom."

"Seriously?" This isn't a story Skylar's ever heard. He always thought his parents met through *their* parents.

"Seriously. We didn't know that until our second date, though. After we made the connection, it was like...." He shrugs and pours more syrup over his pancakes, even though they've reached saturation. "Fate. Close enough to fate for me, at least."

Skylar's father has always seemed like one of the least romantic people on the planet. The soft, wistful shine in his eyes tells a different story. "I miss her a lot," Skylar mumbles.

"Me too." Dad reaches over and pats Skylar's shoulder. "She'd be so proud of you. I was terrified I was going to screw everything up, but you turned into one hell of a man."

"Twenty-eight and divorced," Skylar reminds him, though the praise, and Dad saying that Mom would be proud of him, stokes an ember that's tucked into his ribs.

"Do you think it would be better if you were stuck in an unhappy marriage?" Dad asks. "Is that success? Sticking with something and making yourself miserable? Cutting your losses isn't failing. You and Cody made each other happy until you didn't. I'm glad you got divorced. Any parent who'd rather see their kid stuck in a bad marriage because they shouldn't give up or some shit like that is a bad parent."

Tears prickle behind Skylar's eyes. "It felt like failure. And I'm flirting with bankruptcy too, by the way. I'm horrible at the business part of running a business. Walt's good at it, but I might have wrecked that. And god, I shouldn't depend on another person to keep my business afloat, should I?"

"Nope," Dad says.

Which is what Jett told him all along. He owes Jett a drink or three. Maybe a gift card to a spa.

"It felt like *our* farm with Walt, though. It didn't feel like him figuring things out for me. It was like we were doing it together. Like we each had something we were good at, and we were a team."

"What's with all the past tense? You're talking like it's over."

Shame squirms in Skylar's stomach. "I said… a bunch of stuff. I wouldn't blame Walt if he wanted to break things off. It's not like we've known each other that long." Even if it feels like they have. Even if every part of Skylar feels settled and right with Walt in his life.

Dad makes a noise. "Sure you would. I would too. No one gets to break my son's heart."

"Who said anything about my heart getting broken?" Skylar mumbles. It's maybe the least convincing thing he's ever said in his life.

"Me. I saw how you two look at each other. And I think you shouldn't rush so fast to assuming the worst. Walt didn't seem like a guy who was going to run off just because you guys had a fight."

Skylar picks at his bacon, mostly crumbling it instead of eating it. "I wouldn't even call it a fight. I kind of had a freakout."

"About?"

"It's stupid."

"I'm your dad. I've seen you do plenty of stupid things."

Skylar can't help cracking a smile. "Thanks a lot."

With a shrug, his dad says, "There's nothing dumber than a teenage boy. That's a life lesson for you for if you have kids."

That makes Skylar's chest hurt. Kids. Yeah. He'd like that someday.

Giving Skylar a very parental look, his dad says, "So? Do you want to talk about it or what? I might actually have some good advice for you."

With a groan, Skylar summarizes the whole thing. The short-lived fake dating scheme, their plan to use social media to boost Blue Skies Farm's profile, the stuff with Mario, and everything Skylar said to Walt in the parking lot, even though it's mortifying to repeat.

When he's done, he adds, "Oh, and people videoed him coming out to his parents, so they pretty much outed him to the whole world. And I know that's not my fault, but he might be upset about it anyway, and I don't blame him for that, either."

Dad sops up as much syrup as he can with his remaining pancake pieces. "This is a pretty easy one, kid."

"It is?"

"Sure. You say you're sorry."

Skylar runs his fingers through his hair. "Except I pretty much just broadcast the fact to Walt that I'm a fan of apologizing without meaning it."

"So?" Dad shrugs. "Apologize and mean it. If you can't do that, maybe you shouldn't be together. You're sorry for what you said, right?"

"Yeah," Skylar says quietly. "I lost it on him."

Dad holds up his plate and tips his bacon onto Skylar's. "Sounds like there wasn't an easy solution and you both had good points, but maybe you also both had some baggage you were bringing into the situation. So maybe you could have sat down once you both cooled off and figured it out together?"

Skylar shoves a slice of bacon in his mouth. It's the perfect level of chewy and crunchy. If this place entered their bacon in Spring Fling, they'd win a blue ribbon. Mouth full, he says, "You make it sound like it's the simplest thing in the world."

Shrugging, Dad says, "Simplest thing in the world? Sure. It's simple. I didn't say it was *easy*. I don't have to tell you, relationships ain't easy."

No. Skylar learned that the hard way. That was part of getting married too young too—he expected it to be easy, and then it got hard in a hundred small ways that neither he nor Cody knew how to deal with.

"I just hope Walt didn't leave," Skylar says.

Dad fishes his wallet out of his back pocket. "He doesn't seem like the kind of guy who'd leave without saying anything."

That first weekend, the one with the blizzard that brought them together, flashes through Skylar's mind, but things are different now.

"Yeah." Skylar stands, feeling a spark of hope for the first time since their argument in the parking lot. "You're right. He's not."

After Dad pays the check, they head back along the dark highway to Windham. Skylar pulls up alongside Dad's car where it's parked in town and gets out of his truck to hug him. "Thanks for coming. I know it's not your thing."

Returning the hug, his dad says, "Wouldn't be much of a parent if I wasn't open to learning new things for my kid. If it's your thing, it's my thing too."

A lump lodges in Skylar's throat, and he can't think of a single thing to say that expresses how much that means to him. In the end, he just hugs his father tighter and says, "Thanks, Dad."

He waits until his dad gets in the car and drives off before climbing back into the truck to go home. On the way, he practices what he's going to say to Walt: variations of "I'm sorry" and "let's figure this out together," and "I love you" and "I'm pretty sure I want this forever." Too bad Main Street Market closes so early or he'd stop in and get some flowers. Skylar doesn't know if Walt is a flowers guy, but anyone who loves interior design as much as he does has to have an appreciation, right? It's a moot point, though, because unless he wants to drive back to Route 87 for a Price Chopper, he's not going to find fresh cut flowers on Saturday night in the Catskills.

The headlights cut an illuminated swath as he swings the truck into the driveway, casting the barn and the house in a washed-out glow.

And it turns out that thinking about flowers at all was a moot point. So was practicing what he was going to say to Walt.

The house is dark. The driveway is empty.

Walt's gone.

Chapter Thirty-Two

WALT'S NEVER going to like driving in New York City. There are few things in life that he hates more than Manhattan traffic, but Tad lives in Manhattan, and Walt needs to talk to his brother.

Should he have stayed in Windham? Maybe. Probably. He has a feeling he screwed up by deciding to drive down to the city, but he got back to Skylar's house (big thanks to the license plate birdhouse lady from the market for the lift) and Skylar wasn't there. The longer Walt waited, the more worried he got that he'd screwed things up beyond repair—that he'd been inflexible, or he hadn't taken Skylar's concerns seriously, and that Skylar wasn't going to come back.

The notifications rolling in about the scene at the market didn't help. They were mostly positive, but it was too much. So he sent a long text to Skylar explaining where he was going and that he'd be back, and he headed south to Manhattan.

Once he's walking toward Tad's and Lewis's building from the parking spot he miraculously found a couple blocks away, it occurs to him that obviously Skylar wasn't going to run off and not come back. He has a farm. Animals. *Baby* animals.

Walt was stupid about this again. On the other hand, Skylar hasn't texted him back—Walt was half watching his phone during the two-and-a-half-hour drive, and the screen never lit up. It's killing him not to check right now, but if he hasn't responded, he obviously needs space. Walt would be a huge hypocrite if he couldn't respect that, considering he just drove to the city. That's less because he needs space, though, and more because he needs advice.

Or maybe just to talk. He doesn't have a clear idea of what advice he's looking for.

When he gets to the building, a resident holds the door open for him, even though he says he'll call his brother to let him in. "My arm's getting tired. Just get in here," the man says, which is… nice? Jesus, New York is so not his place.

Luckily, Tad seems happy to see him when he opens his apartment door. "What are you doing here?" Tad asks after ushering him inside. His black cat leaps off the back of the sofa and streaks into the bedroom, which is par for the course. Walt's never gotten more than a quick glimpse of her.

Walt opens his mouth to explain and has to close it immediately. Mortifyingly, he realizes if he speaks, he's going to cry. The two-and-a-half-hour drive was the time for that, not when he's here to talk shit out!

He clears his throat and rakes a hand through his hair, and Tad's expression cycles from worry to sympathy. "Want a beer?" Tad asks.

"Maybe something stronger," Walt says, his voice hoarse despite his efforts to sound normal, but he shakes his head and waves Tad back to the living room. "No, I'm driving back tonight."

Tad chews his lip before jerking his head toward the sofa. "Sit down. What's going on?"

Walt sits, but instead of telling Tad why he's here, he looks around. The apartment is as full of plants as ever and smells green and fresh, very unlike the rest of Manhattan. "Where's Lewis?"

"Working out in the building gym."

"Oh. That's nice you have that."

"Uh-huh." Tad arches an eyebrow. "Interested in renting in the building? I think a unit just opened up."

Walt makes a face. "No, and like you want me living in the same building as you, anyway."

With a laugh, Tad says, "What?! I can't believe you'd say that." He cocks his head. "If you don't want to talk about it—"

"Who says there's something to talk about?" Walt asks, even though it's obvious there is. Even if he hadn't shown up unannounced, it's real, real obvious. He sags against the back of the sofa. "I fucked up with Skylar. Wait, Jesus Christ. No. I have to back up. So, it was this spring market today in Windham, and Mom and Dad showed up…."

Once he starts talking, the words won't stop. Reliving it all is both painful and a relief. Painful, because—well, of course it's painful. It all sucked. But putting all of it into words, giving voice to all of it, gives him some distance and perspective. Saying the words, he feels in his bones the obvious fact that he's not the only one to face rejection upon coming out. He's in good company, shoulder to shoulder with generations of queer people whose loved ones turned away from them, but who went on to find their happiness anyway.

Man, he has a community, doesn't he? Even if he doesn't know them, there are millions of people out there who'd have his back, because they know how it feels.

When he gets to the part about Skylar, though, it hurts. Before he finishes telling all of it, Tad yanks him into a hug. Walt doesn't realize until his face is mashed into Tad's shoulder, dampening his brother's shirt, that there are tears on his cheeks.

With a deep breath, he sits back up, wiping his cheeks with the back of his hand. "I seriously fucked up, didn't I?"

Tad looks like he's processing, and Walt doesn't blame him. It probably wasn't easy for him to hear about the scene their parents made at the market—not after Tad's own coming out to their parents had gone less than ideally.

"I don't think you did," Tad says slowly, and kind of like he can't quite believe what he's saying.

Thanks, Tad. But Walt latches on to what he said and asks, "You don't?"

For a moment, Tad remains silent, a thoughtful look on his face. "I don't think you owe Mario an apology. Even to help Skylar out. I mean, there's apologizing to smooth over an argument, and then there's allowing someone to treat you badly." He wrinkles his nose. "Not to be all 'I told you so,' but I've always thought Mario was a jerk."

Deep down, Walt kind of always knew he was too. He just thought their history mattered, but maybe it doesn't. Maybe their history is just that—history, and maybe it's possible to outgrow friendships the same way you outgrow clothes.

That's not the happiest thought in the world, but then, part of being an adult is taking the good with the bad. Walt's not sure he's done very well with that.

"I want to be with Skylar," Walt says, because that's the simple truth. "But I… I don't think I can compromise on this. I don't think I can apologize for being who I am. What would I even say?"

"'Sorry for being bi?'" Tad offers with a scoff.

"'Sorry for being bi, but I'm not going to stop sucking dick.'"

"Oh my *god*! I don't want to hear about my brother's sex life!"

Giving Tad an earnest and maybe slightly shit-eating look, Walt says, "What, don't you do it too?"

Tad's face is red. This is way better than noogies and wedgies. "Stop! This is a hate crime. You can't come here anymore."

Walt laughs and throws an arm around Tad's shoulders. Tad punches him in the arm but doesn't move. Sobering, Walt says, "You really don't think I should suck it up and try to smooth things over with Mario?"

Emphatically, Tad says, "I really don't."

"I'm worried Skylar's going to hate me."

A fierce look settles on Tad's face. "If Skylar hates you for not compromising who you are, then it's his loss. You deserve someone who won't ask you to be someone you're not, not even for a second."

A sudden lump in Walt's throat makes it impossible to respond. Finally, he gets out, "Thanks, Taddy."

Tad's auburn hair falls in his eyes as he ducks his head. "Nothing to thank me for. It's true. I really liked seeing you so happy the last few months. You know that, right? Or maybe you don't. I'm still not very good at telling you stuff. But I did. I do. And for what it's worth, I don't think Skylar will hate you."

"You don't?"

Tad shakes his head. "I saw how he looked at you."

Embarrassingly, Walt feels his face heating. Apparently he can talk about blow jobs with his brother, but not feelings. Yeah, that checks out. "Not sure he looks at me any certain way."

"Oh, come on." Tad rolls his eyes. "He's obviously crazy about you. And you're obviously crazy about him, by the way. There's literally zero mystery about how you two feel about each other."

"You can't really talk. You and Lewis are gross."

"You're gross," Tad retorts.

Walt snorts with laughter and Tad bites down a smile that becomes a guffaw. They're in full-blown hysterics when the door opens and Lewis says, "Babe, you're never going to believe what's trending on Insta—oh! Walt! Hey, you're famous again!"

Walt gets himself under control and twists around to look at Lewis over the back of the sofa. "Huh?"

Lewis drops a pair of earbuds in a dish by the door and comes over to the sofa. As he plops down on Tad's other side, he wraps an arm around Tad and pulls him in for a quick kiss. "You're sweaty," Tad says, not sounding all that upset about it, which Lewis pretty much confirms by murmuring "You love it." Gross. Walt's pretty sure he wasn't supposed to hear that.

Luckily, it doesn't go any further—though maybe this is Walt's comeuppance for talking about blow jobs?—before Lewis says, "Congrats on coming out to your parents. But also that seemed really rough. Is that why you're here?"

"What are you talking about?" Walt asks. "How do you know about me coming out to my parents?"

Now Lewis looks confused. "The video."

"Video?"

"Yeah," Lewis says slowly. "The video of you coming out to your parents? That's all over Instagram? Isn't your phone blowing up?"

"Uh, no." Walt gropes for his phone, which hasn't buzzed a single time since he got here. "What are you talking about?"

"Oh my god." Lewis puts a hand over his mouth. "You don't know?"

"Lew, can you spit it out, please?" Walt says. Tad's face twitches. Okay, there's definitely some comeuppance going on. "What do you mean, the video of me coming out to my parents that's all over Instagram?"

"It doesn't get much clearer than that," Tad points out. Walt glares at him.

Holding up his phone, Lewis says, "You're trending. I mean, hashtag-farm-boyfriends is trending."

On the screen, a video of Walt confronting his parents is playing, sound off. Ice-cold heat, then burning cold, slides down Walt's spine. Seeing the scene from a different angle, from an outside perspective, is horrifying, disorientating, and thrilling all at once. He'll never be able to take this back! He'll never be able to take this back....

"Did you watch it?" he asks, his voice feeling far away.

Lewis looks guilty. "I, er... yeah. And I got told to shut up by the super serious, grunty guy deadlifting, because I cheered out loud for you!"

"You talked to Grunty Deadlifting Guy?" Tad asks.

"Not really? It was more like he told me to keep it down and I said sorry."

Walt clears his throat. "Can we talk about this video of me?"

"Do you want to watch it?" Lewis asks, holding his phone out.

No, he doesn't, but he probably should. Right? The scene keeps playing out silently on the screen. His gaze isn't drawn to himself or even to his parents. It's Skylar he can't stop watching: the fierce, overwhelming love on his face. Walt's never seen someone so ready to jump into the middle of a metaphorical MMA cage to fight.

And suddenly he knows that both things can be true—he didn't fuck up, and he'll do anything for Skylar. They'll talk through what happens if Mario goes through with his threat to start shit and what it will look like if he manages to affect Blue Skies Farm. But they'll do it together, as a team. Walt can't fathom not doing anything to keep Skylar in his life.

Forever. He wants Skylar in his life forever. He wants the goats and the peacocks and the guard llama, the early mornings and the chores, and the future. Maybe there are a couple dogs on the horizon. Maybe they expand the farm. Maybe they have kids.

Walt really, really wants to find out.

"I don't need to watch the whole thing," he says, standing up. As he reaches for his phone in his pocket, he adds, "I actually think I need to get back to Windham."

Tad gives him an encouraging nod while Lewis looks confused. Walt will let Tad explain everything to him after he leaves.

It's… maybe not a great sign that Skylar hasn't texted him back. Is Walt rushing back when Skylar wants him to stay away?

His phone screen doesn't light up, so Walt taps it. Nothing. He hits the lock button. Still nothing.

A pit sinks into his stomach. His phone. Wasn't his battery barely hanging on before the call with Mario? By the time he got back to the farm, waited for Skylar to come home, and wrote his essay of a text explaining where he was going and why, it would have been down to just about nothing.

Like an idiot, he didn't charge his phone in the car, and now he's been out of contact for hours. What if Skylar's been texting him, wondering why the hell he's not responding?

An even worse thought slithers into his gut. What if Walt's text never went through in the first place, because his battery died?

Shit, shit, *shit*.

"Thanks for the advice, bro!" Walt says, almost tripping over his feet to get to the door. He's yanking it open before Tad finishes responding and rushes down the stairs to the lobby instead of taking the elevator, like the building's on fire and he has minutes to escape.

Everything else, with the farm and Mario and social media? They can figure that out. If Skylar thinks Walt ran away again, though....

He's not so sure their relationship can handle that.

Chapter Thirty-Three

SKYLAR SPENDS as much time in the barn doing chores as he can get away with before it's obvious he's being avoidant. But Walt ran away again, and Skylar's tempted to curl up against Squirrel's soft, warm side while the llama hums soothingly. Maybe that's all he needs—the affectionate hum of a llama while he feels sorry for himself.

No. He's not going to do that. Sleeping on the floor of your llama's stall is something a much more depressed person would do.

For the millionth time, he checks his phone. There's nothing from Walt, and thankfully this time there's also nothing from Instagram. After the first ten thousand notifications from the videos of Walt's confrontation with his parents, Skylar turned them off.

It was surprisingly hard to do. Not like, challenging—though the app makes it harder than it needs to be—but emotionally difficult. Emotionally difficult with a weird physical paralysis. His brain was saying *You really should turn this off* but his hand kept hesitating, because what if he missed something? What if there was some comment, some share, some interaction, that he needed to see and respond to or risk tanking his business?

The physical compulsion keeping him from flipping notifications to Off was what finally jolted him into action. It freaked him out. Being so caught up in social media may have helped Blue Skies Farm, but it sure as shit isn't making Skylar any happier.

Skylar says good night to the animals, making sure each goat and Squirrel gets an extra pet. Several of the goats butt their noses up into his palm, and he can't do anything but smile. His animals' love has the power to make even the worst day a little more bearable.

As he's locking up the barn, texts come in from Jett and Skylar's dad. Dad made it home to Jersey safely, and Jett's wondering how Walt and Skylar are handling the attention from the video. The lure of checking Instagram sucks at Skylar like an undertow, but he makes himself type back to Jett that he's disconnected from social media for tonight.

He can't bring himself to tell Jett that Walt pulled his running away act again. There aren't any texts from Walt, even though Skylar has texted him several times. Too many times. He wishes he could take them back, but he also keeps desperately hoping Walt will respond.

When he does—*if* he does—they're going to have a serious conversation, and Skylar can't bring himself to think too hard about that, either. If there was a way to rewind this day back to the beginning and do it over, Skylar would.

There's no going back, though, only forward. But going forward is for tomorrow. Tonight, he's going to eat ice cream and rewatch as much of *Gaslamp Market* as he can before he passes out from exhaustion.

The credits are rolling on episode two, the timer in the corner of the screen counting down until the app advances to the next episode, when the bright beam of headlights swings across the drawn curtains and Skylar hears the crunch of tires outside.

He's on his feet without conscious thought. His bowl, now sadly empty of ice cream, tumbles to the floor, bouncing off the wood with a clang as the spoon rattles away. His legs carry him to the kitchen, a disconnect between his brain and the rest of his body making him wonder if he's having some kind of episode. A car door slams and within seconds, heavy footsteps thunder on the porch steps.

There's a rattle and thunk of a key in the lock before the door flies open. And there's Walt, hair messy and sticking up in all directions, eyes wide, and phone clutched in his hand. "Sky!" he gasps. "Did you get my text?"

Words refuse to come out of Skylar's mouth at first, before he manages, "What text?" Then, since his voice is cooperating for the moment, he adds, "You *left*."

Walt closes the door, cutting off the chilly draft it's letting in. "I didn't mean to." His voice cracks. "I mean, I meant to, but I was coming back. I sent you a text and told you everything, even though you weren't here so I thought maybe you were done with me, but I swear, Sky, I wasn't running away."

"I didn't get a text," Skylar says, barely keeping his own voice from cracking. He fucked up, he knows he fucked up, and even though Walt's absence was a horrible repeat of their first weekend together, deep down he's been sitting here wondering if he deserved it.

Brandishing his phone, Walt says, "This stupid thing ran out of battery. It must not have sent. Sky, I'm so sorry."

There's an infinitesimal moment where Skylar considers making him prove it: the phone being dead, the text sitting there undelivered. But Walt's blue eyes are locked on him, earnest and pleading and the truest thing Skylar can imagine, and it's inconceivable that Walt's lying.

"I'm sorry too," Skylar says, and god, he is. Sorry for the day Walt's had, sorry for making it worse, sorry for being a wobbly table leg when Walt needed someone solid and immovable. He wants to throw himself into Walt's arms, but maybe they both need a minute—

Walt crosses the space remaining between them and wraps up Skylar in a tight embrace, pushing his face into the crook of Skylar's neck. His lips feather across Skylar's skin in frantic kisses.

Skylar pulls him close and buries his face in Walt's unruly hair, breathing deep. He smells like the shampoo in the shower upstairs and like himself, and it makes Skylar's chest hurt as it hits him all at once that he'd assumed they were done, but they aren't. Walt's back, he's here, and he's hugging Skylar and dragging down the neck of his shirt while he kisses a line along his collarbone.

The T-shirt can only withstand so much, and anyway, desire is unfurling in Skylar's stomach. He reaches over his shoulder to pull the shirt off, not thinking of anything except Walt's insistent mouth, dipping under the hem and nipping at his skin.

He flings the shirt away and Walt groans, dropping to his knees. He grabs Skylar's hips and presses his face to his stomach, licking and kissing along the ridges of Skylar's muscles and over to the ledges of his hips. Skylar's pajama pants are sitting low, exposing the band of his boxer briefs, and Walt's fingers slide up to hook into the elastic.

There's barely any time for anticipation. Walt rubs his face against Skylar's crotch, where his rapidly stiffening cock is tenting his pants, and then he pulls both pajama pants and boxer briefs down.

Skylar's cock bounces free and Walt swallows him down to the root, until his nose is buried in Skylar's pubic hair, pressed up against his skin, and he's gagging. A bolt of shattering pleasure rips through Skylar so hard that he flails a hand out for something, anything, to grab on to for support. They're in the middle of the kitchen, though, and there's nothing to hang on to except for Walt.

Desperately, he clutches Walt's head, fingers twisting in his messy red-sand hair. Walt moans around Skylar's cock at the tug. The vibration of his throat is one of the best things Skylar's ever felt, and shit, he's going to come any second.

With a gasp, Walt pops off Skylar's dick. His lips are swollen red and sheened with spit and pre-cum. Tears streak his cheeks and mat his eyelashes together, making his eyes look bigger and bluer and darker with lust. "Fuck my face," he orders hoarsely.

And Skylar does, ramming into Walt's mouth as Walt swallows him again. The wet slurp of Skylar's thrusts keeps time with Walt's moans and choking sounds.

It's enough to get Skylar there in under a minute. Walt on his knees in the kitchen, right there in front of the door, lips stretched around Skylar's dick, taking it like he was made for this. Walt cups his balls, rolling them around in one big, callused hand, and Skylar goes off like a rocket.

An orgasm so sharp and sudden that it's painful slams into him. A keening cry of pleasure tears itself from his throat as he empties himself down Walt's, while Walt milks him with one hand and swallows and swallows and swallows.

Sensitivity and aftershocks overwhelm him. His knees buckle and he slides free from Walt's mouth to land on the floor. "God," he gasps.

"Just Walt's fine." The goofy smile on Walt's face is hidden behind his hand for a second as he wipes his mouth.

Skylar can't decide between groaning at the dad joke, laughing, or kissing Walt. His brain fires the signals for all three at the same time, and he ends up messily groan-laughing against Walt's mouth. The laugh turns to mostly groan as he tastes himself on Walt's lips and tongue, and that turns into popping the button on Walt's jeans so he can push his hand inside, wrap his hand around Walt's cock, and jerk him tight and fast until Walt's gasping and shuddering too.

They kiss again, slower and softer this time. Then, Walt flops back to lie on the floor and pulls Skylar on top of him. When Walt makes a satisfied noise, Skylar brushes a thumb across Walt's lips, cheekbone, eyebrow, before threading his fingers in Walt's hair. "Where'd you go?" Skylar asks, not accusatory, but genuinely wondering.

"I needed to talk stuff through with Tad." Walt hooks a leg around Skylar's. "I should've made sure my stupid phone actually sent the text. I guess it was so long that it killed the last of my battery."

Skylar lets his head fall so it's resting on Walt's broad shoulder, so his heart thuds in Skylar's ear. They haven't actually fixed anything, have they? But it feels like it's going to be okay. Like it's already okay, and they just need to go through the steps of finalizing the okay-ness. Does that even make sense? Probably not. Probably Skylar's just blissed out on sex endorphins, relief, and happiness that Walt's here again.

He didn't leave.

"You know your phone can also do this cool thing where you can talk to a person who's far away, right?" Skylar teases, raising his head. "You can see their face and everything."

"What?" Walt's eyes widen. "Wow, that sounds amazing. They can do anything these days." He strokes up and down Skylar's spine for a long, quiet moment before he says, "I just needed to talk to him in person. I just—I don't know. He's better at stuff than I am. Emotions, I mean. And knowing the right thing to say when it matters."

Putting his head back down on Walt's shoulder, Skylar says, "I think you said a lot of right things this afternoon. To your parents and Mario. And me."

Walt heaves a huge sigh. "I got mad at them—"

"They deserved you being mad at them. Have you ever gotten mad at them before?"

The beat of silence is all the answer Skylar needs. Splaying his hand across Skylar's back, Walt says, "I didn't take what you were saying seriously. I brushed off the things you're worried about with the farm and social media."

It does sting to hear Walt confirm that he hadn't taken Skylar seriously, but they're talking now, and that certainty that they're going to figure it out is still sitting placidly in Skylar's chest. "I shouldn't have thrown all that at you right then. I just—"

The conversation with Dad flits through his mind. *It's simple. I didn't say it was easy.*

"I'm probably not totally over the way my marriage fell apart," Skylar says. "Or the way I let Cody run the business side of the farm. Getting a big following on Instagram felt like something I was doing myself, and like I was finally good at the business and financial stuff.

But then Mario threatening to try to tank us…. I guess it was like getting slapped in the face with the fact that I still wasn't good at it."

A silence follows these words, long enough for Skylar to feel a pang of worry that Walt's going to nope out now that Skylar has dragged his baggage into the open. Except Walt's still stroking up and down Skylar's spine, and his heart's still keeping a steady, calm rhythm.

"You run a farm," Walt finally says. "You know how to take care of your animals. You helped Jane give birth when it was going to shit. You literally have a whole farm-to-table business, and you're kicking ass. There's nothing wrong with needing help with parts of it."

"What part of your fence company did you need help with?" Skylar asks, half-expecting Walt to say he ran the whole thing on his own.

Walt snorts, though, and says, "Are you kidding? A ton of stuff. I needed a crew—putting up residential fences is a lot of work. And I'm bad at the tax stuff. One of my buddies helped me out for the first couple years, and all he asked for was some help replacing a couple boards in his fence. The scheduling is a pain in my ass too."

Skylar wants to argue that it's different, even though it's obviously not. Or, it is, but the difference is that he's so emotionally invested in Blue Skies Farm that every rise and dip in its fortunes feels like a reflection on him personally. How can it not be?

"How do you keep from feeling like not being good at every part of your company isn't like… a personal failing?" he asks.

"Probably because I kind of hate my company," Walt says.

There's a silence like a held breath after that, and then Walt lets out a gust of air, part laugh, part sigh, part gasp. "I don't think I've ever said that out loud. I *hate* residential fencing." He makes another noise, closer to a laugh this time. "What am I supposed to do about that?"

Pushing himself up on his hands so he can look Walt in the eyes, Skylar says, "Sell it. Move down here. Be my partner running Blue Skies Farm. And start a home remodeling company, because you do amazing work."

Wait. Did he just ask Walt to move in with him?

"Did you just ask me to move in with you?"

Skylar's face heats. He could backpedal, hedge and say that's not what he meant. Instead, he replies, "I think I did, yeah. But if you're not ready—"

"Hell yes!" Walt takes Skylar's face in both hands and kisses him enthusiastically. Skylar covers one of Walt's hands with his, interlacing their fingers and deepening the kiss, heart pounding like he's just run a race, run a race and *won*. Walt helping him run Blue Skies Farm doesn't feel like failure; it feels like things finally falling into place.

When the kitchen floor gets uncomfortable, they clean themselves up and curl on the sofa together. With Walt stroking his fingers through his hair, Skylar drifts into a happy half-doze.

"I've been thinking about what to do about Mario," Walt murmurs.

That wakes Skylar up. "Me too."

Walt holds him closer. "I can talk to him. Figure out where all this came from and move on from it."

"But you're not going to apologize, right?" Skylar can't help flinching. "I know I said you should, but I was being an idiot."

"I'm not apologizing," Walt says firmly. His fingers combing through Skylar's hair are a soothing counterpoint to this conversation, but they falter as he adds, "I'm not sure what to do if he doesn't calm down, though. He might go through with trying to expose us or whatever."

Covering his face with his hands, Skylar can't help but laugh. "It sounds so stupid! 'Expose us.'"

"I know," Walt says with a snort of his own laughter. "But... I mean, he might. And I know social media can be brutal. So if he says something—"

"Then he says something." Skylar uncovers his face and kisses Walt's cheek. "I muted notifications from all my socials tonight, and you know what I realized? After the first few times I reached for my phone to check it, I didn't miss any of it." Straightening up so he can face Walt, he goes on, "I know getting big on social media helped the farm a lot, but I want to pull back and build business the old-fashioned way. Obviously there will still have to be some social media in there. But I want to do more events. Markets and pop-ups and stuff. Maybe getting a little section of goods in the touristy stops along Route 87."

"That sounds amazing," Walt says, so much enthusiasm in his voice that Skylar would think he was laying it on too thick—if he was anyone but Walt Pierce.

"So if Mario says anything...." Skylar steels himself, because saying this out loud is the first step toward doing it. "If he says anything, we aren't going to respond. Anyone can say anything on the internet."

"Are you sure?" Walt asks. "We can have a statement if you think it would help."

"I'm sure. We're going to make Blue Skies Farm amazing on our own. No celebrity endorsements or internet fights needed."

Walt smiles softly. "It's already amazing."

The best response to that is a kiss—so that's what Skylar does.

Chapter Thirty-Four

THE FIRST challenge in pulling back from social media is Walt's coming-out video. Walt may have let go of a lot of his internalized shame, but this isn't the way he would have chosen for everyone in his life to find out he's bi. But they know now, and so do a bunch of strangers. Messages pour in from both the people he knows and the ones he doesn't, and he decides to ignore all of them. If people want to talk to him, they can text him instead of DMing him on his socials.

Plus, by noon the next day, he's deleted Instagram.

He does get texts from most of his friends. They're all positive, though once Walt's initial rush of happiness at that fact fades, he realizes the people who aren't going to have a positive reaction just won't text him. His buddies all give him some variation of "congratulations," and it's a huge relief.

Mario doesn't text. Neither do Walt's parents. It's fine. It's not like he expected any of them to initiate contact with him today. Mario might not even be a friend anymore—in the cold light of day, Walt can't think about him without anger smoldering like a coal in his gut.

His parents, though? He'd really like to not lose his parents over this. Some people do, he knows that. On some level, he's always been afraid he would. Why else would his dad's shame at catching him with Cam have burrowed itself so deeply into Walt's brain? Not just his brain—his entire sense of self?

Keyboard clacking draws him out of his thoughts. He and Skylar are sitting at the kitchen table hunting down events for Blue Skies Farm to attend. Skylar gets the final say in whether they commit, but so far they've signed up for all of them. Weekends are going to be busy, and as the weather gets warmer, so are weekday afternoons. With plenty of farmers' markets in the Catskills, they can be at one every day, if they want to be.

Being at farmers' markets in the Catskills means Walt can't be in Watertown putting up fences. He already sent an email this morning to his carpenter, Lizzie. She's mentioned to Walt that she'd like to run her own business. It might be too soon for her, but Walt would prefer to hand the business off to someone he knows and trusts.

"Is two hours too far to drive every week?" Skylar asks, propping his chin on his hand.

"Why?"

"Because this farmers' market in Callicoon is looking for a vendor to be there all summer, and they're offering a lower rate if I can commit now." Skylar squints at his laptop and after some click-type-click, he makes a face. "That's Pennsylvania!"

"Really?" Walt gets up and comes around the table to look at Skylar's computer. The very squiggly blue line of Google's suggested route seems like it should take more than two hours to drive.

Pointing to the screen, Skylar says, "I mean, no, but basically. It's right on the border."

Walt hasn't heard of Callicoon, but judging by where it is, on the Delaware River and in the foothills of the Catskills, it's probably pretty gorgeous. Maybe a good spot for a romantic getaway, if they can carve out some time for it.

"Let's find out if it gets big crowds," Walt says. "It might be worth the drive if it does."

A car door slams outside, and they look toward the window. It's mostly obscured through the curtains, and so is the driver, who's currently headed for the porch and the front door, but Walt's heart leaps into his throat as his brain identifies the visitor as Dad.

That's dumb, though. Dad doesn't know where Walt is, and even if he did, he wouldn't come here when a phone call, or even a text, would work just as well.

The doorbell chimes and Skylar rises to see who's there. As the door opens, Skylar says, "Oh!"

And then Walt's on his feet, because the other voice he hears, the one saying "Sorry to just show up like this, but I was wondering if Walt's here" is his father's voice. Skylar opens the door wider, and it's also his father standing there, his bulk taking up the doorway, the day bright behind him.

"Walt," Dad says.

"Dad," Walt says back, his mind wiped clean of any other response.

Skylar steps back and gestures to Dad. "Come in, Mr. Pierce."

Walt's father, who's *here*, steps through the door and stomps his feet on the doormat to shake off the mud from the driveway. He looks up, his eyes moving from Skylar to Walt, and Walt just… stands there. His dad is at Blue Skies Farm, and Walt's having a hard time getting a handle on that.

Helplessly, Skylar looks at Walt, his eyes wide. After a few tries at making sound come out of his mouth, Walt manages to say—again— "Dad." Which, judging by the increasing desperation in Skylar's eyes, wasn't helpful. "Um, you can—yeah, come in. What are you doing here?"

That, at least, is moving things from an awkward standoff to a conversation. As his dad wipes his feet again and slowly enters the kitchen, he replies, "I wanted to talk to you. Yesterday, things got…." He stops, like he can't think of a good word to describe how things got at the market. Walt doesn't blame him. He can't think of a way to describe it either, not without resorting to profanity.

When Walt doesn't chime in, Dad sighs and rubs a hand over the back of his head. "I think we should talk about yesterday."

"Okay." Walt's mouth is dry. Why does he feel like a teenage boy again? God, what he wouldn't give to not be hurtled back to that horrible moment from his adolescence.

Skylar comes close and puts his hand on Walt's arm gently. "I'll be upstairs."

Walt wants to kiss him, but he just covers Skylar's hand with his own. That means it's just Walt and his dad again, standing in the kitchen awkwardly, like… like….

Okay, like a father who found out about his son's bisexuality during a shouting at a quaint makers' market, which got recorded from multiple angles and posted on social media. Like that.

"You want something to drink?" Walt asks. "We have some beer from a brewery in town."

"Sure." Dad sounds more grateful for beer than Walt's ever heard—and that's saying something, since Walt can't remember a single Sunday from his childhood where his father didn't have a can of beer next to him.

Walt grabs a couple from the fridge and motions for Dad to come through to the living room. The sun is streaming in from the west-facing windows, putting the mantle in a spotlight. The mantle, where there are peacock feathers and a Pride flag.

They sit, Dad in the armchair and Walt on the sofa. Dad knows he's bi. Dad's known longer than Walt has. Dad is the reason it took Walt so long to figure it out. "You probably have something to say, right? You probably didn't come all the way back here if you didn't."

"Your mom and I got a hotel," Dad says.

Not the point. "Dad."

Dad lets out a slow breath. Walt knows he's overwhelmed and out of his depth. His parents have always been easily overwhelmed, and normally Walt's good at managing them, helping smooth the way for all the curveballs life throws. Not this time, though. He can't manage how his parents deal with him being queer. They'll either handle it or they won't.

He hopes they handle it.

"You never told us," Dad says—fast, like if he doesn't get the words out as quickly as possible, they'll never see the light of day. "About—well. The gay thing."

"I'm bi," Walt says, trying not to sound weary. "I like women and men. Or... everyone, probably, but women and men for sure."

Dad nods, then nods again. "Thought you might be gay. After...."

The word trails off to silence. Walt waits to see if his father will own up to that afternoon all those years ago, and when he doesn't, when he lets the sentence flap in the wind, Walt says, "After you caught Cam and me in my room."

"Yeah." Dad takes a long drink of beer. When he takes the can from his mouth, he dangles it between his knees and looks at the floor. "I always thought... I don't know what I thought. That you were experimenting. Or it was a phase, or... or you decided not to be that way."

There's something hard and painful in Walt's chest. "You knew. All this time, you knew damn well that I wasn't straight."

The beer can crinkles as Dad flexes his fingers around it. "I guess I did," he replies quietly. "But I didn't want to admit it to myself."

With a bitter laugh, Walt says, "Well, that makes two of us."

He can't remember ever speaking to his father this way. It's not that Dad was ever stern or forbidding when Walt and Tad were kids, it's just... he was raised not to talk back to his parents, not to question them, and he's never let go of that upbringing.

Upstairs, floorboards creak as Skylar walks from one room to another. There's a basket of laundry up there that Walt's been meaning to put away; maybe Skylar's doing that as an excuse to stay up there.

Finally, Dad speaks again. "I've been thinking about that day a lot ever since your brother told us he's gay. I've been thinking… maybe I didn't handle it right. I probably should have said something. It probably doesn't mean much, now that… well, my hand's kind of been forced. But I should've said something."

Tears burn Walt's eyes, but he blinks them back. "I was so ashamed of myself for so long."

Dad looks old and sad. "I was wrong, Walt."

Walt's normal reaction to his dad looking like that and admitting to being wrong is to back off, be the good kid. The peacemaker. This time, he says, "Yeah. You were."

"I'm sorry." Dad shakes his head. "I know that doesn't change anything, but I am."

For a minute, Walt can only sit there, his hand clutched around his sweating can of beer. "You don't care if I'm bi?" he asks eventually. "Or if I end up with a guy? Because I'm pretty serious about Skylar, and I want him to be around for a long time. But I'm not going to be ashamed of myself, and I'm not going to let you make Skylar feel that way, either."

Making speeches isn't his thing, but man, it feels good to say that. It will feel better if Dad doesn't say he can't handle both of his sons ending up with men, but even if he does? Walt stood up for himself and Skylar. It doesn't fix what happened all those years ago with Cam, but at least he's doing the right thing now.

"I want you to be happy," Dad says gruffly. "That's all I've ever wanted for you and your brother. I'm bad at showing it most of the time. I'll work on that."

"This is a good start," Walt says, offering a tentative smile.

Just as tentatively, Dad returns it. "If Skylar makes you happy, that's good enough for me." He pauses before adding, "And I know there's all sorts of ways you can have kids now, so your mother doesn't even need to worry about grandchildren."

With a startled laugh, Walt says, "I'm serious about him, but we haven't had that conversation."

They could, though. Walt's… kind of ready to talk about that? Kids are something he's pretty sure he wants, with Skylar, specifically.

Dad shrugs. "When you do, then. You can talk to me about it. Ask for advice, or whatever you need to do. Want to do, I mean. I'm probably going to need some help saying the right thing and being supportive the right way."

Those tears sting Walt's eyes again. "Pretty sure you're doing it exactly the right way."

There's never been much hugging between Walt and his dad, but he doesn't know what else to do right now *except* hug, even though it's awkward since they both have to put down their beers and stand. But Dad holds on tight, and Walt maybe holds on a little tighter.

"I'm proud of you, Walt," Dad says. "So damn proud of the man you are. I'm sorry I ever made you feel like I wasn't."

The man Walt thought his father wanted him to be wouldn't have cried—but the man Walt is finally gives into the sting in his eyes. Tears slide down his face and he lets them, hugging Dad harder.

When they both let go, Walt wipes his eyes with the back of his hand. Dad sniffles and looks at the ground while he clears his throat a few times. If Walt didn't know better, he'd think Dad's crying too.

"Do you want a do-over on meeting Skylar?" Walt asks.

"You think we need a do-over?" Dad replies, and holy shit, is he joking around with Walt about Walt's *boyfriend*? What a weird world.

So Walt calls for Skylar to come down, and Sky and Dad shake hands again and introduce themselves like they're meeting for the first time. They are, in a way—it's obvious that Dad's evaluating Skylar on a completely different set of metrics now, not as a friend, but as a romantic partner.

Pointing to Dad's beer, Skylar asks, "How do you like it?"

"It's good. Fancier than what I usually drink. Walt said this stuff is brewed in town?"

"Yeah!" Skylar sounds eager, and Walt loves him all the more for it. "We can send some home with you, if you want."

"Wait, we're giving away my Windham Ale?" Walt asks in fake outrage.

Clapping Skylar on the shoulder, Dad says, "I like you."

And that… somehow is all it takes. Within a couple minutes, Skylar and Dad are joking around like old buddies. When Skylar asks if Dad wants a tour of the farm, Dad gives an enthusiastic assent. Even though Walt's never known his father to be much of an animal guy, he pets Squirrel and all the goats who crowd around him looking for head scratches and treats.

It's unquestionably a success. But Walt can't help noticing, and worrying about, the fact that his mom isn't here with Dad. When Tad came out to their parents, Dad was pretty cool about it right away. If not for the baggage from his teen years, Walt probably wouldn't have been so paralyzed about coming out himself to Dad. Mom, though… she's obviously still not okay with Tad being gay. Yesterday she made it clear that she doesn't want two queer sons.

At least she's still in town. That has to be a good sign, right? Maybe he should go talk to her. Especially with the way Sky and Dad are yukking it up. Skylar's offering to show Dad the commercial pasteurizer in the basement next to the washer and dryer, and Dad looks like he's always dreamed of seeing one. If Dad tells him where he and Mom are staying, Walt could drive over there right now—

His phone rings and a jolt goes through him when he sees *Mom* on the screen. Did he just manifest this call by thinking about her?

He blurts out something about needing to take the call, flashing the screen probably too fast for either Skylar or Dad to read it, and jogs up the stairs to the bedroom.

"Hey," he says when he answers the phone.

"Hi, sweetie," Mom says.

Walt goes to sit at the foot of the bed, at a loss for words. If he'd driven over to a hotel to talk to her, he would have had time to rehearse what he wanted to say. Now his mind goes blank, and though his lips part, nothing comes out.

There's a scratchy noise on the phone, like maybe Mom just blew her nose. "Is your father there?"

His heart plummets. So that's why she's calling. She just wants Dad, who isn't answering his own phone. Maybe she wants to tell him that they have to present a united front of not being too accepting of their kids. "Oh. Uh, yeah. I'll go get him."

"No!" Mom sounds panicked, and Walt sinks back down onto the bed. "No, I was just wondering. Making sure he got there all right, I guess. But no. I wanted to talk to you."

"Oh," Walt says again. His heart hammers. Dammit, he really wishes he'd gotten that rehearsal time in the car. Turns out he's even less ready to talk to his mom about this than he was his dad. Assuming they're going to talk about him being bi? Maybe she's calling to talk about dinner plans. Maybe they're going to pretend it never happened.

There's a silence before Mom asks, "Is this a good time?"

"Yeah, I can talk."

Another silence, but this time it feels heavy. "I just got off the phone with your brother" aren't the words he's expecting to hear. Maybe that's obvious, because she goes on, "He called me. He saw... what happened yesterday. It's on the internet. Apparently someone filmed it and put it on Instagram."

"Okay...." Walt prompts when she stops talking. Where is this going?

Mom's indrawn breath is audible. "He, well. He gave me an ultimatum. He said I could accept you for who you are, or I'm not welcome at his wedding. Or in his life."

Walt's stomach lurches. Tad did that for him?

Just as quickly as affection and wonder rushed through him, a wave of shitty reality crashes down. "So you're going to be nice because you want to plan Tad's wedding? I guess that's better than nothing, Mom. But you probably should have kept the ultimatum to yourself so I'd think you just had a come-to-Jesus moment."

"Maybe." Mom laughs a little, but she doesn't sound amused. "I think I wanted you to know how much Tad cares. You two were so close, and then you grew apart.... It's been nice seeing you get along again. But you're right. My first thought when he said that was that I need to be nice so he doesn't cut me out of the wedding."

Somehow, the weight of shitty reality gets heavier and shittier. "Great. Well, glad to hear you're going to be better about me being bi. I guess it doesn't really matter why you're being better about it, except it makes it kind of meaningless when I *know* you're faking it."

"No!" Her voice is flustered before she repeats in a more measured tone, "No. I'm not faking it. I'm sorry, I'm not saying this well. I don't know exactly what I want to say, except I don't want to drive you away. You or Tad. Or Lewis, or... Skylar?"

"Skylar," Walt confirms, surprised to hear his future brother-in-law and his boyfriend included.

"I'm so sorry about the things I said yesterday," she says in a rush. "It's been an adjustment with Tad… I just never thought…. And now you, too, and—No, I'm not saying this right," she interrupts herself before Walt's able to. "I've never had a problem with the LGBT, but I didn't know any, so it was easy for me to be accepting. To think I was accepting. And I didn't react well when Tad told us about himself. I know I didn't."

"If you knew that, why did you react so horribly when *I* told you about myself?" Walt asks, a hard lump sitting behind his sternum.

"I don't know. I don't know how to explain what I was thinking, except that it was about how I felt. Not about how Tad felt, and not how you must have felt seeing the way I treated Tad." She takes a juddering breath. "I had an image of our family, and I never imagined husbands for you or Tad. Only wives. Bridal showers and baby showers for my daughters-in-law. Maybe it's not right for me to mourn losing that, but I did. I just… I mourned too long. And I made both of you part of it, when it wasn't about either of you. I don't know if I'm making sense."

"You are," Walt says. He exhales harshly, and the lump in his chest loosens. "And… I get it. I thought I was going to have those things too. It would've been easier. And a lot less terrifying."

"I made it scarier for you, didn't I?" Mom asks softly.

Telling her she didn't would be easier too. Pre-Skylar Walt would have. Instead, he says honestly, "Yeah. For Tad and me, both."

"I'm sorry, honey."

Walt lets out another breath and hangs his head. "I appreciate that. But it only means something if you change. Are you going to?"

"I have to," she replies. "Otherwise I'm going to lose my children."

He's not going to argue with her there. Yesterday was too eventful for him to have given much thought yet to how he was going to move forward with his parents. Would he have gone as far as Tad did with his ultimatum?

The thought of his mom cold-shouldering Skylar the way she has Lewis makes him see red, so—maybe. Maybe he would have.

"Will you let me try?" Mom asks. "I won't be perfect. I know I'll make mistakes, but if you're happy, Walt—you and Tad—that's the only thing that matters. You're my children and I love you no matter what. I've done a bad job of showing you that. But I'm going to do better."

"Okay, Mom." Walt breathes in, holds it. Exhales. "You don't have to be perfect. You just have to accept us for who we are. And the people—the men—we love."

"I will. I do."

Voices float up from downstairs as Skylar and Dad return from the basement and the thrills of the pasteurizer (sidebar, the pasteurizer *is* pretty cool). Walt's not a prove-it kind of guy, but he can think of a pretty great way to make sure Mom keeps this promise. "Come over and have dinner with us tonight," he says. "You and Dad with Skylar and me. I think we have one of Skylar's pot pies in the freezer that we can heat up."

She blows her nose before she says, "I'd like that. If Skylar doesn't mind?"

Skylar will probably grumble at him when they're alone later, but Walt will make it up to him. "He'll be okay with it. We've had so many surprise visits from parents this weekend that we might as well add one more."

That gets a watery laugh. "Okay. I'll have to have your dad come back to pick me up. But I'd like that. Thank you."

Walt listens to Skylar and Dad downstairs. The knot behind his sternum breaks up and melts away.

Yesterday, it seemed like nothing would be okay again. Now, though? Now, he knows it will be.

Chapter Thirty-Five

"I NOW pronounce you husbands. You may kiss each other."

The guests arrayed in the New York Botanical Gardens' Stone Mill burst into applause and a few wolf whistles as Tad and Lewis lean toward each other for a chaste kiss. Wait—the wolf whistle is Lewis's best man and best friend, Stacy. Walt sees her grin through his sheen of tears, which he refuses to be embarrassed by. How could he be embarrassed, anyway, when his brother looks so fiercely, radiantly happy?

Walt blinks to clear the tears and glances at the guests. Skylar is in the front row, seated between Walt's and Tad's father and Lewis's mom, and he's beaming at Walt. The May sunshine makes his hair so black that it's almost blue, and he's in a suit that fits him like a glove, with a smoky eye look that made Walt trip over his own feet when Skylar came out of the bathroom at the hotel this morning.

His heart trips over itself looking at Skylar right now. The concept of soul mates is cheesy, and Walt totally doesn't believe in that. At the same time, though. If something like soul mates *did* exist. Walt's not saying Skylar fits the bill, but he's also not *not* saying that.

By the time they get through all the post-ceremony formalities, Walt's ready to sit down with a beer and the pizza Tad and Lewis decided on for the wedding dinner. There's no head table for the wedding party—instead, everyone is seated with their friends or family. Walt's at a big table that includes the parents of the grooms, Lewis's sister (and bridesmaid) Taylor, and Skylar.

The next table over is Lewis and Tad's main friend group: Stacy and her husband Alang, Tad's bridesmaid Ava and her wife, Lewis's other best friend Matthew and his husband, and, sort of awkwardly, Lia and her plus-one. Walt gives her a nod and a smile and she responds with a little wave. Maybe things won't always be awkward between them. It's not like Walt ever thought about whether soul mates existed or not when they were dating.

He groans as he sinks into his chair. Skylar puts a hand on his leg and squeezes. "Since when does being on your feet and talking to people wear you out?" Skylar asks, smiling fondly.

"This is Tad's wedding. I have to bring my A game." Thankfully, there's already a beer on the table, and Walt takes a grateful sip. It's crisp and cold and exactly what he needs after shaking hands and chatting with every guest that came through the receiving line. The guest list wasn't huge, but Lewis has a big Italian family and they're all extra boisterous today. Walt also wants to make a good impression on Lewis's friends.

Most importantly, he wants Tad to look back on today and remember nothing but love—his and Lewis's, obviously, but also how much their families and friends love them.

Walt's mom leans over and says, "It was such a beautiful ceremony." Her eyes are red-rimmed and there's a crumpled tissue sticking out from her sleeve, one of the full pack she went through during the ceremony.

"Yeah, it was." Putting an arm around her shoulders, Walt says, "You, Tad, and Lewis did a great job."

"Oh, it was mostly Tad and Lewis," Mom demurs, but it's obvious she's pleased to be included.

It's only been a month and a half, but Mom has tried hard to let go of the ingrained homophobia that's been such a wedge in their family for—well, ever. Walt's proud of her, and Dad too. Dad offered out of the blue to call in some favors with business owners in Watertown that he's friendly with to ask them to carry Blue Skies Farm products, and they're in discussions now about the logistics of that with a couple restaurants and one of the upscale grocery stores in town.

The fact that Tad asked Mom to walk him down the aisle was the biggest endorsement of the new leaf she's turned over. Lewis's mom walked him down the aisle, and the symmetry was nice. And Walt would be lying if he said he didn't get choked up at how tight Tad and Mom hugged when they got to the front of the terrace.

From across the circular table, Lewis's mom says, "You looked very handsome up there too, Walt."

Ducking his head, Walt says, "Thanks. Can't really take credit for it since Tad picked the outfit."

Skylar gives him a look that's just this side of heated. "You can take credit for looking good," he murmurs.

The parents at the table share a look—the kind that says, *there's probably another wedding coming up*.

Applause ripples through the room, starting at one end and growing louder as one after another, guests see Tad and Lewis entering. Hand in hand, the two of them cross to the empty seats waiting for them at the Pierce/Mancini-Sommer/Dangda table.

Tad's face is bright red when he slides into his chair, but he's also smiling irrepressibly. Lewis looks like he could float away, he's so happy.

"Done with pictures?" Taylor asks. "I don't mean to sound hangry, but I'm going to chew my arm off if we don't eat soon."

"I thought you brought emergency pregnancy snacks?" Lewis asks.

Taylor sighs. "I ate all of them."

Fiddling with his cufflinks, Tad says, "Thankfully yes, pictures are done. All the high-pressure stuff is done! We're married and we can finally eat."

"We're married," Lewis repeats giddily, which makes Tad's face get gooey before he dips his head forward to kiss Lewis softly.

The grooms sitting down was the signal the caterers were waiting for, because within minutes, they begin bringing out pizzas for the buffet line. It's hard to say if it's because they're at a wedding, because they're in the city, or because it's Tad and Lewis, but the pizzas are fancier than any Walt's seen in his life. They're also delicious, which he knows from accompanying Tad and Lewis to the taste test months ago.

As they move along the pizza lineup, Walt slings an arm around Tad's shoulders in a one-armed hug. Who knew weddings turned him into such a hugger? "I'm really happy for you, bro."

Tad returns the hug. "Thanks for everything. I, um. I'm really happy you're my best man. It means a lot."

Walt scoops a piece of eggplant and artichoke pizza onto his plate to cover the fact that a lump is rising in his throat. He's only had one beer! Weddings turn him into a hugger *and* a crier. "It means a lot that you asked me."

"We have a thanks-for-being-in-the-wedding present for you," Tad says. "Well, it's really for both of you. If you don't like it, though, we have a backup plan. But you and Skylar have mentioned it a few times…. Okay, I'm just going to tell you, and if it's dumb, I won't be offended by you saying so."

Tad reaches into his inside jacket pocket and unfurls a sheaf of papers. As Walt takes them and scans over the first sheet, the only thing he feels is confused. "This is… a printout of all the dogs at a shelter?"

"A no-kill shelter in the Catskills," Tad says. "You guys have been talking about getting a dog, so we thought… well… we'd love to adopt a dog for you and get all the stuff you need. It doesn't have to be from this shelter! This one seemed nice, but anywhere you want. And no expiration date on this, so if you aren't ready yet—"

The lump is back in Walt's throat, so instead of speaking, he pulls Tad into a hug again, this one so enthusiastic that he almost loses his pizza. "That's amazing. Wow. I mean, we'll talk about it, but—"

"Yes!" Skylar says from in front of them in line, eyes lit up and a huge, excited grin on his face.

"—but I'm pretty sure he'll be on board," Walt finishes, returning Skylar's buoyant smile.

With his own bright smile, Tad says, "Yay! Our backup present was much lamer, so this is good."

He's tempted to ask about the backup present, but between balancing his plate and trying to look at the dogs (there's one named Willis!), he's too distracted. After they load their plates with more pizza than Walt's eaten at one time since college and are heading back to their table, Tad says, "I ran into Mario when I was in Watertown last weekend."

Wincing, Walt says, "I bet that was awkward."

Tad lets out an unamused laugh. "I don't know if I've had an interaction with Mario that I wouldn't describe as awkward."

Walt and Skylar had watched for Mario's threat to out their relationship as fake, but it never materialized. Maybe he realized it sounded silly to start drama over a relationship that was only fake for a day. Maybe he wasn't willing to completely burn bridges. Who knows? Whatever the reason, he hasn't reached out with an apology, either. And Walt's decided he needs that, at the very least. He's done sweeping things under the rug to keep the peace. There are people who accept him for who he is; who don't need him to keep parts of himself bottled up and locked down for their comfort.

Those are the people he wants in his life. People who are capable of changing their views and working at holding up their end of the relationship. Walt's parents are proof of that. Walt thinks he might be proof of that, himself. Six months ago, he couldn't even have an honest relationship with himself. Now he's selling the company he doesn't like to start a home renovation business, plus turning into a goat farmer with the man he loves.

And they're getting a dog!

So, yeah. It hurts to lose a friendship that meant so much to Walt for so long. But things run their course. The things that he thought were important once don't seem so important anymore. He's pretty sure he's getting better at figuring out what the really important things are.

Later, once everyone's stuffed full of the most delicious pizza on the planet, and there's been cake and champagne toasts and speeches and the first dance, Walt and Skylar rock gently to Etta James. The warm weight of Skylar's arms on Walt's shoulders feels like home, and Walt pulls him closer. "Today was good," he says.

"Yeah," Skylar agrees. He takes Walt's hand and spins him. Sort of. They've both had a lot of champagne. They're better off sticking to school-dance-style shuffling.

As they crash together again, laughing, Walt knows he's going to spend the rest of his life with Skylar. It's not like a bolt from the sky or anything, just the settled, warm certainty of knowing when something's right. There probably *is* another wedding coming up.

"Fun fact," Skylar says, his arms wound tight around Walt's neck again. "Ninety-nine percent of all fake dating schemes end in the relationship turning real."

"They keep statistics on that?"

Skylar grins. "No, I made that up. Anyway, I don't think this relationship was fake long enough to go into the official count." Skylar pulls him in for a deep kiss, and they sway to the music, pressed tight together. "Think this will ever be us?" he murmurs against Walt's mouth.

"Pretty sure," Walt murmurs back. His eyes are closed, so he feels Skylar's smile instead of seeing it. "There'll be one big difference, though."

"What?"

Walt opens his eyes and draws back far enough to gaze at Skylar. "When we do this, there's no way we're not having one of the goats as our ring bearer."

Etta croons a few last notes before the music segues into Whitney Houston. Skylar's looking at him like no one's ever looked at him—not like he's perfect, but like they're perfect together. Walt would kiss him again, except Tad and Lewis come over and raucously insist on a family dance party.

And that's perfect too.

Keep reading for an excerpt from
Strangers to Husbands
by Lee Pini

Chapter One

LEWIS IS drunk off his ass when he decides riding the mechanical bull is an awesome idea. After finding his pockets disappointingly empty of cash, he gets Stacy—also super fucking drunk—to spot him ten bucks.

When he gets back, some guy is handing over a ten to the operator. Lewis leans his elbows on the railing to wait his turn, and the guy looks over and meets his eyes.

Lewis's stomach swoops, and it's not just the six shots of tequila he chased the pitcher of beer with. The guy has this beautiful head of auburn hair, curly and thick, gorgeous cheekbones, longish, pointy nose, a sharp chin, and an even sharper smile. He's T-A-L-L, taller than Lewis, all legs in tight black skinny jeans. Jesus fuck it should be illegal for someone to walk around with a bulge like that.

The guy smiles slowly and says something to the operator, who shrugs and nods. "Wanna join me, cowboy?" Tall, Dark, and Gorgeous drawls to Lewis.

"Um," Lewis says. The guy unsteadily crosses the crash pad to the bull and puts one foot in the stirrup. Lewis's eyes go straight to his ass.

Damn. He is tooootally not a one-night stand kind of guy because he believes in LOVE, that's L-O-V-E Love. Or wait, no? He doesn't, not anymore. Love is dead! Love is dead, so he should blow this guy in the bathroom.

Hot Mystery Man's shimmery black tank pulls taut across his chest. Muscles in his forearm pop as he holds the pommel on the bull's saddle. The divots of his collarbone look like the perfect place for Lewis to put his tongue.

Does he want to join? Um, *yeah* he wants to join. He wants to join so bad he trips over his feet as he stumbles across the crash pad.

"How's that going to work, though?" Like he cares about anything except getting closer to this man.

The guy's gaze travels from Lewis's head to his feet and back up, lingering at his hips, his chest, his shoulders, and his mouth. Heat floods Lewis. His jeans tighten as his cock stirs.

"You'll know what to do once we start." The guy swings into the saddle and pats what little space is left beside him.

Yeah! He will, totally. He will, and—oh shit. Lewis knows he shouldn't ogle but he gets an eyeful of what's between the guy's legs, and. Nnnng. That is. He is. Okay they're in a western bar so the joke is *right there* but—

Okay. Fine. Yeah. The guy is well hung. And Lewis's mouth is literally watering.

If he was sober, he'd wait his turn. But he's not sober. He is not at allll sober. So he climbs on and finds himself basically in his new friend's lap, Lewis facing forward and the man facing backward. The heat of his legs pressing into Lewis's brings the stomach swooping back.

"Shouldn't we face the same way?" Lewis asks.

Up close, he can see Mystery Man's blue eyes and a thick scatter of freckles that start on his cheekbones and spill down his neck. How far down do they go?

The guy's smile gets wicked, and he leans forward. His lips brush Lewis's ear. And then it's all hot breath and gravel as the guy says in a low, dirty voice, "I like to look at men when they're giving me a good, hard ride."

"Fuck," Lewis breathes.

The guy draws back, looking ridiculously pleased with himself. And ridiculously drunk.

Lewis puts his hands on the guy's knees, and at his nod, slides his palms up his thighs to his waist. The man arches into his touch, and his body is warm and firm and Jesus—will Stacy be cool if he bails on the bachelorette party to take this gorgeous man back to his hotel room?

The mechanical bull starts rocking slowly, swinging in a gentle circle, and Lewis absolutely cannot tear his eyes away from the way the man moves. His hips roll, all fluid sex on legs, and one of his arms loops around Lewis's back as he shifts closer. He slides into Lewis's lap, and they're moving against each other, grinding their hips, and Lewis is so hard it hurts.

There's a rope overhead, and the guy pulls himself up with it. Lewis gets a view of his abs and treasure trail, and he wants to put his mouth there and lick and suck his way down, down, down—

His mouth waters. The guy's legs hook around his back, and he rubs his hard cock against Lewis's stomach.

Lewis can't breathe.

There's a shrill whistle and a couple catcalls. Without looking, Lewis knows it's the bachelorette party. A small, slightly more sober part of his mind informs him he's never going to hear the end of this—he's basically fornicating on a mechanical bull in the middle of a honky-tonk during his best friend's bachelorette party.

But as Lewis pushes the guy down to the bull's neck and ghosts his lips over the man's jaw with its prickle of stubble, it's pretty hard to care.

He smells like gin and rose; spice and wood; *sweat*, and Lewis has never wanted to take someone to bed so bad in his entire life.

The bull slows and stops. Lewis is still on top of the man. Their faces are inches apart. The man's freckles are like stars. Lewis's pulse pounds in his fingertips and in his crotch. His skin is on fire.

"Lew!" Stacy yells. "Who's your friend?"

The guy grins, and where before he was all sultry and sexy, now he looks a little shy, a little giddy, like maybe he can't believe he just did that. It's adorable.

Lewis grins back. "I think I should probably ask your name?"

"Tad," the man says, biting his lip and watching Lewis's mouth.

Lewis shifts off him as Stacy's friends keep whooping. "I'm Lewis. And I would really, *really* love to buy you a drink, Tad."

"I would really, really love if you bought me a drink," Tad replies. He slides to the ground and helps Lewis down, and the two of them stumble into each other's arms, crash pad undulating beneath their feet.

Lewis laughs and leans into him, Tad's arm goes around his waist, and before Lewis knows it, they're jammed together at the bar, doing shots. "Aren't you here with someone?" Lewis asks.

"My brother and his friends." Tad flaps a hand. "They're not *here*. I left them at some casino."

"You left them to come ride a mechanical bull?"

"I left them because they're boring."

"What about me? Am I boring?"

Tad's hair falls in curly wisps over his forehead. He has the clearest, prettiest blue eyes Lewis has ever seen. "I don't think you're boring. You're like, the least boring person I've ever met."

Leaning into him, Lewis says in his ear, "I don't think you're boring, either." He trails a finger along the line of freckles on Tad's neck, down to where they disappear under the neckline of his tank. "I like these," he adds, because it seems really important for Tad to know.

"Really?" Tad sounds awed.

"Mm hm." Lewis leans in. It's easy to dip his head to Tad's neck, because Tad is taller than him. He kisses the spot where the freckles spill onto Tad's collarbone and disappear under his clothes.

It's happening, isn't it? Finally. Love at first sight *is* real. Take that, Jonah! And Diego, and Liam, and Jayden, and every other ex-boyfriend who ground him down and made him doubt true love was out there waiting for him. The rom-coms and Disney movies he loves are right, after all! Because his stomach's fluttering and his heart's pounding and every inch of his skin has this buzz pulling him toward Tad.

Sure, Lewis is drunk right now—really, really drunk—but Tad is definitely a person Lewis falls in love-at-first-sight with.

Tequila seems like it will make him fall even more in love with Tad, so he gets another one of those. And so does Tad, and the night turns to a hazy blur of dancing and singing along to Garth Brooks and Dolly Parton and Carrie Underwood. Tad yells to Stacy at one point, "I'm sorry I didn't get you a gift!"

Stacy yells back, "I'm just really happy you're here, Chad!"

"It's Tad!"

Slinging an arm around Lewis's neck, Stacy pulls him in for a sloppy kiss on the cheek and shouts over the music, "Lewis looooooves you, I can tell! Maybe someday you guys will get married! Lewis, I really want us both to be married."

Goddddd Lewis wants to get married so bad. Ahhhh it would be *amazing*. Stace is getting married, which he is like, *so* happy about! They can both be married to the loves of their lives, which Lewis is now like 99 percent sure Tad is. Stacy will marry Alang, and Lewis will marry Tad, and everyone will live happily ever after.

Tad presses into his side. He laughs and nuzzles his face into Lewis's. "We'll have a long engagement."

Which is like the funniest thing Lewis has ever heard, and now he knows he's in love-at-first-sight with Tad.

They leave the bar, and—stuff happens? Stuff must happen, because Lewis is having a blast, he's having so much fun; his hand is in Tad's, he's kissing Tad, and there's champagne. It's the best night Lewis can remember having in forever, even if he already can't remember most of it.

DESERT SUN on his eyelids wakes Lewis. His mouth is gummy, his stomach is sour, and his eyes are sandy. Something is twisted around his legs. Hotel sheets? Hotel sheets. The air conditioner is blowing on him, which is when Lewis realizes he's super naked.

He rolls over, groaning—and discovers he's also super not alone.

But hey, if you're going to wake up in bed with a man you've only known for twelve hours, it might as well be the most beautiful man you've ever seen.

The most beautiful man Lewis has ever seen opens his eyes groggily. His hair is in curly snarls on the pillow. A flash of hot memory scorches through Lewis's body—his fingers twisted in that hair, a warm, wet mouth on his cock.

Mr. Beautiful, He-Of-The-Best-BJ-Lewis-Is-Pretty-Sure-He's-Ever-Had, stretches, and Lewis's eyes track down and back up his body. He's lean and gorgeous, rangy strength, legs for days, *very* nice cock currently providing a nice display of morning wood. The freckles are all over his body. Lewis vaguely remembers trying to kiss all of them before getting distracted by the aforementioned very nice cock.

Lewis hopes his breath isn't toxic. "Hey."

Looking sated and wrecked, Mr. Beautiful says, "Hi."

What are you supposed to say in the morning to the gorgeous guy you drunkenly hooked up with?

"It's Tad, right?"

Which isn't his best effort, but he's rewarded with a bright, beautiful smile. "Yeah. Lewis?"

Well, Lewis doesn't remember a whole lot else about last night, but at least they remember each other's names.

He extends a hand for a handshake. "Lewis Mancini-Sommer."

Tad's smile gets a little crooked and a lot mischievous, and Lewis's heart swoops. "You don't do this very often, do you, Lewis Mancini-Sommer?"

"Dry hump a stranger on a mechanical bull and then hook up with him? Not really."

Tad laughs. It's hoarse, but—it's such a nice laugh. Sounds out of practice. His hand slides into Lewis's and they shake, which is when Lewis realizes there's definitely cum caked in the creases of his palms. Like. Kind of a lot.

"I don't," Lewis says. "I mean, obviously not the mechanical bull stuff. But… yeah, the like, drunk hooking up."

There's a sad little twist to Tad's mouth for a second and he pulls the sheet up to his waist. Maybe Lewis is still drunk, but the sight of Tad being unhappy makes him want to fix it. "Hey, um. Is there, like. Anything you want to… do? Like breakfast? Or, I don't know, coffee?"

Or sex? Because Lewis is leaving Vegas today and obviously never going to see Tad again. So… sex?

Tad's eyes flick to Lewis's. "Can we do each other?" He bites his lip. "Sorry! God. I'm actually usually not like this, like, at all. Slutting it up isn't really my thing. I mean, it's fine if it *is* your thing, like, no slut-shaming! I'm just, like, not that way. Usually. I was last night I guess? Sorry, I just—I was here with my brother and his friends, and they make me feel invisible, and—wow, did I really just ask if you want to fuck and talk about my brother in the same breath…?"

That's a lot of words that Lewis's brain can't really process, not after the ones at the very beginning. "I think we should do each other." He slides a hand over Tad's stomach and up to his chest. His stomach is just defined enough, but still soft. His pecs, on the other hand, are hard and warm, and Lewis has a faint memory of sucking Tad's nipples and him really, *really* liking that.

So he brushes a thumb over one. Tad's eyes close and he breathes in hard, and Lewis rolls on top of him. Tad grabs his hand and brings it to his mouth, then stops. His eyes widen.

"You're married?" he demands.

"What?" Lewis laughs. "Um, no."

Tad jabs a finger at one of Lewis's. "You're wearing a wedding ring. Why would you be wearing a wedding ring if you weren't married?"

"I'm not—" But Lewis's eyes flick to his own hand, and—

He is. He *is* wearing a wedding ring. He's wearing a rose gold band (gay, wow) with a viney, scrolling pattern.

"What the fuck?" Lewis asks, looking at Tad, even though Tad's made it pretty clear the existence of the wedding ring was unknown to him until this moment.

"I don't sleep with married men," Tad says in the same tone you might say *I don't sleep with serial killers.*

"I'm not married!" Lewis repeats. Tad rakes a hand through his hair and starts to get out of bed, but Lewis grabs his wrist. "Um, hey, excuse me, Mr. I-Don't-Sleep-With-Married-Men? What's that on your hand?"

"What's *what* on my—" Tad looks at his left hand. There's a ring there.

Tad stares. "What the hell?"

"Fuck if I know," Lewis says. "I don't know where mine came from, either."

Their eyes meet. Lewis's mouth goes dry, and Tad scooches back into bed with him, holding out his hand until it bumps against Lewis's.

Tad's is also rose gold, with the same pattern of vines and flowers.

The rings match.

The rings. Fucking. *Match.*

"Do you remember what we did last night?" Tad asks slowly.

"Well." Lewis looks at him meaningfully. "I remember doing a lot of things."

Tad's face colors. "Before that."

"Um." Lewis is saved from answering by his phone buzzing. He dives for it and opens the text from Stacy.

"Oh," he says. "Fuck."

I found this in my purse??? Stacy's text says. Beneath it is a photo of a marriage certificate. Lewis can only see four pertinent words on it: Lewis Mancini-Sommer... and Thaddeus Pierce.

Scan the QR code below to order

LEE PINI is a queer author who has been writing since they could pick up a pencil. They have lived in England, Northern Ireland, and Florida, and currently live in their home state of Minnesota with their wife and cat. Lee studied archaeology at the graduate level but currently uses their degree primarily to chuckle knowingly at classics memes. When they aren't at their day job or writing, they're reading vociferously, listening to music, enjoying nature, or nerding out. Their dream is for someone to one day write fanfiction about their characters.

Connect with Lee:
Website: www.leepini.com
Instagram: @leepiniwriting
Bluesky:@leepini.bsky.social
Facebook:http://www.facebook.com/lee.pini.is.writing

OWL YOU
NEED IS LOVE

HOO SAYS YOU CAN'T
GO HOME?

LEE PINI

Gordon Schumacher couldn't get away from the small town of Sawmill Lake fast enough, but all the big city got him was a dead-end job and a fiancée who dumped him as soon as he came out as bisexual. The last thing Gordon wants is to return to his hometown, so he's stunned when his estranged grandfather dies and leaves him 300 acres and a house. He plans to sell the land to the first big-box store to make a decent offer, pay off his student loans, and never look back....

But that's before an eerie sound draws him into the Minnesota woods, where he meets beautiful, awkward, and fiercely intelligent Charlie Gustafson. Charlie is an outcast and a loner, but he shared a passion for owl research with Gordon's grandfather, Ibrahim. Gordon is drawn to Charlie's passion and quick wit. He finds himself regretting not knowing his grandfather, and he wants to know Charlie much better. He even discovers his love of banding owls matches Charlie's.

Gordon knows selling the land where Charlie conducts his research will break Charlie's heart. Is the attraction growing between them enough to pull Gordon back to the one place he couldn't wait to escape?

Scan the QR code below to order

Six Places
TO FALL IN LOVE

LEE PINI

Percy de Villiers has it all: wealth, status, and a famous name—until his father's political scandal brings everything crashing down. Struggling with the fallout, Percy retreats to the South African wilderness to focus on his passion, nature photography. But even in the vast beauty of his homeland, he can't escape the weight of his family's disgrace or the loneliness that shadows him.

Rob Hale, a Hawaiian travel writer by way of Atlanta, has spent years idolizing Percy from afar. When an assignment brings him face-to-face with his photography hero, he doesn't expect their connection to spark more than professional admiration. But a chance encounter leads to an unexpected hookup, and the chemistry between them is undeniable.

As Percy grapples with the emotional wreckage left by his father's arrest, and Rob struggles with his own self-doubts, their fling starts to feel like something more. Navigating cultural differences, class divides, and the looming cloud of Percy's family drama, the two men must decide if they can turn their brief romance into something lasting—or if their relationship will fall apart before it ever truly begins.

Scan the QR code below to order

Strangers to Husbands

LEE PINI

A New York State of Love

They say what happens in Vegas stays in Vegas, but when Lewis wakes up married after a wild, drunken night at his best friend's bachelorette party, he's worried he's affected the rest of his life. Tad might be sweet, drop-dead gorgeous, and so easy to be with, but the obvious solution is a speedy divorce. The fact that they both live in New York City should make the process easy… so why is it taking them so long to sign the papers? Or even take off their rings? And why do they keep ending up in bed?

Tad's anxiety and fear of coming out to his family has driven guys away before. Can he dare to believe Lewis is different? Lewis, his friends, and his loud, loving Italian family support Tad in a way he's never experienced, and it's easy to imagine a lifetime of that unconditional love. But life isn't a romcom…

Or is it?

Scan the QR code below to order

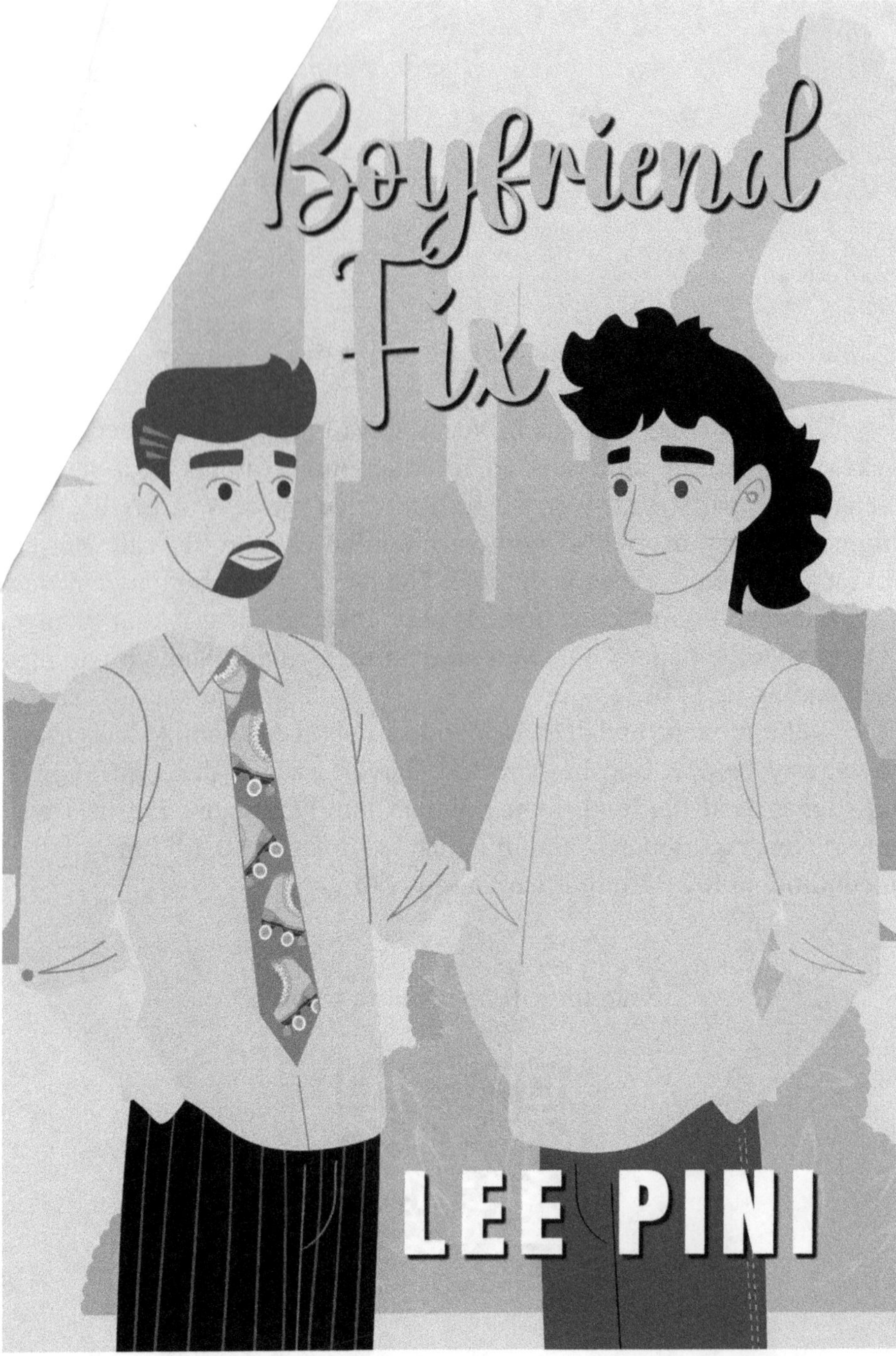
Boyfriend
Fix
LEE PINI

Renowned surgeon Ben McNatt is up for the job of his dreams, and when he gets it, he'll be the youngest chief of neurosurgery in his hospital's history. His success rate is flawless, but his perceived lack of compassion is hurting his chances. He's always viewed relationships as a distraction, but a loving partner might change his colleagues' ideas about his heartlessness. He'll do whatever it takes for this promotion— even pretend to date. The natural choice for his fake boyfriend is the cute guy at the coffee shop.

Jamie Anderson is in student loan debt up to his eyeballs. He has three roommates, and not in a quirky found-family way. He works sixty hours a week as a barista, and his boss won't stop hitting on him. He's even given up on love. He makes do with fantasies about the hot doctor that comes in for coffee every day like clockwork.

A fake relationship might solve Jamie's handsy boss problem too. And there's no way it will lead to real feelings when that's the last thing either of them wants.

So why are they having so much trouble convincing themselves they aren't falling for each other?

Scan the QR code below to order

FOR **MORE** OF THE **BEST GAY** ROMANCE

DREAMSPINNER
PRESS
dreamspinnerpress.com

A New York State of Love

They say what happens in Vegas stays in Vegas, but when Lewis wakes up married after a wild, drunken night at his best friend's bachelorette party, he's worried he's affected the rest of his life. Tad might be sweet, drop-dead gorgeous, and so easy to be with, but the obvious solution is a speedy divorce. The fact that they both live in New York City should make the process easy... so why is it taking them so long to sign the papers? Or even take off their rings? And why do they keep ending up in bed?

Tad's anxiety and fear of coming out to his family has driven guys away before. Can he dare to believe Lewis is different? Lewis, his friends, and his loud, loving Italian family support Tad in a way he's never experienced, and it's easy to imagine a lifetime of that unconditional love. But life isn't a romcom...

Or is it?

Scan the QR code below to order

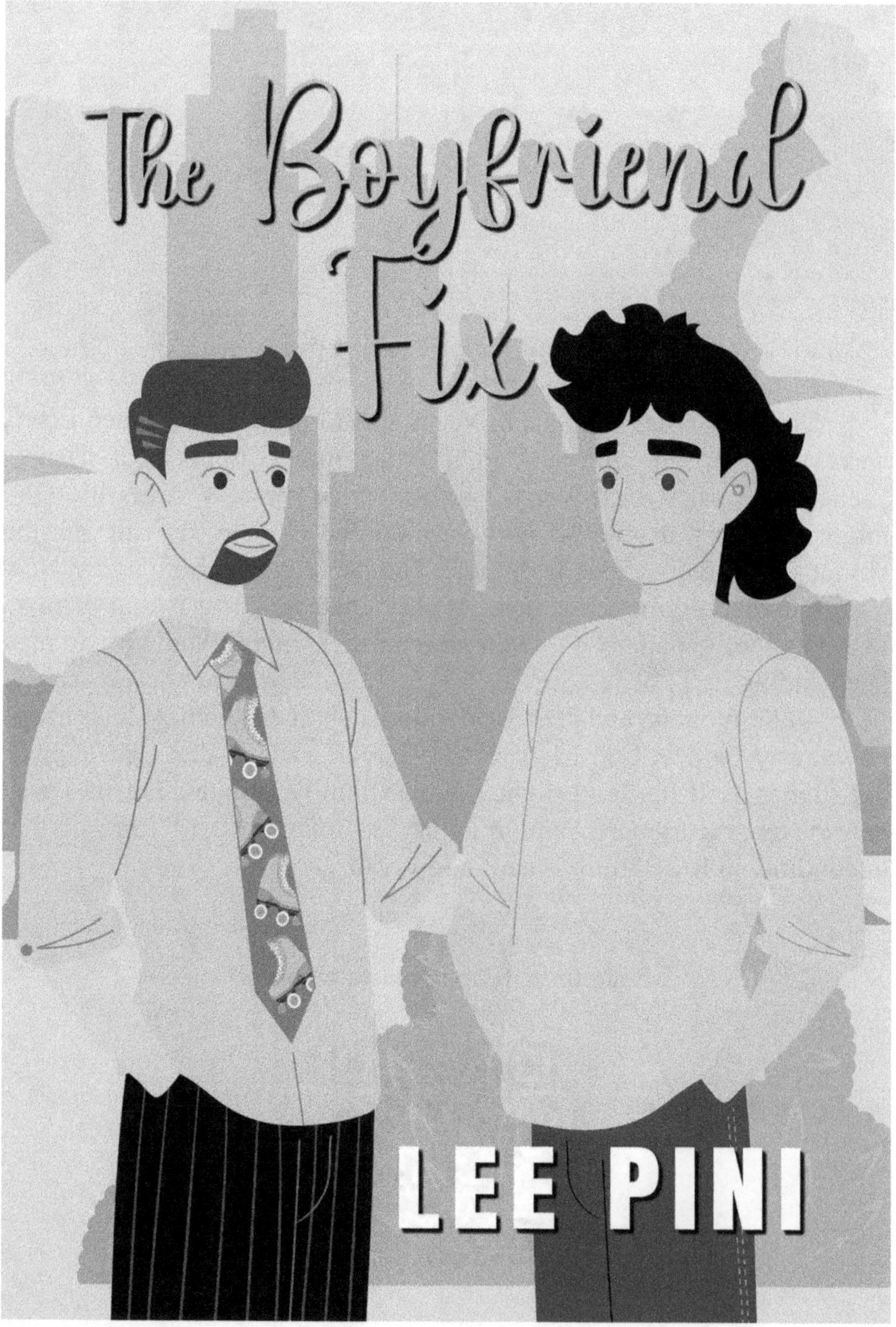
The Boyfriend Fix
LEE PINI

www.ingramcontent.com/pod-product-compliance
Lightning Source LLC
Chambersburg PA
CBHW072118020726
47501CB00003B/882